FATE *Heals*

TWIST OF FATE - BOOK 2

TINA SAXON

Fate Heals

Copyright © 2017 by Tina Saxon

ISBN Digital: 978-0-9987762-2-4
ISBN Special Edition Print: 978-1-7353272-4-2

Edited by: Max Dobson @ The Polished Pen
Proofreading by: Elaine York @ Allusion Graphics
Cover design by: Y'all That Graphic

PROLOGUE

Yesterday was one of the worst days of my life. Fate had illuminated the dark path known as my life and gave me the answer to a question I now wish I never asked.

My father, Travis, wanted me to visit him in jail. I never should have gone. I should have stayed as far away from Travis as humanly possible.

I never planned on him telling me why Aiden's parents were murdered or that the man I saw when I was ten, the man who killed my mother and then walked away smiling was Aiden's father.

I could feel the shards from my broken heart, tearing me apart inside. Aiden and I would never survive this. But there he was, waiting for me outside of the jail. He begged me not to let our fathers' actions determine our future.

Could our love survive the pain of our pasts? Could we build a solid foundation and bury the past so deep it doesn't shake the ground we walk on?

Yesterday, my thoughts were consumed with surviving through heartbreak.

Today, I'm just trying to survive.

1

ADDISON

I've danced with the devil.
I've made him bleed.
I've made him regret his sin—*taking me.*
For about two seconds.

"Y ou will learn, *mija,* that you are not the boss here," he says in a thick accent as he runs his hand down my face, almost affectionately. *His* touch makes my skin crawl. Bile threatens to rise as I jerk my face away.

I spit on his face. "Go to hell," I seethe.

He *tsks* me. "You will soon learn that that is exactly where you are," he roars as his hand strikes my face. I moan out in pain, spitting out blood. He split my lip. The metallic taste churns my stomach. "Your fight is impressive."

"They're going to kill you when they find me," I say between clenched teeth. He steps forward, and he fists my hair, yanking my head back to look up at him. I grunt as I can feel pieces of hair being ripped from my scalp.

"When they finally find you, it's not me who will be dead," he whispers into my ear. I try and fight against his hold but it's too tight. I can't move my head.

Shut up, Addison. I berate myself for instigating his anger. Today is day three of my hell, and by now I should have learned to just shut the fuck up. My arms and legs are chained to a wall, leaving me only enough room to go from the toilet to my single bed. I'm stripped naked. Which is my fault, I'm sure.

When I awoke from my drug-induced kidnapping, I fought with everything I had. My body aches all over from fighting and being beaten. A bitter laugh escapes my dry, cracked, bleeding lips when I remember the look on *his* face when I kicked him in the head, taking him down. First it was surprise and then a flash of fear. My foot connected to his ribs, not once but twice. His groans fueled my adrenaline. His men had to rip me off of him. I focused on that look when they beat me repeatedly while he watched with glee. It was then I was stripped of my clothes. So, yes, it was probably my fault.

I watch him open my prison door, and he looks back at me. "It's those eyes, *mija*. Those eyes are your hell." His wicked laugh echoes through the walls, sending burning rage throughout my body. I scream and fight against the shackles holding me in place. Pure hatred runs through my veins. My bruised wrists don't even hurt. At least not yet. That time will come soon enough, but right now I'm a caged animal trying to fight my way out.

I collapse into a ball on the filthy floor, willing myself to calm down. My chest hurts from my erratic breathing. I tap my head against the exposed cinder block wall.

Calm down, Addison.

I start counting back from a hundred. I figure ten isn't going to give me enough time. Closing my eyes, I breathe in deep through my nose, blowing it out through my mouth. I always sucked at yoga, except at the end when we did breathing exercises to relax. I'd give anything to be lying on a mat on a wooden floor, focusing on just my breathing. But that doesn't happen in Hell. In Hell, you only think about devils, saints, and angels. Why and how you got there. It's hope. It's torture. It's my life.

I think about Aiden. How he's probably going out of his mind right now. I just need to hang on for a little longer. Someone will find me.

Aiden will find me.

When I'm not fighting or being knocked unconscious, I listen. I try to figure out who took me and why. The man, *his* name is Rico. He speaks about my eyes and calls me *daughter,* so I'm assuming I'm here because of Travis. But who knows about me? Who knows I'm his daughter?

If it's some sort of revenge on Travis … how long are they going to keep me here, keep me alive? Every time one of Rico's men looks at me like I'm a fucking toy just for them, especially now that I'm naked, my heart stops beating.

Their fingers have groped me. They've rubbed their hard cocks against me when they've held me down and beat me. But it hasn't gone any farther. I'll take broken bones over a broken spirit.

I try to remember what happened when I was taken but it's all a blur. The last thing I do remember is something was thrown over my head then I was shoved into the back of a van. Everything after that runs together. Screaming, gunshots, squealing tires. Not always in that order.

Tears start running down my face, involuntarily. I don't want to cry. It shows weakness. Each night, I hold back the waterworks until I can't anymore. My body is tired of fighting; it's telling me I need to emotionally recharge because tomorrow is a new day where my brain will take over and I'll end up with new bruises, new scars. I only hope that I'll be found before those scars become irreversible.

2

AIDEN

Beep ... beep ... beep.

"Doc, is he going to wake up soon?"

"Please tell me he's going to wake up."

"Katie, he's tough. He'll wake up."

Voices fill my head. Where am I? Darkness surrounds me. I try to talk, but nothing comes out. Soft hands touch my arm.

"Aiden, please wake up," the quiet voice says. Katie?

Why can't I move?

Beep ... beep ... beep.

What is that fucking noise?

"Everything looks great," a male voice says. "He just went through a tough surgery. Give it some time."

Surgery? Why can't I remember anything?

"Have you guys got any leads?" That sounds like ... *Jaxon?* Leads on what?

Someone sighs. "They went underground with her. But we'll find her," Max says.

Her? Who's missing?

Think, Aiden. Think.

"I love you, Aiden." I watch her walk away. A black van. Screams. Blackness.

No, Addison!

Beep ... beep ... beep ... beep.

I will my body to move. To do anything. I need to wake up. I need to tell them who has her. I know who has Addison. FUUUCKK!

"Nurse, what's happening?" Katie's voice is rushed.

"Not sure, but his blood pressure is spiking. We're going to give him some pain meds."

My body heavies and my head feels light. Thoughts spin around in my head like a kaleidoscope and I'm falling back in slow motion. Sleep finds me at the bottom.

"AIDEN, CAN YOU HEAR ME?"

I feel like I'm walking through a tunnel and someone is at the end, calling out to me. The male voice echoes. Something pulls me to it.

"Aiden, can you open your eyes?" There it is again.

Trying to understand what he's asking shouldn't be this hard. I swallow. Holy fuck that hurt. My body tenses up.

"Are you thirsty?" the voice asks. I nod my head. "I have a drink right here."

Something touches my lips. I slowly open my eyes, squinting as the bright light floods my vision. I see someone holding a drink in front of me and feel a straw touch my lips. I cautiously take a sip, afraid it's going to feel like glass going down my throat. Out of fear, I blow out the breath I was holding, but it doesn't feel as bad as I expected.

I clear my throat as I look around the room. My sister, Katie, sits right next to my bed. The soft smile doesn't match the tears running down her face.

"Don't cry," I mumble. My voice is hoarse and it *sounds* like I swallowed a cup of broken glass. I clear my throat again.

"Aiden," the doctor says. I turn to look at him at my other side. "I suggest you don't try to talk for a while. Your throat is going to be sore for a couple days." He continues to ask me questions while he checks me over, wanting me to nod yes or no. I look down at the tube coming out of my chest and wince when I try to sit up.

A nurse behind him comes around and pulls out a remote from the side of my bed. The bed starts to move to an upright position.

"Why—" I stop talking because it hurts too much. I point to the tube.

"Do you remember what happened?" the doctor asks.

I pinch my eyes closed and nod my head. I was shot. The bastard who took Addison from me shot me.

Addison.

I croak as I try and sit up farther. I need to find Addison.

A hand stops me, pushing me back against the bed. "Aiden, you need to sit back." I look at the person who has a hand on each of my shoulders. I do a double take because the hands belong to a petite nurse. I shake my head. It must be the drugs making me weak because she's practically holding me down.

I exhale quickly, whipping my head toward Katie. "Get Damon. Now," I grate out in a whisper.

Katie stands up, watching me cautiously. "Aiden, I think you need to relax and focus on getting better. You've had a rough couple days," she says softly, laying her hand on top of mine.

I shake my head. "Now or I get up myself." I try to swallow the pain.

She twists her lips and rolls her eyes. "Such a brat. I'll be right back." I smirk as she walks out of the room. She's never been able to win an argument; I'm not sure why she thinks she'll start now.

"So I'm assuming you remember getting shot?" the doctor questions. I look at the doctor and nod once. "While we were removing the bullet from your chest, your lung collapsed, which is the reason for the tube. Once we determine that your lung can stay inflated on its own, we'll remove the tube. This can happen anywhere from a couple days to a week. We need you to focus on getting better." He gives me a pointed look. *I get it, doc.* It's really not beneath me to roll my eyes, but instead I nod. If this tool thinks I'm going to sit back while Addison is in danger, he's an idiot. I'll be a good patient for now so I can get out of this place.

As if the doctor can read my mind he says, "Aiden, you'll be here for at least one week, maybe two, depending on your recovery."

I fist my hands thinking what could happen to Addison in those two weeks if we don't find her. The beeping coming from the machine that is attached to me starts to beep faster. The beeping reminds me of something, but I can't pinpoint what. I shake the thought from my head. My focus right now is Addison.

Only Addison.

The doctor blows out an exasperated breath. "Don't make this more difficult, Aiden. Try and calm down. We'll get you out of here as fast as we can." He writes on my medical record and hands it to the nurse before he turns to leave.

"Alright, my pocket full of sunshine," the nurse says, "how is the pain right now on a scale of one to ten?"

I take in a deep breath and release it, self-evaluating my pain. It's not bad enough for pain meds. I need to be fully awake when I talk to Damon, so I hold up three fingers. It's probably more a seven, but hell, I don't need her to know that. Her eyes squint as she twists her lips.

"I don't believe you," she says, smirking as she adjusts a few things on the machine, "but when it gets to be too much, let me know. Tomorrow you'll start respiratory therapy to get that lung stronger, so don't use up all your energy this afternoon." She finishes writing whatever she needs to and then walks out of my hospital room. Damon's in the room before the door closes.

He pulls a chair up to the bed. "I guess I should skip all the *'I'm glad you're okay'* and *'you fucking scared us'* bullshit," he says with an eyebrow raised. "I know you want to get right to business."

I nod and clear my throat. My fists are still clenched. "I know who took her," I whisper. Whispering is a hell of a lot less painful than me trying to talk.

Damon's eyes go wide. "Thank God, because we've hit a dead end. Who?" His voice is rushed.

I slowly blow out my cheeks. I need to decide real fast how much to disclose. Addison is in a lot of danger, but having it known that she is Travis's daughter could be even more dangerous.

"Get Max." Damon angles his head. Max has been my best friend since elementary school. We joined the FBI together, but he didn't care for rules, so he opened his own security company, Shaw Security. His team is filled with ex-military and ex-law enforcement. Maybe with Max we can keep it under wraps about Travis. Damon is still staring at me intently. "There is stuff about Addison that I need to keep a lid on right now." I swallow to wet my throat before I continue. "We need Max and his team on this."

"You know as soon as the cops know you're awake, they'll be in here asking questions," he says.

"So fucking hurry up and get Max."

Not even five minutes later, Max and Damon stride into my room. Max smirks. "Good to see you alive, brother."

"Good to be alive," I reply.

"So, I hear you have some things to tell us. You know I already have my guys on this," he says. "We'll find her." It doesn't surprise me to hear that Max is already involved. Max grabs a chair and straddles it, leaning forward against the back with his arms crossed. Damon sits in the chair next to my bed. Both guys stare at me, waiting.

I close my eyes and pinch the bridge of my nose. Here goes nothing.

"Both of you know that Addison was at Travis's house last summer." They both nod in agreement. "What you don't know is ..." I pause and look around the room. I feel like I'm breaking some kind of trust between me and Addison, but I'm not sure how to save her without doing it.

"Aiden, if you know something that can help us find Addison, you need to tell us," Max says.

I clench my jaw and growl. "You need to talk to Travis." Both guys look at me with confusion.

"Why?" Damon asks.

I sigh. "Because Addison is his daughter." Damon's eyes widen as Max drops his head onto his arms. "The person who took Addison used to work for Travis. He tried to attack Addison while she was staying there. His name is Joe Lopez. Travis—"

"Wait," Damon says, interrupting me as he puts together who Joe is. "Please tell me this isn't the same Joe Lopez who you built your whole case against Travis and the reason he's sitting in jail right now."

I nod. "The same one. I don't know what the hell happened, or whose body we found, but it wasn't Joe." My voice is still raspy, but talking is getting easier.

"You know what this means, right?" Damon asks.

Fuck yeah, I do. If we find Joe, Travis goes free. I built my entire case against Travis based on one thing: he had Joe killed. We found a body at the bottom of the Hudson River. The bodyguard who was instructed to kill Joe spilled his guts one drunken night. That was it. I took hold of that one mistake

Travis made and built my case. Obviously he didn't have him killed if he's still alive, but I don't have time to think about that right now.

"So this guy has a huge score to settle, then. With Travis *and* Addison," Max says as he stands up and starts to pace. I nod, fisting the white hospital sheet. "Give me all the info you can on this guy Joe. I'll have Stone start digging."

Max is on the phone with Stone, relaying all the information that I gave him, when Damon asks, "How are we going to play this?"

"I'm going to tell the cops who took her, but I'm going to leave out that Travis is her father." Damon leans forward, his arms on his knees.

"I'm kind of surprised you didn't tell me."

I shrug. "Wasn't my story to tell."

He slowly nods. "Okay, we'll go talk to Travis. You know that it'll be on record that we're there. People might start asking questions."

"I'll deal with that if it becomes a problem. Everyone knowing that she's Travis's daughter won't help her be found. They'll know who took her and that's what is important. If you guys can—"

"Oh, my God, Aiden, you're awake." Sydney comes flying in the room, landing on my bed. I have to scoot over to make a little room for her. This bed is small enough as is. "Please tell me you have information that will help us find Addison," she pleads. Her eyes are bloodshot red. She wrings a Kleenex around her fingers, waiting for an answer. I grab her hands. They're so tiny my one hand engulfs both of hers.

"I will find Addison, Syd. I promise," I say, squeezing her hands.

I hear Max get off the phone. "We're all set to see Trav—" Max stops when he sees Sydney on my bed. I can't believe he didn't see or hear her when she came in. He looks her up and down, studying her. "You must be Tink?" he says as he sticks his phone into his front pocket.

Her eyebrows crease, and she looks from Max to me and back to him. "I don't know who you are, but my name is not Tink." She crosses her arms as she stands up, trying to make herself look taller. I chuckle to myself because she's not much taller than when she was sitting.

"Well ..." Damon starts to say something.

"You be quiet." She points her finger at him, and he laughs.

Max walks over, holds his hand out, and says, "Max Shaw."

She shakes his hand. "Sydney Owen." Max seems to hold Sydney's hand a moment too long for Damon's liking. He stands up and walks around to Syd, rubbing her shoulders. Max pulls back his hand but looks from Syd to Damon, smirking.

Syd shakes off Damon's hands. "Would you stop? This is not the time to try and mark your territory. My best friend has been kidnapped and you all need to find her. Now!"

Sydney looks back to me with tears in her eyes. "Syd knows everything I just told you both, so you can finish what you were saying, Max," I say, not looking away from her. Her eyebrows shoot up. "I had to tell them. I'm sure Addison told you about Joe from last summer." She looks down, trying to recall.

I can tell the moment she realizes who he is because her head whips up and tears run down her face. Damon wraps his arms around her as she buries her head in his chest.

Max clears his throat. "So, Jaxon is getting us in to see Travis. Stone is already digging to find anything on Joe." He glances at Sydney still embraced in Damon's arms. "We won't stop looking until we find her." Sydney pulls her head away, peeking at Max, and nods.

All of us look toward the door when it swings open. The petite nurse from earlier walks in. "Alright, visiting hours are over. My patient needs his rest."

That's the last thing I want to do, but I can feel my body agreeing with her. Max nods once and then leaves. Damon squeezes my shoulder. "Focus on getting better and let us focus on finding Addison. I'm glad you're okay. You fucking scared the shit out of us." He smiles before turning around and leading Sydney out of the room.

3

ADDISON

Like clockwork, my meal arrives. At least I *think* it's around the same time every day. The eyes of a creepy guy scan my body making me shiver from disgust. He puckers his lips, sending a kiss through the air. My body convulses as if it can feel his lips. I watch him with caution, my handcuffed hands clenching as I try to breathe through his heinous stare without saying something that will only egg him on.

He bends down slowly, placing my food and drink on the ground, his gaze never leaving me. Chills run down my spine. I can sense something is different. The way he carefully lays my food down, it's almost *too* cautious. He licks his lips when he stands, stretching his hands out and cracking them. I flinch at the sound, which makes him smile.

I'm already on my bed, sitting up, but I scoot back trying to separate myself from the monster. A deep growl erupts from his lips as he sticks his hands down his pants.

Panic rushes through me, and I nervously glance around the room. This can't happen. He laughs at my obvious state of terror then pulls his dick out and starts stroking himself. He moans as his hand increases its speed, his dark eyes never leaving my body. I want to close my eyes and not watch the pervert get off, but I'm afraid if I do, I won't be ready if he decides to attack me. So my eyes lock with his. I will not give him the satisfaction of looking *down*.

"You want this dick, bitch?" he growls. "You want me to come down that dirty mouth of yours?"

I clench my teeth, willing myself to *shut the hell up*. Don't say anything. Just let him get off and he'll leave. His groans intensify as his orgasm rips through him. His eyes finally release their hold on mine as his body convulses. Mine does the same but in revulsion.

His evil smile widens as he puts his dick back in his pants. "I'll see you tomorrow, bitch," he snickers. When he leaves and I can hear the second door slam, I blow out a ragged breath. My heart is racing. I drop my head and the tears run down my face.

Hurry, Aiden. I don't think I have much more time. I've been here a week already. They have to be close to finding me. *Please, God, lead them here.*

I must have fallen asleep from the adrenaline crash. I don't know how much time has passed. It's still light outside, so it must not have been that long. I stare at my food waiting for me. Cheese sandwich and water. My stomach grumbles at the sight of food. I uncross my legs and stretch. My legs ache from falling asleep with them underneath me. I push off the bed and walk slowly to my food. I inspect it, making sure he didn't come all over it. I gag just thinking about it.

I walk it back to my bed, looking over the whole thing. Everything seems okay, so I eat. Slowly. I've learned if I eat too fast, I can't keep it down. Taking small bites, I watch the sky through the small, dark, dusty window. I can tell the sky is clear today. I wonder if it's hot or cold outside. The air is humid down here, but I'm not sure if that's because I'm in a damp basement or if I've been taken to a warm environment. New York is freezing right now, so I don't think I'm there anymore.

I finish my food and water, placing the dishes as close to the door as I can get so whoever comes in and gets it won't need to get close to me. I go to the bathroom before sitting back down on my bed. I should walk around, but for some reason I'm still tired.

I blink a few times as my eyesight starts to blur. I pick up my hands, looking at them. They feel heavy. I feel heavy. When the room starts to spin, I panic. No. No. NO! I lean over the bed and stick my finger down my throat. Nothing comes up, so I keep trying. My world starts to go dark and I know I've been drugged. *Again.*

I CAN FEEL my quick breaths as I open my eyes. A piece of errant hair lies on top of my face, so I lift my hand to move it but it stops when the handcuffs catch my wrists. My chain must be stuck on something. I wiggle my wrist around again and pull, but I can't move any farther. My eyelids still feel heavy and my body weak. I drop my hand, tired of trying to unhook it, and close my eyes.

I take a deep breath in, getting a whiff of … *soap?* The new smell sends a surge of energy through me. I pry my eyes open and try to sit up. Again, my hands are stuck above my head. I shake them violently, trying to get loose. The bed squeaks and scrapes the floor the harder I try.

A deep, familiar laugh causes me to freeze. My heartbeat is about to jump out of my skin. The room is dark as I scan it. I know that laugh, but I can't place it. Movement in the corner catches my attention; I can see the outline of a large man sitting there. The smell of soap invades my senses again, and I look down my body. *It's clean.* It's then I notice my hair is clean and still wet.

Realization dawns on me that my hands aren't caught, they are tied to the bed. The man stands and comes into the light shining in from my little window.

Panic shoots through me like I've been electrocuted. No, it can't be. I pull on my restraints as hard as I can. I can feel my skin ripping, but it's the least of my concerns right now.

"Still a feisty one," he snarls, walking closer to me. "But this time, no one is going to save you."

I let out whimper. I know what's about to happen, and I can't do anything to stop it. Joe is going to get what he wanted last year.

He grabs one of my legs. I scream, kicking and thrashing against his hold. It only spurs him on as his laugh booms louder. He's much stronger than the last time I saw him.

He straddles me, sitting on my thighs so I can't move anymore. His gaze moves up and down my body. "You're still beautiful, *Emily*." He chuckles. "Or should I call you Addison?" He digs his thumb into my broken rib. I writhe and scream out in pain. "I see you've met my dad, Rico. He wasn't too happy when *your* dad ordered a hit on me. You remember Bill, right? Travis was an idiot who trusted the wrong people. He's getting soft in his old age. He had no idea who I was. It's too bad everyone has a price." He laughs out loud. "Bill was a dumbass thinking we would help him disappear with a ton of money and a new identity if he didn't kill me. We were definitely going to help him disappear alright; he just needed to stick around until the dust settled after I was gone. But, fuck, did it go a lot better than planned when he told Jett, a fucking undercover FBI agent, I was sitting at the bottom of the Hudson River. Who knew? Thank God he waited long enough for the poor motherfucker's body we used to decompose." His bitter laugh sends chills across my body.

I clench my jaw shut. I don't hear most of what he's saying as silent pleas run through my head. *Please don't do this. Please let someone find me right now. Please bring back the guy who jacked off watching me.* Tears sting my face as they fall.

"This is how you thank me for washing you?" he says softly, catching a tear on my cheek and slowly running his finger down my body, all the way to my clit. My body burns where his finger touches, yet trembles like it's freezing. I bite my lip so the panic can't escape as I squeeze my eyes shut.

He *tsks* me, yanking on my pubic hair. "Open those eyes, bitch. See the real man who is about to show you how it's done."

Anger takes hold of me when my eyes open. My temper takes over. "You are nothing," I seethe. "You have to kidnap and tie up a woman to get what you want. That is NOT a man, that's a fucking troll. You're not worthy of the title *man*. Aiden will kill you when he finds you."

His jaw tightens and his eyes narrow as he pulls back and punches me in the face. I shriek as the blinding pain shoots through me. I hear the crunch of bones. My whole face is on fire.

"Aiden." He laughs as he sits back on my thighs. "Princess, he's dead." It's hard to focus on what he's saying through the pain and my sobs. But I heard *Aiden* and *dead*. "I guess you don't remember. I shot the asshole in the chest. I'm sorry to tell you, *he didn't make it*," he says mockingly as he shrugs.

No! He can't be dead. The flicker of hope that I was holding onto starts to burn out. My whimpers increase to a full cry as I shake my head back and forth.

"But it doesn't matter. You are mine now," he says, grabbing my breasts. My mind is still mourning Aiden so much so that I don't even acknowledge his invasive hands.

I hear him unsnapping his jeans as he leans over me. "The best thing about this," he gloats, getting close to my face, "is the revenge I get on everyone. Travis is in jail for killing me, I killed Aiden, and now I'm going to own this cunt." He grabs me, shoving a finger inside me. I scream again and wiggle at the intrusion.

"That's it, princess ... fight me," he barks, pulling down his pants and fisting his dick. I squeeze my eyes shut again. One eye is swollen already. I try and squeeze my legs together, but he forces them open with his legs. When he shoves into me, I scream.

His painful assault continues as he forces himself inside me over and over. My mind borders on the present and dissociation. When he flips me, pulling my ass in the air and slamming back into me, I yank on the handcuffs. I can feel the warm blood dripping down my wrist. My face is against the mattress, I'm almost catatonic as I try and focus on the feel of the handcuffs. I don't even flinch as Joe slaps my ass.

When he pulls out and comes on my back, I close my eyes in relief. His fingers start to rub through his cum. "Your ass is begging for me," he says, moving his cum-covered fingers to the pucker of my ass.

My mind slams back to the present. "No!" I scream, trying to wiggle my ass out of his grasp. But his hold on me only tightens.

"This ass is mine, Addison."

One finger slams inside of me. The pain coils up my spine as the screams come out of my mouth involuntarily.

"Scream my name, Addison. Scream who fucking owns this body."

"Fuck you!"

He slams another finger in, doubling the pain. "Scream my name, Addison, or next it's my dick."

It's in that moment that my hope dies. Everything in me breaks. "JOE!" I scream.

4

AIDEN

"Where the fuck can she be?" I scrub my hands over my scruffy face. I haven't shaved in days. It's been nine days since Addison was kidnapped, and we haven't a clue where she is. Max's guy, Stone, was able to find some chatter in the black web that she's being held somewhere in the south.

But that's it.

Travis said he'd tell us anything he knew or found out. We haven't heard a peep from him, either.

I'm exhausted. Lying back on the couch, I stare at the ceiling. Between physical therapy and trying to find Addison, I haven't had much time to sleep. And when I do, her screams fill my head. So yeah, *screw sleep.*

We set up base camp at my apartment. I think Max and Damon did it just so they could watch over me and make sure I made it to all my doctor appointments. Since my lung decided to start working on its own, I've been working my ass off in physical therapy. Anger from not being able to find her has fueled my need to push myself.

"You need sleep, Aiden," Ryan says, hovering over me.

"Fuck you," I mumble. "I'll sleep when I know Addison is safe."

"Well then, sit the hell up and let other people have a place to sit." He hits my legs off the couch. I curse him under my breath, but manage to sit up. He and Jax sit on either side of me.

I look around at the guys sitting around me. Ryker, Jaxon, Damon, Max, and Ryan. My five best friends who are all close enough to be brothers. I met all of them except Max and Damon during our first year of college. Max has been my best friend since I was little. Damon joined our group back in our days at Quantico. Our personalities couldn't be more different, but we all share a common interest in law enforcement. Even though we took different paths after college, everyone here knows the odds of finding someone the longer they are gone—they're not good.

I'm going out of my mind. Every second that she's gone is a second that I hate myself more. I failed her. I try not to go down that rabbit hole of thinking what's happening to her, but it's like a magnet pulling me down there. Max tries to keep me busy, keep me focused so I don't go there ... but it still happens.

That's why the guys are here. They're on Aiden duty. I'm being fucking babysat. If I weren't still weak and tired, I would kick Max's ass for setting this up.

I don't need a babysitter. I just need to find Addison!

5

ADDISON

My body won't let go.
Just let me die.
My body hurts. Everywhere.
It hurts to exist. It hurts to fight.

The roughness from the bare mattress burns my cheek, but I'm too weak to change positions. I lie flat on my stomach, naked and bruised. I slowly blink and look toward the door where plates are piling up with rotten food. I can finally see out of both eyes. One was swollen shut from getting punched. I wouldn't be surprised if my nose was broken; I've given up trying to breathe through it. My stomach turns just thinking about eating or drinking.

I'm afraid. Afraid that I'll wake up again after being drugged. Afraid *he'll* come back like he promised. I'd rather die than touch the food or drink they give me. The rattling of keys in the door when my food is dropped off sends a bolt of fear through me. Every. Time.

Hope of being rescued dwindles every second that I'm here. I have no idea how long I've been down here. Maybe two weeks, guessing from the amount of plates on the dirty floor. Since Joe, though, no one has said anything to me.

My mouth is open as I breathe in and out slowly. The air is humid tonight. Sweat runs down my back. The moon must be full because it's casting a glow in my dark dungeon through the small window. Dust particles float in the light. I watch them dance around the room and wonder if they feel as trapped as I do?

I sigh and then suck in a quick breath, wincing. Trying to release it as slowly as possible, I groan from the pain radiating through my body. I'm pretty sure I have at least one broken rib.

A bitter laugh escapes my lips. *I think I'm just broken.*

My eyelids flutter closed. I welcome sleep. It's the only time I get to see Aiden. We're happy and in love. It's only us. No barriers. I finally know why fate brought us together.

We'll be together soon. Forever.

If my body would just let go.

"*I* MISS YOU," *Aiden says, cupping my face.*

"*You say that to everyone.*" *I giggle. We're in a grassy field. I spin in place and notice it's the spot we made love after skydiving. The sun's warmth wraps its arms around me.*

"*Nope, only you. I'm waiting patiently for you. Who knew I was such a patient man.*" *He smirks and tickles me, taking me to the ground.*

"*Stop or I'll have to hurt you,*" *I scream between laughs.*

He rolls on top of me, his emerald green eyes shining bright.

"*I knew you'd wait for me. I love you forever,*" *I whisper as I pull his lips down to mine.*

In the distance I can hear thunder clap. It halts my kiss.

"*Is it supposed to rain?*" *I ask.*

"*No, it's always sunshine, sweetheart.*" *His lips caress mine, and I quickly forget about any thunder.*

"*Add cat?*" *A whisper jolts me.*

. . .

THE SLAMMING of a door makes me jump, fear pricks inside me like needles all over my body. I look around frantically, but all I can hear are my labored breaths. The moon's light is bright enough I can see that no one is in here with me.

I look at the ground and notice a fresh plate of bread and a cup of spilled water. I shake my head. That must have been the noise I heard that woke me up. My hands shake as I lay my battered body back down.

I close my eyes again, but sleep doesn't come. Instead, I wonder why I would dream about Frankie. I haven't seen Frankie since I left Texas last year.

6

AIDEN

"Do you really think he has information?" Max asks, looking at me in the rearview mirror. Damon turns and looks back from the front seat.

"It's been two weeks of *nothing*. I don't care what kind of lead he has, at least it's a lead." Travis's attorney called Max this morning saying Travis wanted to see me, that he might have some information.

Max nods. "I just don't want you to get too excited. I mean you put this guy in jail. He doesn't like you," he says in a matter-of-fact tone.

"Addison is his daughter. He won't lead me on a snipe hunt. He wants Addison found just as badly as I do. He also wants Joe found as soon as possible, too." I rub my hands down my jeans. At least I hope so. It feels like it's been months since I saw Travis, yet it's only been three weeks.

When we get to the jail, we're directed to a room where Travis is already sitting, and there's a guy next to him. *Who the fuck is that?* I know that's not his lawyer. I look the guy over. Bald, as tall as me, probably as fit as Max. Being caught off guard has me second-guessing why we're here. Travis better not be screwing with us.

They have set up three chairs for us to sit in across from them. The metal chairs scrape against the concrete floor as we take our seats. I'm in the middle, Max and Damon on each side.

"Who's your friend?" I say, looking at Travis. He's not looking so good. It looks like he's getting as much sleep as I am.

"It doesn't matter. What matters is *he* knows where Addison is." I can't decipher his hard stare. Can't tell if he's lying or telling the truth. I fist my hands under the table.

"It does matter," I grind out. "I need to make sure you're not sending us on a wild goose chase. I need all the information I can get. Starting with who the hell he is." I nod my head in the guy's direction.

"Frankie Sanchez," he says, sitting back in his chair with his arms crossed. The name sounds familiar, but I can't place it. Satisfied with a name, I look back to Travis.

"Where is she?"

Travis looks down, taking a few deep breaths. When he looks up, his eyes are filled with turmoil. Regret. Hate. *Tears.*

I can feel the weight of whatever he's going to say. *It's already suffocating me.* I briefly look away from the pain in his eyes, knowing my world is about to come crashing down.

"Is she alive?" I murmur as I lean forward on my elbows, my voice barely audible.

"She is." The reply doesn't come from Travis. I jerk my head to Frankie and wait for him to expand on that. When he doesn't, anger takes hold.

"Well, where the fuck is she? Someone tell me where Addison is!" I scream, jumping up from my chair. The sound of the chair screeching takes me back to when I was here just a few weeks ago when I found out my dad killed Addison's mom and then *Joe took her from me.*

The breath I can't seem to grasp has me feeling lightheaded. Damon must notice because he's standing by my side. "Sit down, Aiden." His hand pushes my shoulder down, forcing me back into my chair. *I hate that I'm still weak.*

I pinch the bridge of my nose, taking in deep breaths. My eyes are closed when Damon starts asking questions.

"Where did you see Addison, Frankie?"

"I work ... worked for Rico Santiago." I tense immediately at the name and look up to Travis.

"What? This is your fault," I say with a chill in my voice, pointing at him. "You told me he wasn't an enemy anymore, that you were on neutral ground." I remember when I worked undercover and came across Rico's name. He told me I didn't have anything to worry about with him. He wasn't a threat. They had come to a mutual agreement. *Seems that agreement was only one fucking sided.*

"You don't think I know that? Don't think I blame myself the entire twenty-four hours a day I'm in this hellhole? It seems I trusted the *wrong people!*" he yells, pulling on his cuffed hands attached to the table.

"This isn't helping," Max says calmly, interrupting us. "Frankie." Max motions for Frankie to continue. Frankie looks between me and Travis, twisting his lips, and slightly shakes his head. I narrow my eyes at him, and I'm about to fire off some words, but he starts talking instead.

"I was there at his house doing some ... business." He glances our way but when we don't say anything he continues. "As I was relaxing with some sweet sugar in my lap, Rico came in the room and told me to take some food to someone. He told me the guy who normally does it wasn't there." He shrugs. "So, I was like, okay. I was definitely not going to say no to the boss. I didn't know it was in the basement though." My fists are so tight that my nails dig into my palms. I know where this is going. I can feel the anger seep into my veins. Anger that erases any oath I've made for justice.

Anger that makes me want to kill.

I jolt up out of my chair, pacing the room. I haphazardly run my hands through my hair. I can't even bring my eyes to look at anyone. Even when Frankie continues.

"When I opened the door, I thought I'd see a man. Some schmuck who did Rico wrong." Frankie's voice becomes hard and angry. "When I saw her ..." He pauses, slamming down a fist on the table. I jerk my head in his direction. His eyes are black and filled with fury. "When I saw Addie lying there ... it took everything I had in me not to pick her up and leave."

"How did she look?" I whisper and swallow the lump in my throat, afraid to hear his answer. He looks away from me as his eyes water. He shakes his head, closing his eyes. My fears have just become reality. I know what he's not saying. I know what goes on in those basements. I've been on numerous cases rescuing people —the ones who lived—from those basements.

"So, you left her there?" I seethe.

"I would have gotten us both killed." He directs his glare at me. I nod, knowing he's right. "Instead, I left her food and the rest of the night I tracked every motherfucker there. Got as much information as I could about security, rotations, layout of the house. And I felt like the biggest asshole the entire time, knowing she was down there suffering." He pushes off his chair, standing toward the wall and hangs his head. "I would do anything for my Add Cat. I owe her my life."

What the hell? Add Cat? Not yours. Mine.

I want to jump over the table and punch his teeth out of his mouth. Damon's words halt the rage ready to explode. "How do you know Addison?"

How does he know Addison? The nickname. I've heard that before. Where have I ... "I know who you are. You got Addison shot." My eyes widen, remembering when Addison told me about the scar on her leg. That's why his name sounded so familiar.

He slowly turns around and lets out a low chuckle. "I did not get her shot," he grumbles. "I was so pissed at her for getting involved. She's always been a firecracker."

Confusion reflects on everyone's face as I look around, waiting for him to continue. Even Travis looks surprised. I guess he doesn't know everything about his *new* friend.

"How do you know Addison? And when the hell was she shot?" Damon asks and glances my way. I jerk my head toward Frankie. Let him explain. I doubt I've heard the whole story.

"Let's just say we saw each other a lot while she was in college." Bastard. *She was never yours.* Why he's making it sound that way grates on my nerves.

"She worked at the courthouse, and Frankie here was a frequent flyer." I raise my brow in challenge.

"Something like that," he says. I don't have time to argue about why he was at court. So I let it go. "Anyway, one night some guy who thought I snitched found me at the courthouse. He somehow got a gun inside and shot me in the leg. Addison thought her *bad-ass self* could take the guy down before he killed me. She didn't know he was hyped up on opiates. He ended up throwing her against the wall and took a shot at her. Before he could take another one, security got there and killed him. The shot grazed her leg." I can hear the anger in his voice as he retells the story.

Damon sighs. "Only Addison," he says, shaking his head. "Why am I not surprised?"

Everyone takes a moment to refocus. "You were right to do what you did," Max says, getting back to why we're here. "When did you see her in the basement?"

"Last night," he murmurs. "When I found out she was there because she was Travis's daughter, I thought for sure they had the wrong person." His bleak eyes meet mine. "I flew here the second I could get away without my absence being noticed."

"Are you sure they didn't suspect anything with you questioning things?" Max asks.

Max's leg starts shaking. He's getting impatient. The reserved guy is losing control. Out of the five of us, he's the one who never shows his cards. He's also the most lethal. He left the FBI because he wanted to do things on his terms, not theirs.

"No, I made sure to get a few guys trashed last night to find out information. Even if they recall anything about it this morning, they won't say shit to Rico. They fucked up running their mouths. They'll want to live."

"Either way, they're already dead," Travis grates out slowly. *Old man*, that is one thing we can agree on.

Max and Damon stand tall and talk to Frankie before the three of them exit the room. I look down at Travis and his head hangs low. I close my eyes and exhale loudly. As much as I want to blame the guy, guilt slaps me in the face.

"I'm sorry I couldn't keep her safe," I murmur. His tear-filled eyes, which show their age, find mine. "Thanks for coming to us. I'm sure you'll be getting out soon."

"Aiden, the only thing I regret right now is not making sure he was six feet under." He sighs before continuing. "I told you I'd come to you if I found out anything. But I promise you, if you don't burn that place down, I will." His voice is gruff, filled with vengeance. I nod slowly. I know better than to say out loud what I really want to say. I silently promise to make sure everyone pays with their life, especially Joe.

I GROWL. "What do you mean I'm not going in?" I stand up and get in Max's face. Instead of backing away, the asshole takes a step closer. We're almost nose to nose.

"You are not in any shape, physically or mentally, to go in there," he says calmly. "You're still healing from a gunshot wound, and you are too emotionally invested to think clearly when going in there. You'll get yourself—or someone on the team—killed. No."

I turn away from his cold stare. "Fuck you."

It's all I got. I slump into the chair. We're on our way to Texas in Max's jet. When I found out where the house was, south Texas, I couldn't believe she was that close to her home.

"At least you'll be alive when you do it." He smirks. I flip him off, shaking my head.

Frankie sits across from me, studying me. It doesn't worry me because I have nothing to hide. *Unlike him.* I tilt my head, twisting my lips with my fingers, and stare right back. I wasn't surprised that he wanted to come. I was surprised that Max let him.

"Why'd you go to Travis?" I narrow my eyes in accusation. "Not come directly to us."

He shrugs. "I don't like cops."

I slowly nod but don't believe him for a second. Something is off.

"Who do you work for?"

"Aiden," Max warns me from his chair. He, Damon, and Stone sit around a table going over the plans for tonight. The table is behind Frankie's chair, to the right. His eyes are on mine and the slight shake of his head tells me this isn't the time.

"Right now I'm working for myself," Frankie says, pulling my attention back to him.

"I bet you are." Sarcasm drips from my voice. He smirks at me as he stretches his legs out. I know I should be kissing the ground this guy walks on for taking us to Addison, but he has an ulterior motive. I start to wonder if he's leading us into a trap but I remind myself that Max would have picked up on that already, so that's not it.

Our stare off is interrupted by Max. "Now's not the time to fight over who has the bigger dick." Max's glare should scare me, *it does most people*. I know I've pissed him off.

"Here's what's going to happen. We have the rest of the team meeting us there. A couple of my guys are already in place, watching to make sure they don't move Addison. I've contacted another Texas security company I trust to help. You'll both be with Stone and one of their guys in the van. You'll be our eyes." He continues to go over the plan with us. My foot starts to shake as my anxiety climbs to toxic levels. I've tried to not focus on what has happened to Addison, which is probably the reason my focus has been on Frankie.

We're close. We're close to bringing her home. And I'm scared out of my mind what we're going to find.

7

ADDISON

Another loud noise pulls me out of my dream. I try and focus my eyes in the darkness. Looking around, I don't see anything. I shake my head. I feel like I'm walking the line of reality and make believe. I don't know where one ends and the other begins. My eyelids are heavy, and I welcome the sleep. Sleep takes away the pain.

Two more loud pops and my eyes fly open. *Gunshots.* I try and sit up, listening to the silent air, but I'm too weak and my arm gives out. The door flies open, and I scream. A shadow moves across my room and a gloved hand covers my mouth as fear takes hold of me. Curse words are muttered under his breath. It's hard to even see him as he's covered in black from head to toe.

"Addison, it's okay. I've got you," his words are whispered into my ear. I don't know if my mind is playing tricks on me again. Am I going to wake up from this dream? Am I going to wake up to this hell again? My body starts to tremble as I squeeze my eyes closed. I hear metal against metal and my hands are set free from the handcuffs. A blanket is thrown around me, and I'm lifted into strong, warm arms. I moan out in pain as I'm reminded about my broken rib. The pain finally subsides as my body starts to pull me under.

Sleep ... I welcome sleep.

I hear words, but they float around in my head. I'm dreaming. I have to be dreaming.

"I need a fucking medic, stat."

"Keep the package warm."

MY EYES FLUTTER open to a bright room. I feel pressure on my left arm. I look at the IV in my arm and follow its path to a bag filled with liquid. I hear numerous beeps but other than that it's quiet. My mind is having a hard time forming a coherent thought. Instead, I focus on the beeps. I lick my lips and they have something gooey on them.

I grunt at the horrible taste. Where am I? I look down at my wrists and both are wrapped in gauze. I exhale shakily when the fog starts to clear, and I understand where I am. I'm in a hospital.

I was rescued.

"She's still not awake," Aunt Amy whispers as she walks into the room. When our eyes meet, the phone slips from her hand and falls to the floor. She rushes over.

"Oh, my God, Addison," she cries. "You're awake." She grabs my hand as tears fall down her face.

The relief from being rescued doesn't come. Instead, I look away in shame. I can't take the pain in her eyes. I close mine as she tells me that she's going to get a doctor. A petite female doctor comes in by herself. I stare at her for a moment then turn to face the large window. The sun shines bright, and I can see a tree blowing in the wind. I watch the leaves move with the wind, and I wonder where I am because it's winter. Most trees are bare right now.

The doctor is talking, but my mind focuses on the tree. Are the leaves changing color at all? My gaze moves from branch to branch.

"Addison?" the doctor says, interrupting my tree assessment. I look at her.

"Can you hear me?"

I nod my head.

"Are you able to talk?"

I know I don't really want to. I know once I start, they'll ask questions. Never-ending questions. Questions I don't want to answer. I just want to enjoy the peace and quiet right now. I shake my head.

She narrows her eyes at me. "Able to but don't want to?" she asks, studying me. I nod my head this time and look back out the window at my tree. I can hear her pen scribbling something on my chart.

As soon as she leaves, Amy comes back into the room. She doesn't say much, just holds my hand. I appreciate the time she's giving me to remain silent. She does force me to take a couple bites of my breakfast. After taking two bites, my stomach protests the nourishment it's been deprived of for the past couple weeks.

It doesn't take long for my body to tire. I resist the urge to sleep, afraid of who is waiting for me behind closed eyes. My eyelids grow heavy and sleep is unavoidable. In my dream, I wake up and Aiden sits by my bed, holding my hand. I wish we were back in the field. I liked that better than my hospital bed. When I squeeze my hand, he looks up and our eyes meet.

He flashes a warm smile. "Hi," he whispers.

I know I'm dreaming but this feels so real. I can feel the warmth in his hand. I look down at our linked hands, confused. I don't think I've ever *felt* someone in my dream. My gaze moves back up to his face. My brows furrow.

"Do you need anything?" he asks, tilting his head. My gaze

quickly darts around the room and when I see my tree swaying in the wind, reality hits. I'm not dreaming. I yank my hand back. The ground underneath me shifts, throwing me off my axis. *Everything changes.*

"Get out!" I yell. I feel betrayed, but I don't know why. Aiden stands up, taking a couple steps back. His face twists and his shoulders drop.

"Addison, it's okay." He shoves his hands into his jeans pockets.

"No. No, you're supposed to be dead!"

"I'm not, sweetheart. I'm here." He takes a huge step in my direction, pulling his hand out of his pocket as he tries to touch me again. I flinch away from him. He clenches his hand, steps back, and starts to pace the room.

"Please leave," I whisper. I choke back my tears. *I mourned you. I thought you were dead.* My mind twists between reality and what I believed. I'm having a hard time processing this new reality. I watch him pace. My eyes shift away when he looks at me. I feel like I'm drowning in disbelief. I can't breathe. I roll away from him, cradling my body as emotions overtake me. My body shakes violently from my cries. Guilt starts to strangle me as my thoughts turn to wishing he had died rather than him being here and seeing me like this. I hate myself for even thinking that. *God, why didn't you let me die?*

Amy sits down in front of me, blocking my view of the window. I hadn't even heard her come into the room. I have no idea if Aiden is still here, but at least I can't see him if he is. She grabs my hand and wraps her other arm around my body while I cry. Exhaustion pulls me under. This time there aren't any fields of love in my dreams, there's only the feeling of rejection from being broken.

I wake up before my eyes open. I'm afraid Aiden will be in my room, so I cover my face with my hands like a shield, digging my palms into my eyes. It's still daytime because the sun still shines its bright rays into my room.

"Look who's awake," I hear Ted say. I peek through my fingers and see Ted sitting at my side. His face is unshaven and his eyes are turned downward. I can see how tired he is. He flashes a weak smile as I move my hands away.

"Hi," I say, sighing.

"I was instructed that I had to get you to eat a couple bites when you woke up." He stands and walks over to a tray filled with food. My eyes widen, wondering why the hell they would bring that much. He must see my reaction because he says, "They just bring what the lunch is for the day. The doctor just wants you to eat a couple bites, though." He puts it on a roll cart and swings it in front of me. I let out an audible gasp and hold my broken rib as I try to sit up. "Wait. I'll lift the bed," he says, softly putting his hand on my shoulder. I exhale sharply, lying back. The bed slowly reclines. Ted sits back down as I pick through my food.

The silence that surrounds us is awkward. I know he has a ton of questions, but doesn't want to ask them. Out of the corner of my eye, I see him open his mouth to say something only for it to snap back shut.

"Thank you for being here," I quietly say, looking over at him. He angles his head and takes in a deep inhale then lets it out slowly.

"Addie, I wouldn't be anywhere else."

"Is … did they …" I can't say his name. Even though my body is scarred by every mark left on it by *him*, I'm afraid if I say it out loud I'm acknowledging it. I stuff a spoonful of mashed potatoes in my mouth. I glance at Ted and his hands are firmly grasped in his lap. His jaw clenches. My gaze turns downward, and I close my eyes. I hate seeing the pain this has caused.

"He's dead," he says, his voice strained.

Those two words should make me feel better. But they don't. I wish I had been the one to kill him. To see his eyes plead for mercy while I took the life from them. A warm hand covers mine. When I open my eyes, Ted nods as if he understands.

"Eat," he whispers.

I take a couple bites of applesauce and push the cart away. Ted pushes it to the side. The door to my room opens, and I abruptly pull my blankets up over my chest. When I see that it's my doctor, my shoulders relax as I lean my head against the pillow. I haven't seen Aiden since this morning, but I know it'll only be a matter of time. I don't want him to see me like this. I know I'm not thinking clearly because he's already seen me, but seeing the pain in his eyes cuts me deep inside. It's a reminder that I need to let him go.

She checks me over, happy that I've decided to start talking. She inspects my food to see how much I have eaten and writes it down in my chart. Amy walks in with a Target bag and gives Ted a hug. He smiles at me and winks before leaving.

The doctor sits down and discusses the tests that were run when they brought me in—including a rape test. I cough as my lunch threatens to come back up. Embarrassment creeps through me as Amy wraps her hand around mine. I close my eyes as tears roll down my face freely.

"Addison, it's okay," Amy says softly.

I shake my head. "No, it's not. Everyone knows I'm broken," I cry.

8

AIDEN

"Keep the package warm." We hear Max growl through our headphones.

Rage burns through me. I know there is only one reason that Max wants Joe alive. *Revenge*. And that must mean one thing. I run out of the van, needing to get to Addison. She's my lifeline. She can't die.

I run the two blocks, full speed. Cold air hits my face as my feet pound the pavement. When I see Max start to get into the medic helicopter, I pick up my speed, pushing through the pain in my chest. They are not leaving without me.

We had a plan for me to meet them at the hospital, but it's two hours away and I was supposed to drive. Fuck. That. I yell for Max to wait, but the helicopter's blades start to turn, drowning out my yelling. I wave my arms, catching Max's attention. I see him say something to the pilot. Thank God he's waiting for me.

When I jump into the helicopter, Max scoots over, making room for me. "You almost got yourself shot. Dumbass," he grates.

I don't hear a word he says. My world blurs at the sight of Addison. I thought I was angry when I didn't know where she was. That was like an open wound. This feels like someone is pouring acid on it. It burns through my core. I fall to the ground by her lifeless body. Half her face is unrecognizable. It's swollen with yellow bruises covering the entire side. I go to reach for her but then stop myself. She's covered with a blanket, and I'm afraid to see what is underneath. The medics already have her hooked to an IV.

"Hold on, sweetheart," I whisper, laying my head down by her body. I don't want to touch her not knowing what might be broken. Max has his hand on my shoulder. My body shakes as I silently cry.

Addison is rushed into a hospital room as we're instructed to wait in the waiting room. I can't sit down. My body is so revved up that there isn't a single muscle inside me that will relax. I've had to pull myself back from punching a hole into the wall. I stalk around the room like a caged tiger waiting to pounce.

While we were in the waiting room, FBI agents come and go as well as the police. Once we got the initial report from Addison's doctor, that's when things got a little fuzzy. Dehydration, broken rib, broken nose, and lacerations here and there ... the list went on and on. When my eyes scanned over the word rape, my entire body froze. I thought I knew what revenge felt like before. It doesn't come close to how I felt at that second.

Next thing I know we're on the helicopter headed back. Back to get the revenge I need to unleash. The beast grows by the second, my restraint slipping every second we got closer.

As soon as our feet hit the ground, I follow Max's heavy footsteps toward a small guesthouse on the same property of the house we found Addison. I can see the main house in the distance, but it's not close enough to hear the screams coming out of the small house right now. My hands twitch, knowing who those screams belongs to. I want in on the action.

Joe is tied to a chair, stripped of his clothes, except his underwear. When I see his beaten body, the angry monster inside me wants *more*. There is not enough pain in this world that can make him suffer for what he did to Addison.

When he sees me, he smiles wickedly through the blood dripping down his face. I step forward, planning to wipe that smile off his face. Max's arm halts me.

"Not yet," he growls.

Hudson, one of Max's men, continues his barrage of assault. I stand with my feet planted and arms crossed, enjoying every fucking second. Every scream that comes out of his mouth makes my heart beat faster. I've never been one to torture, but this right now ... it's like my body is inhaling his screams and energizing every nerve within me.

While Hudson takes a break, deciding what to do next, Joe lifts his head. His gaze finds mine. He coughs up blood through his laughs.

"Your Addison is one good fuck. How's it feel to know I've claimed her as mine?" He coughs again. "Every part of her. The best part was her ass."

My body lunges forward, and my fists connect with his face over and over. Max pulls me off of him, dragging me back. My chest heaves from the rage.

"You can finish him off, but not yet." Max nods to Hudson. I jerk out of Max's hold, nodding my head as I lean against the wall.

I look over at Hudson and he clutches a hammer. His nostrils flair as his face is hard as stone. When the end of the hammer is slammed down *onto* his groin, Joe's high-pitched cries makes *me* even clench my ass.

Max can sense when I've had enough. He calls off Hudson and

hands me his gun. I don't waste a second as I walk up to Joe and pull the trigger.

The blades of the chopper turn. Tonight's events run through my head. The last couple of hours have been a blur. I look out the window into pitch blackness except for the flames of the little house lighting up the darkness. Fitting for the Devil himself. I take a deep breath in and blow it out slowly. *That was the easy part.*

Max and I hop out of the helicopter when we reach the hospital. Max stops me before we walk through the doors.

"You okay?"

I exhale loudly. "No." I shove my hands in my pockets. The sting of my raw knuckles reminds me I need to wash up. I pull them back out and look down at them.

"She's tough. She'll pull through this," he says.

"Max," I howl. "I'll do everything in my power to help her through this, but you and I both know what this does to a person. We've seen it. The destruction from the pain."

"Time, brother. Just give it time." He grips my shoulder as I hang my head.

"I'll give her an infinite amount of time." My hand covers my face as my sobs wreck through me. Max embraces me, holding me up. I take a deep breath, pulling myself together, and stand. I can do this. I can be strong for Addison. Max glances at me, tilting his head in question.

"I'm good."

As we walk down the white, sterilized hallway, I lean into Max and quietly say, "Remind me never to piss off Hudson."

Max nods. "He was definitely a crazy, pissed-off motherfucker." He jerks his head toward the bathroom so I can go clean up.

When I walk into the waiting room, Amy and Ted stand. Amy wraps her little arms around me and her body shakes. "Thank you for finding Addison," she says through muffled cries. I swallow hard trying to keep my emotions at bay.

Ted looks at my raw hands and our eyes lock. His jaw clenches, and he nods slightly. He's been in law enforcement his whole life. He's not stupid. He already knows that Joe wasn't found in the raid. He also knows there was a reason I wasn't here when he got here. I know what he's asking without it being asked. *Did he suffer?* I grit my teeth and nod. He drops back into the seat, sitting forward with his elbows on his knees, and drops his head into his hands. I'm sure he was holding in the worry of Joe still being out there. His emotions flow freely now.

NOW

"Fuck! Fuck! Fuck!" I scream into the empty car, beating the steering wheel with my palms. I can't believe that asshole told her I was dead. No, I can believe it. Psychopaths play mind games all the time, but when it's the woman I love being lied to, being told that I'm dead, it makes it hard to see straight. I pound on the wheel a few more times before I fall into it and let it hold me up. I dig my head into the leather. What am I going to do?

I roll my head to the side when I hear tapping on the passenger window and grunt when I see Max. I'm really not in the mood to talk to anyone. There's a reason I'm out here alone.

"If you don't unlock it, I'll do it myself," Max says, smirking. I flip him off then press the unlock button. I roll my head back, sighing. Max gets in and shuts the door but stays quiet. I take a few deep inhales and exhales before sitting back up.

"I don't know what to do," I say, looking straight ahead. The wind is strong. I watch a couple walking to their car, the woman gripping her dress preventing it from flying up.

"Like I said before, it's going to take time, Aiden."

"*Before* I didn't think she thought I was dead. Who knows how long she's had that in her head messing with her."

"Well, you're obviously not," he says, matching my snide tone. "So she just needs time to process it."

"When I was holding her hand while she was asleep, I felt like everything was going to be alright. She's a fighter. She's been through so much that I thought she'd be able to get through this. Then when she opened her eyes and realized I wasn't dead, I felt every singe of betrayal radiate off of her. I felt helpless. And then seeing her cry without being able to comfort her, killed me."

"She is a fighter." Max grips my shoulder. "And she'll need all the help she can get from everyone to help her fight. Including you." I sigh heavily and nod in agreement. "Let's go get something to eat, hospital food sucks."

9

ADDISON

I wake when a nurse comes into my room to check my vitals. The sun is barely peeking over the horizon and emits a soft glow into my room. I told Amy to leave my curtains open last night. I like knowing that I can focus on my tree when bad thoughts start to creep into my mind. The wind has died down so the leaves barely shift.

My body feels so much better as fluid runs through me. If it weren't for my broken rib, sitting up would be easy. Unfortunately they took out my catheter, so I have to walk by myself to the bathroom. As much as my body is thankful for all the fluids, my ribs hate me right now. I walk slowly with the help of the nurse.

"Would you like to take a shower?" she asks quietly. A shower sounds wonderful, but I'm not sure if I'll be able to stand for that long. I groan with frustration. "I could help you if you want. If you want to sit on a chair, I could wash your hair for you."

My first thought is Amy can help me. Then I think about all the bruises on my body that I'd rather her not see. "Yes, I'd like that," I whisper as my emotions stir within me. A tear falls down my face. She glances at me and smiles warmly.

As awkward as it is having someone wash me, I feel amazingly better afterward. Amy brought me some pajamas so I won't have to wear the hideous hospital gown and my breakfast is a success; I finish my entire Jell-O cup and my stomach doesn't protest. Proud of myself, I lie back and watch TV. I look toward the door as it opens, hoping it's not Aiden.

Damon knocks and peeks in. "Can I come in?"

"If I say no, are you going to listen to me?" I say sarcastically. He shrugs and walks in anyway. See? I don't even know why he asked.

He pulls out the chair from next to my bed and sits forward on his knees. "You look better today. How are the ribs?"

"Hurts like hell," I answer dryly. I narrow my eyes at him. I can't think of one good reason why he's here. It doesn't matter if he's here for Aiden or because he's FBI and needs to question me, either way, I don't want to talk to him about it.

He exhales loudly, looking down. "I'm assuming you don't want to talk to me about what happened." *Really?* What gave that away? "I'll send someone you don't know personally if that'll help. I just wanted to see how you are doing, if you needed anything …" he says, lifting his head up with furrowed brows. I look away from his pained stare.

I stare at the TV. "No, I'm fine."

"Addison, I'm only here for you. So, if you need anything …" he pauses until I look at him, "… please let me know." I nod once and he stands. He looks back over his shoulder giving me a crooked smile before pulling the door open and leaving. Unwanted tears fall down my face. I can't even tell why I'm crying. Maybe it's because I was just a bitch to a friend or maybe because anything or anyone associated with Aiden messes with my emotions. I may be clean on the outside, but the filthiness I feel inside of me that won't go away consumes me whenever I think about Aiden. I'm not the woman he fell in love with. I'm not the woman he wants.

Damon doesn't waste any time sending someone in. A female FBI agent comes into my room and asks questions that are so painful to say out loud, that my broken rib feel like kisses on my skin compared to that pain. When she leaves, I'm exhausted from my body being tense the whole time. I press the nurse call button and request some pain meds. I know it's not going to make the emotional pain I feel go away, but it'll help me go to sleep. So much for a successful morning.

I can hear the quiet hum in my room before I even manage to open my eyes. My eyelids are still heavy from the pain meds, so I keep them closed. I would know the person behind that melody anywhere. *Sydney.* I hesitate because I need to prepare myself. Sydney is as much my sister as Amy is my aunt. They are not my family by blood, but by choice. I know she must have been going crazy the entire time I was missing.

I take a deep, quiet breath before I pry open my eyes. Sydney sits on the chair next to my bed, looking down at her phone. She has black circles under her eyes and her messy hair is pulled back in a clip. I slowly scan her face. She doesn't have any makeup on and her face is pale. My heart hurts knowing how much anguish she must have been in. My gaze moves down her body, and I notice her plaid leggings don't match her flowered tunic. It's so hideous that people might actually think she meant to do it. But I know Syd. She didn't *mean* to.

Her fingers fly across the screen as she writes out a text. Her polish is chipped on numerous fingernails; she's been picking it off. The melancholy melody coming from the back of her throat brings tears to my eyes. She's sad because of me. When I sniffle, her face jerks up, meeting mine.

She softly smiles and says, "Hi."

"Hi." I manage a small smile. We stare at each other for a couple seconds before her eyes fill with tears.

"Fuck!" she says. My eyes go wide at her sudden burst of a curse word. "I'm sorry. I thought I could put on a strong façade because I know you." Tears run down her face, and she wipes them away. "I know you don't want anyone looking at you and feeling sorry for you, b-b-but I can't do it," she stutters and climbs on the bed, lying on her side so we're face to face. My eyes sting as the tears fall freely down my face. "I'm so sorry this happened to you. I can't even imagine the hell you were in these last couple weeks," she hiccups. She wraps her hands around mine and falls silent. She's right. I don't want people's pity, but if there is anyone who I can be myself around, it's Sydney. I close my eyes and let my emotions pour out of me.

My body shakes as my cries fill the room. She moves closer and wraps herself around me. I don't even notice that someone else is in the room until I hear Syd say, "Not now." I wipe my tears away and turn toward the door. No one is there so I turn back around.

"Always so bossy," I say, sniffling.

She smiles and shrugs. "You needed this more than that person needed to come in here."

I take a deep inhale and exhale, nodding. "Who was it?"

"I'm pretty sure it was your doctor."

I smirk. "I'm having a déjà vu moment right now."

"Nope. She's definitely not as hot as Dr. Parker was," she says with a laugh. I chuckle when I think about the last time I was in the hospital after being shot and Syd hooked up with my doctor.

"Thank you for being here," I say softly.

She squeezes my hand. "Nobody could have kept me away from you. I love you, Addie."

"I love you, too, Sydney." I take a few more deep breaths to calm myself. I need to change the subject because I can tell my emotional state is barely hanging on. "So, did you get the job?"

Her gaze flicks over my shoulder before coming back to meet my eyes. She chews her lip while she contemplates what to say. I can already tell what her answer is going to be.

"That's great," I say, not wanting to wait for her to tell me she got it but that she's not going. That will never happen. She will not put her life on hold because of the mess I'm in.

"Addie—"

I shake my head. "No. When do you start?"

She stares at me for a minute and sighs. "I'm supposed to go next week for orientation."

"Then you're going," I deadpan. She sticks her tongue out. "I'm fine. I'm alive and I'll eventually go back." She narrows her eyes. "I need someone to take care of my apartment anyway."

"I don't want to go there without you," she pouts. "And you need me here with you."

"I can't live with any more guilt, Syd. I need you to go."

"You shouldn't feel guilty for anything, Addison. None of this is your fault. None!" She bolts out of bed, making me jump. I wince at the pain in my ribs. "Oh, oh, oh … I'm sorry," she quickly says, laying her hand on top of mine, holding my side.

I close my eyes and lean back, taking in a big breath and letting it out slowly. "It's okay, Syd. I just need to know that you are going to New York."

She huffs. "Fine. I'm going to New York." I want to tell her to take Aiden back with her. I have a feeling that he's going to be more determined than Syd to stay. He can't. That guilt I shouldn't have, *I do*. And a lot of it has to do with Aiden. "I'll leave when you get out of the hospital. Until then, you're stuck with me."

She leans back and I turn on the TV. The next time the doctor comes into the room, Syd moves off the bed so she can check me out. It's not until the psychologist enters that I ask her to leave. It's not because she'll hear something that I don't want her to know, it's actually the opposite. She'll see the wall I let down go right back up. I don't want to talk to anyone about what happened. Telling it to law enforcement is as far as I'll go. And that was only so if Rico and any of his men were arrested, they wouldn't be getting out anytime soon. The agent didn't elaborate on what happened when I was rescued. I'll have to get that out of Damon later.

My unwillingness to talk makes the doctor's visit short. She promises to be back tomorrow, or sooner if I need her. I promise her I won't need her. After she leaves, I focus on my tree. I always get a sense of calm when I watch it. The sky has a mask of gray clouds and it looks like it's going to rain any minute. Clouds swirl in the sky and my tree holds onto her leaves for dear life as wind rushes through her. I forgot how volatile Texas weather can be in the winter.

I hear my door open. I don't look over because I'm sure it's just Sydney coming back in. When I don't hear any noises, I turn my head in the direction of the door. Aiden is leaning against the wall, his hands in his pockets and his head slightly downcast, but his eyes are pinned on me. His pain radiates off of him. I feel the waves pulsing around my heart, constricting it. I can't do this. I look away, blinking away my tears.

"Addison, look at me," he quietly commands. I close my eyes and shake my head. I hear him push off the wall and his heavy steps approaching my bed. I flinch when I feel his hand on top of mine and whip my head back to his direction.

Yanking my hand away from his, I whisper, "Please, don't touch me."

"Why are you pushing me away? Addison, I love you. Please let me be here for you," he murmurs as he falls into the chair. His hands fist my sheets. I feel the slight tug on them.

"I can't do this," I say, looking back out the window to my tree. *I can't do us.* His touch I once craved now makes my stomach churn. He won't want me anymore after the guilt settles. Why can't he see that? I will not be with someone out of a sense of pity or obligation. I'm not going to saddle him with a broken woman. He deserves more. "Syd is moving to New York next week, you should go back with her," I say flatly.

"What? I'm not going anywhere." He stands abruptly. His chair scrapes against the floor. The amount of anger inside my body surprises me. The feeling of being trapped again is irrational, but it's exactly how I feel.

I jerk my head toward him and sit up, wincing again from the damn broken rib. It only adds fuel to my raging fury. "That's not a decision for you to make, Aiden," I seethe. "I don't want you here. You're not helping me." His eyes go wide and the hurt reflecting in them squeezes my heart a little more. I'm being a bitch, I know I am, but if it'll make him leave, then it's worth it. He'll understand one day.

"Addison—"

"No!" I scream, interrupting him. I fist my hands and slam them down on my thighs. "Get out!"

The door swings open, and Max walks in. "Aiden," he says in a low, commanding voice, motioning to the door with his head. Aiden's eyes narrow as his jaw tightens. His hands fist at his sides, and I wonder if he's about to hit Max. He turns toward me and the tension in his shoulders fall. His eyes water, and he takes a sharp inhale, blowing it out slowly through his nose.

"I'm sorry," he says, his voice shaking. I watch as he pivots and paces out the door, not once looking at Max. Guilt and relief collide within me. *This is what you want, Addison.*

"Goddammit!" I scream, jumping out of bed. I sway from getting up too fast. "Whoa," I say, grabbing the side of my bed. Max is by my side immediately, steadying me and pushing me back to the bed. I slouch over the side of it and rub my temples. My head is dizzy, and I'm not sure if it's from lack of oxygen or the fucked-up mess in my head.

"Addison, you need to rest." *You think?*

"You need to make Aiden leave." I look down. I don't want to see the disappointment in his eyes. He's not going to understand. He's Aiden's best friend.

"Addison, I can talk to him, but he won't listen to me." He sits down in the chair right in front of me. I sigh, lift my head, and look at him. "He loves you."

"I know that," I murmur. "But it's too much when he's here. There are expectations that I can't handle right now. Please talk to him about going back," I plead.

"I will." He leans forward on his elbows. I swing my feet back up on the bed, wrapping them in the blanket. Max's eyes scan my body. His scrutiny embarrasses me, so I bring the blanket up to my chest. The blanket settles over my body, outlining it.

"It was you, wasn't it?" I whisper. I wasn't sure who rescued me since the man was dressed all in black, but seeing Max in front of me right now, there is no mistaking that it was him. I remember how huge and hard he was, like he was built of stone, when I was in his arms. I look over at him and he nods. "Thank you."

"It would've been Aiden had I let him." He sits back in his chair and crosses his arms while he watches me. That doesn't surprise me at all. I'm glad it wasn't. It would've made everything so much worse. He already knows I'm broken; seeing the hell that I lived in would be etched in his head. *Forever.*

"You look better."

"Yeah … water, food, and a shower does a body good," I say sarcastically.

He sighs. "They won't ever touch you again, Addison," he says through gritted teeth. I close my eyes and nod. Just the thought of them *touching* me again makes my heart start pounding. I take in a few deep breaths, trying to calm myself. I'm safe. I focus on that.

"Will I have to testify?" I know that Joe is dead, but I'm still not sure about Rico. When Max doesn't respond, I glance his way. His head hangs and his hands are balled into fists. I can tell he's trying to control his anger.

After a few moments, he gathers himself and looks up. "No."

I nod in understanding and my eyes start to water. *Thank God.*

THE NEXT FEW days I can really feel the effects of food and fluids. Each day I have more energy. Well … *physical energy.* Mentally, I still don't want to get out of bed. If it weren't for the nurses and Sydney making me walk around the hospital, I would stay in bed. I've tried to take less pain meds, thinking that is what's making me feel so blah. Joe invades my sleep more frequently. I wake up more tired than when I went to sleep. Last night my doctor prescribed me a sleeping pill. When I woke up this morning, I felt like my brain was as heavy as a bowling ball. I didn't want to lift my head off my pillow.

But at least I had a dreamless sleep.

Aiden visits my room at least once a day. We don't talk. We *definitely* don't touch. Each morning he comes into my room with a chai tea latte and banana bread. He watches me for a couple moments, says *"I love you"* and then leaves. I can't bring myself to eat or drink his gifts. I want to tell him to stop, because the pain I feel for him is almost too hard to bear. This is entirely my fault, so I'll bear the pain if it will eventually make him see that I'm not worth it. My soul is tainted with hate that Joe forced into me. I can't take that back. It'll always be there. *He'll always be there.*

"I see Aiden's visited this morning," Syd says, walking into my room and glancing at the table. I nod. "You should drink it. You know you want to." Her voice is light as she sings the words. I think about that. Do I? I shake my head to my own question. I really don't. She stares at me and sighs. "Well, I brought you some clean, comfy clothes, so go take a shower and we'll go walk around." She throws a bag on my bed and claps to hurry me along.

We've been going outside the last two days, but the weather changed again. *Typical Texas*. The rain and dreary weather is back. It's exactly how my head feels, dreary with a hundred percent chance of fog. I grab my clothes and trudge to the bathroom. I already know that no matter how much I whine, Sydney won't let this go. The faster I get this over, the quicker I can wrap back up in my warm bed.

My day with Sydney was uneventful, but now I'm lying in bed, watching the sky light up like fireworks from the lightning. Rain taps on the window and it lulls me to sleep with its rhythmic beats. The sound of a loud clap jolts me out of me sleep. I look around frantically, confused about where I am. My heartbeat is erratic and my breathing is labored. I blow out a huge breath when I recognize that I'm in my hospital room. Another loud clap of thunder hits making the lights flicker out in the hallway. I lie back. *It's just thunder, Addison.* It's not long before the effects from my earlier sleeping pill pulls me under again.

I can feel the heat of the sun on my face before I open my eyes. I let the warmth cover me for a few moments before I begin another day. When I finally open my eyes, the first thing I see is my tree. My eyes fly open wide.

"No, no, no," I cry as I jump out of bed and run to the window. I don't even register the pain in my ribs. I lay my forehead against the cold window and stare at my tree. *My broken tree.* The tree is split in half, one part leaning on the ground. Tears run freely down my cheeks as I mourn Mother Nature's destruction. Lightning must have hit it last night. Anger bubbles up inside. "Why do you take everything from me?" I cry out to the sky, pounding on the window with my fist. When will fate finally stop with the blows? I can't take much more. Is that what she wants? Because this is killing me. I'm done living in agony.

"Addison, are you okay?" Aiden's concerned voice asks from behind me.

My shoulders drop, and I let out an exasperated sigh. "Not now, Aiden."

"When then? Addison, when will you talk to me? I'm hanging on by a thread waiting for you to see me. See that I want nothing more than to help you."

I spin around and plant my feet firmly on the ground. The hateful words are out of my mouth before I can stop them. "Aiden, I can't be with you. Every time I see you, I see your dad's face. I see the smirk he had the day my mom lost the light in her eyes." The venom in my voice frightens me. I can't believe I'm saying this, yet it's coming out of my mouth. *Stop, Addison!* You don't mean it. *But I can't.* I throw my hands out. "I thought Travis was the poison inside of me, but he's not. My life has been destroyed by the blood that runs through your veins." I can't even see straight. The irrational part of my brain that is controlling me right now is blinding.

The door swings open. Syd walks in, rounding Aiden, and stands in between us. "Aiden, I think you need to leave," she says softly.

He grips his hair and mumbles a few curse words. He spins around and starts to walk out the door. I sharply inhale, gripping my chest, and hold in the cry that wants to come out. He turns around and pins me with his stare. "You don't mean that. I know you don't," he growls, pointing at me. I stay frozen in place, afraid of what else might spew out if I open my mouth. "I'll leave, Addison." He swallows back his emotions. "But don't think for one fucking minute that we're done." His shoes squeak when he turns, slams the door open, and walks out.

The cry I was holding in breaks free, and I collapse onto the ground. Syd wraps herself around me and I cry not only for the man who I love but also for the man I just destroyed.

10

AIDEN

I stuff my hands in my pockets to keep from punching something or *someone*. My steps are heavy and I'm breathing so hard the bleach undertones in this fucking hospital burn my nostrils. I need to get out of here. I hear footsteps behind me, and I'm almost positive it's Max; I caught a glimpse of him at the nurse's station when I stormed out of Addison's room.

I yank my keys out of my pocket when I approach my car, unlock the doors, and slide inside. Max jumps into the passenger seat without saying a word.

"I don't think you want to be around me right now," I grate out.

"Not a chance in hell I'd let you be alone," he says as he pulls out his phone. When he finds whatever he's searching for, he looks over at me. "Let's go."

I jerk my head in his direction. "Asshole, I'll need more information than that." He sarcastically presses the start button with his index finger on his map app, and a woman's voice comes on and says *turn left onto Sage Parkway.* I blow out a ragged breath and shake my head. "Max," I warn. I am not in the mood for jokes.

"Just follow the damn directions, Aiden."

I sigh and turn the car on. I don't know where the hell I'm going, but at this point I don't care as long as it's away from this hospital. The directions lead us to a biker bar not too far out of town. A few bikes and an old, red, Ford Pickup are parked in front. The sign above the door reads Stokers and it flashes blue every couple seconds.

"How the hell did you know about this place?" I ask, turning the car off and getting out.

"I didn't. But your options of open bars are limited at this time of morning."

I flip my wrist, looking at my watch. It's only nine in the morning, and I don't give a flying fuck. My heart was just ripped out by the woman I love, stabbed a few times, then handed back to me on a silver platter. Bring on the liquor.

The stench of cigarette smoke clears the lingering ammonia smell as I take in a deep whiff when we walk in. Only a couple of patrons sit at the bar. They glance our way as light from the outside fills the dark room from the open door. The female bartender looks us up and down and tells us to sit wherever. Max walks to a booth in the corner and we slide in.

"What can I get you two gorgeous men?" a female waitress purrs. Her voice is raspy, like she's inhaled cigarette smoke too long. She has tats splattered all over her chest and arms, and I'd bet all over her body, too. Her bleach-blonde hair is braided to one side, which is in stark contrast to the black tank top she has on.

"Two shots of Jack," Max tells her, knowing it's my drink of choice. I stare at him. Only two? Max shakes his head. "Bring the whole bottle." He whips out his wallet and slaps down a fifty-dollar bill. That's more like it.

The waitress brings back a couple shot glasses and a brand new bottle of Jack. "Y'all need anything else..." she says with a deep southern drawl and winks at Max, "...my name's Lace." Max flashes a smile.

"We'll let you know, Lace. Thanks."

I'm already opening and pouring the drinks before their short conversation is done. I don't hesitate to down a shot. The quicker I can get drunk, the quicker I can stop this feeling of heartbreak. The sting from the liquid running down my throat is a slow burn that I crave right now, needing to erase Addison's words that repeat in my head. Max watches me pour shot after shot. He takes one every now and then, but for the most part he watches.

As I'm bringing another shot to my lips, he says, "She didn't mean it." I toss the drink back. The sting is starting to numb. Unfortunately, the pain is still there. I slam the shot glass down on the table and hang my head. Squeezing my eyes shut, the words still slice through me like a double-edged knife.

I sigh and look up. "How do you even know what she said," I spit out.

"Sydney and I were outside the room."

"Fucking great. It's so *awesome* that everyone knows that my dad killed Addison's mom." Sarcasm drips from my voice as I pour and down another shot.

"Aiden, no one else heard. I already knew. Sydney didn't, but I'm sure Addison would've told her at some point."

"What were you doing there so early?" I can feel the effect of the Jack as my words come out slower.

"I was there to find you. I have to go back to New York for some business." Max pours himself a shot, wincing as it goes down. I'm jealous of the burn. This numbness is a joke. I'd rather feel the sting because the only thing that's numb is my throat.

I slam my fist on the table. "I can't fight anymore," I say. Addison's words are my biggest fear. She's right. My dad *is* a part of me, and if she can't look at me without seeing him, we're done.

Max raises his eyebrow at me. "When have you ever backed down from a fight?"

"This is different," I say with resignation. "Addison's right. We're not meant to be together." I toss back another shot, having lost count. Max runs his hand across his jaw; I can tell he's thinking what to say. *Brother, there's nothing to say.*

I look around the bar. Lace and the woman bartender are leaning against the bar, looking in our direction and talking. The bartender smiles wide when our eyes meet. I return a lopsided smile before looking back at Max.

"I think you need a break away from everything," he says, shifting his gaze to the girls and back to me. "I have a case up in Washington. It's surveillance only. Four months max. You can take a personal leave of absence, especially since you were just shot three weeks ago."

The thought of leaving Addison makes my stomach twist. Which pisses me off more is because I don't think I have a choice. I can't stay. She doesn't want me here. I'm a fucking man; I should have some sense of dignity. Maybe it is a good idea to get out of dodge. I'm a fool though if I think time will help me forget Addison. She's embedded into my heart. It'll take a lot longer than four months.

My lips start to feel numb, so I push the shot glass away and lean back against the cracked pleather cushion. I look up at the ceiling looking for answers. They always say stuff is written on the walls. Instead, a dirty, yellow ceiling looks back at me.

"I'll go. What else do I have to lose?" I say, sighing and looking back to Max. He nods. "When do I leave?" I slur.

He smirks as he pushes the Jack farther away from me. "Wheels up in three hours."

Panic rushes through me about leaving Addison. "Fuck!" I slam my head down on the table. "Why can't my heart just go numb?"

"Aiden," he says. I lift my head and push myself back up to a sitting position. "I don't think for a damn minute that this is the end of you and Addison. But you're going to need to get your head straight and let her have some time to heal."

I cross my arms. Can't he see that the more time that goes by, the more obvious it is that the world is working against us? It scares me to think what it might throw at us next if we stay together. So why am I panicking about leaving Addison? I should already be packed and on my way back. *Man up, Roberts.*

"Fuck. Let's go," I say, stumbling out of the booth.

A few hours later, with a headache from hell, I lean my seat back and watch from the airplane window as Texas get smaller and smaller. Regret bubbles up from inside of me. I shouldn't have left. What if she's looking for me, wanting to apologize? She'll never forgive me for leaving in her most desperate time of need. I rub my hands over my face and remind myself that she hasn't reached out to me. It's not like she's lost my phone number.

"It's not forever, Aiden," Max says, sitting across from me, looking at me over his computer.

"I just need to accept that it might be." The harsh reality hits me like a brick wall. It might be over and there isn't a damn thing I can do about it. I need to move on. I will always love Addison, but she's right; Fate didn't mean for us to fall in love. "Are you going back?"

He nods. "Make sure she's okay?" I ask.

"I'll keep you informed, brother."

"Can you give her something?"

He nods again. I pull out a random receipt from my wallet and write on the back of it.

YOU'RE NOT BROKEN, *just a little bent. You can fix bent.*

Fight for yourself. I'll think of you always, love you forever.
~A

I FOLD it and hand it to Max, instructing him to give it to her when she leaves the hospital. It's time to move on with my life.

The bullet in my chest hurt less than this.

11

ADDISON

The weather is abnormally warm outside for a January day, even in Texas. I've been told that the sun can help improve your emotional state. But what if you don't feel anything? Only numbness.

I push off with my foot to keep the swing in motion. The two-seater swing sits out in the front yard. It's the place I go when I'm feeling claustrophobic inside. We've established that when I'm out here I want to be alone, meaning leave me alone, people.

I lean back, lounging across the swing, and cross my legs on the armrest. The slight breeze blows over me, swirling my hair around. It's been three weeks since I've seen Aiden. I'm not sure if it was the broken tree or the look on Aiden's face as he was walking out the door, but that day was the last day I felt something.

The doctors want to try anti-depressants, but I don't want any more drugs than I already take. I tell them I'm fine, hoping they'll believe me. Who am I kidding? *I'm not fine*. But I'm not ready to be thrown back into my life. The best thing about country life, you don't have to deal with the hustle and bustle of the outside world. Out here I don't have to think, I can just *be*.

I hear the squeak of the front door. Amy comes into my sight, and she looks down at me. "You want to go to the barn with me to feed the horses?" Her smile is hesitant. She already knows my answer.

"Not today. I'm tired," I say, looking away from her. I hear her softly sigh and walk away.

It's been a long month. The holidays sped by without a lot of celebration. And I was perfectly fine with that. Amy and Ted tried their best to get me excited. Christmas is usually my favorite holiday. Not this year. This year, I don't feel like celebrating. I'm finding it hard to feel anything. I'm stuck at blah.

Joe doesn't visit me too often in my head. Although, I feel him waiting for the chance. It's like playing with a jack-in-the-box toy. My days are like the turning of the handle and he pops out of nowhere when it's least expected. I'm still a prisoner, but now it's my own thoughts keeping me captive. I continue to take a sleeping pill at night. I feel like a child, though, when I'm *given* one at night. They worry about me taking more than one. It's degrading they think I might want to end my life. I can't say the thought has never crossed my mind, but it's never been more than a thought.

I stick my leg off the side of the swing to push off again. The motion soothes me. Closing my eyes, I breathe in the fresh air. I can hear the horses neighing in the barn. Amy wants me to ride with her, but getting on that huge horse gives me anxiety. I have an overwhelming need to be in control at all times right now.

I lift my head up at the sound of a car coming down the driveway. Not recognizing the car, I sit up and watch it come to a stop. I tense. I look toward the front door and back to the car. A fleeting thought of running inside flashes through my mind. My hand squeezes the chain of the swing as I place both feet on the ground, readying myself to run. I watch the door of the car swing open. When I recognize who gets out, I release the breath I was holding.

Tony? Why would my Krav Maga instructor from New York City be here?

I push off the swing and stand, folding my arms across my chest. He shuts the door and starts walking toward me, smiling.

"Hey, Addison," he says, like he's a regular around here.

I open my mouth and then shut it. "Hey?" He laughs at my surprised look. "Tony, what are you doing here?"

He walks over to the swing and sits down. I watch him and then glance around, wondering what I'm missing. He's a couple thousand miles away from home, yet he's acting like this is where he should be.

"Sit with me?" he asks, gesturing to the empty spot on the swing.

"I think I'll stand."

He clasps his hands together in his lap and looks up at me. I don't feel like I'm in danger, but I don't like this feeling of confusion. I don't have unexpected visitors.

"You look good," he says warmly.

"Tony, can we get to the part about why you're here?" I say snidely. I don't mean to sound like such a bitch, but that control issue I have is rearing its ugly head.

He flashes a crooked smile and shrugs. "I was just in town. Wanted to see if you felt like working out with me."

My eyes go wide. Really, *just felt like dropping by to see if I wanted to work out?* I might not be in a good place, but I'm not stupid. That's coming a long way to just work out.

I run my hand through my hair and put it up in a bun because the wind keeps whipping it in my face. *Not* because I plan on working out. I purse my lips, trying to get a read on him. Is that really why he's here?

He stands up, and I take a step back. "I think it'd be good for you." He takes another step in my direction. I furrow my brows, taking another step back.

"No thanks, Tony. I'm *really* not in the mood." My heart starts to race as he takes another step. Why is he pushing this? Chills run up my spine thinking of any man right now touching me. I glance to the front door again, rethinking that I should make a run for it.

He twists his lips and slowly nods. His eyes never leave mine. He suddenly lunges for me leaving me no time to react. I tumble to the ground with him on top of my back. My chest heaves as I lie there, feeling paralyzed.

"Fight, Addison," he says in my ear. I shake my head over and over.

"Please get off of me," I snarl. My nose starts to tickle as tears fill my eyes.

"No," he says sternly. "Make me get off of you." He grabs one of my hands and shoves it between us against my back. I cry out and squeeze my eyes shut, my forehead on the cold, dead grass. What is he doing? Why is he doing this? Can't he see I don't want to fight him?

"Addison, I know you're in there. Fight me, dammit!" he barks out.

The tears burn my face as confusion blurs my mind. I dig my free hand into the grass, grabbing a piece of the earth. His body is heavy on top of me, and I can feel the heat from his breath on my neck. It's not until his hand grabs my ass that my whole body hardens. The thin string that is holding my entire world together snaps.

Unexpected rage flows through me, and my body heats up. *Fuck this!* I plant my foot and a free hand on the ground and push with everything that I have. "NO! Get the fuck off of me!" I scream as I flip us over onto his back and then jump off of him.

He doesn't waste any time, he's back on his feet within a second, coming at me again.

Nothing but our grunts and occasional curse words can be heard as we spar in the grass. My focus is no longer to flee, but to take him down. I don't even know when it changed. I can tell I don't have as much energy as I used to have, but I have enough to fight.

Sweat runs down my forehead as we both lie on our backs, panting heavily. Maybe it's just me panting; I can't tell right now. My breaths are too loud. I can't believe I just did that. Even though my body aches, I feel more alive right now than I have in the last month. The adrenaline pumping through my body feels awesome.

Tony sits up, craning his neck to look back at me. He flashes a sly smile. "Training starts tomorrow. Be at Luke's Gym by nine," he says. He stands and watches my stunned look for a second before he walks back to his car.

I continue to lie on the cool grass, hearing his car drive off. *What the hell just happened?*

EVERY DAY, I feel one step closer to feeling normal. The fog that permeates my mind has started to lift. I've been training almost daily with Tony for a month now. I still haven't got out of him why he's here, or why he's staying, but I have a feeling it's because of Aiden. Max continues to visit weekly, and he won't say anything either. Last week when he was here I asked how Aiden was doing. His reply? *Call him, he'll answer.* That night I stared at my phone for an hour trying to muster up the courage to dial his number. I couldn't do it. I said horrible things to him, and I wouldn't blame him if he hated me. The consequences of my words have no doubt haunted me daily. I'm not ready to hear his voice. And I'm definitely not ready to hear him reject me.

Obviously Max told Aiden about our conversation because I just got a text. I need to remind myself that Max is Aiden's best friend, so I need to keep my mouth shut if I don't want it getting back to him. I look down at my phone once again and sigh.

Aiden: *"One Call Away"* **by Charlie Puth**

I wiggle my earbuds in my ear, lean back on my bed, and press play on my phone. With my eyes closed, I imagine Aiden singing me this song. His deep, raspy voice. God, I miss his voice. *Why can't I just call him?* He obviously doesn't hate me. I guess I'll need to take a few more steps, a few more days, to get back to *that* normal.

"Addie," I barely hear. If I weren't being shaken, I probably wouldn't have even heard it. I open my eyes to Amy standing over me. I must have fallen asleep. Aiden's song is still playing through the earbuds, so I slip one out of my ear and look at Amy.

"What's up?" I ask.

"I thought we were going out riding, and I know how much you hate missing out on riding Rusty. It'll be dark before too long," she says, sitting down on my bed.

"Oh, sorry. I must have fallen asleep." To a gorgeous, green-eyed man singing to me. I don't tell her that, though. I know what she'll say. *Call him.* It seems to be the consensus. There is still so much I need to work through before I go down that road. The song is playing on repeat, so I grab my phone and press stop, then swing my legs over the bed. I grip Amy's hand, pulling her up.

"Let's go. I don't want to keep Rusty waiting."

Rusty, a big, stunning, chestnut gelding, has become my best friend. I chuckle when I think about the reason I wouldn't ride before, that I wouldn't have control. When I'm on Rusty's back, the saddle in between my legs, the leather straps in my palms and we're flying through the open fields, I've never felt more in control of everything. My body. My life. My sanity. It's a feeling of being free. I yearn for that feeling so I'm out riding Rusty whenever I can.

"Syd is coming out next weekend," I tell Amy as we trot along the banks of a creek that runs through the back part of the ranch.

"That's awesome. I can't wait to see her," she replies. "Is Max coming, too?"

"No. I told him Syd was coming so he didn't need to *check* up on me." I roll my eyes. "I mean, he can call to see how I'm doing. I still can't believe he flies here almost every weekend to see me."

"You have a lot of people who care for you and want you to get better."

I sigh and nod. I know I'm on the road to recovery. The scars on my body have faded, and I'm working on the emotional ones. They may never go away, but I'll make damn sure they don't ruin my life.

12

ADDISON

"You ready?"

I gaze out the small airplane window, watching the bags get loaded one by one up the conveyor belt.

"Hey," Tony says, hitting my leg with his. I look over at him. Poor guy. He barely fits into his seat, and not because he's overweight. He's built a lot like Max, just a slight bit smaller. "I asked if you were ready, but you seem somewhere else."

"Sorry, I was just zoning out," I say, smiling at him. Tony has been by my side for the last two months, pushing me to get better every day. I don't think I'll ever be able to thank him enough. "Yes, I'm ready. Thanks to you." I grab his hand and squeeze it.

"Nope, I will not take credit for it. You're the one who pushed through. I just guided you."

"Tony. You gave up two months of your life for me. And even though I'm sure you were here on behalf of Aiden, you're still one of the most amazing men who I know."

"Aww, thank you," he says, blushing, looking down, then leans over and whispers, "But I'm still not telling you why I came." I bump him with my shoulder. It's a question that I have asked repeatedly. He's been here so long though that I gave up trying to find the answer.

"I didn't ask." I chuckle. He gives me a pointed look. "I just said that I'm sure it was Aiden."

He shakes his head. "You know you could have easily found out if that's what you thought."

Here is the main reason I think he's never told me. He *wants* me to call Aiden. Hell, everyone wants me to call Aiden. And while I thought about it many times, what if it wasn't him? Then I'll make him feel guilty for not doing it himself. I blow out a breath. I don't want to make him feel guilty for anything else. I'm sure the guilt between us weighs so much it could ground this seven-thirty-seven airplane.

"I guess I never thought to ask you if you left anyone behind in New York," I say, trying to change the subject. "Are you dating anyone?"

"Why, you interested?" he asks, wagging his eyebrows. I laugh, knowing he's joking.

"Oh, yeah, that would go over well."

"Right? I'd like to keep my life, thanks," he teases. "I mean I'm a big man and can protect myself, but I've got to say, Max scares me."

I laugh louder. "Max seems to scare a lot of people. Hey, you know Harper? You guys should go out."

His hands clap and his laugh echoes. "Oh, Addison. Yes, I know Harper." I turn my body toward him and lift my brow. I obviously haven't heard this story. "She's never told you?" I shake my head. He wiggles his arm so his watch moves down a little and then steeples his fingers, placing his elbows on the armrests.

"Come on, tell me! Harper usually tells me everything. Why haven't I heard about you two?"

"It happened before you moved to New York," he says, turning his head my direction. I gesture with my hand for him to continue. "So, we went out a couple times and ended up at my apartment one night. Things were getting hot and heavy between us and as I'm carrying her to my room, we pass some pictures."

I'm trying to decide if I want to hear the details, because I don't know how detailed he's about to get. Curiosity wins. "Who was in the pictures?"

"My mom and dad," he says, looking down.

"What's wrong with that? I think it's sweet that a guy has pictures of his mom and dad in his house."

"Well. Come to find out, my dad is Harper's doctor."

"Hmm. Okay?"

"My dad is a gynecologist, Addison."

I gasp, covering my mouth with my hand silencing my laugh. Oh, my! *Wait, who's my doctor?*

"So what did she say?"

"She thought it was really awkward that my dad has seen her *vajayjay*—her word, not mine—and that it was just too weird for her." He shrugs.

"Wow."

"Yep. Story of my life. You'd be surprised at how many women who I've met that go to my father."

I grab his arm and squeeze. "I'm so sorry, Tony. I can't imagine," I say, trying to hide the humor in my voice; I can't for long and bust out laughing.

"You don't know how happy I am that he's retiring next year. It sucks that I have to ask a woman who her gyno is before I date them."

The plane takes off and we talk the entire way home about what it was like having a father as a gynecologist. By the time we start our descent into La Guardia, Tony has everyone around us doubled over laughing.

It feels weird walking into my apartment building. Like it's not mine. I've been gone three months. Even the security guard is new. He stops me before I make it to the elevator.

"Excuse me, miss, who are you here to see?" he asks as he stands up.

See, even he thinks I don't belong here. "I'm Addison Mason. I live here."

"Oh, I'm so sorry," he says quickly. His face flushes.

"That's okay. It's been awhile since I've been here."

"I'm Stan Bishop. It's nice to finally meet you." I can only imagine what he's heard about me. "If you need anything, please let me know."

I nod and thank him. As I wait for the elevator, I watch my reflection in the glass. I've changed so much since the last time I stood here. The feeling of melancholy washes over me when I think about the last time I was in my apartment. I was wallowing in sorrow thinking that Aiden had left me. He disappeared for a few days to the beach house. *So much change.*

My reflection vanishes when the doors open and pulls me back to the present. When I step off the elevator, I see a sign on the door that says *"Welcome Back."* I told everyone not to be here when I got home. I needed to do this myself, so if there is a group of people in my apartment, I'm going to kill someone.

I breathe a sigh of relief when I slowly open the door and peek into an empty apartment. I look around at everything. *Well, life, we're back in business.*

I may have wanted to be alone when I got home, but everyone might as well have been here because my phone has been ringing nonstop. Did you get there? How are you feeling? When can I see you? Are you sure you're okay?

I settle back into my couch and take a breather between phone calls. I need to get out of here, go for a walk. The liveliness of the city has always energized me.

"Addison." I whip around at the sound of my name and see Marco swiftly walking toward me as soon as I walk out of my building. I smile but quickly grab my phone like I just received a text. I half expect him to want a hug, so I make my hands look busy. Even though I feel like my old self, I'm definitely not in the mood for flirting. I text Sydney random stuff. She'll just think I'm bored. "It's so great to see you," he says, standing in front of me. He looks down at my phone and then back up to my eyes. I keep both my hands on my phone.

"Hey, Marco, it's good to see you, too." I force a smile.

"I heard you were home." My back straightens. There are only a few people who knew I was coming back, and I just got back today. "I mean, I overheard someone in the restaurant say that you might be coming back soon," he says backtracking.

I guess that could've happened. I stuff my hands in my jacket and stand there, not really knowing what to say. "Well, it was really good seeing you. I need to go back up to my apartment; I think I forgot to turn off my stove. I just needed some fresh air so I walked out without thinking." I shake my head and wave my hand around. "Silly me."

His eyes assess me like he's trying to gauge if I'm telling the truth. I put my hand on the door and his eyes follow my movement.

"Okay, beautiful. Come see me soon. I want to make you your favorite meal." His smile reaches his striking, dark eyes. He is really an attractive man. Why he's not taken already surprises me. I blow my cheeks out as I walk back inside. Maybe I'll skip the walk.

13

ADDISON

They say time heals, but what if time seems to be standing still? The day changes, but my life feels like it's staying in one spot. I'm caught in a loop and can't seem to move forward. The colorful blur of people's lives pass me while mine seems to be stuck in black and white, motionless.

I get up feeling groggy every morning after taking a sleep aid at night. I've tried to stop taking it a couple times because I hate that feeling, but it seems my mind doesn't want to move on either when I sleep. Why does it want to keep reliving that hell?

Coffee is a must now. Before, I rarely drank it. My chai tea latte was all I needed, and I tried that once but ended up wearing two different pairs of shoes to work. Definitely not strong enough to pull me out of my sleep-induced funk.

Speaking of work, I know everyone there has good intentions, but I'm tired of people walking on eggshells around me. It's been three and a half months. They are still afraid to talk to me and when they do, their voice drips with pity. I hide out in my office all day.

Sydney is worried about me. At least she's not treating me like

I'm going to break. She's trying to make me push forward out of my merry-go-round of a life right now.

Syd's on her way up now. I'm lounging in my pajamas, watching Chip and Joanna on *Fixer Upper*. I've never wanted to live in Waco before, but it's very tempting watching this show. I want them to do a house for me.

I hear the door open and close. My eyes stay on the TV because the reveal is coming up. I can't *miss* that! Syd walks around the couch and plops down.

I look over at her quickly. "Hey," I say.

"This again?" she says, staring at me.

"What's wrong with Chip and Joanna?"

She purses her lips and rolls her eyes. "I can't believe they're making Waco out to be this fabulous place," she says, waving her hands toward the TV.

I laugh at her. It's true. It's a college town and not much else. Well, if you Google Waco, it's definitely a known town. But good on Chip and Joanna for helping make it a better place.

I shush Syd when the reveal starts. I'd love to have a fixer-upper. I think of Aiden and his beach house, all that work they did and how proud he was of it.

I think of Aiden a lot, wondering how he's doing and if he's thinking of me. I've picked up my phone so many times I've lost count. I mean to call him or text him, but then chicken out. He probably hates me for what I did. The guilt eats at me every day. It's not my fault … that's all I ever hear from people. Nothing seems to be my fault, but everything keeps happening to me. Can't they see it's *me*? I've been doomed since I was born. Bad luck, bad karma, bad fate … whatever, *it's all BAD*.

I get pushed over by Syd's foot. "What the hell?" I snap.

"It's over. What are we going to do today?" she asks, still pushing me with her foot.

"I'm going to break your foot today, if you don't stop," I answer. I grab her foot and start tickling her.

"Okay, okay!" she squeals, pulling her foot out of reach.

She tucks her feet under her and stares at me expectantly. I lay my head back and look up. Can't I just sit here and watch the *Fixer Upper* marathon? I don't dare ask because she'd never let me.

I shrug, tilting my head in her direction. "What's Damon doing?"

She shrugs back. "I don't know. He said he had a date tonight." My eyes widen.

"What? I thought you two ..."

She waves her hand in the air. "I don't even know what to think. He's hot one minute, the next he's cold. I don't know what he wants. I don't think *he* knows what he wants."

"Well, he's a stupid man not to see what's right in front of him," I say, smiling at her.

"Yep, his loss," she says quietly, looking at the TV. I watch her for a few moments. I know they like each other so I'm confused. Seems there's a lot more to the story than she's telling me. Typical. It's the same with everyone. They only tell me things they *think* I can handle. I sigh as I push off the couch.

"I'll go take a shower so we can do something," I say, dragging my feet to my bedroom.

As I turn off my hair dryer, I hear voices coming from the living room. I freeze, trying to hear who it is. Sydney laughs and then I hear a male voice. My hands fist and my body tenses up from anxiety. I take a deep breath and close my eyes. *Addison, calm down.* Syd wouldn't be out there laughing if it were someone to worry about.

It's not until I hear the male voice yell, "Add Cat, get out here," that I know who's here. My lips curl when I recognize Frankie's voice. I walk out of my room and a surprise stops me in my tracks. A Caribbean, blue-eyed surprise.

"Travis," I say. I look around the room as Travis, Frankie, and Syd all watch my reaction. I don't even know what I feel. I haven't seen him since the day I was kidnapped, and I didn't leave there with any warm and fuzzies. But I know it's because of him and Frankie that I was rescued, so there *is* gratitude. And a small part of me recognizes that he is my father, even though I know we can't have a relationship.

He stands up from the barstool. "Addison, it's good to see you," he says, embracing me in a hug. My arms hang at my side because I'm confused about what to do. Do I hug him back, push him away, or just stand here hoping he'll stop soon?

It's not until I take a deep breath and his scent reaches me that I break. I wrap my arms around him as tears begin to fall. His embrace tightens. It feels surreal that I'm in my father's arms. So many years I wondered what he was like and now he's right here, holding me in his arms. Wavering emotions flow through me.

"I'm so sorry," he repeats softly into my hair.

I blink my tears away and draw in a breath. My arms go lax as I step back, and I smile up at him.

"Thanks," I say sheepishly.

"Anytime," he says as he wipes away a tear on his own face. "You look great."

I nod and let out a soft sigh. I look at his dark denim jeans and off-white sweater. If it weren't for his salt-n-pepper hair, I'd have a hard time thinking he was old enough to be my father. He definitely looks better than the last time I saw him.

"You do, too. Orange definitely wasn't your color."

His powerful laugh echoes in my small apartment. "I hope to God I never have to wear it again," he chuckles.

"C'mere and give me a hug," Frankie says with his arms open wide. I walk over, laughing at his big, goofy smile.

As soon as my arms wrap around his neck, he picks me up and spins me around. I cherish the moments when someone does something, not expecting me to break. I think that's why I like to go to the gym a lot with Tony. Shit, sometimes I think he's actually *trying* to break me—but in a good way.

"Well, I guess we're even," I say when he puts me down. If it weren't for Frankie, I would have died in that prison. It's eye opening to think about why a person was placed in your life. When I met Frankie, I would have never figured that he would be my angel. I thought I was his. But our relationship was bigger than that. And I'll forever be grateful for him.

"We're not keeping tabs, Add Cat," he says, his voice turning serious.

"I know," I whisper. "Thank you. For everything." He nods in understanding. "So, do y'all want something to drink?" I ask, needing to do something. I walk to the kitchen, grab a bottle of water, and hold it up. "I have … water." I laugh when I look back into the refrigerator and notice it's almost empty except for the waters. I guess I should go grocery shopping today.

Grabbing one for everyone, we all sit in the living room. I sit in the cushioned chair, Sydney and Frankie take the couch, and Travis grabs a kitchen chair. He sits in it, leaning back with his leg propped up on his knee.

"So what brings you to New York City?" I ask, looking between the two guys.

Travis opens his mouth to answer and then snaps it shut. He's thinking about what to say. "Just some business," he answers.

"Oh. That was vague," I reply sarcastically.

Frankie laughs out loud, clapping his hands. "I see it now," he says, nodding his head.

"See what now?"

"Similarities," he says, smiling.

I roll my eyes, shaking my head. "What … they're both smart asses?" teases Sydney.

"Girl, *that's* for sure," Frankie boasts, high-fiving Sydney.

"It's best you don't know anything about what I do, Addison," Travis says, ignoring the chuckling duo on the couch. "But since I was here, I wanted to stop by. I hope you don't mind."

"I don't. But you're right," I say, looking at him. "It's probably best that you don't make this a habit either. Coming here," I clarify.

"I won't," he says, looking down, playing with the water bottle in his hand. "I just wanted to see you. Make sure you were okay."

"I'm glad you did." When he looks up, I smile at him.

"Well, I wish we could stay longer..." he glances at his watch "...but we have to be somewhere in half an hour." The guys stand and they each give me another hug before leaving.

I shut the door and lean back against it. My feelings for Travis catch me off guard. A small part of me would like to get to know him better.

"Well, that was interesting," Syd says as I walk to the couch. "It's crazy how you don't look anything like him, but you definitely have his eyes."

It's those eyes, mija. Those eyes are your hell.

I snap my eyes shut, shaking my head. I fall into the couch and drop my head between my legs as my body starts to shake, hearing Rico's words.

"Addison! Look at me," I hear Syd say. She grabs my hands off my head. "Addison, it's me, Sydney. You're safe. You're with me. Open your eyes," she commands softly.

Her words start out muted but the more she talks, the closer I get to her. When it's just her voice I hear, I pry my eyes open.

"That's it, Addie. You're safe," she says, nodding, expecting me to understand. I nod back. She grabs my water, untwists the top, and hands it to me. I can feel drops of sweat running down my back. I hold out my hand for the cap. When I twist it back on, I run the bottle across my forehead. The coolness helps as I do my breathing exercises.

"What just happened?"

I exhale slowly. I always feel pathetic when I have flashbacks. "Rico would always mention my eyes. He told me they were my hell," I say, picking at my jeans.

"Your eyes are beautiful, Addie. Your eyes are not your hell. He was." I nod, agreeing with her. Yes, he was. *Him and his spawn.*

When I calm down, I glance at Syd sitting across from me on the coffee table. "I'm sorry," I say and look away from her.

A pillow slams against my head. "Ouch," I say, rubbing my head. "What was that for?"

"Stop saying you're sorry. You don't have anything to be sorry for." She tries to hit me again, but I duck this time. I stick my tongue out at her. "Dr. Price told both of us that this might happen. It's part of your healing. You know you're safe," she says, standing up. "I'm starving, so let's go eat."

That is what I love about Syd. She's direct and moves on. As we're walking out of my building, she says out of the blue, "Frankie is so hot." I laugh when she starts to fan herself. "I mean seriously. It's a good thing you came out of the bedroom when you did, because I was about to jump on the man."

"Speaking of them being here, did you let them in?" I ask, just now remembering I never buzzed them up.

"Yes, but don't be mad," she adds quickly. "I just thought you'd want to see Frankie. And I was being really nosy wanting to see Travis in real life." She bites her lip, waiting for my response.

"It's okay," I say, bumping her with my hip as we walk. "It was good seeing them both."

"Excuse me."

Syd and I both stop walking and turn to the voice behind us. There is a woman a little shorter than me with long, dark brown hair and striking emerald green eyes. I tilt my head while appraising the woman, definitely not missing the uncanny similarities to Aiden. They both have a strong jaw line, although hers definitely looks feminine.

"Are you Addison?" she asks, fiddling with her purse strap. She's wearing black slacks, black boots, and a pink sweater. She's as beautiful as Aiden is gorgeous.

I nod. "And I'm assuming you're Katie?"

"How did you …" she stops when she looks at my face. "Oh, well, I guess we do look a lot alike." She flips her hand out and an awkward laugh escapes her lips. I can tell she's nervous.

I glance around to see if there is anyone else with her. I'm not sure who I expect but a little flicker of hope is that I'll see Aiden standing somewhere close by. He's not here. I look back at her. "What brings you to New York?" I ask.

I'm having another déjà vu moment right now. It seems everyone is visiting New York today. And me.

"I was here visiting … a friend," she answers.

I look at Sydney. "What is with all the vague answers today?" She laughs while Katie's eyebrows furrow, obviously confused. I'm not sure why she feels like she needs to lie. She could have just said she was here on business, and I wouldn't have thought twice about it. *But now I am.* Is Aiden back? No. I'm certain Max or Damon would've told me.

"Katie, this is my best friend, Sydney," I say, looking between the two.

"Aiden's mentioned you," she says as she shakes Syd's hand. My heart patters. Did he mention her recently? Maybe he *is* back. I narrow my eyes at her.

"Is Aiden back?" I ask.

"Oh. No," she says, sighing when she sees my lips turn down. "I'm sorry. I didn't mean for you to think I've talked to him recently. I haven't talked with him for a few months."

"That's okay. I was just wondering," I say. I don't want to let this connection go, though, not yet. "We were headed to lunch. Would you like to join us?" I offer.

"Are you sure?" she asks, looking at Syd and then back to me. "I don't want to intrude."

Syd smiles at her. "I don't mind. I'm kinda tired of being with her all the time by myself," she says, giggling.

"*Hmph* … I love you, too," I huff, wrinkling my nose.

Syd laughs again, wrapping her arm around me. "I love you lots and lots," she says, looking up at me with puppy dog eyes. I roll my eyes at her dramatic flair. Even if I wanted, I could never stay mad at her.

Katie agrees to go to lunch with us. We're walking down the street, passing Bella Mistero, when Marco comes rushing out of his restaurant.

"Addison!" he boasts. He walks up to me with his arms stretched wide and wraps them around me. I feel a little irritated because he takes away my control by not waiting to see if I even *want* a hug.

It's okay, it's just Marco. I tell myself. He's always been a hugger. He's not going to harm me. I take a deep inhale and blow it out slowly. Sydney saves me, pulling me out of his embrace and saying it's her turn, then gives him a hug. When our eyes meet, hers bore into me.

He pulls back quickly, looking back to me. "Please come in and have lunch, ladies. I have a new dish I need to test out," he says, smiling wide at us. He's always been a happy guy, but he seems a little over the top right now.

Syd glances my way, her eyes wide. "Thanks, Marco, but we were going—"

"Nonsense," he says interrupting me. "I promise that you will have an amazing lunch with wine or anything you want, beautiful." He opens his door, ushering us in. Syd is still staring at me, throwing fire with her eyes. I shrug. What am I supposed to do?

Katie walks in behind Syd, not having a clue as to what is going on.

We're seated out on the terrace. The sun is out in full force, but the cool spring breeze keeps it perfect. I close my eyes and take a deep breath of the fresh air. It feels rejuvenating. Things that I took for granted before, like fresh air or the feel of the sun's warmth, I now covet.

"Are you okay?" Syd asks, sitting across from me. I keep my eyes closed and nod. I just need a moment for a time out. I've learned to meditate, especially right after situations that I feel uncomfortable. Marco's hug is definitely one of those times. And it's not really him; it's me and my levels of comfort right now with men.

"Addie, we don't need to stay. I can make up an excuse for us to leave," Syd says as she squeezes my hand on top of the table.

I open my eyes and sigh loudly. "No, I'm okay. I can't keep running and hiding when I feel anxious. Marco is harmless." I look to Katie, wondering if I've made it uncomfortable for her. Instead, her eyes crinkle with a warm smile.

Lunch ends up being amazing, which doesn't surprise me. The food here is always getting rave reviews from foodies. Our conversation is light with lots of laughs and flows throughout lunch. I feel relaxed and really like Katie by the time we finish with lunch. She doesn't bring up Aiden, which surprises me. I thought that was the whole reason she wanted to find me. She admits she was here for a man but doesn't disclose any other information, and we tried to pry it out of her. I'm not exactly sure why, but I get the feeling she's hiding something from Aiden. She tells me that she's wanted to meet me for a while now, but for obvious reasons hasn't. Since she's in town, she said she thought she would look me up. I'm so glad she did.

As we get up to leave, Marco comes to our table. This time when he moves forward to hug me, I step back. "I'm sorry,

Marco," I say holding up my hand. The hurt in his eyes makes me second-guess my decision. *Don't be a bitch.* The man just gave us an incredible meal, on the house, and this is how I treat him. "I just ..." I pause trying to gather my thoughts. "I'm just not ready for a lot of touching," I explain the best I can.

"Beautiful, I understand," he says softly. His body language says something different though. His posture is stiff, and I notice the flex of his muscles. I tilt my head, watching him briefly, before Syd takes it upon herself to say our goodbyes. As we're leaving, I glance back at Marco and offer an apologetic smile. He scowls until he realizes that I'm looking at him. His expression instantly changes to a smile, and he waves goodbye. Shit, I hope I didn't make him mad. He's always been so nice to me, I should really come back later and apologize. Without Sydney.

Katie tells us she has to go to make her flight. I give her a hug. "Thank you so much for finding me. I loved meeting you," I say.

Her hug tightens around me before she pulls back. "If you ever need to talk to someone who knows how you're feeling, please call me," she says softly. I'm taken aback by what she says. Her lips curl up slightly and she nods. "They tell you to go to group sessions, but I always found those depressing."

Oh, my God. Katie was raped? Does Aiden know? Does Max know? So many questions run through my head.

"He doesn't know," she says quietly, looking away. "He's already an overprotective brother. It would have just made things a lot worse. But really, if you need to talk, I'm here to listen."

I hug her again. "Thank you."

We hail a cab for her and wave as she leaves. "I like her," Sydney says, leaning into me. I nod. Me, too. "Who I don't like is Marco." She pulls me down the street. I sigh loudly. "Addison, why can't you see it?"

I shrug. "See what? He's just a concerned friend. He's been nothing but nice to me."

"He hovered the whole lunch. More so this time than in the past. And that hug in the beginning. Anyone could see how uncomfortable you were, but he just hugs you tighter," Syd exclaims.

I shake my head. She's being overly dramatic. All I know is today was a good day. I felt normal. A step in the right direction. Maybe time is just moving slower for me, but it's definitely moving.

14

ADDISON

"I'll call you when I'm done running, Syd," I say into the phone, holding it between my shoulder and my ear while I tie my shoe. We hang up and I put my cell phone and gun into a special running belt under my shirt. I double-check that they are both in there snug before heading out to Central Park. The constant feeling that someone is following me has slowly subsided, but I feel more at ease knowing I have my gun.

The air is crisp this spring morning. I'd gotten used to the sticky, spring air in Texas; I'd already be sweating just stretching. As I sit on the grass and stretch my legs, I watch people run past me, lost in their own world. Do they know how lucky they are to be able to do that? Will I ever feel that safe again? Have I ever truly felt that sense of security? I reflect on my life, and I think the last time I felt that way was right before my mom was murdered.

I glance around one last time before sticking one earbud in my ear and turning on my music. I push off the ground and wait until a couple runners pass before jogging behind them. Selena Gomez's "It Ain't Me" blares into one ear. I find the rhythm and my feet fall into pace with it. Working with Tony again has improved my endurance running stamina. Running a marathon has crossed my mind. *For a quick second.* I'm not sure I would enjoy running for *that* long. I start out my run around the reservoir. The view is unbelievable. I've missed the magnificent skyline of Manhattan, but the best part of the view is the blooming cherry blossom trees. They are like puffs of cotton candy against the blue sky. Running along the east side of the reservoir, tiny pink and white petals dust the trail. For a few moments I feel like a princess from a fairy tale, running under the light shower of petals. I always laugh to myself, thinking a squirrel is going to come out and be able to talk to me. Then I pass the pretty trees and I'm back to reality.

I hum the tune of the song as I run along the path. I'm back to my starting point so I know I've gone a little over a mile and a half. I usually veer off and take a different path through wooded areas, but something inside of me tells me to stay on this path. I pull out my earbud and strain to listen to everything around me. I keep my pace, but the feeling of someone following me makes me uneasy. I shake my head and roll my eyes. Of course someone is following me. I mean, I'm on a freaking jogging path; there are probably a hundred people behind me. I take a deep breath, trying to calm my irrational nerves.

I put my earbud in again, hoping I can drown the feelings I'm having with music and get back into a groove. It doesn't work. Instead, there are heavy footsteps behind me that drown out everything else. It's all I hear. Even my heartbeat matches the vibrations of the steps. I don't know if I'm imagining the increase of both or if I'm going crazy. There are a lot of people out here; nothing is going to happen to me. Reaching under my shirt, I run my thumb along my gun to make sure it's still there. I know I'm being ridiculous as my blood simmers with anxiety.

I tell myself to pull off to the side, but my body is afraid of what might happen if I stop moving. I glance at the bench coming up and decide I'm stopping. I sit at the last second before passing it and a tall man plops right down next to me so close we're almost touching, causing me to scream and jump up.

"Oh, sorry, I didn't mean to scare you," Marco says, standing up. I grab my frantic heart, beating so fast that I think I might pass out. "Here, sit down." He guides me back to the bench and helps me sit. I take in deep breaths, blowing them out slowly.

When I'm able to talk, I look at Marco sitting next to me. "Holy shit, you scared me." My eyes dart over his body, relieved to see that he's wearing basketball shorts and a sweat-covered shirt. He's running, just like me. Just like the hundreds of other people here. I cover my eyes with my hand to hide my embarrassment. "I'm sorry," I say with my head down.

Marco's hand rubs my back. "It's okay, beautiful. Nothing to be ashamed of."

My back straightens from the unexpected feel of his hand. Standing up quickly, I look down at him. "So, do you run here often?" I quickly blurt out. Marco chuckles. I close my eyes and sigh. *Good one, Addison.* Way to defuse the situation. Maybe next I can ask him if he has a map, because I keep getting lost in his eyes.

Marco sits back, laying his hand across the park bench, and his gaze moves up and down my body. His apparent gawking has me ready to turn and leave. "I come here sometimes," he replies slowly when his eyes move back up and meet mine.

"How long were you behind me?" I ask, tilting my head, wishing he'd stop checking me out.

"Not long. As soon as I started, I saw you up ahead and I figured I'd catch up with you. But you're faster than I thought," he says as he runs his fingers through his wet hair, smiling wide. How the heck did he know it was me from behind? Is my ass that recognizable? Especially in the sea of people out this morning? I twist my lips and think about that for a couple seconds. Aiden swears he could pick out my ass anywhere ...

"Well, it seems you've caught me on the tail end of my run," I say, trying to sound sincere. I had planned on running another couple miles, but given the company, I'm not feeling it anymore. Marco rubs his bottom lip with his fingers, staring at me. I rock back and forth on my feet under his assessing eyes. When he stands up, he steps right in front of me.

"Addison, go on a date with me," he says. My eyes go wide in surprise. That's the last thing I expected him to say. Although, I'm not sure why I'm surprised. He's made it very clear that he likes me, but he's never acted on it.

"Oh," I say when he looks at me expectantly. "Um, Marco, you're a great guy ... but Aiden and I are still figuring things out." It's not a total lie. I manage a soft smile at the awkward moment. His eyes turn hard and he spins around. He takes a few steps and then whips around again. I wrap my arms around my waist when his eyes bore into mine.

"You are such a tease, Addison."

"I'm sorry. What did you say?" I ask defensively. Talk about a one-eighty about face. I don't know what the hell just happened with his attitude, but that was uncalled for. I have never given him any indication that I was interested in him.

"You know you want me. I can see it in your eyes every time you see me. Why don't you just give me a chance?" His arms go out wide, like he's waiting for me to run into them. My mouth gapes open as my head jerks back a bit. *You know you want me?* Oh, yeah, that's a *great* way to get a girl to go out with you.

I take a couple seconds to pull myself together. I open my mouth and then slam it shut. *Not quite ready.* When I am, I try again. "Marco, I've been with Aiden almost the entire time we've known each other, so what have I ever done to *tease* you? I've always been nice to you because I thought we were friends. But that's it."

He takes a step toward me, and I hold up a hand stopping him from getting any closer. He looks down at my hand and a shadow falls over his face. He blinks a couple times, his temper erasing from his features. I narrow my eyes at him, watching him closely. He backs up. "Well, I feel like an idiot now. I'm sorry, Addison. I must have misread the situation." He tries to sound apologetic but it comes out hollow.

I nod slowly. I don't know what else to say. I frown and sigh. "I don't want to give you the wrong idea again, so maybe it's best if I stay away from the restaurant and if we pass each other on the street, a friendly 'hi' will suffice," I resign.

"No, beautiful," he begs as he reaches forward. I step back again and wince at the name and wonder why he's still using it when five seconds ago he looked at me with pure hatred. "I know now you can't go out with me because of Aiden." I could easily add that isn't the only reason, especially now, but I keep that to myself. I look around at the joggers running past us. I catch the eyes of a few of them and flash a soft smile as they go by.

"Well, I need to go," I say, pointing my thumb behind me in the direction I should be heading. "I'm sure I'll see you around." He nods his head and sits back on the bench. Is he going to watch me walk away? Well this is about the most uncomfortable goodbye I've ever had. I wave and then turn around. I don't think I've ever tried this hard to *not* sway my hips. I know if I turn around, he'll be watching me. To prove to myself that I'm right, I glance back after a few minutes. He's still on the bench and his smile reaches his eyes when our gazes meet. *Fuck!*

15

ADDISON

"Addison," CJ sighs. "We got another one." I look up from my computer. My head tilts to the side.

"Another one?"

"Another family was murdered last night. I need you and Harper out there..." CJ pauses, "...unless you think you need to sit this one out."

"The cereal killer?" CJ nods. We need to find this guy. The media gave him the name *cereal killer* because he always leaves a bowl of uneaten cereal as his calling card. How stupid is that? It pisses me off even more that someone leaked that information. Can't people keep their damn mouths shut? Now we have to worry about copycats.

"No, I can do it," I reply, my voice flat.

Harper walks into my office, twirling the van keys around her finger. "Ready to go get this guy?"

"More than you know," I say, putting on my vest and badge. My motivation for finding this guy has my body heating up in anger just thinking about it. Things like this didn't bother me before, but knowing that he always rapes the wife before killing her has me feeling uneasy.

As we walk out to the elevators, Harper leans over and whispers, "Let me know if you need a breather."

I stand tall and nod. *I can do this. This is my job. I love my job.*

Pulling up to the house, the media already occupies almost every piece of lawn space. The sound of a group of vehicles parking quickly grabs my attention. I look up and find two black SUVs, their doors swinging open. I stop and see who gets out. My head knows that Aiden doesn't come back for at least another month, but my heart skips a beat hoping to see him hop out of the vehicle. Instead, my eyes land on Damon. He gives me a half smile and mouths, "*Okay?*"

I twist my lips, taking a deep breath in and out. I nod.

"You alright?" Harper quietly asks from behind me. I grab my kit from the back of the van and turn toward her.

"Yep. I don't know what it's going to be like when he gets back into town." I sigh.

"If anyone can figure it out, it's you," she says, wrapping her arm through mine. "Now let's go find some evidence to catch this asshole."

As always, we push through the questions being thrown at us with determination. It's not until a reporter yells something about me being capable of doing my job because of what I went through that I almost trip. I tighten my grasp around my field kit as heat crawls up my body. I can't help it when my mouth opens to tell the jerk off, but I stop when a hand wraps around my arm.

"Ignore them," Damon whispers. "You've been cleared to work. Don't second-guess yourself because these assholes are trying to get a story."

I clench my teeth together, and we continue walking into the house. Two detectives join us when we enter, as well as the FBI agents. We're debriefed quickly. Family of four all shot, man, woman, two kids: a boy and a girl. They estimate the time of death at around midnight. All the bodies were found in the bedrooms. When they report the woman was raped, my spine stiffens. I already knew this would be the case, but it still gets to me.

Harper leans over and whispers, "You get the kids' rooms, I'll do the parents' room." I nod in agreement and quietly breathe a sigh of relief. God, I love her.

A few hours later, I'm in the last room to be analyzed. I take out my notepad and start taking notes. Looking around the room, my eyes land on the tiny, lifeless body on the bed. How someone can be so cruel to harm such innocent children always baffles me. I pull out my camera and take a few pictures. I walk around the room, looking at the drawings on the walls of clouds and sunshine, the name Lexi spelled across one wall, little girls' princess dresses thrown all over the floor, the pictures on the dresser. One picture is the victim with another girl. Their smiles brighten the whole picture, but what catches my attention is the other girl. Her eyes match her hair, caramel-colored but outlined in green. I've never seen that coloring in eyes. As I glance from picture to picture, my brows furrow. Why is that other girl in all the pictures, some by herself, some with the family? What's missing is the daughter in all the pictures.

"Something's not right," I whisper. I turn and look around the room again, looking for an answer. I glance to the lifeless child and back to the pictures of the parents. She doesn't resemble them, but there are a million reasons that could be. I look back at the other girl and chills run down my back. She looks identical to the mom.

I turn my head thinking I hear a noise, but it's so faint that I could be imagining it. Focusing on the noise again, I hear it coming from the closet.

Oh, shit.

I walk to the closet, barely leaning my ear against the door, and hear soft sobs. I gasp. *Oh, my*! Knowing what I'm about to find, I slowly open the door. Crouched in the corner of the closet, a pair of huge, caramel-colored eyes look up to me. Tears fall down her face as she hugs her legs close to her chest. I try to look at her body to see if she's hurt, but it's hard when she's curled up so tight.

I kneel down in the closet. "It's okay. You're safe now. My name is Addison, and I'm with the New York Police Department."

She stares at me but doesn't move an inch. "Are you Lexi?" She slowly nods her head. I exhale quickly. "Are you hurt?" She shakes her head. I close my eyes and drop my head.

I glance to the bedroom door, wondering how I should handle this. I can't believe they missed that the little girl wasn't the daughter. I need to let the detectives know that Lexi is still alive. They're going to have a shit storm coming when the parents of the little girl find out. And it won't take long. I also need to get her out of here without her seeing her friend.

As I start to stand up, Lexi lunges for me, grabbing me. Her arms wrap around my waist like a vise. I kneel back down and wrap my arms around her.

"Don't worry, I'm not leaving you, sweet girl." My heart hurts for her. "We're going to have to go downstairs, but I need you to close your eyes really tight and not open them until I tell you." She doesn't say anything but digs her head into my shoulder and squeezes her arms around my neck. I scoop her little body up while I stand and her legs wrap around me. She's like a spider monkey holding on for dear life.

"Okay, I'm going to walk you downstairs. Keep those eyes shut," I say as I back out of the closet. Her little body starts to shake, and I'm not sure if she's going into shock or she's crying. "Shh … I've got you. It's going to be okay, Lexi." I don't know what else to say. It's a load of bullshit because I know firsthand that it's not going to be alright. As I'm walking downstairs, Harper notices me. Her eyes get huge and she's about to say something, but I put my finger to my lips. She meets me at the bottom of the stairs.

"I need you to find Damon. Meet me in the guest room." I already know that the guest room is clear, and we need to make sure to keep her out of sight of the media. For now.

I walk into the room, shutting the door behind me. "You can open your eyes now, Lexi. Can I place you on the bed?" I ask softly. She shakes her head violently, not even looking up to me. "I'll sit on the bed and you can sit with me." She doesn't move so I guess she's okay with that suggestion. Damon comes into the room right as I sit down. His eyes widen in disbelief.

"What? Who is that?" Damon asks as he crouches in front of me, looking her over.

"Lexi, this is Agent Damon Flores. Can you say hi?" Again, she shakes her head. Damon looks at me, tilting his head with an arch of his brow. I can't just come out and say her friend was killed, so I ask, "Lexi, did your friend spend the night with you last night?" She slowly nods her head. Damon nods his also in understanding.

"Can you tell us her name?" Silence.

"Lexi, are you hurt at all? Can I take a look at you?" Damon softly touches her back and the most God-awful scream comes out of her mouth. I jump at the horrible noise and shove his hand away, hoping it'll make her stop.

"It's okay, Lexi. *Shh* ... Damon isn't going to hurt you." I begin to rock her. She quiets, but her vise grip is suffocating. "Alright, sweet girl, I'm not letting you go, but you're going to have to loosen your grip a little bit." She does exactly that, *just a little bit.* Damon finds this amusing. I kick my leg out, kicking him in the shin.

I mouth to him, "What do I do?" He shrugs. I narrow my eyes and twist my lips. I'm seriously in unknown territory here with this kid.

He mouths back, "You're the woman." My mouth drops open. I roll my eyes and flip him off. *Asshole.*

"Stay here, I'll go find out what we need to do."

As I'm rocking Lexi, I feel her breathing slow and her arms fall lax against my shoulders. I'm fairly certain she has fallen asleep. I hesitate to move her because I really don't ever want to hear that shrieking noise that came out of her little body again, but my arms are falling asleep. I gently and slowly stand up and her body is still limp, so I lay her down on the bed as softly as possible. I manage to get her on the bed without waking her up. I shoot my arm in the air. Yes!

I look over her, making sure she isn't noticeably hurt anywhere. I exhale quietly, relieved. My eyes gloss over thinking about the long road this little girl will have to endure. Long, caramel curls with soft highlights frame her little face. She's got the perfect little button nose and her long lashes flutter as she drifts further to sleep. I cover her with a blanket and walk to the door.

Wrapping my hand around the doorknob, I turn it so slowly that I wonder if it's even turning, hoping it doesn't make any noise. When it stops, I turn and look back at Lexi. She hasn't moved, so I pull open the door. Light floods the room, so I quickly shut the door from the other side.

I rub my face with my hands. The heavy burden I feel for that little girl is already messing me up. It has to be because I know what it's like to be in her shoes.

I stay posted outside the door, not wanting to leave Lexi. Damon's watching me as he's on the phone. He's shaking his head, clearly as lost as I am about what to do. Harper comes up to me. "I've started on Lexi's room. What the hell happened here?"

"I don't know. She won't talk, but I'm assuming she might have heard something and hid, and the killer didn't know about the friend," I say.

"How are you doing?" she asks, concern in her voice. "I know this might hit a little close to home for you."

I shrug. "I'm okay. My heart breaks for her because ... well, you know." I take a deep breath and blow out my cheeks.

Damon struts over to join us. "So we need to get Lexi to the hospital to have her checked out. But we need to keep her status under lock and key since we don't know if she'll be in danger when the killer finds out she's still alive. We also need to find out if she saw him. She might be the biggest lead we've had on catching this guy," he says, crossing his arms.

Oh, my God! I didn't even think about her being in danger. I shudder at the thought. "That asshole will not touch Lexi," I say through gritted teeth. My need to protect Lexi catches me off guard.

Suddenly a scream comes from behind the door, sending chills down my back. I rush through the door with Damon and Harper right behind. Lexi is screaming, thrashing all over the bed. She's still asleep. The monster that kids are always afraid of that live in the closet has now invaded her sweet dreams. He's real and he's not going anywhere anytime soon.

I scoop her up in my arms and hold her tight against my chest. Her arms are flailing as she continues to scream. She's fighting her monster. As I'm trying to grab hold of her arms, a small fist connects with my lip.

I let out a groan. Shit, her little hand packs a punch. I grab her hands and wrap my arms around her. "Lexi, wake up. It's just a dream." I automatically start rocking her. After a few minutes she settles down, opening her eyes. When she sees me, she digs her head into my chest and starts bawling.

"I want my mommy," she hiccups through her sobs. It's the first time I've heard her voice. I look to Harper and Damon for assistance, but all I get is silence. Harper's hand is over her mouth, her eyes watering. Damon turns away, aggressively running his hands through his hair.

What the hell am I supposed to say? I am not going to be the one to tell this child that her mom is dead. Since it's obvious I'm not going to get any help from the two people standing in this room, I murmur, "Lexi, your mommy had to go to the hospital." Two sets of eyes land on me in surprise. I shrug, tightening my lips. When they both nod, I continue. "So we're going to take you to the hospital, too. Okay?" I lightly brush the hair off her tear-soaked face. Her bottom lip trembles, but she slowly nods.

"I'll pull the SUV into the garage. We'll load her up in there," Damon says, backing out of the room.

"You go with her. I'll call CJ to update her and have Alyssa come take over so you can finish up here." Harper gives me a soft smile before leaving.

The ride to the hospital goes as smoothly as possible. Lexi's hold on me never lessens. A couple uniformed officers and Damon escort us into an exam room. I try and place Lexi on the bed, but her unwillingness to let go of me has me sitting on the bed with her.

"Lexi, I promise I will stay right here by you, but you're going to need to let the doctors have a look at you." Two doctors walk into the room and introduce themselves. One of them I know, Dr. Terry. She's a psychiatrist who works in the same building as Dr. Price, my doctor.

She gives me a warm smile as she walks to the other side of the room, taking a seat. Lexi lets the other doctor look her over as long as I'm sitting right beside her. I notice Dr. Terry assessing Lexi. I have a weird feeling she's assessing me, as well. I've been going to therapists half my life; *I know that look.* I tilt my head, wondering how much she really knows about me. She writes a few things down then excuses herself, telling us she'll be right back.

I bite my inner cheek, staring at the door. She probably heard that I lied to Lexi, and she's trying to find a way to make me leave. I wouldn't blame her. I'm fighting my own demons, I sure as hell can't help anyone else, let alone an innocent child.

My eyes scan the room and land on Damon. He's leaning against the wall with his arms crossed. He arches his brow. I'm not sure if he's questioning the doctor or me. I shrug. His guess is as good as mine.

After the doctor confirms that Lexi is physically okay, Dr. Terry comes back into the room. She slides a chair over to the bed. Lexi is leaning against my side as we sit.

"Hi, Addison. How are you doing?" she asks, making clear eye contact with me. Her voice is genuine.

I sigh. "I'm doing alright." Please stop focusing on me. My foot starts wiggling as I break eye contact with her. I look down at Lexi, whose facial expression is ghostly. She's pale and her eyes are glossed over. I pick up her hand and hold it. My chest tightens. I hate this.

"Hi, Lexi, I'm Dr. Terry," she says, speaking softly. Lexi stays silent, frozen in place, except she squeezes my hand. Dr. Terry notices the reaction as her eyes trail down to our joined hands. "Lexi, do you remember what happened last night?" Her voice is calm, nurturing.

Lexi's lips quiver as her eyes fill with tears, but she shakes her head. "Lexi, nothing that happened last night is your fault. You did nothing wrong." *Wow, I've heard this spiel before.*

Lexi releases my hand, pulls her legs up to her chest, and hides her face while covering her ears with her hands. "I want my mommy," her little voice cries.

I look up and blink quickly to keep the tears from escaping. Standing up, I feel the need to move around. My mouth feels like I've swallowed cotton, it's so dry. I look around for something to drink. I'm trying to keep my composure, but Damon senses something is wrong and walks up and whispers, "What's wrong?"

"I need some water." He leaves but comes right back with a bottle of water. I gulp the whole thing down. Shit, I need to get out of here. *Too many memories.*

The feeling of guilt stops me. I told Lexi I wouldn't leave her. I just need to suck it up. I take a few deep breaths in and out before I make my way back to the bed. When I sit down, Lexi falls into my lap. I run my fingers through her hair, the same way my aunt did for me all those years ago. It seems to help calm her. Focusing on her helps me turn my thoughts off.

The sound of someone opening the door has me looking up. *Dr. Price?* I tilt my head and narrow my eyes. Well, now I know where Dr. Terry went earlier. *Isn't this just so much fun.* I look at Damon with wide eyes. He sticks his hands in his pockets and shrugs.

"I'll wait outside," he murmurs.

"Traitor," I sarcastically respond.

"Dr. Price, what a surprise to see you here," I say, pointing my glare at Dr. Terry. She flashes me a soft smile. I turn back, "I'm assuming you're not here for Lexi?"

"Yes and no," she states. I continue softly combing through Lexi's hair. I glance down and notice that she has fallen asleep.

I raise my head. "I don't understand. Why would you be here for Lexi? I know you both are state-appointed doctors, but why would Lexi need two?"

"No, I'm not here as Lexi's doctor. I'm here as yours." I sigh and roll my eyes.

"I'm fine," I huff. "This isn't about me. It's only about Lexi."

The door opening has all three of us looking over. CJ walks in first and behind her is Todd, who is Damon's boss, and I'm pretty sure there's a social worker behind him.

I gently lift Lexi off my lap, laying her back on the bed so I can stand up. She remains asleep. "Let's all go out of the room," Dr. Terry says, motioning to the door. I look back at Lexi. "She'll be okay, we'll just be right outside the door."

We all huddle around the door, Damon joining us. Todd starts talking first. "Here's what we have so far. We found out who the little girl was and notified the parents. We still don't know if Lexi will be in danger once it gets out that a friend was killed and not her. With that said, we will have a uniformed guard with her at all times." He looks at the social worker and asks, "Have we found next of kin?"

"We think we found an aunt. Both sets of grandparents are deceased, and the father was an only child. We are currently tracking down the mother's sister, but it doesn't look like they stayed in touch."

"We need to keep her in a safe location for now." He turns to the doctors. "Do you think she'll be able to give any information on the sub?"

Dr. Terry says, "In my professional opinion, based on her reactions I do think she saw something. It's too early to determine what exactly she saw, though. It might take a few days talking to her to get her to open up." She looks at me. "She seems to have bonded with Addison, and it's critical for a child who has been traumatized to be with someone they trust. So I recommend she stay with Addison until the aunt comes into town."

My eyes go wide with panic. "What?" I look around the group. "I can't … I … I don't know anything about kids," I stutter. I look to Dr. Price for confirmation. *Tell them I can't do this.*

Instead she says, "I think it's a great idea." Her lips curl up at my gaping mouth.

"The only reason she trusts me is because I'm the one who found her. She'll trust someone else just as easy," I plead my case. When no one says anything, I add, "What am I going to do with a five-year-old?" My shoulders drop in resignation.

"She'll be safe with you," CJ adds. I send her a pointed look. I hadn't even thought about the whole keeping her safe part. I'm a mess. How can they think that I'd be a good fit?

"They'll be an officer stationed at your building. We've already been there to set up," Todd tells everyone.

Did everyone know about this except for me? I look at Damon, narrowing my eyes, and he quickly looks away. *Really, jackass?*

"Addison, I'll come to your apartment daily to work with Lexi. And Dr. Price will be on call, if you need her." I sigh when I realize I've just lost this battle.

"Keep us informed with any information you get," Todd states to everyone before leaving the group.

Damon nods and mouths, "Call me if you need me." He follows Todd out.

Dr. Terry goes back into Lexi's room. I blow out an exasperated breath, looking at Dr. Price. "Really? You think this is a good idea?" My voice shakes with uncertainty.

She puts her hand on my shoulder. "I do." She smiles. "I also think Lexi will help you as much as you will help her." I look at her like she's grown two heads. "Addison, I know you believe in fate. It comes up a lot in our conversations. Well, I believe fate put you in that exact spot to find Lexi for a reason." She releases her hand and turns to walk away. She stops and looks back over her shoulder. "Maybe instead of hating you, fate is helping you heal."

16

ADDISON

This is good. I needed to get out of my apartment, I tell myself as I run through Central Park. I blow out a long exhale.

Lies. If I hadn't been kicked out of my own apartment, I wouldn't be here right now. I'd be with Lexi, making sure that doctor wasn't making things worse.

How the hell did she think I would act when she told Lexi straight out that her mom, dad, and brother were dead? I mean, what the hell? She's just a little kid who's gone through something tragic. How about showing some compassion for the child. Does she really need to hear that *now*? I shake my hands out trying to calm my anger. My pace picks up just thinking about it again. I was told I could come back at eleven, so I'm glancing at my watch repeatedly.

By the time it's eleven, I'm pacing the lobby.

"It's eleven, Addison," the security guard says, flashing me a warm smile.

"Thanks," I say, running to the stairs. I don't feel like waiting for the elevator. Lexi might need me. When I approach my door, I stop myself from barging in. Putting my hands on my knees, I take in a few deep breaths.

She's fine, Addison.

Dr. Terry comes out, and her lips curl up when she sees me. "Addison, how are you doing?" That's a loaded question. I narrow my eyes at the doctor.

"Doctor, you're not here for me." I have enough of my own doctors so I don't need *another one* psychoanalyzing me.

"I'm just asking the person who is the caregiver of Lexi. Nothing else," she says innocently but grins. I nod, even though I know that's a load of bullshit. "I know you think that I wasn't being sensitive to Lexi's situation earlier, but I need you to understand a few things before I leave. First, kids need the truth. They have active imaginations, so if you're not truthful with them, they will fill in the blanks with their own make believe. Next, Lexi will have triggers. Good and bad. Since we don't know much about what Lexi saw, we don't know what that will be yet. You want to encourage the good and be with her to get through the bad. I heard you experienced an outburst with Lexi when you were with Agent Flores." I wince, remembering the scream. She nods once, understanding. "Also, when she does start talking, don't be surprised at anything she asks. Explain it to her in kid terms, but be truthful."

I sigh loudly. How will I ever be able tell that sweet girl something that will hurt her? I hang my head, but nod in resignation.

I watch Lexi on the couch, staring mindlessly at the cartoons on TV. Today marks the third day she's been here with me, and she still won't talk. She's watching TV, eating, or sleeping. She does respond to me with tiny smiles for certain things, like food or TV shows, but that's about it. Dr. Terry tells me that's progression.

She's had a couple rough nights. I stopped taking my sleeping pills so I can be there for her when she wakes from her nightmares. It seems like my demons jumped ship and invaded her dreams. I'd take them back just so she didn't have to go through it. It's gut wrenching to hear her screams. When I snuggle her close to me, I hum "This Little Light of Mine," and it's not too long before she settles and drifts back to sleep for the rest of the night. I don't even know where I learned that song.

The first night I put her to sleep in the guest bedroom and ended up falling asleep with her in there after a nightmare. The second night I put her in her room again, and the sneaky little girl somehow made it into my bed before I was even asleep, curled up into a ball behind me, and fell asleep. I'm not even sure I'm supposed to let her do that, but hell if I care. There is no way I could tell those pitiful, caramel eyes no. I'm going to totally suck at parenting. My kid will get away with everything. The image of a sweet boy with emerald green eyes flashes in front of me. I gasp in surprise, shaking my thoughts from my head.

Where did that come from?

My phone rings, distracting me from my daydream. I glance at Lexi, and she still hasn't moved. I sigh as I answer the phone. "Hey, Syd."

"That doesn't sound good," she says.

"I don't know what to do to help her. She still hasn't said anything. I need your help. You're so much better with kids than I am," I whine.

She giggles. "That's for sure. Have y'all eaten lunch yet?"

"No, Dr. Terry just left."

"Okay, then I'll bring lunch. See you in a few."

I blow out my cheeks, hanging up the phone. Maybe Sydney can sprinkle some of her fairy dust on Lexi and help her come alive.

Half an hour later, Syd's walking in with a couple pizzas and a grocery bag full of stuff. I inhale the scent of pizza. *Mmm.* She puts the pizza on the island and takes out juice boxes from the bag. I'm gazing at Lexi to see her reaction to Sydney, whom she hasn't met yet, but she doesn't even look over.

"It's going to take time, Addie," Syd says from behind me.

"I know, but I don't know how much time we'll have with her." I sigh. "Her aunt is supposed to come into town in a few days. I hear she's a pretentious bitch."

Syd's eyebrows rise, and I raise my hands in the air. "Hey, Damon's words, not mine. I guess she's a model in Los Angeles or something like that." I shrug. "When she learned about what happened, she was more concerned with missing some photo-shoot than her sister getting murdered and her niece who she's about to inherit," I whisper.

"Well, that stinks for Lexi," Syd says, sticking out her bottom lip. It does. At least Amy wanted me, even though I was a surprise.

Syd grabs the bag and walks over to Lexi. I follow. She crouches down beside her and says, "Hi, Lexi, I'm Syd."

She looks down at Syd. Her expression stays neutral though. Syd smiles at her and pulls out crayons and a coloring book. "Do you like to color?" Now why didn't I think of coloring books? Geez, I used to love to color.

Lexi's eyes widen as she slowly nods. Syd places the Barbie coloring book on the coffee table. "I do, too. Do you want to come down here and color with me?" My pulse picks up as I wait to see what Lexi does.

Come on, sweet girl.

Syd doesn't wait for Lexi's response. Instead she opens the coloring book and flattens out a page, places the crayons on the table, and begins to color a page. Lexi focuses on Sydney as her fingers twitch against her pants.

After a few seconds pass, Lexi pushes her little body to the edge of the couch. I see Sydney look at her out of the corner of her eyes and a faint smile shows, but she continues to color. Lexi's feet are on the ground, but she's still leaning against the couch. Seconds feels like hours, waiting to see if she'll join. I can sense that she wants to.

Sydney rips out a page and places it to her side, right in front of Lexi, spreading out the crayons next to it. The small step Lexi needs to make to the table is one of the largest steps she'll ever take.

When Lexi steps forward and sits on the floor, grabbing a crayon, excitement bubbles up inside me that makes me want to jump and scream. I put my hand on my heart as a tear escapes and rolls down my cheek. I watch in awe as she colors her picture. Syd looks back with a huge smile, and I mouth, "Thank you."

It's so quiet I can hear the cars outside, but the feeling of triumph is almost deafening. While they continue to color, I pull out some plates and load them with pizza. I hear Syd say, "That is beautiful, Lexi."

I glance their direction to watch Lexi's reaction. She looks over at Syd with a small smile and then returns to coloring. "I'll be right back," she tells Lexi.

"Her eyes remind me of yours when I first met you. Mesmerizing, but full of pain." She leans her head on my shoulder while I pour two glasses of wine. Syd turns and looks at me, surprised.

"What's that look for?" I ask as I furrow my brows.

"Wine?" she responds, directing her gaze to the two glasses.

"It's just a glass," I say incredulously, holding up her glass to her. "We're not getting drunk."

"Fine. Just one." She twists her lips, taking the glass from me.

We grab the plates and a juice box for Lexi and sit down around the coffee table. When I put down the pizza and drink in front of Lexi, she looks up and flashes me a smile. That little gesture warms my heart.

Lexi alternates between eating and coloring while we talk

about the funny things kids do in Syd's class. They're working on doing the musical, *Annie*. We're laughing at the things kids come up with these days. I'm so glad Syd came over. I needed this. My attention goes to Lexi as I sit back against the couch and watch her little fingers hold the crayon and color. She's very precise with coloring in the lines. *I'm impressed. I've never been an 'in the line' type of girl.*

Syd stands up, grabbing the wine glasses and plates, humming "Tomorrow" by Alicia Morton. I giggle, thinking I'm surprised she doesn't hate that song by now.

Standing to stretch my legs, I start to walk to the kitchen to join Sydney, but I'm halted by the sound of the most pure, angelic voice singing along with Sydney's humming. Lexi's voice is so soft, the noise from the traffic almost drowns her out. *Almost.*

Syd's wide eyes meet mine as she stops humming. I gesture with my hands for her to keep going. She continues to hum and comes to stand by my side as we watch Lexi in amazement as she sings and colors, not even aware of us.

Her voice is hypnotic. It's like listening to the ocean waves, it's so beautiful and pure; you never want to stop listening. I can't believe that voice is coming out of a five-year-old's mouth. Syd gets to the end of the song, and we wait to see what Lexi does. She looks up with a smile, her eyes sparkling with life. Life she's been hiding inside that little body of hers for the last three days. I smile and try to push back the tears that want to escape. I don't want her to think I'm upset.

I shuffle to her, picking her up, and embrace her in my arms. "Lexi, you have a beautiful voice." Her arms wrap tight around my neck.

"Thank you." Her sweet response shocks me. I shake both of us, feeling an overwhelming sense of pride rush through me.

That's my girl. I knew you could do it.

"Lexi, do you like the movie *Annie*?" Syd asks from behind me.

I pull back so I can see Lexi's face. It beams when she nods her head. "What's your favorite song from the movie?"

I turn around so we can both face Syd. I see her twists her lips, thinking. "Opportunity," she says quietly. Hearing her little voice makes me giddy. I squeeze her again, giving her a kiss on the cheek.

Music fills the room from Syd's phone. I've never seen the new Annie, so I'm assuming this is the song Lexi was talking about. I put her down as Syd walks over and grabs her hand. She picks her up and places her on the coffee table.

"Can you sing again for me?" Syd asks, now holding both her hands. She nods as they sway back and forth to the music.

After a few songs, Syd has Lexi dancing and singing all around the living room. My gaze hasn't left Lexi's face and a grin hasn't left mine. When they start singing a song that I actually know, I jump up and join them.

Syd and I fall breathless onto the couch. Lexi jumps in right between us, but she leans against me. I close my eyes, wrapping my arm around her, and kiss the top of her head.

"Sweet girl, you did it," I whisper.

When I look at Syd, she's wiping away her tears. I blow out a sigh of relief.

"So, do you take voice lessons?" Syd asks, looking down at Lexi.

"Yes. My mommy says I have a voice like an angel," she responds quietly. Syd glances quickly at me as my spine stiffens. Does she remember what the doctor told her about her mom?

She looks back down to Lexi and says, "I agree, you do have the voice of an angel." Syd sweeps her hair out of her face, wrapping it behind her ear.

Lexi is quiet for a few moments then looks up at Sydney. "My mommy is dead," she says matter-of-factly.

Well, that answers my question. She turns her head in my

direction and says, "When can I see her?" My eyebrows furrow, looking at the innocent little face in front of me.

Shit. Didn't the doctor explain what dead means? I blow out a quick breath. Okay, the doctor told me to be truthful, but kid terms. So what the hell does that mean? I glance to Syd and she shrugs. I run my hand through my hair.

"You go to church, right?" I ask Lexi. She nods her head. "Well …" I pause to gather my thoughts. I don't want to do this. I briefly look away.

Looking back to her waiting eyes, I reluctantly continue. "So, your mommy, daddy, and brother went to be with God in Heaven."

Confusion crosses Lexi's face. "Why didn't they take me with them?" I drop my head. What I really want to tell her is that she was the lucky one who got to stay.

I pick Lexi up, placing her on my lap. "Lexi, they didn't want to leave. They didn't want to leave you." The doctor's words echo in my head. *Truth.* Tell her the truth. I sigh. "A bad man made them go to Heaven."

Lexi screams, attaching herself to me in her vise grip, "Don't let him get me," she cries, digging her head into my chest.

"No, no, no, Lexi. I won't let anyone hurt you." My voice hitches as I squeeze her closer to me. So much for being truthful. I'm the worst person ever. I pull out my phone and text the doctor to let her know that Lexi is talking, but I think I messed up. Her reply tells me that she'll be here in half an hour.

"It's all my fault," she whimpers.

I pull her back and lift her chin so she's looking at me. I know what to say. It's been repeated to me a million times in my life. Her bottom lip trembles. "Lexi, none of this is your fault. You did nothing wrong," I say. It sounds weird coming out of my mouth.

"It is," she hiccups through her cries. "My daddy told me and Sadie to go to bed, but we weren't tired. He told me if I got up one more time, I would be in big trouble." She crumbles back down into my chest. I look at Sydney, who looks as lost as I do.

I begin to tell her again that she's not the reason this happened, but she starts talking again, "I got up one more time to get a snack for me and Sadie."

I grab my phone and hand it to Sydney and quietly tell her to press record. When I see that she does it, I ask, "What happened next?"

She shakes her head, almost violently, obviously not wanting to talk. "It's okay, Lexi. You don't have to talk about it."

Her cries echo in the room for a few more minutes before she starts talking again. "I was going to my ... my room," she hiccups. "I saw Mommy and Daddy's light on in their bedroom. I could hear my mommy screaming. I wasn't supposed to be up. She was mad at me."

Her guilty cries are killing me. How can I explain to her that it isn't her fault? None of this is her fault. Her mom was not mad at her. I decide it's probably best to wait for the doctor.

When a knock at the door sounds, Sydney gets up to answer it. She waves goodbye and gestures for me to call her later. She looks at Lexi and lets out a worried sigh before she turns and leaves. Dr. Terry walks in and sits where Syd just left.

A rough hour later, the doctor decides it's time to call it a day. She wasn't able to get much more out of her than what Lexi had already told me, but added that when she heard a noise in her brother's room, she got scared and hid in the closet while her friend was asleep.

17

ADDISON

Laughter is definitely the best medicine. Lexi is the most hilarious five-year-old I've ever met. And she's not even *trying* to be funny. It's just her personality. She reminds me a lot of Sydney. *Sassy and free-spirited.*

"Are you ready to go, Lexi?" I call to her from the living room. She comes running out, dressed in a leotard and a tutu. I tilt my head, studying her outfit. "Hmm. You know we aren't going to dance, right?"

"I know," she says, rolling her eyes, "but I like wearing this." She twirls around. "Do you like it?"

"I do. It's very ... puffy." Her face lights up, and she starts dancing around. I love seeing her smile. It's been a long two weeks of therapy for both of us. My focus has shifted to Lexi, so my mind isn't as clouded with my problems. Dr. Price is making sure I'm not ignoring my issues by replacing them with Lexi's, so we have met a few times this week. We've determined that Lexi won't be able to identify the person who murdered her family. We're pretty sure she didn't see him. At least that is one thing she won't ever have to relive.

Sadness creeps in when I think about the person who killed my mom. I could still draw him. And he's the father of the only man I've ever loved. *Life's a bitch.*

I grab my phone off the counter when it rings. Security tells me that Max is here. I send him up but wonder how Lexi will be with Max. It took her a few days to warm up to Damon, but she really likes him now. Max ... he's a different breed of man. He's huge and might be a little scary to a five-year-old. I chuckle to myself. He's scary to most adults.

"Lexi, my friend Max is coming up. He's really nice," I say, hoping that she won't freak out.

"Do you think he'll like my tutu?" she says, still spinning around everywhere. I shake my head, getting dizzy just from watching her. Doesn't she ever get dizzy? I laugh, thinking Max doesn't seem like a tutu kind of guy.

When I hear a knock at the door, I say a little plea that this doesn't go badly. Max gives me a huge hug when he comes in.

"Max, this is Lexi," I say, turning to find Lexi. She's stopped spinning and her eyes are bugging out looking him up and down. She grips the side of the couch with her little hands. It's hard to tell what she's thinking. "Do you want to come say hi?" I ask softly. She slowly nods her head, her eyes glued to him.

She runs to my side and grabs my hand. Max squats down and holds out his hand.

"Hi, Lexi. It's nice to meet you." She stares at his large hand, slowly letting mine go and slipping hers into his. His hand swallows her. "I like your skirt," he says, smiling at her.

In the next second, I learn how to get a little girl to love you instantly. Tell her you like what she's wearing. Lexi's lips curl into a megawatt smile, and she starts bouncing on her toes. "Do you really like it? It's my favorite color. What's your favorite color? Are you going to the gym with us?" her questions are rattled off one after another. I'm stunned by the amount of words coming out of her little mouth.

"Hey," I say, trying to stop the onslaught of questions. "Are you going to let him answer any of those questions?" She looks up at me and giggles then looks to Max, waiting expectantly. My eyebrow shoots up, and I smile at Max. Okay, Max, let's see if you were really listening.

He smirks at me and then looks back to Lexi. "Yes, I really like it. Blue is my favorite color. I might go to the gym with you. I live …" He continues answering every question she's asked. When he looks up at me with a smartass look, I clap quietly.

When he stands up, Lexi slides her hand in his again and looks up at him with so much adoration in her eyes, it's sweet. He looks down at the little hand and smiles wide. Seems Lexi is pretty smitten with Max.

"Lexi, have you been to the gym before?" he asks, looking at her skirt and feeling the material between his fingers.

"Nope, but Addie is going to show me how to fight," she boasts and kicks out her leg. A laugh escapes my lips. I never told her that. I narrow my eyes at her.

"Hey there, Karate Kid, that is *not* what I said." She giggles. "I told you I was going to go work out with Tony and you could go watch and *maybe* I'd show you a few moves to help protect yourself."

"My brother took karate. I know how to do it," she says, doing a karate chop and screaming *YAAAA*.

Max laughs. "Lexi, you definitely could kick my ass." Lexi's eyes go wide. She sports a Cheshire cat grin and walks to her designated bad-word jar. She made the jar the second day she started talking.

Let's just say it's filling up rather quickly. She holds it up and tells Max that he owes a dollar for saying a bad word. When he looks at me, I nod my head. He narrows his eyes at Lexi while taking out a dollar. "It's a good thing I like you, Lexi." He chuckles and tickles her stomach. She squeals and runs away.

As she runs into my room, I yell at her to go to the bathroom before we leave. "You going to be alright when she leaves tomorrow?" Max asks, putting his hand on my shoulder and squeezing.

"I'll be okay. I liked having her around. It'll be weird her not being here," I shrug. "I hear her aunt is a bitch." I whisper the last part. "So, I'm definitely not excited to hand Lexi off to her."

He nods. "What are you here for anyway?" It dawns on me that Max doesn't live right down the road or even *in this state*.

"I had business to take care of here, so I thought I'd stop in and say hi. Glad I did. I get to finally see how kickass you are." He smirks and squeezes my biceps.

"Well, I'm glad you're here. You can sit with Lexi."

"We'll be your biggest fans." I roll my eyes.

We watch as Lexi comes out of the room, still wearing her tutu but has added knee-high boots to her ensemble. "I'm ready to go," she says, grabbing Max's hand again.

"Well, I know who *your* biggest fan is," I say, smiling.

"Don't be jealous, Addison," he says, swinging Lexi's hand and walking her out the door. I laugh at his overzealous walk.

"I don't think my brother knew how to do that," Lexi says as we leave the gym an hour later. She's catching a ride on top of Max's shoulders, her tutu covering the top of his forehead. *Her and that tutu.* She held everyone's attention the entire time she was there. Tony showed her some self-defense moves and watching her do them in the tutu was the highlight of everyone's day.

I laugh to myself thinking about when Tony had her in a tight hold and she was supposed to grab his wrist. Instead, she started belting out the song blaring from the gym speakers. Tony was so caught off guard, he let her go while he was laughing. She was so proud of herself that she got loose, she danced and sang for everyone.

Then Tony and I sparred. Tony ended up calling it quits because of my *cheering* section. He told me I wasn't playing fair having her around. She was a *little* distracting. I think we were laughing more than we were working out.

"Hey, Lulu, what's for lunch?" Max asks. I glance over at him, tilting my head. Lulu?

He shrugs. "She told me Syd calls her Lulu. I like it," he states matter-of-factly. Well, okay.

"I want pasghetti," Lexi says, clapping her hands.

"You want what?" Max replies.

"Pa-sghetti," Lexi says slowly, leaning down over Max's shoulders.

"Do you mean spaghetti?" he asks, confused. We've already had this exact conversation, so I know that is what she wants, but it's still hilarious when she says it.

"That's what I said," she huffs adorably, sitting straight back up. "Pasghetti."

"Okay then, let's get you some pasghetti."

"Yay." She claps again. "There is this yummy place that has the best pasghetti. It even has the name Bella in it. I wish my name was Bella," she says, resting her head on top of Max's head.

"What? Then I couldn't call you Lulu," Max says, flipping her off his shoulders. She squeals on the way down.

"But Bella means beautiful. I want my name to mean beautiful."

Max scoffs. "Do you know what your name means?" She shakes her head. "It means protector," he says, grabbing her hand.

She looks down. "Well, I don't want that name. I couldn't protect my family." My heart breaks for her. Max squats down and pulls her in close to him.

"Lulu, you're five," he says softly, pulling her chin up to meet his eyes. "There was nothing that you could have done except for what you did. But don't forget that your name is a strong name for a strong little girl."

Tears swim around my eyes as she jumps into Max's arms, and he embraces her. "I want to be strong like you, Max."

"Oh, Lulu, you're the strongest girl I know."

She releases Max's hold and smiles wide. "I need pasghetti to make me stronger." She pats her tummy.

I blink back my tears, smiling down at her, when she looks at me. I wonder if she's talking about Marco's restaurant. I don't know any other restaurant with Bella in it.

"Are you talking about Bella Mistero?"

"Yes," she says, jumping up and down.

I haven't seen Marco since the park incident. And I really don't want to now. Considering Max is going to be joining us, I think it's probably not a good idea to eat there. "How about we order from them and take it home?" We can easily pass by the restaurant walking home from the gym. She nods quickly. I call in our order so it'll be ready once we get there.

Please don't let Marco be there.

"How about you go in and get the food, and we'll wait on the bench. It's such a pretty day." I look at Max and smile innocently. He watches me for a beat and then nods, going into the restaurant by himself. A few minutes later Max walks out with our food. Lexi is jumping up and down singing "On top of Pasghetti ..."

I glance at the restaurant door opening and Marco walks out, flashing a crooked smile, strutting my way. Damnit! I lean over to Max and tell him to take Lexi and that I'll be right behind them. He takes Lexi's hand, but his eyes dart over to Marco. He looks back at me, and I slightly nod that it's okay. Lexi's too busy singing her song and skipping that she doesn't see Marco.

"Hi, Marco."

"Hi, beautiful," he says with a cheerful smile. I blow out a huge breath. I guess we're back to normal. He looks over my shoulder to Max and Lexi walking away. "Why didn't you come in and eat?"

"I have company," I say, tilting my head in their direction. "We're doing a picnic and my little friend wanted spaghetti." He nods and looks their way again. His gaze remains on them for a few moments before he looks back at me. "Well, I guess I should get going before my food gets cold."

"*Beautiful,* you definitely don't want it to get cold." I force a smile and say a quick goodbye before rushing off. I walk fast to catch up, glancing back at Marco as we round the corner. He's standing there watching us disappear behind the building. I exhale loudly. I'm going to need to stop taking this route.

Max doesn't say anything and doesn't let go of Lexi until we get into my apartment. He instructs her to go to the bathroom and wash her hands before we eat. His parental demeanor surprises me. The more I learn about Max and what an amazing man he is, I wonder why he hasn't settled down. I can tell he adores Lexi as he watches her leave the room. Of course, when his gaze lands on me, he's not in an adoring mood anymore.

"Who is he?" he presses. *He doesn't waste any time.*

I sigh. "A friend. His name is Marco. That's it. Nothing else," I exclaim. And really not even a friend anymore.

"He didn't look at you like he wants to be friends, *beautiful,*" he says sarcastically.

"I can't help if someone likes me, Max." I wonder if Aiden told him about Marco. His name doesn't seem to trigger any memories, so I'm not going to tell him how we met. And how he named the restaurant after me. Or our little conversation a couple weeks ago. Max is already overprotective of me, I don't want him to have to worry about something that I can deal with myself.

Later that night, Lexi and I are cuddled up on the couch in warm, soft blankets, watching a Disney movie. I watch her more than the movie. She's so animated. Her hand reaches into the popcorn bowl, missing it the first time. She doesn't look down to try again. She just feels around until she hits the popcorn, grabbing a handful and popping it into her mouth.

I'm going to miss her. Miss this. Those caramel-colored eyes looking at me when I wake up and when I put her to sleep at night. They've sucked me into a world I didn't even know I wanted. *Motherhood.* I can't even figure out my relationship status so being a mom hasn't even crossed my mind.

She scoots closer to me and by the look on her face, wide eyes and shoulders scrunched up, we must be at a scary part. I glance at the movie and I'm spot-on. I chuckle to myself and snuggle her closer. Yep, I'm definitely going to miss her.

When I tuck Lexi into bed, I remind her about her aunt coming tomorrow. Her little lip sticks out as she stares at me. Oh, I know, sweet girl, this really sucks. I play with her hair a little and we sing our song, *"This Little Light of Mine,"* until I'm the only one singing. I lie beside her, listening to her little breaths. Her eyelids flutter and her lips curl up in a smile. I exhale slowly, hoping the dream she's having shines bright enough to keep the darkness away.

"HAVE WE PACKED EVERYTHING?" I ask Lexi, boxing up the last of her clothes. Silence. I turn to find her sitting on my bed, arms and legs crossed, her bottom lip sticking out. *I know the feeling.* If I weren't an adult, I'd be doing the same thing. I jump on the bed and wrap my arms around her.

"I'm going to miss you," she pouts.

"I am going to miss you, too," I reply, pulling her back so she's looking at me. "But you can call me anytime. Do you remember my number?"

She nods and repeats it. I tell her I put it in her bag just in case she forgets it, which I'm sure she will. We talk about how much fun she'll have in Los Angeles. I try to say things that will get her excited about her aunt, talking about mine and what a gift it was to have her in my life. Unfortunately, my aunt wasn't a bitch. I really hope she's not as bad as Damon makes her out to be.

———

"You're going to what?!" I say, gritting my teeth. So much for my high hopes that Damon was wrong. *I hate the woman.*

"It's a great school for girls. She'll love it there," Sophia says with a snobby smile. Her uppity voice grates on me. When Lexi's Aunt Sophia came into my apartment, the first thing that came out of her mouth was how nice my apartment was and how she was surprised I could afford it. I'm standing there introducing her to her niece and *that's* what she's thinking about? My apartment?

"So you're sending her to a boarding school?" I say, trying to wrap my head around what she's telling me. My hands fist at my side. I can't believe I'm sending Lexi away with this woman. At least her assistant is a sweet, older lady and has taken the initiative to pay attention to Lexi because her own flesh and blood can't be bothered. Right now they are downstairs putting all Lexi's stuff into the limo, and I'm trying my hardest not to yell some sense into the aunt. If it wasn't for Lexi's doctor being here and the social worker, I think I would have.

Dr. Terry must notice my angst because she pulls me into my room. "I know this is hard, Addison," she says, grabbing my fisted hand. *Hard?* It's more like cruel and painful. I don't want to let her go with that uppity bitch. I plop on the bed, crossing my arms and sigh heavily. Yep, I'm done being an adult. *I'm going to pout for a second.* When Lexi runs into my room, I straighten and smile.

"Addie, the limo is so huge," she says, throwing her hands out wide. She hops up and down in excitement. "And it has purple lights inside. Ms. Jackie let me play with all the lights and music. It's like a dance party in the back of the car."

My smile remains plastered on my face, watching her animated expressions. I'm seriously going to have Lexi withdrawals when she leaves. There's nothing like seeing the excitement through a five-year-old's eyes.

"That sounds so cool," I say, picking her up. We walk into the living room where a police officer is talking to Sophia and her *bodyguard* about the officer that will follow them everywhere as a precaution while they are still in town. Given it's been two weeks and nothing has happened, we're hoping that Lexi is safe and will be safer when she leaves New York City. That's the only reason that makes me okay about this whole thing. Not like I have a choice.

We hug and tears are shed as we say our goodbyes. "I'll miss you, sweet girl. Keep singing and dancing, okay?"

She nods and sniffles as big tears run down her face. I gently swipe them away with my thumb. "Don't cry. We'll see each other again. So, it's not goodbye, it's I'll see you later." Dr. Terry looks at me. I know what she's thinking. *Don't lie to her.* I smile at her. I'm not lying. I will definitely see her again.

Watching her drive away in the limo, my chest hurts. She made such an impact on me in such little time, I'm surprised how much this hurts. I look at Dr. Terry with my arms crossed. "So, why exactly did y'all think this was a good idea to put her with me? Because this sucks."

Her eyes soften as she wraps her arm around my shoulders. "She brought so much goodness into your life for two weeks, and she leaves you with great memories. Nobody could have bonded with her at the level you did. You understand what she's going through, even though you were a little older when it happened to you." I listen to her words and let them soak in. She's right. And it's a bond that I'll never forget.

18

AIDEN

I run my hand across my unshaven jaw. I'm so fucking tired. Of course, I came home to an empty fridge a couple hours ago, so here I am at the store, waiting in line behind the lady arguing about expired coupons. I close my eyes, shake my head, and sigh. This day can't get any longer.

Ever since I was instructed to come home a week early to help with a case, my nerves have been on overdrive. The last few months have been a true test of my sanity. My heart belongs to someone who might not want it. My thoughts have tormented me daily, from thinking about her sinful body to *her words*. Her words about how the blood running through my veins has destroyed her life. I've tried so hard to move on, but I can't. Now I'm home and I have no clue what's next for us. If there still is an "us." I have no control when it comes to Addison, and I hate it.

I take in a deep breath, shaking my thoughts from my head, bringing me back to the present. I look at the lady still arguing and now asking for a manager. Looking around to see if there's a shorter line, but not finding one, I drop my head onto my arms that rest on the cart.

Don't pull out your gun and shoot her, I say to myself. I just want to go home and sleep.

My head bolts up at the sound of screams and then gunfire. Panic fills the air with more screams and people rushing to the exit doors. I pull my gun out and instruct everyone to get out. The cashier looks at me with a deer in the headlight look. "Go, now!" I growl. He nods and dashes out with everyone else.

I run toward the direction of the shots and stop at the sound of a scream coming toward me. A small girl comes barreling down an aisle. I grab her, needing her to stop screaming.

"Don't touch me!" her little voice screams, hitting me with her tiny fists.

"Shh … I'm the police," I say quietly. When she quiets, I immediately notice who she is. This is why I'm home early. I caught up on the case and read about her on the plane ride home. "Alexandra Collins?" Her eyes widen and she slowly nods. "Is someone after you?" Again, she nods.

Fuck! The serial killer might be here. Where is her detail? I quickly glance around but don't see anyone. I need to put her somewhere safe. Seeing the manager's office, I run over, open the door, and put her down.

"You stay in this room. Do not open the door for anyone. Do you understand?" Tears fall down her little face as she nods. "I need a secret word from you that only I will know. Don't open for anyone who doesn't know the secret word."

She nods in understanding, and I can tell she's thinking of a word. Holy shit, any day now, kid. I scan the area, looking for movement. When I don't see any, I look back to the girl. "Alexandra, I need a word, right now."

"Tater tot," she says.

"Tater tot?" I ask slowly. She nods with a small smile. Okay. Tater tot, it is. "Remember, do not open this door." I close the door behind me, making sure it's locked, and run in the direction she came from.

I hear the sound of sirens outside. As I clear an aisle, I silently run down to the end. Peeking around the corner, I notice a body on the floor. A woman. I creep toward her, my gun drawn and ready. Reaching down to feel for a pulse, I notice a gunshot to the head. She's dead. *Fucking hell.*

I glance around the place. Where are you, asshole? As I'm standing up, SWAT surrounds me. "Hands up!" they scream. "Drop your weapon."

I slowly put my weapon on the ground, lifting my hands in the air. The last thing I need tonight is to get shot. "I'm FBI. Agent Aiden Roberts. My badge is in my pocket." An officer comes over and reaches in my pocket for my badge, inspects it, and hands it back.

"Sorry, Agent Roberts," he says as he bends down and grabs my gun for me.

I report what happened to the officer, station a police officer outside the manager's office, and then call Damon to get his ass here.

"We found Officer Kale." I hear another officer say grimly.

I look at the officer standing with me. "Alexandra's detail?" He nods slowly as he radios it in. *Son of a bitch.* "We need to get security video ASAP. Make sure that asshole isn't hiding in here somewhere," I command. "Get the dogs in here. He couldn't have gone too far." I look at my watch. It's only been fifteen minutes since I heard the first scream. "I need to get Alexandra out of here, but I want to make sure that the unsub isn't in here hiding out. She's safe in that room for now." I glance at the door to make sure an officer is outside, waiting.

FBI's here within a few minutes. It's not too long after that they have the place cleared. The bastard escaped again, but now we know he's after Alexandra. Damon stops me on my way to get the girl.

"Aiden, we need to talk."

"Can't right now. I need to get the girl. She's probably scared out of her mind. Let me get her handled and then we'll talk," I say over my shoulder as I'm walking away. He mumbles something, but I don't hear what he says.

Alexandra. Life sucks for her right now. First her family was murdered and then her only relative is murdered because a psycho is trying to finish the job. I read she was staying in an undisclosed location until her aunt came to get her. We're going to have to take her to a safe house. She has no clue how much danger she's in.

When I get to the manager's door, I knock, but I don't hear anything on the other side. "Open up, Alexandra. Secret word is tater tot." Nothing. I try the door handle, but it's still locked. I look to the officer and he shrugs. I dart to an employee telling him that I need the keys to the office.

Opening the door slowly, I breathe out a sigh of relief when I see a little girl nestled under the desk asleep. I crouch down and scoop her up in my arms. Her eyes fly open in surprise. "Hey there, Tater Tot."

Recognition reflects on her face so she swings her arms around my neck in a tight embrace. She whispers in my ear, "Is my aunt dead?" Her unemotional question stuns me. This little girl shouldn't know death.

I sigh. "She is." She lays her head on my shoulder. "I'm so sorry, Alexandra. We won't let anyone hurt you." I'm at a loss for words. What do you say to a five-year-old who has had her world ripped from her … *twice*? I don't know what else to say, so I try and comfort her until Child Protective Services can get here.

19

ADDISON

Bubbles reach the top of the tub as I lie down to soak in a hot bath. I take in a deep breath, letting the essential oils fill the air. It's been a long couple of weeks. Closing my eyes, I think about saying goodbye to those big caramel eyes. I can't believe Lexi leaves for Los Angeles tomorrow. An empty feeling flows through me, knowing she won't be a part of my life anymore.

I think about how different my life was before Lexi came into it. I was living day to day, but it didn't have meaning. It didn't have life. Lexi brought purpose to my life, gave me something to look forward to. Dr. Price was right; Lexi has helped me heal. I hope I was able to help her as much as she did me. I start humming *"This Little Light of Mine"* and the symbolism of the song surprises me.

Lexi was my light.

My phone jolts me awake. I pick up my hand out of the luke-warm water and look at my wrinkled fingers. I must have fallen asleep. Stepping out of the tub, I wipe my hand on the towel and grab my phone. It's from an unknown number.

"Hello."

I hear whimpering on the other end, but no other sound. "Hello? This is Addison, who is this?" I ask.

"Addie, please come get me," Lexi cries.

"Lexi? What's wrong? Where are you?" I ask, panic in my voice. I grab a towel and dry off with one hand while listening.

"I'm hiding in a room," she sniffles. "The bad man tried to take me."

Where the hell is her aunt or her security detail? I grab the first thing I can, which is workout shorts and a white T-shirt. I slip on my flip-flops, grab my purse, and I'm out the door in less than two minutes.

"Do you know where you are? Are you at a hotel?" I stop at the stairs because I know I'm going to lose my cell service. My heart is about to jump out of my chest, it's beating so fast.

"No, we came to a store."

"What store, Lexi?" I'm pacing now.

"The one with two red circles."

Target. It must be the one that is right by their hotel. At least I hope that's the one. "Lexi, my phone is going to hang up, but I will be there in a few minutes. Do not leave your hiding spot. Do you understand?" I plead with her.

"The man told me not to leave. The secret word is tater tot."

Man? Secret word? What the hell is going on?

I quickly tell her goodbye and run down the stairs, wrapping my dripping hair in a bun.

IT'S May and still a little chilly at night, but the adrenaline running through my blood has me burning up. I have the cab park next to all the cop cars and throw some money at him. Jumping out of the car, I make my way through the crowd. The officers let me by when I flash my badge. I'm walking in as Damon is walking out.

"Damon, where is Lexi?" I quickly ask him, not stopping to hear an answer.

"She's fine, Addison. She's inside with …"

Once I hear she's fine, I speed up to find her. I don't care who she's with, I just need to see for myself that she's okay. When I get inside, I scan the place, looking for that set of caramel eyes.

What I find instead are emerald green eyes. My eyes widen in disbelief. I freeze and inhale sharply. *Aiden.* He's holding Lexi, and she's slumped over his shoulder. He draws in a ragged breath as his eyes drag their way up my body. The heat from his gaze spreads through me like an inferno. Feelings hidden deep inside slowly make their way out. When his gaze stops on my breasts, Aiden arches his brow and flashes a salacious grin.

The inappropriate timing of his perusal of my body shocks me out of my frozen state. I look down to see what the hell he's so fascinated by. *Oh, my God!* I cross my arms over my chest as my face flushes from embarrassment. In my haste to get dressed, I seemed to have forgotten a bra. And my wet hair made my shirt a little wet. Wet hair, wet, white T-shirt, add the cold temperature outside, and it makes me look like I should be entering into a wet T-shirt competition. My nipples are on full display for everyone to see.

When I hear Aiden chuckle, my head whips up. "Really?"

He wags his eyebrows and grins. "Hi, Addison," he says, his voice softening. When Lexi hears my name, her head bobs up, and she wiggles out of his arms.

"Addie!" she screams, running into my arms. I scoop her up in a tight embrace.

"Hi, sweet girl." I close my eyes and let out a soft sigh. I take a deep breath, loving the smell of Lexi. When I open my eyes,

Aiden's eyes are trained on me, assessing me as he stands with his arms crossed. His expression turns serious.

"Hey, Tater Tot, is this your friend who you kept saying was coming for you?" Aiden questions Lexi.

Lexi releases her tight hold on me to looks at Aiden. "Yes. Addie, this is Aiden," she says. "He helped me hide." I look at Aiden and chuckle at her introduction. This is definitely not how I envisioned our first time seeing each other.

She leans her head on my shoulder. "My aunt is dead," she whispers.

I sigh. "I'm sorry, Lexi." My stomach knots, thinking what she went through tonight. How the hell did this happen? "Lexi, did you see the bad man?" She nods her head, still resting it on my shoulder.

"I've seen him before." What? I wonder if she did see him the night her parents were killed or did she recognize him from somewhere else. Her head jolts up like something stung her. "I did what you told me to do, Addie," she says, proud of herself.

"Did you fight and scream?" I ask. The words feel like sandpaper coming out of my mouth. When I told her that, I was hoping she'd never have to do it.

"I did. When I scratched him, he yelled. He was mad," she says as her eyes get huge. "And then I ran. That's when Aiden found me. But he used my *real* name." She scrunches her little nose. I look over at Aiden. He smiles and shrugs.

"Lexi, you said you scratched him?" I say, putting her down. She nods. I grab one of the police officers walking by.

"Who's working forensics?"

"Alyssa and Jennifer," he answers.

"Get Alyssa over here and tell her to bring her kit." He nods and walks off.

"Lexi, you know how I told you about my job. That we look for clues to help find the bad person?" She nods. "Well, because you scratched him, you might be able to help us find the bad person."

Lexi tilts her head with the look of confusion on her face. "I hope he has to go to the doctor and get lots of shots. Because they really hurt." She rubs her upper thigh and then continues. "And then the police will know it's him and they'll take him to jail?"

Aiden chuckles, and I can't help but smile. "Not exactly," I say, trying not to laugh. Little kids and their imaginations. "Remember when I told you about DNA?"

"Yep. You said everyone has a different one."

"Well, when you scratched him, you might have gotten his DNA under your fingernails." She throws her hands in front of her, inspecting her nails.

"Yucky! I don't want his DAN on me." I chuckle as she starts shaking her hands. I grab her hands to stop her.

"Sweet girl, we'll wash them after we're done. Don't you want to help catch the bad man?" Her bottom lip juts out as she nods her head. I hold her hands until Alyssa comes over.

"This is going to be really easy, and I promise it won't hurt. But you need to be still, okay?"

She holds her hands out to Alyssa. "The DAN is hurting my hands, so can you please hurry?" Alyssa tries really hard to hold in her laugh, but she has to turn around to let it out. Thankfully, it's silent. When she gathers herself, she turns back around.

"Okay, Lexi, let's get that DAN off."

"Listen, both of you. It's DNA. D. N. A.," I correct them. Alyssa chuckles. When I stand up, a jacket is wrapped around my shoulders. I look up to see Aiden warmly smiling at me.

"I didn't think you'd want to be flashing everyone." He winks.

I put my arms through and I notice the tags are still on it. "Aiden, I'm not going to get arrested for stealing, am I?" I say, holding out the tag.

He comes over and rips the tags off. "Don't worry, I'll pay for it," he says defensively.

I laugh, zipping up the jacket. He's right, though; I definitely don't need to be flashing everyone. I watch him walk over to Damon. It's the first time I've truly had a chance to look at him. He's wearing cargo shorts and a black T-shirt. My heart shudders as I admire him from the backside. His broad back and powerful shoulders flex as he moves. My eyes gaze downward to his perfect ass. I gasp when my body tingles deep down in my core. Sensations that I haven't had in months and didn't know I'd ever have again are starting to wake up.

I panic and look away, trying to shove them back into the dark corner they've been hiding inside of me. I don't know if I'm ready for that. I can't even make myself have an orgasm. I sure as hell am not ready for a man to do it. I laugh when I think about Dr. Price telling me that masturbation is one of my homework assignments.

I push back all thoughts of orgasm and Aiden when I see that Alyssa has finished with Lexi. "Alyssa, can you take Lexi to wash her hands? I need to talk to some people about what is next," I say quietly and point to Lexi.

She nods in understanding, grabbing Lexi's hand. "Come on, Lexi, let's go wash the rest of the DAN off your hands." I roll my eyes.

"DNA," I yell at her as she walks away.

A group has gathered around Damon and Aiden. They all stop talking when I approach. "Please, don't stop talking on my account," I joke, trying to ease the awkwardness that I'm feeling right about now.

"We were just talking about what we were going to do with Lexi," Damon says.

I look around the group. "Well, I thought she could stay with me again until we figure out what to do with her." It's funny how things have changed in two weeks. Two weeks ago, I was begging for them to not send her home with me; now, I'm suggesting it.

"The fuck she is," Aiden barks out.

I turn to face him. "Excuse me?" I say snidely.

"Addison, she's in serious danger," he seethes.

"I get that, but they'll be guards." I puff out my chest and stand taller. He does not get to show up out of the blue and tell me what I can and can't do.

"She already had detail. Look what happened," he grits out through his teeth as he gestures in the direction of the two bodies.

"It's only until we figure out where we need to take her. And I know how to use a gun," I say defiantly.

"A lot of good that did before."

SMACK!

The sting on my hand from the slap to his face doesn't even compare to the outrage that pours out of me. "Fuck you, Aiden." I shake my hand, turning to leave this conversation before I say something I can't take back.

A hand grabs my arm, and I feel Aiden's hard body at my back. "Addison, I'm sorry," he says softly. His voice hitches. My eyes fill with tears. I yank my arm from his grasp and walk away.

I hear him walking behind me. "Addison."

"Let her go, Aiden," Damon says.

I walk outside, needing air. My breathing is shallow as my body shakes from anger. I tell myself that I'm here for Lexi, not Aiden. He's not even supposed to be working this case. I'm pacing the parking lot, doing breathing exercises, when I hear someone walking up. I glance over and see that it's Damon, so I continue my pacing.

"You know he didn't mean it," he says. "He's just worried about you being in a dangerous situation again." I look at him with narrow eyes. "Hey, I'm not saying he didn't deserve to be smacked. Hell, I almost punched him for that." I smirk, knowing that

Damon would do anything for me. He's been a great friend. I stop pacing when Damon wraps his arms around me. "Have you calmed down enough to go finish our meeting about what we're going to do with Lexi?"

I blow out a long breath. "No, but I'll be okay. Let's go."

When we walk into the store, Lexi sees me and runs to me. "You get all cleaned?"

She shows me her hands. "Yep, I got all the DA … DNA off me." She smiles proudly. I grab her hand and walk back to the group.

Child Protective Services is there. It's the same lady who I've been working with the last two weeks. She warmly smiles at me when she sees Lexi's hand in mine.

"We've decided that tonight Lexi will go to your apartment," she states, looking at me. "But we'll need to decide tomorrow where Lexi can go, somewhere she'll be safe until we catch this guy."

"I'm good with that," I say, looking at Aiden raising an eyebrow.

He shrugs. "And I'm going wherever Lexi is going. So that means I'm coming, too." A smug smile stretches across his face.

My mouth gapes open. "What?" I look around at everyone, expecting someone to remedy the situation. My glare lands on Damon. He must know that this isn't a good idea. My eyes plead with him, and all he does is shrug. I mouth, *Asshole.* Unfortunately, the person who says something is Lexi.

"Yay!" She claps her hands. I narrow my eyes at her. *Little traitor.* She leans her head on my hip and whispers, "I like Aiden."

"Tater Tot, I like you, too," Aiden boasts, holding his hand out for a high five. She smacks his hand. I can't believe this is happening. Everyone, including a five-year-old, is railroading me.

I blow out an exasperated sigh. "Then let's go," I say with resignation.

When we settle into my apartment, Aiden sits on the couch and watches me get Lexi ready for bed. I glance at him numerous times. His body is tense and his expression thunderous. When our eyes meet, his intense glare has me turning away quickly.

"I don't know what the he…heck your problem is, but please stop staring at me. You're making me nervous," I scold.

"Why the fuck didn't anyone tell me that she was staying with you for the last two weeks?" he says, standing and walking toward me. I shrug dismissively.

I see Lexi out of the corner of my eye, grabbing the jar, and giggle knowing what's about to happen.

"This isn't funny, Addison. This is serious."

"Aiden," Lexi says, standing right in front of him, holding the jar in one hand and her other hand on her hip. I put my hand in front of my mouth, trying to hide my amusement.

"Hey, Tater Tot. What's up?" He ruffles her hair with his hand.

"You owe me a dollar." The lost expression on Aiden's face when he looks at me has me busting out laughing. His eyebrows furrow when he looks back down at Lexi.

"Okay, I'll bite." He narrows his eyes. "Why do I owe you a dollar?"

"This is the potty-word jar," she says, holding up the jar. His expression still reflects his confusion. His silence has Lexi continuing. "You said a bad word. A *very* bad word," she scolds.

Aiden glances my way, looking for help. "Don't look at me. You said a *very* bad word," I say, trying to sound serious but ending up giggling. "Do you see all those dollars in there already? Where do you think those came from?"

He peeks in the jar and chuckles. He pulls out his wallet and places a dollar in the jar.

"Thank you," she says, putting it back on the shelf, obviously proud of herself. She goes back into the bedroom to get ready for bed.

"You could have warned me we have the bad-word police here."

"There's no fun in that. Don't worry, it won't be your last. That little girl has long-distance radar for hearing bad words." I shake my head, laughing as I go into my room.

"Alright, Lexi, it's time for bed." She hops on my bed, slipping right into the middle. My heart warms seeing her in my bed again. I know the circumstances of her being here are horrible—and I might be a little selfish thinking it—but I love seeing her in my bed. I lie down beside her, cuddling with her.

"Are you sad about your aunt? You haven't said much about her tonight," I ask while I twirl her hair around my finger.

Her little shoulders shrug. "I don't know her," she whispers, staring into my eyes. "And I don't like her very much. She wasn't very nice to me." I close my eyes and sigh. *Bitch.* Who couldn't love Lexi the minute you meet her?

"Well, if you ever need to talk about it, you can always talk to me."

"Is the bad man going to try and take me again?" she asks, moving her body a little closer to me.

"Not if I can help it."

"I'm scared," she whispers.

"I know, sweet girl, but you're safe here with me."

"And me, Tater Tot," Aiden says sitting on the bed. She rolls over and smiles at him. Rolling back over and closing her eyes, I start humming our song. My eyes are closed as I'm humming when I hear a deep voice softly start singing with my humming. Aiden's singing has always had a profound effect on me, but hearing him sing this song to Lexi ... I can literally feel my fractured heart fuse together piece by piece. I open my eyes when I feel movement, and see Lexi reaching behind her with her little hand, searching for something. When Aiden grabs hold of her hand, she settles. Aiden lies down behind her and together we put her to sleep.

I keep my eyes closed, knowing that Aiden's gaze is pinned on me. I'm afraid if he sees my eyes right now, he'll misread the love that I have for him. I can't deny that I love this man. Our connection hasn't broken. But I am. He might think I'm not broken, but I am. I don't know if I can put him through more than he's already been through. I don't know if I can give him all of me again. I wanted to die because of the love I have for him. It scares the ever-living shit out of me that he holds that much power over me. He doesn't even know it.

We've come too far to start fresh. The past has molded me and while I'm definitely ready to move on with my life, I don't know if I can move on with him. I squeeze my eyes tighter, I don't even know if I'll be able to handle being intimate again.

When we finish the song, I open my eyes and our eyes lock. His eyebrows draw together as he watches me. I nod toward the door and move as softly as I can to get off the bed. Aiden does the same.

I grab us both a bottle of water from the fridge and then sit on the couch. He sits down, laying his arm across the back of the couch, turned toward me.

"Where'd you go in there?" he asks.

I shake my head and look down. "Just thinking about stuff."

"Addison," he commands softly. I look up into his green eyes. "I have no clue where we stand, but the last thing I want to do is cause you more stress. If this is too much..." he gestures between us with his hand, "...you need to let me know. I can request to be sent back out in the field." The thought of him leaving sends a sharp pain to my heart. And it confuses me. I'm all over the place tonight.

I sigh. "Aiden, seeing you has brought on feelings that I haven't had in months. I'm not sure if that's good or bad. I don't know—"

"You're unsure. To me, that's not a no," he says, interrupting me, his voice confident. "I have no expectations other than it's a *maybe*." His lips curl up into a smile.

Can I do a maybe when a couple seconds ago it was more of a no? My thoughts are like walking a straight line, drunk. As much as my mind wants to move forward, it's the needing to sidestep that is stopping me from getting there. *And Aiden's on the side where my body wants to go.*

I softly smile back. "*It's a maybe*. But not right now."

"I agree, right now we need to find the son of a bitch who is trying to kill Lexi." I look at the partially closed bedroom door. "You've become close to her," he says in a hushed voice.

"I have," I say, leaning my head on the back of the couch, looking at him. "How could you not? Have you seen those eyes? It's like her little secret weapon to get people to do whatever the hell she wants you to do." I laugh.

"I know that exact feeling about eyes hypnotizing you," he says, arching his eyebrow. I roll my eyes with a shake of my head. I playfully reach my foot over and push his thigh.

"Stop. We're not talking about me." I narrow my eyes.

"Sorry, I was just saying that I understand," he says, holding his hands in the air. The slight touch of my foot on his thigh makes my heart beat a little faster, but I can't seem to move it away. It's that damn pull we have, *a side step*. The one I'm trying to fight. And seem to be losing at the moment.

"She has helped me so much being here. She's given me a reason to get better. She needs me."

"I ..." His voice falters when he stops midsentence. When he doesn't continue, I already know what he was going to say. He reaches for the coffee table to grab his water and takes a big gulp. My foot loses our connection, and I instantly miss it. The feeling doesn't last long, though, because when he settles back down, he grabs my foot, putting it back where it was. Touching him.

"So, what's our plan of action with Lexi tomorrow?" he asks as he plays with his empty water bottle.

"I've been thinking about that," I say, bringing the water bottle to my lips. After I take a drink, I continue. "The killer obviously didn't know she was here or he would have tried something sooner."

"She can't stay here, Addison," he states matter-of-factly.

"I know that. I'm not suggesting that."

He gets up off the couch, walks toward the window, and pulls back the curtain. I already know who he's looking for. *Security.* I've already checked a few times myself. "If he finds out where she is, you'll be in danger now that we have his DNA. Whoever it is might be more motivated to do whatever it takes to find Lexi and fast." Aiden shuts the curtains and stands tall, folding his arms across his chest. "Maybe you should go with Lexi, wherever we send her."

"Aiden …" I stand up with my hands on my hips, "… I was out of work for almost four months. I am not leaving."

"You know—"

"Stop. Not going to happen," I say, shaking my head.

After a loud sigh of frustration, he says, "You are so fucking stubborn."

I immediately look toward my bedroom door. I chuckle to myself that Lexi has me conditioned at the sound of curse words. When I don't hear anything, I look back to Aiden. "You said a *very* bad word."

The corner of Aiden's mouth twitches. "Do you feel the need to punish me?"

I roll my eyes and launch my water bottle at him. "I'm going to make you sleep outside my front door," I huff.

He catches the bottle and throws his head back, laughing. "Shh!" I whisper yell, pointing to the bedroom door. He covers his mouth to stifle his laugh.

"We're getting off track. We need to go back to thinking about what to do with Lexi tomorrow," I say, dropping back down on the couch.

"We can send her to Max's. You know no one will be able to get her there."

I sigh. "You're right, she'd be safe. But I don't like the idea of sending a five-year-old little girl to a house full of men. Not that I don't trust them, *I trust them with my life*. But none of them have kids and would have no freaking clue what to do with a little girl." I chuckle, remembering how much Lexi loved Max.

"What's funny?"

"Lexi *loved* Max when she met him, like she has a little crush." Aiden's smile disappears and I can see his jaw flex before he looks away. "What did I say?"

He blows out a rough breath, shaking his head. "Nothing."

"No, it's not nothing, Aiden."

"I'm feeling like I've missed so much, especially when it comes to you. Neither Max nor Damon told me about Lexi. Why the hell not?" I can hear the vulnerability in his voice and see the hurt in his eyes. He puts his hands in his pockets.

I bite my lip, thinking how I am going to say this. "I told them not to tell you," I say, looking away from his pained eyes.

"Why?"

"Because. How you were acting a few minutes ago … I didn't want you to worry about me." I look up at him as he comes to stand right in front of me.

"I haven't ever stopped worrying about you," he murmurs, bending over and brushing my hair behind my ear.

"I know," I whisper. He lets out a soft sigh and mumbles something about the bathroom.

20

AIDEN

I stare at myself in the mirror. If I thought the last four months were hard, it's nothing compared to being in the same room as her and not being able to touch her.

When I first saw her walking into the store, it was like my dreams were coming true. Addison, in a wet, white T-shirt with no bra. Holy fucking wet dream. I seriously thought I was hallucinating from being so tired. I grip the sides of the sink and hang my head. And after all she's been through, how screwed-up am I to go there?

I snag my overnight bag that I grabbed from my apartment before coming here from off the floor. Putting on my sweat pants, I think about Addison touching me with her foot. I can see it in her eyes that she still needs me. That connection isn't lost.

Be patient, Roberts, she'll come around.

Patience. *That's hilarious.* I once thought I was an impatient man. I usually got what I wanted when I wanted it. I guess I haven't ever been tested. The past year and a half, I've been nothing *but* tested. I think I deserve an A+.

It still burns me that nobody told me about Lexi staying with

Addison. I can already see how much Lexi means to her. I can't say I'm not a little jealous. Not of Lexi, though. Just that she's been able to help Addison where I couldn't.

I take off my shirt and run my fingers over my scar from the bullet in my chest. It kills me to think that Addison might be in danger again. I sigh, wondering if this is going to be a common occurrence. I need to figure out a plan to get Addison out of town with Lexi. Of course, she's hell-bent on staying, but I don't think my heart can handle her getting hurt again. It's barely hanging on right now.

As I shave, I come up with an idea. I call Max and see if it's even possible. After I get the go-ahead, I make a few more calls. Anxious to share my plan with Addison, I walk into the living room and she's still sitting on the couch messing with her phone. When she looks up, her expression shifts.

She slowly stands up and walks toward me. Her hand softly glides across my scar. I inhale sharply, closing my eyes. Her touch sends a bolt of electricity through me, waking every cell in my body. She looks up, a pained look in her eyes. I know what she's thinking.

"It's not your fault," I whisper, putting my hand over hers.

"I know," she says. "But it still doesn't take away the pain I feel for what happened to you."

"Sweetheart, don't do this to yourself. I'm okay." Without thinking, I take her hand and kiss her palm. She runs it against my clean-shaven face.

Back away. She's not ready.

I mentally know she's not ready. If I continue, it's only going to backfire. But physically, I need her touch. I crave her smell. I desperately need *her*. I blow out a slow breath, removing her hand, and kiss the top of her head. I want all of her. I just need to be patient.

There's that word again. *Always a fucking test.*

I turn to walk into the kitchen and grab another water. I'm suddenly parched. "So, I have a plan for Lexi," I say, sticking my head inside the fridge. I welcome the cool air, leaving the door open a little longer than necessary. When I stand back up, Addison is leaning against the counter, arms crossed.

I wink at her and smile. "Do you want to know what the plan is?" I say, leaning against the opposite counter, twisting the cap off my water and emptying the cool liquid in one gulp.

"What I want is for you to put a shirt on," she says coyly. "I see you've been working out a little extra these days." Her eyes flicker down to my bare chest.

"Had a lot of extra time on my hands." I shrug, pushing off the counter. "Am I too *distracting*?" I say, teasing her as I walk past her. As much as I like her staring at me, if she keeps looking at me like that, I will fail this test.

When I walk back into the kitchen, I yank on my shirt.

"Much better," she says, now sitting on top of the counter.

I lift my brow. "Much?"

"Better that I can have a conversation with you without having dirty thoughts."

"Mmm … I like dirty thoughts, especially with you in them." I flash a huge smile. Shit, this isn't helping my situation. My mouth starts moving before my brain can catch up with what it's saying.

"Well, let's just keep our dirty thoughts to ourselves." She giggles. God, I've missed that sound. "So, tell me about this plan you have."

"We leave tomorrow morning at seven," I say.

"What? Where are we going?"

"We're taking Lexi to your aunt's house." Addison's eyes go wide as she hops off the counter.

Confusion is written all over her face as she looks around. "Did I fall asleep at some point that you had time to plan this all out?"

"It just took a few phone calls. Max is taking us on his jet so we don't have to have Lexi's name on a flight list."

"Did you–"

"I have everything taken care of," I say, cutting her off. "It's all approved and Max will have the plane fueled and ready at seven. All we need to do is be there, ready to go."

She takes a few moments to absorb it all. I can tell the second my plan has been foiled when she narrows her eyes at me in silent accusation.

"I am not staying there with her," she states matter-of-factly. "I'm coming back to help with the case."

"Addison, that's not your job."

"Actually, we have his DNA now, so yes, it is my job," she says, her voice hardening. She stands in front of me with her hands on her hips and she bites the inside of her cheek. She's so seductively hot when she gets mad, and she has no idea.

I grab her by the upper arms and lean down in her face. "You frustrate me, woman," I growl.

"Hey, pot, meet kettle," she says sarcastically, standing taller.

I let her go and pace the room. "Fine. Don't stay," I say, throwing my hands up in the air.

"Now that we got that out of the way …" she says while I shake my head in defeat, "did you call my aunt, too?"

"Yes."

"I bet she is so excited to meet Lexi," she says excitedly. "Lexi will love it there with the horses and cows." My resolve dissipates seeing how excited Addison is. I just wish she was excited enough to stay with Lexi and show her everything herself. I should have known better.

"Well, since you felt the need to make us leave at the ass-crack of dawn, I need to go to sleep." Addison jokes as she walks toward the spare bedroom.

"Where are you headed?" I ask, following her.

"Making sure you have everything you need in here," she says, stopping in the doorway.

"I'm not sleeping in there."

She tilts her head. "Um …" She pauses, looking up toward the ceiling. She's flustered, and I love it. Looking back to me, she exhales quickly and says, "So, where are you planning on sleeping?"

"Are you hoping I'm going to say in your bed?" I whisper in her ear. I see her body shiver. Not that I would, but her reaction makes my dick stand at attention.

"No," she says, her voice vibrating. She pushes me away as a blush creeps up her cheeks.

I wink. "Sweetheart, I'm sleeping on the couch. This is too far away from you and Lexi."

She turns to walk away. "You can figure it out, I'll see you in the morning." I watch her sexy ass sway, and I'd bet a million dollars that she's swaying a little more right now, knowing I'm watching.

"So gorgeous," I whisper.

She stops in the doorway, looks over her shoulders, and blows me a kiss. I don't want to look like a fool and act like I grab it, but I want to.

21

ADDISON

My alarm goes off way too early for me. I set it to vibrate, hoping not to wake up Lexi. I lie in bed a little longer, staring at the ceiling. I blow out my cheeks letting out a silent breath, thinking about last night. So my body definitely isn't broken.

It still *feels*.

It still *reacts*.

It still *wants*.

And it all begins and ends with Aiden. But I'm scared. Scared that when he touches me, I'll go back to that hell. That my mind will take me prisoner again. It would ruin me. Ruin us.

I shake the thoughts from my head. I can't think about that right now. I look over to Lexi, sleeping peacefully. She woke up once last night, screaming *"no"* over and over. It's something I'm used to, but Aiden, he about had a heart attack running in here, gun drawn ready to attack. I silently giggle, remembering it.

Noise in the living room reminds me that I should be getting up. I slip on my robe and walk out of my room. I'm startled and let out a small scream at the sight of a man who isn't Aiden. It's not even light enough outside to brighten my living room and only the kitchen light is on. My reaction happens before I notice that it's Max. I pick up a pillow from my couch and hit him with it.

"Geez, you scared the crap out of me."

"Not my fault you're jumpy," he says jokingly, but he winces as soon as he says it. "Sorry," he says, stuffing his pockets with his hands.

"It's okay. I just wasn't expecting to see you here."

"Addie, what happened?" A small voice behind me asks. I turn to Lexi, and she's rubbing her eyes. When she puts her hands down she sees Max.

"MAX!" she screams, running into his arms. He picks her up and throws her into the air. When he's done, her little arms wrap around his neck.

"Hey, Lulu. I heard you had a rough day yesterday," he says, squeezing her. His enormous arms almost hide all of her. I think Max loves Lexi as much as she loves him. It makes me see Max in a totally different light. He has a soft side that only Lexi brings out. It's sweet.

She lays her head on his shoulder. "Yes, a bad guy tried to take me," she murmurs. Her head shoots up, looking him in the eyes, "But I got his DAN." She looks at me, twisting her lips and then looks back to Max. "I got his DNA. It made my hand hurt until I washed it off. I don't like DNA on me," she whines.

"Good girl." Max chuckles. "Hey, do you like banana bread?"

Lexi's face beams and mine … well, mine frantically looks around because where there is banana bread is where I'll find my drink. When I spot it on the counter, I run straight to it. Max watches me suck half down in one sip and his eyes widen. I shrug and laugh.

"My mommy makes really good banana bread," Lexi says as

Max walks over to the kitchen with her. He looks at me, unsure what to say.

"I bet your mommy's banana bread is a lot better than this store bought one," I say, taking out a slice of the bread and handing a piece to her. "When I was little, my mommy and I used to make brownies."

"Do you miss your mommy? I miss my mommy." Her bottom lip sticks out.

"Every day, sweet girl." My voice cracks with emotion. It gets me *every* time she asks about her mom. I glance at Max and his eyes gloss over. He looks away quickly. Yeah, Max, even big manly men like you can't escape the emotional tug when it comes to Lexi.

The front door opens with Aiden and Damon strutting in. Aiden's eyes meet mine, and he flashes a sexy, half grin, displaying a dimple. The one that always makes me melt.

"Aiden, I got banana bread." Lexi holds out a piece for him to see.

"Let me see that. I need to make sure it's not bad."

"It's not bad," she says, looking at it while she holds it out.

Aiden walks over, holds her arm up, and acts like he's inspecting it. "Hmm … I don't know." Suddenly he eats the piece of banana bread right out of her hand.

Lexi squeals. "Hey, that's mine!"

"Do you want it back," he asks and then opens his mouth.

"Yucky." She wrinkles her little nose. I agree, *that's gross.* He finishes chewing the bite and says, "Well, you're right, it's definitely not bad." He pulls her out of Max's arms, tickling her. She giggles and wiggles right out of his grasp.

Grabbing the rest of her banana bread, she narrows her eyes at Aiden and says, "Mine."

Everyone laughs. She climbs the barstool, but struggles to get to the top. Damon gives her a hand.

"Hey, Lulu," he says, sitting her on the stool.

"Hey, Peter Pan," she giggles.

Max and Aiden both look at each other and throw their heads back, laughing. "Lexi, I thought we agreed, *not Peter Pan*. I'm a Lost Boy," he says, standing tall. Lexi thinks Sydney looks like Tinkerbell, too. Damon came over with Sydney one day so Lexi thought they were together. She started calling him Peter Pan after that. He tried his hardest to get her to call him a Lost Boy instead, but it seems Peter Pan stuck.

She just shakes her head as she pops another piece of bread in her mouth. The guys continue to laugh and Damon flips them off. I'm standing back, adoring the camaraderie with Lexi and the guys, enjoying my drink and the bread. A little girl having three very large men wrapped around her finger is entertaining.

"I think I should check your bread, too," Aiden says, walking up to me. I smile as I break off a piece and put it up to Aiden's mouth. Instead of snatching it like he did Lexi's, he sticks my entire two fingers in his mouth, sucking them as I pull them out. Heat spreads through me instantly. He flashes a sexy grin and winks.

"You're not supposed to eat her fingers, Aiden," Lexi exclaims.

"Yeah, Aiden," I say sarcastically as I wipe off my fingers with the napkin I'm holding.

"I was just making sure it was good." He leans overs and whispers in my ear, "And it was fucking delicious." I notice Lexi hop off the barstool behind Aiden, and I look up at him pursing my lips. "She's getting the jar, isn't she?" I nod, putting my hand over my mouth to stifle my laugh. "Damn, she's got good hearing."

She stands in between us. "That'll be two dollars." She holds up the jar.

"Two?" His eyes start to move around as he tries to recall when he said two bad words. I mouth *damn* to remind him. "That is not a bad word," he replies.

"Aiden, you won't win. Just pay her." Max chuckles.

After Aiden reluctantly pays her, I tell her to get dressed because we're going on a trip.

Her eyes go wide. "Are you taking me far away from the bad guy?"

I bend down and grab her hands. "Yes, very far away. We are going on a plane." Her eyes get even bigger. "Have you ever been on a plane?" I ask, wondering if she's scared.

"Nope. Are we going to Disneyland?" she excitedly asks. Why the hell does she think we're going to Disneyland? When I don't answer her right away, she continues. "My friend went on a plane and she went to Disneyland."

"Sorry, sweet girl, we're not going to Disneyland."

Her shoulders slump. "Oh." She sighs. Holy shit, how do parents deal with letting their kids down?

"But you'll have fun where we're going. You get to meet my aunt in Texas." My words are rushed as I swing her little hands.

"Is she nicer than my aunt?" she asks. That is definitely a yes. I still can't believe what a bitch Lexi's aunt was. It's horrible to say because she's dead now, but *wow*.

"She will love you, Lexi. And she has horses, cows, and chickens. You will have so much fun," I say excitedly. I know I'm exaggerating how much fun she'll have, hoping to make her forget about Disney. "Oh, and we're going on Max's airplane."

She whips around to Max and runs to him. He swoops her up in his arms. "You have a plane?" she asks. It's so cute how animated little girls can be.

"Yep."

She puts both her hands on Max's cheeks and puts her face right up to his. They are touching nose to nose.

"Can you take me to Disneyland?" She stares into his eyes. So much for trying to get her to forget.

"Lulu, for you, I'll take you anywhere." She screams and wraps her hands around his neck. I narrow my eyes at Max and cross my arms. He must understand why I'm irritated because he adds, "But not this trip. You need to go to Amy's house this time."

She looks at him. "Okay. But do you pinky promise you'll take me to Disneyland?" He looks at me, tilts his head, and shrugs. I shrug back, not having a clue.

"Lulu, I don't know what that means."

She sticks her pinky out and says, "You have to wrap your pinky with mine and promise you'll take me to Disneyland."

He does as she says, and then she runs to the bedroom to get dressed. I look at Max and giggle. "You're such a pushover."

"There is no way in hell that I'd be able to tell that little girl no. Those eyes are like voodoo, it's fu…" he stops himself, "…freaking ridiculous."

We all laugh, glancing at her bad-word jar. I doubt she ever had that much money in her jar from home. We're so bad.

"Well, brother, looks like we're all going to Disney after this," Aiden says, getting off the couch, slapping Max on the back.

22

AIDEN

Our flight takes off smoothly leaving Austin. I peek over at Addison while she's looking through her case files. I wish she would've stayed with Lexi. I could tell that she wanted to. It pained me to hear Lexi cry when Addison told her we were leaving. I'm thankful to Max that he stayed behind. He wanted to make sure security was all set in place around the ranch. At least that was his excuse. I'm sure part of him staying had to do with Lexi feeling better. I've never seen Max become so soft around someone, let alone a five-year-old child. It's surprising.

"Where are they with the DNA test?" I ask to break the silence looming around us.

"They put a rush on it. Hopefully we'll have it back tonight or tomorrow," she says, looking up. There are moments of silence before she speaks again. "I'm glad Max stayed."

"Me too." I'm not sure why there's this awkwardness between us right now. It dawns on me that this is the first time we've truly been alone since I got back yesterday. There is so much we need to talk about, but I know this is definitely not the time.

We're about an hour away from landing, and I'm getting

nervous. My leg shakes and I have my arms on the armrests with my fingers pointed on my lips. Just thinking about Addison being here already has my anxiety spiking. She looks over at my fidgeting with a questioning look.

"So, your place or mine?" I spit out.

"What are you talking about?"

"Tonight. Your place or mine?" I repeat.

She looks at me with a blank expression. "Um, I'm going back to my place and since Lexi isn't with me, you don't need to stay." She looks right into my eyes. Rejection fucking stings.

"Addison, I don't think you should be alone."

She sighs. "Aiden, I'll be fine. I already know you have Stone parked outside my building, so why are you freaking out?" Why can't Max keep his mouth shut?

"Why am I freaking out?" I grind out. "Maybe after what happened to you, you should be a little *more* freaked out." I flip my seat belt release button, needing to stand up.

"Are you serious?" She stands up right in front of me. "I'm trying to live my life not in fear of everything because of what happened to me, and I've worked really hard to get to that place. I don't need a daily reminder of it from you," she snaps.

"What am I supposed to do, Addison? I can't function thinking that you might be in the crosshairs of a sick bastard. *Again.*" I throw my hands in the air.

She takes a step back from me. "I don't know why I thought we might have a chance," she mumbles quietly.

My spine straightens. "What are you talking about? Because I'm worried about you, we won't work? Did I miss something, Addison?" I step forward, needing to be closer to her, but she steps back again. Panic fills my eyes.

"That's exactly why," she says, briefly looking away, wrapping her arms around her stomach. "You're too emotionally attached to my wellbeing that you'll always be worried about my safety."

"Let's pretend what happened didn't, I'd still be worried about your safety because I love you," I explain.

She twists her lips, thinking about how to respond. "Aiden, too much has happened between us. You won't know how to let it go. You'll always be overprotective of me. And that's understandable, but that's not what I need in my life right now." She stalls for a moment. "I can't live in the past. If you are constantly worried about me, that's exactly where I'll stay." Her voice shakes with emotion as tears run down her face.

Her words shoot straight to my heart. Like a fucking spear. I'm at a loss of what to say. The airplane shakes from turbulence. I think it's from the weight of my heart breaking into pieces. *Again.*

"Please take your seat as we make our final descent into LaGuardia," the pilot's voice comes over the intercom. Addison turns around and sits down quietly and buckles her seat belt. My hands go to my temples. I can't even comprehend how we got here in just a few minutes. The plane shakes again, reminding me that I need to sit down. I take a seat across from Addison. She stares out the window the rest of the flight.

By the time we land, anger has taken over my confusion. I slam my bag down as I watch her gather her stuff. I've taken two bullets since I've met Addison, and I'd take more to keep her safe. And that's the reason we shouldn't be together? Well then, I suck at this relationship thing.

As we walk off the plane, silence follows. I don't even look her way when I sarcastically say, "I'm taking you home, but don't worry, I won't go in."

"Aiden, I don't want you to be mad at me." She grips my arm.

"I really don't know what you want from me," I say, flexing my jaw, looking off into the distance. "You don't want me to love you. You don't want me to be mad at you. You don't want me to worry about you. Tell me, Addison, what the hell *do* you want from me?" I stop in the middle of the tarmac and pin her with my stare.

"You *could* be a little more understanding," she whispers and then looks down.

"Well, that goes both ways, *sweetheart*," I say with anger, walking away, leaving her standing there. I close my eyes as my shoulders drop, and I let out a heavy breath. I'm a bastard. I turn around to apologize, but she's already walking in the direction of another hangar. I throw my head back, staring up at the sky. Why didn't anyone warn me about this shit when you fall in love? I might have tried to avoid it a lot longer.

I laugh at myself over thinking that was even an option. The second I laid eyes on Addison, I knew something had changed in me. My heart started beating to a different tune that day.

When I look back at Addison, she's almost to the hangar. I take off, sprinting to catch her. "I said I was taking you home," I say out of breath when I catch up to her.

She ignores me as she keeps walking. I shake my head and curse under my breath. I follow a few steps behind her into the hangar. She stops and looks around.

"You'd make this so much easier on yourself if you'd just walk to my car so I could take you home," I say, my voice laced with humor. She continues to ignore me, walking toward a couple of men.

"Excuse me, do y'all have a phone I could borrow? My phone died and I need to call a taxi," she asks in her sweet, southern voice. The guys look at her and then at me. I smirk and slightly shake my head no at them. I'm thankful right now that Addison can't see me.

"Sorry, our phones are having issues today. They're not working," one of the guys says and shrugs. Addison turns enough so she can see me.

"How convenient," she grits out, narrowing her eyes at me. I shrug innocently. She turns back to the guys who are trying to hide their smile. She sighs out of frustration. "Whatever. All you guys are assholes," she says, stomping toward the exit, waving her hands around.

The guys chuckle as I pass by. "Good luck with that, Aiden."

I laugh. "Thanks for your help guys," I say over my shoulder, jogging to catch up with Addison again. I laugh again, thinking that Max will get a kick out of that. The Smith brothers have been our friends for a long time.

When I catch up with Addison, she's already walking toward my car.

Thank God.

Not a word is spoken the entire car ride. When I pull up to her apartment, she hops out and slams the door shut, not even looking back. I watch her walk in and then look the other direction. Stone is sitting in his car across from me with a smirk. I roll my window down.

"Don't ever fall in love," I warn him, shaking my head. He laughs out loud.

"You've been back one day and you already fucked it up?"

"So it seems," I say blandly. "Let me know if something comes up." He salutes me before I peel off. It's almost five but since I don't have anything else to do, I head to the office.

Walking into the office, Cheryl greets me with a smile. "Good afternoon, Aiden." Her cheerfulness is like fingernails on a chalkboard right now.

"Absolutely nothing good about it," I mumble, walking past her, making a beeline for my office.

"Is there a reason you're being an ass?" Damon asks, standing in my doorway with his arms crossed.

I plop down in my chair, leaning back into it, staring at the ceiling. I sigh. "Have we got any leads?"

"Where's Addison?"

"At her fucking apartment," I seethe. I close my eyes and exhale quickly. I fist my hands as my anger brews. I glare back at Damon and say, "Are we going to chit chat all goddamn day or are you going to give me an update on the case?"

A tiny body takes a spot next to Damon in the doorway, holding a file, flashing a concerned look.

Fuck! I drop my head, knowing what's coming next.

"Aiden," she calmly says.

"Dr. Price," I respond, looking up to her.

Damon looks at the doctor and then to me. "Great timing, doc. Maybe you can get the stick out of my friend's ass." He turns around and leaves. *I'm on a roll today.*

"Do you have a minute?" she asks, walking into my office and shutting the door. Seems I don't have a choice in this matter, so I shrug. She takes a seat across from my desk, trying to read me. I'm usually really good at hiding my emotions; shit, I'm trained in that area. So why can't I hide my feelings when it comes to Addison?

"I'd ask you how you are doing, but I think that goes without saying." I just nod again. "So why don't you tell me what's going on?"

I run my hand through my hair, groaning in frustration. I don't even know where to start.

"Isn't this a conflict of interest, you being both our doctors?" I ask. I've had a weekly Skype session with Dr. Price for the last four months. Come to find out, she's been Addison's doctor, too, for the last month.

"I'm assuming you mean you and Addison. I'm very capable of separating the two."

"She is the most stubborn woman." I think my mouth decides to vomit words because once I start, I can't stop. I push off my chair, almost knocking it over, and walk around my desk. "She's being ridiculous. She thinks we shouldn't be together because I'm too *emotionally attached* to her safety. But how the hell should I feel when she keeps putting herself in dangerous situations? And she tells me I should be a little more understanding? Doesn't she know she wasn't the only one who was hurt four months ago? I was shot, almost died, and my heart was torn to pieces!" I bark loudly, slamming my hands down on my desk.

Dr. Price doesn't even flinch. She's sitting back in her chair with her legs crossed, silently letting me have my outburst. I drop back down in my chair, trying to calm the fury.

"Have you both had a chance to talk?"

"No," I mutter.

"You definitely need to talk to each other, but I understand why that hasn't happened yet." Her voice is a constant state of calm, but her eyes reflect compassion. "I do think she might be right."

My eyebrows pop up. "What?"

"There needs to be understanding from both sides. Addison needs to feel in control for her to be able to move on. You suppress that control by constantly trying to keep her safe, which in turn will take her back to the times she didn't have it."

"Do you think I don't know that?" I sigh and drop my elbows onto the desk and rub my eyelids. "I just don't know how to stop these feelings of helplessness. I love that woman more than anything. I just can't *stop* worrying about her."

"Give it some time, Aiden. I think when you both have a chance to sit down and talk, it will help you both understand each other. To make this work, you'll need to set expectations on both ends. But you need to be patient with Addison. I know that you went through a lot, and I'm not discrediting that, but what Addison went through was life altering." She stands up and flashes me a soft smile. "I think it'd be a good idea if both of you came to a session, together." *Of course you do*, I chuckle to myself and nod.

I pick up my phone and call Addison. I need to apologize and see if we can talk. Her voicemail answers, so I hang up. I sigh. She's probably ignoring me.

A few moments later, movement in my doorway catches my

eye. A makeshift white flag is being waved. Damon peeks his head in. "Is it clear? Am I going to get shot if I come in?"

"Come in, asshole," I grunt.

"I am *not* the asshole here." He smirks walking in.

"Sorry. It's been a shitty few hours."

"What the hell happened? Last we talked, you were getting ready to leave Texas and everything was fine."

I sigh. "Addison is being stubborn as ever. And I guess I fucked up."

"That's not surprising. But if there were ever two people who belonged together, it's you two. You're just as stubborn as she is." He chuckles.

"Well, that might be our undoing," I say grimly.

"I don't believe that. But to get your mind off of it, we just got back the DNA results."

I lean forward in my chair. "What are you waiting for, tell me the results."

"We're meeting in the war room now," he says, walking out. The war room is the conference room where the entire case is spread out.

I walk into the room and chatter fills the air. Addison's boss, CJ, my boss, Todd, and a few other agents are sitting around the table. When Todd sees me, he clears his throat to get everyone's attention.

"Everyone's here, let's get started," he says, looking at me. I nod and pull out a chair. "So, the DNA results came back, but we didn't get a match in CODIS." Several sighs can be heard. "But … we did get a DNA match to another case in St. Louis. Seems this wasn't where he started with his murders. Another family was murdered last September. We are working with the office there to see if there might be more unsolved murders that match. So far it's just the one."

"Forensics is running a familial DNA search to see if we get anything there. You never know if there's a family member in the system who might help us catch a lead," CJ states. "We started that earlier today, so hopefully we'll get those results back any time now."

"What we know so far is that the unsub has only killed families of four. He always rapes the wife."

"Are there any patterns with the women?" asks Damon.

"The woman in St. Louis was brunette, but the other three here have all been blonde. So we're not sure if that's a connection or not. Something might have happened or he just doesn't care."

"He must have been following them for a while. Where did he find them? Did they have the same doctor, kids go to the same school? Where's the link that connects them?" Dave asks.

"We have the analysts looking at everything. The three families all live in the city, so there are a few similarities. They all went to the same movie theater, ate at the same restaurant, two of the three go to the same bank. But schools, doctors, employers are all different."

My hands are behind my head as I lean back and think. Something in the back of my head is nagging at me, telling me that I'm missing something. It's like when I have a déjà vu moment but can't for the life of me remember when I had it.

Then the light bulb turns on. Addison … St. Louis … changing of hair color. I jump up out of my seat, startling people.

"What restaurant?" I fire out.

"What?" Todd asks.

"What restaurant did they all go to?"

He starts looking through his notes. Damon stands with me, walking to the computer and starts typing. He knows what I'm thinking.

"Bella Mistero." He tilts his head in my direction.

I look at Damon, and he nods his head. "He came from a town not too far from St. Louis."

"He's going to go after Addison," I say quickly, getting ready to leave.

"Aiden?" Todd stops me. Of course he's going to want more information.

"His name is Marco Aceto."

I quickly tell them about Marco and that when he and Addison met she had brown hair. Then he conveniently moved here, just a couple blocks from her. I give CJ his dad's name to compare the DNA results. His dad currently resides at the Colorado State Penitentiary for raping and killing a woman in the nineties. Fucking apple doesn't fall far from the tree.

I call Stone and tell him to be on the lookout for Marco.

"Someone went inside about ten minutes ago with a delivery from Bella Mistero," I say, repeating what Stone just said and looking up at the team. "Don't go in. We'll be there in five minutes." I gesture with my hands to get a team together now. I hang up, and Damon has already grabbed the SUV keys and is handing me a vest.

"We'll get this son of a bitch."

Hopefully, it's not too late.

We pull up in front of her apartment and start devising a plan of entrance when we hear three shots ring out.

Air escapes my lungs. Time stops. My hand reaches for my chest as I gasp for air. It feels like someone punched me in the stomach, and I can't catch my breath. They are going to have to put me in a mental hospital if I lose Addison because I'm about to crack. Damon shakes me, bringing me back to present.

I suck in a large gulp of air and take off running.

23

ADDISON

My door makes a loud bang as I whip it shut and walk into my apartment. Anger fills my body, thinking about the last few hours. I growl, walking around my apartment, slamming everything I touch. Aiden can be such a caveman sometimes.

I drop down on the couch, letting out a forced breath. Closing my eyes, my words come back to haunt me. I can't believe I told him we couldn't be together.

Then doubt rears its ugly head. Doubts that I can't be the woman he deserves. He's not going to want to live in a constant state of fear, worrying about me. It's not a good place to be. I blow out a breath, willing the insecurities to escape my body.

The rate that my feelings have changed has left me drained. I lie back on my couch, staring up to the ceiling. My breathing slows and I drift off to sleep.

Something wakes me, but I'm not sure what it is. I sit up and look around. Nothing is out of place. Maybe it's just a car horn outside. Glancing at the clock, I see I was only asleep for thirty minutes.

Taking in a deep breath and releasing it, I know I need to call

Aiden. We need to talk. I need to apologize for being a bitch. I see my phone sitting on the entry table. As I'm pushing up off the couch, a knock on my door startles me. It's probably Aiden since the doorman didn't call me. I swing open the door, expecting to meet emerald green eyes. Instead, I'm looking into chocolate brown eyes.

"I'm having a déjà vu moment right now." Why is it that Marco always seems to show up at my door when I'm really pissed off at Aiden?

"Aww, yes. I seem to always be trying to feed you." He holds up the bag of food, sporting a huge smile. "Did you not hear me knocking? I almost left, thinking you weren't home?" The knock must have been what woke me.

"Sorry, I passed out on my couch and didn't hear you," I say. "But, Marco, I'm pretty sure I didn't order anything."

"Your neighbor did," he says, looking down the hallway. "So when I saw the address, I thought … well … I hoped you were home so I could bring you your favorite dish." I'm caught off guard, so I stand there staring at Marco. I feel I need to tread softly because I'm not so sure about Marco anymore. Last time he flipped on the drop of a dime, and I am not in the mood to deal with crazy right now.

"Well, I am starving. Let me grab my wallet." I let go of the door, keeping it open, and turn to snatch my wallet off of my kitchen counter.

"How much do I …" I pause when I hear my door shut and lock. Whipping around, I see Marco looking around my apartment. Like he's searching for something. My spine stiffens. "… Owe you?" I finish, but there's uncertainty in my voice. He quickly turns toward me, setting the food on my coffee table. Dammit, why didn't I shut the door?

There's a flicker of darkness for a second before he blinks and smiles at me. I take a step back as warnings start blaring in my head. I know the look of evil. Shit, I've met the Devil himself. "I've never been in your apartment before, beautiful. It's amazing. It's a big place, though. Do you live here by yourself?" His voice has changed. There's a chilling undertone to it.

That's right. He hasn't been to my home. How the hell does he know where I live? He stands there watching me, waiting for my next move, like a hawk watching his prey.

"Thanks," I say, masking my concern. "Actually, Sydney lives with me. She should be back soon, so she'll be excited you brought food," I lie, hoping that if he thinks that I'm not alone for long he'll leave.

"Really?" he asks sardonically, taking a step toward me. Shit! How do I keep getting myself in these situations? I don't think he plans on leaving anytime soon.

My skin prickles as fear runs through me. He knows I'm lying. I instinctively take a step back. He's five steps from me. I'm five steps from my front door. There is no way I can make it to my bedroom where my gun is, or the kitchen to grab a knife, without getting past him first. That leaves the front door as my only option or to fight. I take another step back. *Four more to go.*

"Marco, is something wrong?" I murmur, trying to sound as calm as I possibly can. My heart races, making my body heat. I can feel sweat forming on my back.

"Oh, *bella*, nothing is ever wrong when I'm with you," he snarls as he takes another step forward. I start to panic, knowing that my front door is locked. That'll take time. *Time I don't have.* My stomach turns, knowing this isn't going to end well.

"Well, thanks for the food. I really appreciate it." I force a smile but don't take my eyes off him. I take another step back. I jump when my cellphone rings on the entry table. I glance at it and can see that it's Aiden. The sound of a gun cocking has me jerking my head back to Marco. There he stands a step away from me, holding a gun to my head.

"Don't answer it, Addison," he demands, his voice cold.

"I'm not," I whisper, holding my hands up to show him I don't have anything in my hand. "Marco, what do you want? Why are you doing this?"

"Have a seat on the couch. I'll tell you all about it." He smiles. *He fucking smiles.*

I'm saying a silent plea, hoping that Aiden will get worried when I don't answer the phone. I internally chastise myself. How freaking ironic is that? *Now* I'm hoping he worries about me. If I make it out of here alive, I promise he can worry about me all he wants.

I slowly walk to the couch as Marco follows right behind. I can feel the gun pressed to the back of my head. Just the thought of it makes my head sting. When I sit, he remains standing. I look up at a man who I thought was once an attractive guy but now there's nothing but pure evil. I remain quiet, crossing my legs and arms.

He growls. "I like you obeying me." He reaches down and runs his hand down my cheek. I smack his hand away.

"Don't fucking touch me," I grind out.

He *tsks* me. "All in due time, bella." I fight the bile wanting to climb up my throat at his words. "This wasn't supposed to happen yet, you know? You weren't supposed to be involved," he says, staring down at me. I don't know what the hell he's talking about. What am I involved in? The *yet* has me really concerned. So, he had planned this … it's just happening sooner rather than later? I squeeze my eyes shut, cursing under my breath. Why does this keep happening to me? I open my eyes and chew the inside of cheek. When I don't say anything, he continues. "But you left me no choice. Where is the girl?"

What? I shake my head, looking down. He can't know about Lexi. And if he does …

I gasp as I look back up at his towering figure looming over me. I scan his face and tense when I see it. Two scratches on his neck. He smirks when he sees that I've noticed them.

"If only I'd done a better job, I would've known that she had a friend over." He shrugs. "But now there are a few loose ends that I have to deal with. *You* weren't supposed to be one of them. I had a different plan for you," he says, pointing the gun at me.

I tense and squeeze my arms around my body tighter. How he says it … I know that plan wouldn't have turned out well for me. Of course, now I'm a loose end that has to be dealt with. It sounds like either way I'm screwed. I try to remain calm. Now is not the time to lose control.

"I'm not telling you where she is, Marco," I sneer, staring up at him. He can do whatever he wants to me, but he will never know where Lexi is. I've already been to hell, I know what it's like. He can't do worse. His eyes bore into me and his nostrils flare. He shakes his head as he sighs harshly. "Why Marco? Why did you kill those families?"

His face twists like I should already know the answer. "Because of you, Addison," he says dryly.

"Me?" My stomach drops as the horror of what has been happening is somehow linked to me. I dig my fingers into my arms so deep I know it'll leave bruises.

He sits on the coffee table, making sure to keep the gun pointed at me. My eyes dart around his face, waiting for his reason. Waiting to find out what I did to unleash this monster. "The day I met you, when your lips pressed to mine, I just knew you were mine. I had already found out everything about you before you came back the second time. It was like you came back for me. You felt it, too." Had I kissed Marco? I think back to that first night. I guess I did give him a peck on the lips. That one kiss led to all of this?

I shake my head. "No. That isn't why I came back into town."

"I figured that out when you rejected me and kicked me out," he growls. I keep quiet so I don't anger him more. "But I knew you just needed time to feel the same way I do." I let out a ragged breath. When will the hits from that fucking trip ever end? Did I piss anyone else off during that time? My attention goes back to Marco when he starts talking again. "I was still angry. And when a family came into the restaurant that night, the woman looked like you. It was like you were cheating on me, happily married with kids," he barks out.

Oh. My. God. My hand flies to my mouth. He can't be saying he killed those families because the women reminded him of me. I grab the couch on each side of me to hold myself up. I think I'm going to be sick. I fight the tears that are threatening to erupt.

"And then when I found out you moved to New York City, I thought it'd been enough time. You would see me and know that I was the one. But that FBI guy kept getting in my way," he snarls.

"You didn't have to kill those families," I whimper.

"You were not going to be happy with anyone but me!" he yells as he stands up, hovering over me. I gasp at his abrupt movement. He's starting to lose it. This is definitely not what I want. I sit back against the couch cushion to add a little space between us. I stare up to him, trying to think about what I should do. Reality sets in. It's going to be me or him. We aren't both walking out of here alive. I take a couple breaths, trying to calm my anxiety. I just need to get to my bedroom.

A wicked gleam in his eyes makes my insides quiver. My eyes flash quickly to the hand holding the gun and back. I follow his other hand down as he starts to unbutton his pants. "I've been waiting so long to feel the inside of you. I think it's been long enough," he says as he pulls the zipper down. A dark room and cigarette smoke fill my senses. I shake my head, reminding myself that I'm not there and my hands and feet are free. I am not a prisoner.

He can't hold you down, Addison. You can fight.

He puts his legs on the outside of mine as he gets closer to me. I lean back, allowing more space between us. My position leaves me few options, but I still have one.

He smirks. "I can see it in your eyes, you want it, too," he hisses, thinking I'm giving him room to get on top of me. He finds out quickly when I swing my leg up as hard as I can, connecting my knee to his groin that that is definitely not what I was doing. He cries out, doubling over. I jump up and run to my bedroom, slamming the door and locking it to give me a couple more seconds to get ready.

I grab my gun from my nightstand. Rocking on my feet in a squatted position, I tell myself I don't have any other options. I hate him for making me do this. I hate him for killing all those women because of me. I hate him for trying to kill Lexi again. I hate him for making me feel like this is all my fault.

As soon as my gun is in my hand, I steady myself and wait. I don't wait for long, though.

The door is kicked open. "You think this door will stop me, Addison?" he laughs wickedly.

No, but this will. I take three shots.

24

AIDEN

The shower has been running for an hour. I've stopped myself from checking on Addison over a dozen times. But enough is enough. I knock on the door. No answer. I blow out a ragged breath, leaning my head on the door. *Please don't hate me for coming in.*

I turn the doorknob slowly, pushing the door open even slower, but it's when I don't see the outline of Addison's body in the frosted glass that I start to worry. *Fuck being careful.* I run to the shower.

When I round the corner and look in, she's sitting in the corner with her hands wrapped around her legs. Her head is against the wall and her eyes are closed. She looks like she's meditating. I turn the shower off, surprised that the water isn't ice cold, and she opens her eyes. Her red-rimmed eyes lock with mine.

"I'm sorry for going to my apartment," she whispers.

Words that come to mind, I don't dare say. Yes, I'm pissed. I'm pissed she is so goddamn stubborn. If she had let me go home with her, or she had stayed with me, I could've been there to protect her. *You can't always be there.* The rational part of my mind reminds me of the one thing that I hate to admit, but I seem to think with the irrational part when I'm around her.

I want to be her protector.

I want to be her hero.

And I keep failing. But I'll settle for being the person she needs to lean on right now. Help her get through this. So instead of saying anything, I grab a soft, white, cotton towel. I lift her up and wrap the towel around her. She gives me a soft smile as I lift her in my arms and carry her into the bedroom.

She sits on the bed as I dress her in a pair of her panties and a T-shirt that I had grabbed out of her bedroom before we left. When I'm done, she lies back and snuggles into my covers. I lie down beside her, pulling her into my chest. I can feel the warmth of her breaths on my shoulder.

"Why didn't you become a musician?" she asks softly. So softly I almost didn't hear her.

I jerk my head back, looking down at her. Where the hell did that come from? She looks at me expectantly. The randomness of the question still has me in shock; I'm more concerned with why she's asking than to actually answer the question.

"Aiden, I'm okay," she says. "I was just thinking about all the times you've sang to me, and you have an amazing voice. And you seem to love to sing."

I stare at her apprehensively. I know she's not okay, but maybe not thinking about it for a while will help her relax. "I don't love to sing," I say. She stares at me. Okay, so that wasn't entirely correct. "I love to sing to *you*."

Her smile widens. I run my hand down her arm until I reach her fingers, then I weave our fingers together. She squeezes my hand. "So, answer my question."

Touching her has temporarily wiped my mind clean, so it takes me a few seconds to remember what the question was.

I nod slowly when I remember. "Before my mom died, I sang

all the time," I say. I chuckle to myself, remembering that I used to piss Max off by always singing. I tell her a couple stories of the times I embarrassed Max with my singing. It wasn't until I started to attract the girls that he decided it wasn't so bad.

"I played the guitar, so he learned to play the drums so we could play together. He'll swear to this day it was only because the girls loved it."

"How cute! You guys had your own little band," she says. "What was the name?"

"What makes you think we named our band?"

She laughs. "Oh, please. You and Max and your overzealous egos. It was probably called something like..." she pauses to think, "...Audacious Flames."

It's my turn to laugh out loud. "Audacious Flames? We were *thirteen* when we named it. We didn't even know what audacious meant. Hell, I'm not even sure I do now."

"See! You did name your band!" she says, poking me in the chest. "Tell me."

"Okay, okay. We used to deliver newspapers, so we went with Delivery Boys."

"Oh," she says blandly. "It's catchy."

"Well, sorry our name doesn't live up to your Audacious Flames," I say, tickling her.

She grabs my hands, begging me to stop. Instead, I flip her around and pull her into me, spooning her.

"Are you okay?"

She inhales deeply, blowing it out slowly. "I will be. I'm really surprised that I didn't see it. I'm usually so good at reading people. I had him pegged so, so wrong."

I stay quiet because I don't want to tell her what I'm really thinking. I warned her. She didn't listen. Silence consumes us for a few minutes before she talks again. Here I was thinking that she was deep in thought about the events of tonight, but instead she says, "So, did you stop singing because your mom died?"

"Are we on that topic again?" I ask.

"Yes! You never told me why you stopped."

"When my mom died, my whole life changed. My priorities changed," I say. I hug her tighter. I definitely don't need this conversation adding weight to her already grieving body.

She nods her head slowly. "I understand," she whispers. "It's a shame. You could have been famous."

"Then I would've never met you."

"Oh, I'm sure I would've been your number one fan," she giggles.

"Would you have flashed me while I was up on stage?" I say into her ear. My dick twitches, and I tell myself to shut it down. Just thinking about her glorious tits while she dances to my singing has me scooting my ass back a little bit so she can't feel how hard I'm getting.

I don't know why I thought having her in my bed, so close to me, would end up any other way. Any self-control flew out the window the second she asked me to take the handcuffs off her at Travis's.

"For you, definitely," she says, laughing again. I thank God she doesn't wiggle her ass back. "You seem to get me to do things I normally don't do."

The irony of that sentence isn't lost on me. She has flipped my world upside down and sideways, leaving permanent marks in its place. I've never given someone this much power over me. *Given.* I chuckle to myself. More like *taken.* I would do anything she asks of me. Except leave.

I thought I would never sing again. I hadn't sung in over twelve years before I met Addison. Now I can't seem to stop. I've always thought the words that come out of music impact us more than just saying them. I was always able to express my feelings through music. That was before though, when I had feelings. When my mom died, everything went numb. I didn't want to feel the words, definitely didn't want to express them.

I wanted revenge.

But the first sight of Addison's gorgeous body and her hypnotic, Caribbean-blue eyes ... *fuck,* I was goner. I can tell from her breathing that she has fallen asleep. I kiss her on the head and whisper, "I love you." She softly moans and scoots closer to me. Wrapping my arms around her, I drift off to sleep dreaming of concerts and her perfect tits.

25

ADDISON

I've been given a few days off. More like mandatory days off because I didn't ask for them. Staying at Aiden's apartment probably isn't the best idea, but I don't want to be alone at night just yet. Having his arms wrapped around me the last couple nights has made me feel more at peace than I've been in a long time. Just this morning I've received at least five texts from him checking to make sure I'm okay.

I'm fine.

More than fine.

Too fine.

What's there to not be fine about? Lexi's safe. I'm safe. Oh, well, *maybe* it's the fact that I killed someone a few nights ago. Someone I thought I knew. Someone who was going to rape me.

I shouldn't be fine. That's why I have an appointment with Dr. Price today, at the suggestion of the department, Aiden, Sydney, and every freaking one else.

Okay, people, I'm going!

I'm always going. I already have a standing monthly appointment with her. I think I paid for that new Jaguar she bought a couple months ago. When I tease her about it, she laughs awkwardly. See, even she knows I come a lot, she just won't admit it.

Therapy days seem never ending. I'm tired, starving, and ready to relax. When my cab drops me off, I notice Aiden's beamer at the curb in front of his apartment. Hmm, that's weird. I wonder where he went today that he needed his car. Walking into the apartment, the smell of Chinese food greets me.

I can feel Aiden's eyes on me before I know where he is. I turn around after putting my stuff down on the entry table and find him in the kitchen. He's leaning against the counter drinking a beer, his emerald green eyes pinned on me. My whole body tingles as I drink in his gorgeous body.

"Hey," I say softly.

"Hi," he replies, flashing a sexy, half grin. "Want some wine?"

"Some? I'll take the whole bottle, please." I sigh as I walk over to him.

Instead of grabbing my wine, he sets down his beer and pulls me into his hard body. I settle between his legs as his arms bind my upper body to his chest. Wrapping my arms around his waist, I melt into him. He presses his lips to the top of my head, resting them there. The love I feel through his touch, floods through me. My broken heart and body that I thought would never be whole again … I can feel it mending. Coming back to life with just his touch.

"Want to talk about it?" he murmurs.

I inhale a deep breath, letting it out slowly. "No," I say somberly. "I've done enough talking about it today."

"Addison …" He pauses for a moment. "I know what it's like to kill a person. Taking someone's life changes you. Please talk to me," he says, pulling back so he can see my face.

When I look up at him, his eyes are pleading. "I will. Just not tonight." I sigh, looking down. He places a soft kiss on my head again, steps out of our hold, and grabs my wine.

"Hungry?" he asks, nodding in the direction of the food.

"Very."

After dinner, Aiden suggests watching a movie, so I grab some pillows and a blanket while he sets it up. Glancing out his bedroom window, I remember his car being out front.

"Aiden," I say, walking out of the bedroom, "what is your car doing out front?" A mischievous smile crosses his face. I tilt my head and raise my eyebrows. "What are you up to?"

He laughs. "You're too observant."

I shake my head. "Um, you do know what I do for a living, right?" I giggle, laying the pillows and blankets on the couch.

"Well … since you're off for the next few days, and tomorrow is the weekend, I thought we'd do something."

"Something …?" I narrow my eyes.

"Will I ever be able to surprise you?"

"More than likely not," I say, wrinkling my nose.

"Fine. Have it your way, spoil sport." He laughs, poking me in the nose. "We're leaving in the morning. You, Sydney, Damon, and I are all going skydiving."

I squeal and jump into his arms, not even caring that I spoiled the surprise. He falls back on the couch with me straddling him. Not being able to contain my giddiness, I wiggle my ass in excitement, grabbing Aiden's face with my hands.

"You are amazing," I squeal.

Aiden's hands grip my hips. "Sweetheart, you *really* need to stop that."

I wasn't even aware I was doing anything, but now that I am, the feel of his arousal against me causes a myriad of feelings. I gasp as heat streaks up my body at the same time my brain takes me to a place I don't want to go.

I'm not ready.

"Sorry," I say, jumping off of him. He grabs me and pulls me back to his side.

"That is not something to be sorry about. *Ever*," he says, smirking. He leans over slowly and his lips are a whisper away from mine. My pulse increases as he remains there. Waiting for me.

The rise and fall of my chest intensifies as I close my eyes. "Open your eyes, sweetheart." Aiden whispers. The warmth of his breath has my body shivering. I pry my eyes open. "It's just me. The man who loves you more than anything in this world." My eyes start to water at the depth of his words. "We won't do anything you're not ready for, but I want to feel your lips on mine. Meet me halfway," he pleads, still whispering.

A lone tear falls down my face. He catches it with a kiss as soft as a feather, making my breath catch, but then returns to hovering over my lips. My resolve weakens as I lean in, our lips fusing together. I can feel Aiden's breath hitch when I lean my body into his. The kiss is sweet and soft.

Aiden pulls back, cups my neck with his hand, and brushes his thumb across my bottom lip. He inhales sharply and brings his forehead to mine. We stay like that for a few moments before he places a kiss on my forehead and then stands up.

"I need another beer. Need more wine?" he asks quickly and heads to the kitchen. I turn to look over the couch and watch him. He adjusts himself, whispering something. I chuckle because I swear I hear him say Katie's name.

"How was Syd's reaction when you told her?" I ask while arranging the pillows and spreading out the blanket.

"Much like yours," he says, shrugging, walking back to the couch.

"Well, if she jumped in your arms, too, you better not have had the same reaction you did with me." I smirk. He sits down, handing me my wine.

"I didn't tell her, Damon did. And I can promise you that if she did jump into his arms, I'm almost certain he'd have the same reaction." He grabs the remote and looks over at me. "But I love that you're jealous." He winks and flashes his megawatt smile. I stick my tongue out and lean back into my pillow.

"Why in the world did you set up our pillows so far apart from each other?" He pouts, leaning back into his own pillow. He stares at me, waiting for an answer.

Placing my glass on the table, I shrug. "I just thought—"

He grabs both my legs and yanks me over to him. I yelp. Lying flat on my back, I look up to Aiden's gorgeous face. One that I will never get tired of looking at.

"Well, you thought wrong," he says, pulling me up against his chest. "I need you beside me." He kisses my nose and then turns me around, leaning my body against him. I feel like a ragdoll being tossed around. He exhales. "That's much better."

"I don't know what just happened, but you could've just asked me to sit next you," I say, playfully elbowing him in the stomach.

"What fun would that have been?" he says, tickling me.

I squeal as he continues to torture me. When he stops, I breathlessly ask, "Can I grab my wine now, or are you going to manhandle me again, thinking I'm moving?"

"I like to manhandle you," he whispers in my ear. My whole body trembles. Ugh, this is exactly why I thought it was better if I was *across* the couch.

"How about you manhandle the remote and turn the movie on already." I giggle, moving to grab my wine. I empty my glass trying to drown the heat tickling deep down in my belly.

Avoiding sitting back down right away, I go to the bathroom, fill my wine back up, and turn out the lights. By the time I sit back down, I feel like I've seized control of my body.

But how stupid am I? Aiden wraps his arm around my waist,

resting his hand on my stomach, and that control I thought I had flies out the window. As he watches the movie, he's not even aware of how his simple touch affects me. I'm so confused right now. How can I have an incessant craving for his touch, yet when I think about having sex I start to tremble? It's like my body is playing a really twisted game. And I'm definitely not the winner.

"Stop thinking," he whispers.

I try to relax and watch the movie, but every time he moves, my body reacts. His thumb mindlessly rubbing my stomach. The slightest touch of his head against mine when he takes a sip of his beer. Just the feel of his chest moving from breathing has my overstimulated nerves on fire. *Is there a movie playing?* I wouldn't even know because I'm so wound up.

Baby steps. My therapist says take baby steps. For the sake of my sanity I have to do something. Right now I'm so turned on that if he just said the word pussy, I'd have an orgasm. I want to grab his hand and stick it down my pants. I shiver just thinking about him touching me. I blow out a shaky breath, standing to get some air. As I stand, the effects of downing wine are apparent. I'm not sure though if it's the wine that's burning me or the gorgeous man staring up at me.

"What's wrong, Addison?" I'm pacing, fanning myself.

"Be right back," I murmur, walking to the bedroom, the wine fueling my courage.

Baby steps, it is.

There is only one thing that's going to satiate this fire. I just hope it doesn't fuel another one. I unzip my bag and grab a small pouch. I noticed it this morning when I was getting my stuff to take a shower. It must have been in there since we went to the beach last year. When I walk back into the living room, Aiden has paused the movie and is watching me with eagle eyes.

I sit down next to him, and I'm suddenly nervous. How do I

ask him this? I inhale deeply, letting it slowly out. "So..." I pause for a second, "...I have a homework assignment."

He raises a curious eyebrow. Grabbing his hand, I empty the little black bag's contents in his hand. He looks at it and his tongue darts out to lick his bottom lip. Wrapping his hand around the small bullet, he looks back up to me. A salacious grin spreads across his face.

"So, what exactly is your homework assignment?"

"I'm supposed to masturbate," I say quickly as I feel the heat of embarrassment spread over my face. I bite my lip, looking away from his grin. *Shit, this just got awkward.*

He cups my face with his hand, lifting it so my eyes meet his. "You sure you want my help?"

"Five minutes ago I was sure." I let out a nervous laugh.

He leans forward. His lips brush mine and any awkward feelings I have diminish. I lean into the kiss and open for him. He moans when our tongues touch. He explores my mouth with such a soft caress as his hand runs through my hair. Nipping my bottom lip when he pulls back, he softly says, "If it gets to be too much, tell me to stop." His eyes swirl with concern, lust, and love. I can only nod.

My breathing accelerates, not from being scared, but anticipation. He sits on the edge of the couch, lying me down. He lies to my side, head resting on his hand, and his eyes never leave mine. His hand travels painstakingly slow down my torso. As soon as his hand cups my sex, my back arches off the couch. I moan out with pleasure.

Aiden leans over and whispers in my ear, "*Fuck.* Still so responsive to me."

My body shudders at his words. He moves his hand back up, moving it inside my shorts. I bite my lip, staring up into his eyes. He lowers his head and sucks on the lip I was just biting. My hips move of their own accord when Aiden's fingers graze my clit.

My thought process becomes hazy as my body takes over, giving my mind the night off. My insides quiver when his finger skirts over my opening. The touch of his fingers are light, yet they have a purpose. His eyes stay glued to mine. It's hard for me to keep my eyes open as the feelings rush through me. A feeling I've missed. A feeling I took for granted before. A feeling I thought I never would get back.

I can feel the wetness pooling as his finger's pressure intensifies. I'm practically humping his hand, wishing he'd just get inside me.

"Aiden," I plead. He slightly nods and smiles.

When his finger finally presses inside of me, I moan loudly. His fingers tease in and out of me. When I feel the vibration of the bullet on my clit, my body starts convulsing almost immediately.

"Oh, God! Aiden," I scream and contract around his fingers, and he lets out a moan. My nails are digging into his muscular arms as I hold on through my release. I feel lightheaded and my breaths are erratic. He kisses me like he's trying to breathe for me. Deep and passionate.

I did it. Well, I didn't do it, Aiden did. I giggle to myself. The post orgasmic haze starts to clear, and I open my eyes to find Aiden staring intently at me.

"Thanks," I say softly.

"Sweetheart, any ... and I mean *any* time," he chuckles, leaning down and pressing his lips to mine in a sweet kiss. When he leans down, the feel of his hard bulge rubbing against my leg has my body humming already. The need to satisfy him has me pushing him on his back, straddling him.

His eyebrow arches as he watches me in silence. My hands rub his taut chest, slowly working their way down, gliding over his muscles. When my fingers gently slide beneath the waistband of his underwear, his hand stops me.

"Addison, you don't need to do this. Tonight was about helping you," he says sternly.

"You're right, it is about me. About me taking back control. And right now, I want to feel you. So let me," I softly demand.

He releases my hand and brings his hands behind his head. "By all means then, feel away. My body is your playground." He flashes his megawatt smile, dimples on full display, and winks.

I undo his jeans, pulling them open. His hard cock presses against his black underwear. I slide my fingers underneath, brushing the tip. His growl has me looking back at his face. His breathing has accelerated and his lust-filled eyes are almost completely black with desire.

I stare into his eyes, completely mesmerized by how I can cause this gorgeous man to completely give himself to me. I wrap my hand around his cock, slowly stroking him. It's the first time my body has felt another man since …

I freeze and squeeze my eyes shut. Begging myself not to go there. *Think about Aiden.* Instead, my mind takes me to a dark, musty room. The smell of cigarettes …

"Addison, open your eyes." Aiden commands. His deep voice erases the room, bringing me back to the present. I exhale shakily and open my eyes. His hand is on top of mine, still on his cock. "Keep those blue eyes on me," he says as he runs my hand over his still-hard dick. "Stop thinking. You are in total control here, you want to stop … we'll stop. But it's just me and you here right now."

I wrap my hand around him, adding more pressure as I stroke him. *I definitely don't want to stop.* As long as I stay here with him, I want this. He moans as he moves his hand off mine and slides it up my shirt. He runs his thumb over my hard nipple poking out of my bra. I lean into his touch, needing more. He licks his lips as his fingers find their way inside the cup.

Yes, please put your lips on me, I silently beg. As if he can read my mind, he sits up and yanks my shirt off. The second his mouth is sucking my breast, I arch my back, moaning out in pleasure.

The feel of his hard cock on my stomach reminds me that I was supposed to be relieving him of his needs. I bring his face up to mine, and we kiss deeply before I push him back into the couch.

"Stop distracting me."

26

ADDISON

I hear Aiden's front door open, and I can tell from the high-pitch squeals that Sydney has arrived. I'm just finishing zipping up my bag when she comes barreling into the bedroom.

"I can't believe I'm going skydiving today. Eeek!" she screams. She's called me every day, checking on me. But I haven't talked to her since we had been told about skydiving, so I wasn't sure what her reaction was. Her voice seems a little higher than normal today. I mean, don't get me wrong, Syd is usually an excited person, but this is *different*.

Realization dawns on me. "You're scared," I say surprisingly. I smile wide. Sydney has never been afraid of doing things. Truth or Dare growing up, she *always* chose dare. She accepts things and takes them head-on. Well … maybe not some of my ridiculous stunts at trying to find bad people. She's never quite understood my need for that.

She shakes her hands as she shifts from one foot to the other. "I'm scared to death," she admits. "Look, I'm shaking." She holds out her hand to show me the noticeable shaking. I grab it, holding on.

"You'll be fine. Damon and Aiden have jumped hundreds of times. You will love it," I say, trying to reassure her.

She waves me off. "Rationally, I know that. I'm super excited, but that's not helping my nerves. I mean nothing like thinking I'm going to fall to my death from ten thousand feet in the air."

"Let's go prove you're a real pixie and can really fly." I laugh as I grab her hand again and pull her out of the room.

Aiden's on the phone saying good luck to someone and then hangs up. He looks at Sydney and then back to me, and I can tell something is off.

"So, Damon got called out on a case today, so he won't be able to go …" *Well, this sucks.*

"I've already been. Why don't you take Sydney up," I suggest, interrupting Aiden. I know she's scared, but I also know she really wants to do this. I'd hate for her to miss this opportunity.

"No. I can just go next time," Syd says, looking at me. But I can already hear the disappointment in her voice.

"Would you two be quiet and let me finish?" We both whip our heads in Aiden's direction. "Max is going to go with Syd, so we're still good."

Syd lets out a small laugh. "Oh, Damon will love that."

Turning my attention back to Syd, I cock my head to the side. "Is there a *reason* Damon would be upset?"

"No," she states. "He's always been a little territorial." She rolls her eyes. "Anyway, he's dating a girl he met online."

What? I look at Aiden. His eyebrow raises. This must be news to him, too. He flashes a mischievous grin. *Oh, shit.* Damon will never hear the end of this.

I'm still secretly hoping he and Syd get together. They have a connection. And if he's getting jealous of other guys, then he still likes her. I was thinking this weekend might help move things along, *but I guess that won't be happening.*

"I don't want to be a third wheel with y'all at the beach house."

"You're going. End of discussion. Let's go," I say, picking up my bag.

"Wow. You're sounding more like a mom every day." She scrunches her nose at me, picking up her bag. I don't know why, but hearing that makes me miss Lexi. I've talked with her already this morning, and she's loving every second on the ranch. Hearing her tell me that she misses me pulls at strings I'm not even aware I had. Feelings that make me questions things.

I file those away for another day. They won't be answered today. Aiden comes up and hugs me, and I melt into his arms. Memories of last night run through my mind. I shiver, remembering how worshipped I felt. My memories of that horrific night are slowly being replaced and pushed back into a dark place I'll never let see the light of day again. I know I'll never be able to forget those ten days, but the pain associated with the memory will eventually disappear. Time will heal my mind.

Aiden will heal my heart.

Aiden pulls me from my thoughts. "Sweetheart, as much as I love you in my arms, we need to leave." He presses his lips to my forehead and whispers, "I love you."

"Yes, because I'm *already* starting to feel like a third wheel," Sydney says sarcastically.

THE CAR RIDE is definitely not as eventful as the first time we drove up. I can tell Aiden is thinking about it, too, from his wicked smile and wagging eyebrows, his hand squeezing my thigh when we pass the spot where he pulled over when I had my mouth on his cock.

The memory sends heat straight down to my core, making me wiggle a little in my seat. His laugh is deep and sexy. The car's atmosphere turns electric, evident by the exaggerated sigh coming from the back seat. I feel bad at first, then remembered all the times I had been subjected to the screaming of her current boyfriend's name in the middle of the night during our college years. *Yep, don't feel bad anymore.*

Syd's eyes get huge when we park, and she notices the plane. "We're going up in that thing?"

"Did you think we were going up in a seven-thirty-seven?" Aiden jokes.

"No … but I guess I thought it'd be bigger than that," she says, pointing to the plane. I wrap my arms through hers as we walk to the hangar. I can tell she's getting more nervous by the way she's biting her fingernails.

"Why aren't you dating anyone?" The memory of hearing her sex noises throughout the night make me realize she hasn't mentioned any boyfriends since I've been back. Granted, it's only been a couple months, and I've been busy with Lexi, but I'm hoping it's not something I just missed.

"I've been on a couple dates." She shrugs. "I just haven't really had a connection with any of them. It just hasn't been a priority these past few months."

I sigh and my shoulders drop. I hate knowing people put their lives on hold because of me.

"Don't think it's been all about you, girlfriend." She laughs as she bumps my hip with hers. "I had a new job, moved to a new city. I had a lot going on." The new job she almost lost because she was flying back and forth to see me. "Addison Grace Mason," she says sternly, stopping me. She had to go there, didn't she? It's been years since she's used my whole name. I think the last time was when I learned Amy wasn't my real aunt. Her big, ice-blue eyes look up at me. "Stop. Right now. You would have done the same thing for me." I nod, knowing she's right. I would have fought with everything I had to find her. "You have so many people who love you. You need to stop thinking you're alone in the world, because you're not. People worry about you, deal with it."

She spins on her foot and pulls me forward again. I squeeze her arm. "I love you, Syd," I whisper, blinking back the tears that are forming.

She replies softly without looking at me, "I love you, too, Addie."

Aiden kept walking while we stopped. *Smart man.* He's talking to Max up ahead. I smile to myself, thinking that Syd is right. I have so many friends who have become my family. Since my mom died, it's always been hard for me to lean on people. If I didn't get too close, I couldn't get hurt when they left. I learned to just rely on myself. Not let people in. Syd wiggled her way in and never left.

I think about the people in my life now and I know that I would do anything for them, and *they would do anything for me.*

When we walk up to the guys, Max looks at me and says, "You okay?" The concern in his voice just reiterates my previous thoughts.

"I'm good. Just ready to jump." I look at Aiden. I'm ready to jump with him. Wherever it leads. If anyone should know how life is so unpredictable, it's me. I'm not wasting it anymore. Aiden flashes a knowing smile and pulls me in for a tight embrace.

"It's just you and me, sweetheart," he whispers in my ear. My hands squeeze around his neck, pulling him closer to me.

Max clears his throat, "So, it looks like you're with me, Tink." I pull back from Aiden and laugh loudly. *He thinks her nickname is Tink?*

Syd sighs loudly. "Tell me again why I'm putting my life in the hands of this man?" she asks, gesturing to Max with her hands.

"No, I think he's just remembering me telling him you looked like Tinkerbell." I giggle.

"Uh-uh, he knows darn well that is not my nickname. He's just being an ass." Syd rolls her eyes. Max barks out a loud laugh. What the hell? I didn't know Max and Syd really knew each other.

"Your boyfriend going to be mad you're jumping with me?" he asks with amusement.

"He's not my boyfriend," Syd exclaims with her hand on her hip.

"Max," Aiden says, "seems Damon is dating someone he met online."

"No shit," Max says, looking down at Syd who's crossing her arms and has a red face.

I glance between Max and Sydney while they're having a staring contest then to Aiden. What am I missing?

"Max is just being Max." Aiden chuckles, grabbing Max's shoulder. "Let's go, children."

Max growls under his breath. "I'll show you *child*. I'm a hundred percent man," he says, grabbing his crotch.

My eyes go wide. I would expect this from Damon, but Max? *Never.* He's more of the reserved guy, likes to watch from the sidelines, and you never see him coming until it's too late. *That's* Max.

"Oh, my God! I'm going to die," Syd says dramatically.

"Max, play nice. Sydney is nervous, and you're not helping," I grind out, pushing his arm.

Max stops and looks back at Syd, who hasn't moved from her spot. "Tink, I wouldn't let anything happen to you." His voice turns serious, but I'm still surprised he's using that nickname. He walks back to her and surprisingly throws her over his shoulder. "Stop sulking and let's go fly."

She screams and kicks her feet, yelling his name. A large hand lands on her ass, smacking her silent. I gasp, waiting for the shrill voice to come. When he keeps walking past us, Syd's submission shocks the hell out of me.

I turn toward Aiden, and I know what he's thinking. The

devilish glint in his eyes as he bites his lip has my body wanting to jump on him and run away at the same time.

"Don't you dare. I told you already what would happen to that hand," I say instantly, already backing away from him.

His emerald green eyes gleam with challenge as his lips curl into a salacious grin. I twist my lips, watching his every move. *Challenge accepted.*

The second I see movement of his foot, I turn and run toward the hangar. He's close, but not close enough. Instinct has me turning to see where he is. Unfortunately, instinct doesn't know about the rock I'm about to trip over.

"Shit," I scream on my way down onto the grassy area. I roll as much as I can to avoid the hard impact on my knees and hands. *Thanks, Tony, for teaching me that trick.*

"Nice dismount," Aiden jokes as he reaches me.

"Haha, funny man. Help me up," I say, putting out my hand for him to grab.

Aiden holds both his hands up in the air, shaking his head slowly. "Nope. I fell for that once." He smirks. "Last time I got kneed in the nuts and shot."

"You're still bitter about that, huh?" I giggle, pushing myself off the ground. He's serious. He is not going to help.

He picks the grass out of my hair as I dust off the dirt and grass from my clothes.

Aiden stands really close to me, leaning down to my ear. "No, the real reason I didn't help was because watching your tight ass run in front of me got my dick hard, and if I would've helped, I would have thrown myself on you." He bites my ear before sucking it. Chills spread over my entire body.

"But we need to go," he states quickly, grabbing my hand and pulling me forward. He adjusts himself with his other hand as we walk, and I chuckle. He looks down at me with an amused smirk.

"You should know not to run from me," he jokes, squeezing my hand.

I roll my eyes. "If it wasn't for the damn rock, I would have made it." I stick my tongue out at him.

"I'm about to give you something to do with that tongue." His threat sparks a desire deep within me. I let out a soft mewl. "Addison," he growls. "Your best friend is going to get a little show here in a minute if you don't cut that out," he says, adjusting himself again.

"So, how's Katie?" I say, trying to get his obvious hard-on to become *not so obvious*. He looks down at me again and throws his head back, laughing. God, his laugh is as gorgeous as he is.

As we walk up to the hangar, I quickly glance down. "We're good. For now," he says, winking at me.

Walking into the hangar, Max is helping Sydney put on her jumpsuit. It's super quiet in here. I tilt my head. I mean, Max is usually quiet, but Syd ... she's abnormally silent.

She looks up and catches me watching them. Her lips curl into a small smile, and she rolls her eyes at Max. "The dominant asshole doesn't think I can do it myself, so he's doing it for me."

I hear Max growl something under his breath, but I can't make out what it is. *But Syd does.* Her face turns red and her eyes get huge.

"Ugh. Not in your lifetime," Syd sneers, stepping away from his grasp. He stands up with a wicked smile and walks over to put on his jumpsuit. "I'm burning up in this thing. I'll meet y'all outside," she says, obviously flustered. Max lets out one of his booming laughs.

I'm so enthralled with what's happening right now I don't notice Aiden standing beside me, holding my jump suit.

"What's so interesting?" he whispers in my ear.

"I'm just ..." I twist my lips, turning to look at Aiden. "Never mind," I say, shaking my head. I don't even know what to think.

I grab the jumpsuit out of Aiden's hand. Max walks by me, suited up already.

"I'll be outside with Tink. I need to go over everything with her and get her harness on." Max's playfulness is gone. He's all business now. *This* is the side I'm used to.

"Why do you insist on calling her Tink?"

He shrugs. "Why not?"

"Really?" I say, my brows furrow. "Maybe for one, it pisses her off."

"No, when I call her little girl … *that* pisses her off." Max chuckles, walking out the door.

I whip around to Aiden. "When did he call—"

My words are cut off by Aiden's lips pressed to mine. Naturally, I fall into him. I let him explore my mouth with his tongue as our kiss deepens. He bites my lip before pulling back.

"Don't worry about them. Syd can handle Max, I promise." He leans his forehead on mine.

I sigh. "If you say so."

"I do. Now hurry up so I can get you into the sky." He reaches around and slaps my ass then grabs a handful. "God, I love this ass." A low growl erupts from his lips as he gives me a quick peck.

"This ass is mine." My body freezes as my mind takes me back to my hell. *"I bet Aiden never had this ass, but I will. I will own this virgin asshole."* The stench of cigarette smoke and the pain as he forces his fingers in me have me gasping for air.

"No!" I scream out. *Fight, Addison.* "Get the fuck off me!" I push off, fighting to escape the pain.

"Addison!" Aiden's voice commands, grabbing my arms and wrapping himself around me tightly. When I pry my eyes open, the smell and the pain is gone, but the memory is right in front of me. My body is shaking so badly I'm lightheaded.

"I need to sit down," I whisper. Instead, Aiden squeezes tighter.

Max and Sydney are standing in the doorway, staring at me,

concern in their eyes. I want to close mine out of embarrassment, but I'm afraid of who will be waiting for me behind the darkness. I fight back the tears, but I don't have enough strength. They fall freely down my cheeks. I bury my face into Aiden's chest. Both our chests rise and fall with heavy breaths.

"I'm so sorry, Addison." Aiden's voice hitches.

Guilt spreads through me like a raging inferno. My tears break into waterfalls. Just when I think the memories are fading, reality proves me wrong.

"I don't know how to make it stop," I hiccup through my tears. "I'm sorry."

Aiden's arms release me, his hand hooking around my neck. As he guides my chin up with his thumb so I'm looking into his eyes, he says, "Do not apologize. You didn't do anything wrong." His voice is soft, but his hardened face tells me he's fighting his emotions. Anger. Sympathy. Guilt. All of them tear at my heart. I don't want him to hurt. I want him to be free of my nightmare, but I don't know how to do that if we're together. I squeeze my eyes shut in frustration. Why is it the second something goes wrong, I doubt us being together?

I look down and dig the palms of my hands into my eyes. Shaking my head slowly, I groan. I hear the door close, so I assume Syd and Max went back outside.

"Addison, I love you," he whispers in my ear. "We'll get through this. Together." He raises his voice to make sure I hear the last part. I sigh. If only it was that easy. "*Stop*. You remember last time you tried to run from me? *You fell*." He chuckles. I look up to his eyes and softly smile. His eyes glisten with wetness. "Let me be here for you. To catch you and lift you up. Let my love fill your dark spaces. If you would just let me in and stop fighting with yourself." I exhale shakily as his thumb caresses my cheek. "Fuck, Addison. That's for me to decide. And I choose you. I will always choose you. *So stop running.*"

The depth of his words reach deep inside me, his love encompassing my fractured heart, sending pulses through it to wake it the hell up. Any doubts that I have about Aiden start to shred, piece by piece. This man in front of me, who is handing himself to me without any reservation, is the breath I need to help me heal. I can't live without it.

I can't live without him.

A tear escapes down Aiden's cheek. I take a deep breath in and out. "I can't believe I'm saying this, but I'm happy that fate led me to you." He laughs, bending over and kissing my nose. *He knows how I feel about fate.* He's silent as he waits for me to gather my thoughts. "I can't imagine you not being in my life. The love that I have for you scares the shit out of me." I look away from his emotional eyes as I declare one of my biggest fears.

"I understand that," he says softly as he guides my face back to his.

"We … we have so much more to talk about, but I can't right now," I say with so much vulnerability in my words. I'm emotionally drained. I need to be more stable to talk about how deep that love is. "But…" I pause, taking in another deep breath, "…I'll stop running. Please be patient with me."

"Addison, there's no rush. As long as I'm by your side." He holds my face in his hands and pours his love into a kiss. *A beautiful kiss.* Tender, soft, and loving.

"I'm going to need a few moments to gather myself," I say. He smiles and nods in understanding. I walk to the bathroom, letting it close behind me.

I look like hell, I say to myself when I see my reflection in the mirror. I redo my ponytail, pulling it into a bun, and splash cold water on my face. Gripping the outsides of the cold sink, I stare at myself in the mirror.

You are not a victim. You are a survivor.

I close my eyes and repeat my mantra over and over. A soft knock interrupts my current pep talk.

"Addie," a voice as soft as the knock says, "I'm coming in." Syd walks in and closes the door behind her. I sit on the toilet seat, and she props herself up on the counter. "Hi." She smiles. Her jumpsuit is unzipped halfway, hanging off her hips.

"Hi," I say back, folding my hands in my lap.

After a few silent seconds, she asks, "Wanna talk about it?"

I know I should talk about it, at least that's what the doctors say. I shouldn't keep it bottled up inside. Their words run through my mind. I blow out my cheeks. "Aiden said something and it triggered a memory." I start rubbing my temples. "I don't want Aiden to feel he has to walk on eggshells around me, not knowing what he'll say or do that causes one."

She twists her lips and nods her head, thinking about what to say. "I know you don't want to talk about ..." She pauses, but I gesture that I understand where she's going. "So maybe you need to tell Aiden certain *things* that might trigger a memory."

"I was doing so well with Lexi around, not having these memories or nightmares." I sigh.

"It's not a surprise that you're having them with Aiden," she says, looking at me with her eyebrows up. "Y'all's relationship is on a different level than yours and Lexi's."

"Okay, smartass, I know that," I say sarcastically. She laughs. "I'm sorry I'm putting a damper on today."

She hops down and stands in front of me. "Stop apologizing, Addie. I heard what you were saying to yourself. You are a survivor. So don't let what happened to you run your life. You are in control, even if you do have a few missteps along the way. And you have a gorgeous, bad-ass man who loves you more than the air he breathes." I smile. That's exactly the way I feel about him. "Now let's go out there and get ready to watch me get smashed by the Hulk himself." Leave it to Syd to make me laugh. "I mean really, if he so much as trips when we land, I'm doomed," she says with wide eyes and flailing hands.

"Max is not going to trip," I say. "But speaking of Max, he acts *different* around you." I don't even know how to explain it. Syd's description of him as *dominant* seems to be right on target. I stand up and walk behind her out of the bathroom.

"He's just an annoying, overgrown boy. That's all," she says, handing me my jumpsuit.

You sure that's it? I narrow my eyes at her vague explanation. She shrugs.

A sound of popping grabs my attention out the window. I don't see anything, and I can tell it's not super close, but I can definitely tell it's gunfire.

I turn to find Syd zipping up her jumpsuit. "Did you hear that?"

"Yeah. That's Aiden and Max," she says scrunching her nose. "He needed an … outlet." Her voice is hesitant. I know she would never lie to me, but I understand her hesitancy.

I pound back the guilt that wants to surface. He just needed a minute, too. A song comes into my head that I heard the other day. I wanted to send it to Aiden then because it's exactly how I feel, but I chickened out. I wasn't ready. *I am now.* I grab my phone to text him.

ME: *Unsteady* **by X Ambassadors**

27

AIDEN

I unload thirty rounds before I calm down. When Max found me outside pacing with my arms around my neck, he didn't ask questions. He just brought me to the gun range.

It's exactly what I needed. To put power back in my hands when all I felt was failure. Failure to protect Addison. Failure at not watching what I say. *Just plain failure.*

I know everything that happened. I read the goddamn report. *I know.* I put the gun down, dropping my head, as I lean on the table. The sun beats down on me as sweat beads form on my forehead.

"Fuuuckk!" I yell.

"You feeling guilty about this is about as fucked-up as Addison feeling guilty." Max's words come from behind me. I turn to see him leaning against a post with his arms crossed.

"It's my fault she went back there." I rest against the table, my shoulders dropping. "To see the pain in her eyes, the fight in her body ... I wanted to kill someone, *again*," I grind out, scrubbing my hand over my face.

"You and me both, brother," he says. He clears his throat. "But you don't have a clue what's going to set her off, so it's pointless to think it's your fault."

Fuck. He's right. I think. I don't know. I should know what *might* set her off and avoid that at all costs. I groan in frustration. How the hell am I going to do that when I can't keep my hands off of her?

"I don't know what to do," I say, kicking dirt around.

"What you're going to do is hold on tight and be there for her. You both are so stubborn, it amazes me how perfect you are for each other." He chuckles. I blow out a breath, giving him a slow nod.

My phone dings. Pulling it out from my pocket, I see I have a text. I close my eyes and shake my head. *This woman.* The smile on my face doesn't even come close to how I feel right now. I pull up the song and listen.

How ironic Max is telling me to hold on. Like letting go is even a possibility. She reeled me in the second I saw her. Then I had to taste her and I was lost. *Gone.* I never knew what it felt like to crave something so badly and not be able to have it until she left. She's slipped through my fingers, *twice.* I will make damn sure it doesn't happen again.

I type a few responses, deleting them just as fast as I type them. *Grow some balls, Roberts. Tell her how you really feel.*

ME: I want forever, so letting go isn't an option.

I tuck my phone back into my pocket and notice Max waiting for me in his Jeep. I hop in and put my aviators on.

"You good?" he muses.

"Little nervous," I reply, running my hands down my shorts. "I hope I didn't just run Addison off."

Max laughs out loud, grabbing my shoulder. "You haven't run her off yet, and that's saying a lot since she shot you." He laughs again as he starts the Jeep and drives back to girls. I'm never going to live that down. I can just imagine everyone telling our kids *that* story one day. *Our kids.* Damn. I've never even thought of having kids, but just thinking about Addison having my kid excites the hell out of me.

My leg is shaking. I check my phone just in case I didn't feel it vibrate. Nothing. Why am I so nervous? It's not like I asked her to *marry me.*

Fuck, might as well have, I told her I wanted *forever.*

I throw my head back on the seat, looking up at the clear blue skies. I can't think of one emotion that I haven't had in the last couple hours.

Lust. Fear. Pain. Guilt. Anger. Excitement. Love. *Nervousness.*

To say she owns me is an understatement. We park and I let out a long sigh. I stand tall. I'm a confident man. Even if Addison doesn't see forever right now, she will.

When I walk into the room and see her zipping up her jumpsuit, her eyes dart up to mine. I stare at her, looking for … anything. *Everything.*

"Stop trying to read me." She smiles, inching toward me.

"What? That's my job," I say innocently.

"Well, Agent Roberts, what do you see?"

"I see a gorgeous woman who wants forever *with me.*"

"I didn't say what do you *hope* you see," she giggles, standing right in front of me.

"Ouch." I clutch my chest, looking down at her. "You wound me, woman."

"Well, let me fix that." She stands on her toes, bringing her lips to mine. Her lips are soft and full … and perfect. I try to hold back and not devour her. Let her take the lead. When she pushes into my body and her hand wraps around my head and runs through my hair, I lose that battle.

I pick her up and her legs wrap around me. I can't get enough of her addictive taste. I'm starving for her; every second I'm not with her, the hunger is insatiable. That can't be normal. *Right?*

"Oh!" I hear Syd say as she opens the door. "I guess I'll give y'all a minute." She giggles, backing out of the room.

"I need more than a minute," I murmur, pulling back, gazing into her eyes.

"How about forever?" she whispers.

I think I just felt my heart skip a beat. I think the flush of adrenaline tingling throughout my body has left me speechless. Hearing those words come out of her mouth spins my world off its axis.

I wait for a *but* ...

Instead she smiles. "Did I shock you that much?" She chuckles.

"Yes. No. Yes."

She raises an eyebrow. "I've never heard you so indecisive."

"I was just waiting for your stipulations. You're never easy." I grin.

"I don't know about *that*. You got me in bed on day four."

"If you think that was easy, you need to experience a hard-on for four days. I was in fucking agony."

Our laughter must be Max and Sydney's cue. They both walk in.

"If you plan on us getting to the beach house before midnight, we need to get moving," Max states.

Syd's face jerks to Max. "What? You're going to the beach house?" She looks quickly to me and Addison, her eyes wide.

Addison hops down out of my arms and shrugs. "I didn't know, but there are three rooms there. Plenty of room," she says, trying to reassure her. She mumbles something under her breath, and Max laughs and shakes his head.

Addison doesn't get it. Doesn't see it yet. But I know Max better than anyone. There's a shit storm brewing, and I'm not sure I can even stop it. Damon and Max are going to have to figure this out on their own.

Addison claps her hands. "I'm ready. Let's go," she says, grabbing my hand.

After going through our checklist of making sure everything is set, we head to the plane. Stone is checking off his own list with the plane. I'm relieved he'll be flying us up. Hudson, the other guy on Max's team who can fly, thinks he's Evil Knievel. I'm all about an adrenaline rush when I'm by myself, not so much with Addison.

Stone wraps his arms around Addison and gives her a hug when she comes up. I tilt my head, wondering what the hell. *Jealousy*. I can mark that one off the list now. He looks at me and winks. I narrow my eyes. He laughs, letting her go.

"You doing okay?" he asks her. I'm not surprised by his question. Hell, he knows everything she's been through.

"Better than I have been in a long time," she says, looking at me. I stand a little taller hearing her say that. I want to beat my chest and yell, "*She's mine*."

Then, I about fall over when he says, "Hey, Syd, you're looking pretty hot in that jumpsuit."

She giggles and says in her southern accent, "Thanks, Stone." *Oh, shit*. I shake my head. Stone has no idea what's about to happen.

I glance over at Max, waiting. *Because it's coming*. His expression is solid. I've been trying to read Max for over half my life. I still don't know what the hell he's thinking half the time, but I know his reactions. Precise and to the point.

"Stone, I need you to do the parameter check when you get back. Hudson had something come up this afternoon."

There it is. Stone's eyes go wide in surprise, but he knows not to question it. I want to laugh at the whole situation, but I think it's best I keep quiet.

The parameter check is the shit job. And usually you get it when you screw up. Max has acres of land, and the check consists of riding along the parameter, checking each of the security checkpoints for hours on an ATV in the rain, sun, snow … doesn't matter. It sucks no matter what the weather is.

I help the girls get on the plane after Stone stomps his way to the front of the plane. When Max gets behind me, I turn and smile. "Strong-arming it, huh?"

He pats me on the back. "Don't have a clue what you're talking about." He laughs.

"Well, you could've waited until we were ready to jump to issue a punishment, *asshole*." Now I have to fly in a plane with a guy who's really ticked.

He freezes, just realizing his mistake. "He wouldn't dare." I shrug. Too late now.

The engine starts up. "Maybe I should get Hudson."

"No fucking way. I'm more afraid of what he'd do than Stone," I say, hopping in the plane. He's right behind me because I'm sure he agrees.

I sit behind Addison, pulling her into me. She relaxes, rubbing her hands down my legs. We watch out the window as the ground gets farther and farther away and the sky opens up, welcoming us. The ride is smooth, and we reach our targeted altitude.

I make sure we're attached and whisper, "Just you and me, sweetheart. Leave everything else up here."

28

ADDISON

larity. I've decided to name my jumps. This one is definitely clarity. My mind is free of the fog that has been taking up space for too long. Eight seconds of free falling seems to clear my mind. *At least for the moment.*

I'm a survivor. What happened to me, *happened.* Nothing will change that. But I am in control now. Memories can trip me, but I won't let them make me fall. I'm breaking free. It's time to let go. *Free fall.*

As we drift closer to the ground, Aiden instructs me to hold the handles. This time, I'm excited to be in control. I know exactly what'll happen if I move them side-to-side. Instead, he weaves his fingers through mine. The warmth of his hands covering mine feels good. Everything about Aiden feels good.

"Oh, wait," I say, removing one of my hands. The tug it takes for me to pull my hand back from his has us turning a little. I laugh out loud at the unexpected thrill. He straightens us out.

"What are you doing?" he asks as I unzip the pocket on my side. I pull out my phone, hoping like hell I don't drop it.

"I told Lexi that I'd take a picture of us while we were skydiving," I say, turning it on and finding the camera app. Doing it all with one hand usually isn't difficult, but with the pressure of not dropping it, it's a lot harder than I thought.

Aiden chuckles. "Only a woman would think to take a selfie while skydiving."

I hold it up, finding the perfect position that doesn't make me look ridiculous. Because there's always that one angle that makes anyone look bad. *Click. Click. Click.*

"Damn, woman, I think you have enough."

"You always have to take more than one," I say incredulously. "I mean, what happens if we get on the ground and the *one* we took looks horrible or blurry?" I put my phone back in my pocket and make sure to zip it back up.

"I can't imagine you'd look bad in any picture," he whispers in my ear, goosebumps cover my body.

"Oh, come on, Agent Roberts, you can do better than that corny pick-up line." I giggle.

He barks out a laugh and instead of trying again, we're suddenly in a tailspin. I scream in excitement.

This, I love.

We straighten back out as we get near the ground. I see Syd and Max a little higher than us. I laugh to myself, hoping Max really doesn't fall on Syd.

With our feet on the ground, I start to take off my harness and find Aiden watching me with a salacious grin. Remembering our first jump floods my memory. The first time I told him I loved him. The first time we made love. So much has happened since then, but my love has only grown stronger for this man.

Putting my hands on his face, I stand on my toes and bring my lips to his with a soft brush of my lips.

"I love you, Aiden," I whisper on his lips. His lips curl against mine.

"I don't know what I did to deserve you, but I won't ever let you go," he whispers back. His hand puts pressure on my back, pulling me into him as it moves into my hair. He pulls my ponytail out, releasing my hair, only to wrap it around his hand.

He pulls it back, giving him full access to my neck. His soft lips slowly kiss across my neck. After each kiss, he whispers, "I love you."

My already overly sensitized nerves from the adrenaline are crawling with desire from his heated breath, soft touches, and loving words. My eyes roll back, feeling *everything*.

Birds are chirping above us. The sun is low in the sky, but its rays are still heavy with heat. My body soaks it in. I'm burning up. I can't seem to catch my breath.

But I don't want Aiden to stop.

I grip his shirt to steady myself. My breathing is heavy as he assaults my neck. He drags his lips up to my mouth, kissing me deeply. I start to get dizzy. I have to pull back to gasp for air. I'm drowning from the heat of his love. He rests his forehead on mine, panting just as heavily as I am. He closes his eyes, draws in a few deep breaths. I know he feels it, too.

"Forever," he says breathless, tucking his head into my neck.

"Forever," I repeat.

We stand there, embraced in a hug for a few more minutes. Aiden looks down at me and softly smiles.

"Let's go find Max and Syd."

Oh, shit! I totally forgot about them. My eyes go wide as I look around. Aiden chuckles.

"They're in the next landing spot, right past those trees," he says, jerking his head toward a line of trees. He kisses me on the forehead before releasing me.

We pack the parachute and head their direction. As we clear the trees, we find Max and Sydney. I gasp in surprise, bringing my hand to my mouth.

Sydney is in Max's arms, and they are lip locked. Aiden clears his throat. Sydney immediately stops, hops down, and runs to me, jumping into my arms.

"Oh, my God! That was so … unbelievable!" she screams, jumping up and down in my arms. I'm still staring at her with wide eyes, wondering when we're going to address what we just walked up on.

She finally sees the surprise on my face.

"Oh, that was just a thank you for not getting me killed." She waves her hand in Max's direction. His laugh echoes in the field. "Adrenaline and all that." She laughs, still jumping up and down. "That was insane. I could see everything. The ocean! The *ocean* was so captivating. Everything was amazing."

I can't even keep up with her rambling. She's talking so fast that I give up and laugh.

"I'm glad you loved it." I hug her tight. She needed this as much as I did. I know she's been through a lot these last few months, even though she'll never admit it.

"Alright, women, our ride is here," Aiden says, pointing to the two Jeeps coming our way. Max finishes packing his parachute and walks past us.

"You're welcome, *Tink,* and any time." He winks at Syd.

Syd rolls her eyes, giving him a dismissive wave. Then starts talking nonstop about the jump again. I'm still stuck on them kissing that I don't even hear what she's saying as we walk to the Jeep. I shake my head. It must have been the adrenaline.

Syd and I hop in the back seat. With the other Jeep in front of us filled with a couple of Max's guys, we head back to the hangar. Syd and I stand up in the back of the open Jeep, letting the wind rush past our outstretched arms.

"Shit," I say, spitting out dirt that flies in my mouth. Well, that was fun for about one minute until dirt started to peg us from the Jeep in front of us.

The guys up front are laughing, shaking their heads. *Oh, he thinks that's funny, huh?* I squeeze in the middle of the front seats and bring my dirt-filled mouth to Aiden's. He doesn't skip a beat though, pulling me forward and pulling me up top of him. I'm straddling him, and he kisses me like he can't get enough.

I move back, biting my lip as I stare at him through his avia-tors. Reflections of myself shine back at me with his smug smile.

"*Sweetheart,* nothing … and I mean nothing would stop me from kissing you." He rubs his tongue on the inside of his mouth and smiles again. "Gritty."

I shake my head, laughing, and try to push off him to return to the back seat. His hands grab my thighs, not allowing me to get up. I tilt me head and raise a brow.

Aiden leans forward and whispers, "You're the one who came up here, now I'm rock hard from your hot pussy rubbing against me. So *now* you're staying up here to keep it hidden." As he sits back, he thrusts up into me while pushing down on my thighs. Heat curls down my spine as I try my hardest not to react. I mean hell, Max is sitting right next to us.

He flashes a slow, smug smile, his sexy dimples on full display. Oh, he is not going to win this one. I lick my lips, biting the bottom one.

I have to grab onto the side of the Jeep as the unpaved road has us bouncing everywhere. Well, that and the fact that every bump has Aiden's cock hitting me in that *oh so perfect* spot. I need to steady myself. It's weird watching myself in his sunglasses but a little erotic at the same time. My cheeks flush and my mouth is slightly open, wishing his lips were on mine right now. But I *won't* be the first to give in.

We continue our standoff, or rather *sit-on*, with no words. Just body language. Desire radiates between us. The tenseness of his jaw. The bite of my lip so hard I'm surprised it's not bleeding. His hands grip my thighs, and I'm sure they'll have bruises. The wetness pooling in my panties, right on top of his hard cock. Nothing exists around us. It's only him and me.

I gasp audibly as we hit something in the road and Aiden thrusts up hard. *Bastard.* His lips curl and then his tongue darts out, licking his bottom lip.

He mouths, "I want you." I exhale shakily.

I slightly shake my head. *Cheater.* I didn't know words were allowed.

I mouth back, "I want your cock in my mouth." My mouth waters just thinking about last night and how he felt in my mouth. How much power I had making him lose control.

Just like I'm doing now. He's barely holding on. His jaw is clenched and his grasp is almost painful.

A booming laugh makes me jump. "Brother, I don't even know why you try." Neither of us look over, but Aiden busts out laughing.

He leans forward and tells me in my ear, "He can read lips." I jerk my head to Max, and he has a devilish grin on his face. *Oh, shit.*

Heat rises to my face from embarrassment as I fall into Aiden's chest. Thank God we're parking a minute later.

Max hops out. "Come on, Tink, they're going to need a few minutes to finish their game," he says with humor in his voice.

I watch Aiden to see what he's going to do. My breathing accelerates with anticipation. He pushes up my sunglasses. "I hated not seeing those beautiful eyes." His hands move up my ass and ascend to my back, pulling me closer to him.

I give him a curious glance. "What next?"

"You're about to find out." He smiles, hopping out of the Jeep with me still around him. I squeeze my legs to hold on and wrap my arms around his neck.

We walk past Max and Syd, who are taking off their jumpsuits.

"Meet you at the car in fifteen," Aiden says with authority. He's on a mission. My body shivers. *I'm the mission.*

He takes me into a room with a bed inside the hangar, kicking the door shut behind him. I don't have an ounce of fear right now about what we're going to do. All I want are his hands, his mouth, his cock on me. *In me.*

"You better hurry. We only have fifteen minutes." I giggle.

The second my ass hits the bed, we tear at each other's clothes.

"Sweetheart, I hate to admit that it'll only take five." He growls. "Now wrap your hand around my cock," he demands.

"How about I—"

"No." He interrupts me, his stare is hard. "I hate saying this, but this is purely one hundred percent for *me.* I have been hard since you had my cock in your mouth last night and that fifteen minutes of you bouncing up and down on my cock about killed me," he says, his voice straining. His hand grabs my breast, thumb flicking my erect nipple. I moan, lifting my chest off the bed. "I need to taste you. I have homework to finish." He winks at me, sliding his hand down my stomach to my clit. Who knew homework could be so exciting?

I drag my fingers along his impressive cock. He jerks and almost falls over on me, cursing under his breath. A growl escapes his lips as I rub my thumb across the tip. He whips his body around so his cock is at my lips and his face is planted between my legs.

I've never been a fan of sixty-nine. It's really hard to concentrate on pleasing a man while he's tongue fucking you, but with Aiden, sign me up! *Every day.*

"I think Dr. Price is going to give me an A-fucking-plus," he says confidently as we lie side by side, sated and panting. I giggle. *I know I do.* I didn't realize how much I missed those fingers and that tongue. How much I needed his touch.

"Honor Roll, right here," he says, leaning up on his elbow. He looks down at me and flashes a sexy grin.

I narrow my eyes. "I think you're supposed to have more than one A to be on that list," I tease.

"Exactly." He nods as his grin widens and reaches his eyes. He bends down and gives me a quick kiss before pushing off the bed to get up. While putting on his clothes, he mumbles, "Never got so many A's in my entire life." Then he chuckles to himself.

I'm sitting up on my elbows, wondering what he's talking about. Of course, I'm enjoying the view, too. I definitely give his body an *A-plus-plus*. When he notices that I'm not moving, rather watching him, his eyes rake over my naked body.

He inhales sharply and moans. "Now that's a picture I wouldn't mind taking." My eyes grow as big as saucers. I don't think I've ever jumped up so fast in my life.

"That would be a no," I say quickly, picking up my clothes. My luck, that picture would be leaked somehow. That's all I need. My life is already too public. "And, *Agent Roberts*, you of all people know that someone could easily find that picture." My words are rushed as I hop into my shorts.

Aiden grabs my hips while I'm slipping my top on. "Hey. *Calm down*, Addison. I was kidding," he says, his tone turning serious. He leans down so he's eye level with me. "I would never put you in that position." I exhale loudly and drop my head, leaning against his chest. Why would I even think Aiden would do something like that? I know he wouldn't.

"I'm sorry. I just …" *I want to go back to just being Addison Mason.* Not Travis Stein's daughter. Not the girl who went missing and was found beaten and raped. Not the girl who killed a serial killer. Just plain, old Addison.

"No need to explain," he says, putting his finger over my lips. When I nod, amusement fills his face. "We'll talk later about *exactly* what positions I'd like to put you in though."

And just like that, all seriousness is gone.

WE WALK in the beach house right as the sun is about to disappear into the horizon. I don't even have time to drop my bags before Syd is dragging me to the back door.

"Wow," she says in amazement when she steps outside. Aiden steps behind me, wrapping his arms around my waist. He rests his head on my shoulder, and we watch in silence as the sun disappears.

Lights turn on and illuminate the backyard and pool. I look up to Aiden, sending him a curious glance.

"Max."

I forgot Max knows everything about this house.

"What the hell happened in here?" Max asks from inside the house.

Aiden's head falls back and he mumbles, "Fuck."

I turn in his arms, wondering what Max found. My spine stiffens thinking that Jessie did something. I peek around him and see Syd walking in. "Oh, my."

I try and get out of Aiden's grasp, but he squeezes a little tighter.

"Aiden? What are they talking about?" I don't see anything out of the ordinary. Well, with the way Syd immediately dragged me outside I didn't see anything at all.

"So ..." He pauses looking down at me, biting his lip. I lift an eyebrow wondering where this is going. "Remember when I left for those few days?" I slowly shake my head, not having a clue what the hell he's talking about. "When I found out what happened with my dad and your mom?" *Oh, those days.*

"Yes," I say slowly.

"Well, I came here to the house." He sighs. I'm waiting for

whatever the hell he's holding back, so I stay quiet. He shakes his head. "Come on, it's best if you just see." His shoulders drop as he grabs my hand.

When we walk into the house, I gasp audibly. I look at him and he shrugs. I look back to a wall that has five holes punched into the sheetrock.

"Please tell me that none of those are for the same reason that one is," I say, pointing to the hole still there from the last time we stayed here together. My voice is strained. He looks at the hole, I'm pointing to and jerks his head back and his eyes soften.

"No, no, no," he says quickly, shaking his head when he realizes what I'm implying. "I didn't even see Jessie." I feel a sense of relief but then wonder what the hell happened.

"I'm surprised you didn't break your hand," I say, looking at the holes.

"I really don't remember even doing it."

I whip around to him. "You don't remember?"

He shoves his hands in his pockets. "I was so pissed. I thought I'd lost …" His eyes tell me everything even when he stops talking. *He lost me anyway.* "I was piss-ass drunk the entire time I was here. When I decided I needed to get back, I sobered up and that's when I saw it." He looks over to Max. "Ryan said he'd fix them. I guess he hasn't gotten around to doing it yet." Max nods.

We haven't even talked about that day. That one day that I went and saw Travis. The *one day* that changed everything. The day that made everything irrelevant, except surviving.

I place my hand on Aiden's chest. "We can neither change the past, nor can we blame ourselves for what our parents did," I say.

He places his hand over mine and squeezes. To change the subject, because I'm really emotionally exhausted from today and I'm ready to relax in Aiden's arms, I say, "What are we ordering for dinner?"

It's like a switch turned everyone back on.

"Pizza," Syd says.

"Barbeque," Max says.

"Chinese," Aiden says.

All in unison. I laugh. "Can anyone narrow that down?" I say, looking at all three of them.

"I'm good with pizza," Aiden says. I look at Max and he nods. I walk to the drawer that holds all the menus. I surprise myself when I remember where it was.

After I order our pizza, Syd and I change into more comfy and warmer clothes. The breeze coming from the ocean is chilly. I come out of the bedroom with yoga pants on and my oversized NYPD sweatshirt.

"Hey, sexy," Aiden murmurs, bringing his beer to his lips. He takes a drink, keeping his eyes on me. The way he makes me feel every time he looks at me, like I'm the only one in the room, is indescribable.

He's leaning against the counter with his bare feet crossed. He changed into a pair of dark blue jeans and a long-sleeve T-shirt. *Mmm* ... he's so gorgeous. I saunter up to him and kiss him, leaning into his hard body. He tastes like beer.

"You taste good," I say, taking his beer from his hand and bringing it up to my lips, my eyes never leaving his. Beer has never been my drink of choice, but tasting it on his lips—*his tongue*—is definitely moving to the number one spot.

I lick my lips and watch his eyes move down to my mouth before he blinks his gaze back up to me. His eyes darken as he pulls me forward. My body shudders.

I feel like a love-struck teenager who can't get enough of her boyfriend. Butterflies flutter in my stomach every time he looks at me. My hormones are having a field day with his sexy looks. Sexy body. Sexy voice. *Everything* about him is pure sexy.

And to think just a week ago, I was afraid I couldn't be intimate again. Now all I can think about is *how* intimate we can be. I giggle to myself. Five months and not a trace of desire in my body. Zero. Zilch. Thinking of it alone made me sick to my stomach.

But one look from Aiden and it's a visceral need.

It's like my body forgot the trauma. Maybe it instinctively knows that Aiden would never hurt me.

"What's so funny?" Aiden asks, taking his beer back. *See?* Just the touch of his fingers across mine when he grabs his beer has my heart beating faster.

I smile at the *sexy* man in front of me. "Just thinking."

"Well, *stop that.* Tonight isn't about thinking. It's about relaxing," he says, giving me a quick kiss. "And letting me touch you all night." He wiggles his eyebrows.

Touch away.

We walk out to the back where Syd and Max are. Max is starting a fire in the fire pit, and Syd is finding music to play on her phone. Aiden walks over and shows her where to hook it up to play over the speakers.

It's a gorgeous night. Cool, crisp air swirls around me. The sound of the ocean's waves is perfect background noise. The stars twinkle in the sky, demanding attention, calling for people to look up and wonder what else is out there.

The pool looks inviting. Blue lights in the pool glow against the dark blue sky. I wonder if it's heated. I bend down, sticking my hand in the water. Chills run down my back as I shiver. *Nope, not heated.*

"Are you wanting a repeat of our last pool experience?" Aiden asks, pressing his body to the back of mine when I stand back up.

"Not in that water. It's freezing."

Aiden chuckles. "It'll start getting warm in about a month, when the nights aren't as chilly."

As we eat and unwind around the fire pit, we talk about our jump today. The guys tell us some crazy things they've done when jumping.

I don't even notice how much I've been drinking, but when I stand it hits me.

"Whoa." I giggle, trying to balance myself. I make sure to balance in the opposite direction of the fire.

"Sweetheart, you okay there?" Aiden chuckles from the chaise lounge that we share. *Our chaise lounge.*

"I'm fine," I say, waving my hand around. "It just hit me a little. I think I need to move around a bit."

"I think it's *time* to go to church." Syd jumps up out of her chair. My smile widens.

Aiden tilts his head to the side, his face filled with amusement. "I bet you two were huge trouble makers growing up."

Syd laughs from behind us. "We were more *entertaining* than trouble makers," she says. I would say that's pretty accurate. But there was definitely some trouble mixed in there.

"I don't doubt that at all," Aiden says, sitting up and pulling me back down on him. I squeal when he tickles me.

His torture continues, so I scream, "If you want me to *entertain* you later, you better stop tickling me." His hands stop immediately and shoot up over his head. "That's what I thought," I say, trying to catch my breath. When I roll off of him and stand, Syd and Max are staring at us.

Max laughs out loud, shaking his head. "You're so pussy whipped."

"Hell yeah. Look at her," he says, grinning up at me. Max looks at me, his eyes perusing my body. My eyes go wide. He's actually looking at me. Like he *wants* me. "Asshole, I didn't mean like *that*," Aiden growls, throwing his pizza crust at Max.

"Eww … yeah, Max," I say. "You're like my brother." Especially after all we've been through.

He shrugs. "He told me to look at you," he says defensively, pointing to Aiden with his beer bottle. "*I did.*" He smiles innocently.

Mine and Syd's song flows through the speakers. Syd runs up and grabs my hand, pulling me to a little platform by the pool. I guess it's more of a tanning ledge but without any chairs, it's the perfect stage.

As we sing *"My Church"* by Maren Morris, we dance and move to the music. It reminds me of the past.

Reminds me of the old me.

Music has a way of touching places that are hidden inside of us. It evokes forgotten memories. It can turn the simplest action in our daily life into a major one. It rouses feelings. It can make you love. It can make you hate. The effect that music has on our mind is amazingly profound.

I tuned it out for months. I was numb to it. I didn't want to hear the music. I didn't want to attach music to any memory.

Until Lexi.

Lexi's enchanting voice and innocence opened my heart to music again. The feelings that I desperately buried are starting to be released.

I glance at Aiden. He locks eyes with me. He's relentless in his gaze. When he brings his drink to his lips, I close my eyes momentarily, grinding my hips to the song. When I open, I gasp audibly at the sight of Aiden standing right in front of me.

He pulls me to him and grinds his straining erection against me. My body starts to hum as we dance. His hand grabs my ass, pulling me into him harder. A moan escapes my lips.

Aiden flashes a sexy half smile. He leans down and says, "If I knew this was a type of church when I was younger, I would've gone every damn day."

I don't have time to answer before his lips crash onto mine. Clapping and whistling interrupt us. And it's not from Syd and Max.

I look around Aiden and see two guys standing in the doorway of the house. Aiden looks to the sky and curses under his breath.

I'm not sure if these guys being here is a good thing or a bad thing by his reaction.

But I catch his huge smile as he turns around. "What the hell are you guys doing out here?" he says, hugging each of them. Syd is standing by my side as we watch the guys. The excitement in Aiden's voice makes me smile. It's not until they step out onto the patio that we both get a good look.

"Holy shit," Syd and I both say at the same time.

Syd grabs my hand. "That's ... that's ..." she says, stuttering, not quite able to get it out.

"Ryker Dallas," I whisper. As if he heard me say it, he looks right at me. His signature smile spreads across his face. The one girls will do anything for. The one he flashes when he wins a game.

Ryker Dallas, the quarterback for the New York Giants, is standing a few feet away from me. He's gorgeous. Short, sandy blond hair with green eyes, and the perfect smile that is probably insured. Syd and I have always had a crush on him. We've secretly wished that he would play for the Cowboys so we didn't feel we were crushing on the enemy. I mean, it only makes sense that he was on the Cowboys ... his last name is freaking *Dallas*.

And he's here. Smiling at me.

Oh, shit, he's walking this way. Syd squeezes my hand and a small whimper can be heard under her breath. I'm so star struck that I don't even notice Aiden at my side.

Until I hear him.

"Addison," he growls. "You're making me feel a little inade-quate here."

Max and the other guy, who I haven't even looked at yet, laugh out loud, breaking my trance. I glance at Aiden and then back to Ryker. He's standing in front of me with a shit-eating grin.

"You must be Addison?" he says, holding his hand out. His voice is sweet with a slight southern accent. It surprises me. I guess I've never paid attention to him when he talks on TV. I smile, placing my hand in his. It's rough and huge. "Nice to finally meet you."

Finally? Like he's been waiting to meet me?

"It's great to meet you, too," I say and then look toward Aiden with a raised brow. He's staring hard at our joined hands. Oops. I pull my hand back, biting my lip.

I can feel my cheeks burn from embarrassment.

"Fucking hell," Aiden groans as he picks me up and throws me over his shoulder, carrying me inside.

I scream in surprise but don't say anything. I can't say I blame him for being jealous. Hell, I'd be pissed if he reacted that way to a friend of mine. But it's Ryker Dallas! And this is *his* fault. If he would've told me in advance that they were friends, I could've been prepared.

Keep telling yourself that.

He stomps through the house, taking me to the bedroom. He throws me on the bed and crawls on top of me. I blink innocently, trying to gauge how mad he is before I say anything.

His lips slam down on mine, and I immediately open my mouth, letting him take anything he needs. His hands roughly explore my body in urgency. They're up my shirt, down my pants, *in me*, without any warning. I moan into his mouth at the feeling of his thick fingers pumping into me. My hips buck, feeling the tingle working its way down my spine, about to explode. My whole body trembles as pleasure explodes through my sex. My screams are muffled by Aiden's kiss. My chest heaves as I gasp for air.

Aiden pulls back, but is still an inch away from my face. "You are mine," he says unapologetically. I see the pain in his eyes before he has time to react. He jumps up and walks around the room. He runs his hands through his hair while he mutters curse words under his breath. I don't even know what he's so upset about. I'm so confused at everything that just happened.

"Aiden." He stops and looks at me. My brows furrow as I stand and walk to him. I run my hand over his jaw. It clenches under my hand. "What's wrong?"

"I'm so sorry," he says quietly, putting his forehead against mine.

"For what?"

"I didn't mean to be so rough." His voice cracks. *What?* "I just … there was this feeling that was so strong that I just acted on it without thinking."

I look up in disbelief. "Okay, first, I should be the one apologizing. I didn't mean to act all stupid in front of Ryker. I was just surprised to see him standing there. He's like a celebrity to me." I shrug, softly smiling up at him. Concern is still etched on his face. I blow out a breath. We haven't ever talked about this, and I don't want to now, but he can't beat himself up every time he *thinks* he's done something wrong. "Second, nothing you do, and I mean *nothing*, will ever be close to what *he* did to me. You could never hurt me, Aiden." I stare into his eyes, making sure he's hearing me. "Please don't misconstrue our intimacy as anything but love. I promise you, if I feel uncomfortable, I'll let you know. But I don't want you to hold back with me, ever."

I run my hands up his chest. His muscles tense under my palms. I stand on my toes and kiss him softly. "I love you, Aiden. Only you. It's only ever been you," I say into his lips. I can feel his body relax. His arms wrap around me, pulling me closer.

"I love you, too, Addison. I'll work on number two. It might take me a little time, because I don't know what I'd do if I ever hurt you. Even unintentionally." His hands cup the back of my head as his thumb caresses my cheek.

I smile and nod. "Now that we got that out of the way, Mr. Caveman, what the hell?" I playfully hit him in the chest. "I can't even believe inadequate came out of your mouth. You are the sexiest, most confident man I know."

"You were looking at him like you wanted to have him for lunch and then you started blushing when you had his hand in yours."

I roll my eyes, shaking my head. "Really? That's a little extreme." He shakes his head slowly. "I told you *already* why I had my reaction. Why are you being so jealous? He's your friend. One that you have never mentioned before, by the way."

He shrugs. "I did tell you about him. He's one of the guys I went to school with, and he would come to the house. I just didn't tell you his name."

"So he's one of your *best* friends, yet you never told me his name. Why?"

"I don't know, Addison," he says, throwing his hands in the air. "I guess there was just never a good time to name drop, that one of my best guy friends is Ryker Dallas."

My eyes widen. "Oh, I don't know, how about the time we had a *bet* during one of the games that we watched together," I say sarcastically with my hands on my hips.

He exhales loudly, pinching the bridge of his nose. "Addison why are we fighting about this?"

"Oh … uh-uh. You don't get off that easy. Why were you so jealous? I've seen you jealous before. It's playful. Back there …" I say, pointing to the patio, "was a totally different reaction. Do you not trust me? Do you actually think that I want Ryker in *that* way?"

"No. Yes. No!" he growls. I take a step back. *Wow.* There was a *yes* in there. What the hell is happening here? Just because I got a little star struck, he doesn't trust me now? Aiden looks away from my hurt eyes.

I look at the closed bedroom door. I should just leave. No,

screw that. I didn't do anything wrong to make him not trust me. I cross my arms and wait for Aiden to figure his shit out.

He doesn't even look up when he starts talking. "In college, Ryker and I used to ... *share*."

"O ... *kay*. We've all passed around at least one guy before, Aiden. Typical college life," I say. He still won't look at me.

I see his shoulders drop before he stands up straight. His eyes meet mine. "At the same time."

My eyes get bigger. "Oh."

Lucky woman.

Oh, my God, I did *not* just think that. I bite my lip, trying to get that image out of my head. His eyes scan my face. I really don't know how to respond.

"All the time?" my voice squeaks out.

His lips slightly curl up. "No. It wasn't ever planned. It just would happen every now and then."

I bite the inside of my cheek, deciding what to ask next. I've never had a three way, really never had a desire to do so. I can't say I'm surprised though. All the guys are gorgeous.

"So ..." I start and then stop. I'm still confused. What does this have to do with anything about what happened tonight?

When I don't continue, Aiden says, "When I saw how you were looking at him, it brought back a lot of memories. Before when I didn't give a fuck who the girl was."

Now I get it. I drop my arms and reach for his hand. "I don't want Ryker, Aiden," I say, pulling him toward me. "And I would hope that since he's your best friend, he knows how much I mean to you that he would never try anything with me."

"Fuck, Addison. I know that. He would never. You would never. *I fucking know that.* I've just never felt like this for anyone, and I didn't know how to handle the jealousy." He releases a forced breath, looking down at me. I hate seeing the vulnerability in his eyes.

"I think you *handled* it just fine." I lick my lips and bite down.

"Only fine?" He flashes a confident smile, pulling our joined hands up to his lips. The vulnerability quickly vanishes, replaced with desire.

"*Hmm* … I think it's been too long for me to give an accurate statement on that."

He rubs my knuckles against his lips. "I guess I'll have to refresh your memory."

"Yes, please." I giggle as he pushes me back down on the bed.

Yep, it's definitely more than *fine*. More like spine-tingling amazing. Two orgasms later, we lie on the bed wrapped in each other's arms. I want to return the favor, but he says this is about me and proving that he is more than *fine*. I laugh out loud. He can prove that point any time he wants.

"Are you ready to go back out there?" Aiden asks, gently rubbing my hand with his thumb. I'm lying to his side, my neck resting on his shoulder. It's my favorite spot. Where I can hear his heart beat. I can hear the music blasting and laughter coming from outside. I'm a little afraid to see what trouble Syd has gotten herself into.

"Are you sure?"

"I'm sorry, Addison," he says, sighing. "I don't want you to feel uncomfortable around Ryker, afraid I might misinterpret something. It was a gut reaction based on our past. He is one of my best friends, and I want you to get to know him."

I look up from his shoulder and smile. "I want that, too. And *not* because he's a NFL football player, but because he's your friend," I say. I really try to sound sincere because it's *mainly* true. I can't help it. He's freaking Ryker Dallas.

We walk out to the patio, and Aiden holds me close. I have a feeling even though he trusts me, he's going to hold me a little tighter tonight. And I'm okay with that.

29

AIDEN

"You good?" Max asks as we sit on our lounger.

I nod. Max knows me better than anyone here. He knows I freaked out. I'm pretty sure everyone knows it. I'm embarrassed I acted that way. I hated it even more seeing the hurt in Addison's eyes when she thought I didn't trust her.

That foreign feeling burst through me like a fireball when I saw Addison look at Ryker. My mind didn't even give me a chance to rationalize it. I just saw red. Raging, jealous red. And of course, Addison saw it right away.

I scrub my hand over my scruffy face. I need to talk to Ryker. I'm sure he thinks I'm an asshole for what I was thinking. He knows I love Addison.

"Hey, I'm Jaxon. We didn't have a chance to meet before you were hauled off."

Jaxon is at Addison's side, extending his hand. He briefly looks at me with his brow cocked and an amused grin. Asshole, I'm not worried about you. I shake my head.

"Addison. Nice to me you." Addison shakes his hand and takes it back immediately then scoots next to me a little more while still smiling up at Jax.

Normally, when she is close to me it makes me feel like I'm the luckiest guy in the world. Right now, I feel like an ass. I give her a quick kiss on the lips and push off the lounger, standing. Jax and Addison both look at me.

"Where's Ryker?" I ask Jax.

"Inside, getting us beers."

I look down at Addison and she nods. I wink and walk off. As soon as I walk through the door, Ryker slams his beer down on the counter.

"What the hell, Aiden?" he asks, staring me down.

Walking over, I curse under my breath, and he hands me a beer. He must know I need it. I think I'll need a few more. I put it to my mouth and take a long drink. He stands there, crossing his arms, waiting.

I chuckle. It's the exact same stance Addison gave me earlier. He lifts his eyebrows. I'm sure he's wondering what the hell I find so funny.

"I fucked up," I admit.

He just nods.

I finish my beer, throwing it in the trashcan. The bottle shatters, causing a loud noise.

"It's been years since we pulled that shit," he grits out.

"Fuck!" I bark out, running my hands through my hair. "*I know that.* I can't explain where that came from. I know how much Addison likes football and when she smiled at you, I just lost it." I sigh.

"The mighty Agent Aiden Roberts is jealous of *me.*" His voice is full of humor. "Who would've thought that would ever happen?"

"Fuck off," I laugh, grabbing another beer.

He grabs my shoulder and squeezes. "If I didn't believe that you fell in love with this woman, I do now. And remind me never to fall in love, because that girl has your balls in a vise grip." He chuckles.

"Don't I know it." We tap bottles and take a swig.

"Did you tell her?"

"She wouldn't let it go, I had to." I shrug.

"Fuck, man. You know it's going to be awkward between us now." My eyebrows furrow. "Not me and you, asshole. Me and Addison."

"Ryker, that's the last thing that I want. I told her the same thing. You're like my brother. It was a knee-jerk reaction," I say, irritated. Goddamn *feelings*.

"By the look of the holes in the house, it seems like you've been having a lot of those," he says, looking around.

"Balls. In. A. Vise. Grip," I repeat slowly.

"How is she doing? She looks good," he says as we stand looking out to the back patio. She and Syd are dancing around. My cock twitches. I don't know what I was thinking earlier, not taking her up on her offer. I guess I was punishing myself for acting like a fool.

I can see Ryker's serious reflection in the glass. Max told me he had talked to the guys. They don't know everything, but they know enough.

"She's doing well. She has her moments, but she's working through them. If she'd stop putting herself in danger, I might be able to breathe."

He looks over at me, confused.

"Did Max tell you about Lexi?" He shakes his head. At least I wasn't the only one.

I tell him the short version about what happened. How Addison and I met back up and how Lexi has become part of Addison's life.

"Fuck."

"I question the world we live in sometimes," I say, shaking my head. "Well, after we got back from Texas, Addison went back to her place. Come to find out, she knew the perp and he ended up in her apartment with her." One hand fists at my side and my other one grips my beer tighter.

"Holy shit! How can one person have *that much* bad luck?"

"Don't even ask. Her life has been one *fuck you* after another."

"So, what happened? This had to be pretty recent because I just talked to Max at the beginning of the week and he didn't say anything."

"It happened on Tuesday." He looks out at Addison and then back to me with a look of surprise. "She shot and killed him. That's why we're here. I was trying to get her mind off of it and relax."

"How is she even managing? She killed someone a couple days ago." He looks outside again and points to her. "*That* does not look like someone who just killed someone. Aiden, I'm a little concerned for you." He chuckles nervously. If he only knew that she already shot me, he'd think I was insane.

"She didn't have a choice. She did it out of self-defense. *But* ... I also think she's not dealing with it like she should be, emotionally."

"Only you would fall in love with La Femme Nikita." I laugh out loud. "So what's up with the sidekick?" He nods his head in Syd's direction.

Not you, too?

"Why?" I ask cautiously.

"Back when you were in the hospital, I heard about her through Damon. He made it sound like they were a thing. Tonight, I asked about him, and she made it very clear they weren't and never were. She's hot, so I thought what the hell ..." I drop my head, shaking it. "Yeah, well, I got the message loud and clear." He takes a drink. I smirk, knowing what he's going to say. "I happen to glance at Max and if looks could kill, I wouldn't be five feet under, I'd be chopped up and fed to the wolves."

I clap him on the back, laughing. "It's best you stay away from that one. I have a feeling this is a train wreck waiting to happen and you don't want any part of that," I say, pointing at Syd.

"Whatever happened to bros before hoes?" he laughs.

"I've been gone for a while so I don't know what's happened between Damon and Syd, if anything. Syd says he's dating someone he met online."

Ryker spews his drink everywhere as he coughs. "Shut the fuck up."

"Seems to be the consensus. I'm definitely going to give him shit about it on Monday." I'm not surprised that he found someone online. I'm surprised he went looking there. "And she and Max ... I don't have a clue, but he has his sights on her."

"She should run. And *fast*."

"She's pretty feisty. I'm thinking she can handle Max or else I'd say something." I look at Max, and he's watching us like a hawk. A huge grin spreads across his face. I had a feeling he'd be watching, reading us. I mouth, *"Asshole."* I can hear his loud laugh from inside.

"Goddammit. He did his spy mouth reading bullshit, didn't he?" I swing my arm around Ryker and nod.

We head outside and sit around the fire. The girls are still dancing and singing, so it's just us guys sitting around the fire, bullshitting.

Syd walks over to her phone. "Hey, Max, wanna sing?" she says, looking over her shoulder. That's hilarious. If she gets Max to sing, I'd cut off my right nut. I tried for years to get him to sing. It is not happening.

"Little girl, I don't sing," he says, smirking and leaning back in his chair. She huffs and picks a song before turning to go back to where Addison is.

The sound of splashing water has me looking over at the pool and then to Max. *Oh, shit.* Max lowers his head to look at his wet shirt. My gaze turns to Syd standing by the pool with her arms crossed and a scowl.

"Stop calling me a little girl," she says, giving him a dirty look.

I scoot to the edge of my seat, not sure how this is going to play out. Ryker is biting his lip, trying not to laugh. Jax's eyes are wide as he drinks from his beer. It's a wait-and-see game now.

"Tink, that water is cold. If you don't want to—"

Jesus Christ!

I don't even have time to react. I'm not even sure what made her do it again. But she did. *Stupid girl.* He's up out of his seat in a second flat, grabbing her and jumping in the water.

Addison screams at Max. Jax, Ryker, and I stand, but we don't move. It's too late. There's nothing we can do about it now. He won't hurt her, but she's going to be pissed.

A couple seconds later they both bob up. Sydney is gasping for air. Max swims around like the water is actually enjoyable.

"You ... fucking ... bastard." Syd gasps between each word. Yep, she's pissed.

Addison runs into the house. I go to the edge of the pool to help her out. Addison comes out and wraps a shivering Syd in a towel, throwing a couple down by the side of the pool. I look at Max, twisting my lips.

He shrugs. "I tried to warn her." He puts his hands on the side of the pool and pulls himself out. His strips out of his shirt dropping it onto the ground.

Syd whips around at the sound. Her eyes widen when she looks at Max. Her pupils dilate for a fraction of a second before they return to anger. She curses under her breath as she spins back around, stomping to the door. Addison follows her. *Oh, Syd, you're playing with fire.*

"I need a hot shower," she says, her voice shivering.

Addison is about to say something when Max beats her to it. "No." Max's voice booms. "She shouldn't—"

"Max," Addison says in a cold voice, shooting him a look of frustration. "I'm fully aware of how the body works." Her stare is icy. Max sighs and nods, holding his hands up. I think Max forgot that Addison, a forensic scientist, definitely knows that you should never change your body temperature from cold to hot that quickly to prevent heart damage or shock.

The girls disappear into the house, and we erupt in laughter. All of us except Max.

"This day needs to go down in history," Ryker says, clapping. "Aiden's jealous of me *and* you just got put in your place, *by a girl!*" He points at Max.

Max flips us off as he walks back into the house. He's back with dry clothes and a beer within a few minutes.

"Check on the girls?" I ask.

"Are you kidding me? I'd like to keep my nuts tonight," he says, plopping down in his chair. He drains his beer in one gulp, placing it on the ground in line with the other empty bottles.

"Seriously?" I look toward the patio door where the angry voice is coming from. "What the hell? I'm feeling a little left out right now."

We all bust out laughing at the butt-hurt whine coming from Ryan.

"I'm not kidding! I haven't seen y'all in four months. We get a couple calls saying there are some concerns that teenagers might be partying at Aiden's house. *THIS* is not what I expected to see! Assholes!"

I bite my lip to contain my laughter. I do feel a little bad. Ryan was always the sensitive one, which is probably why he was the first to settle down. He walks over and I give him a hug. "Hey, brother. It's good to see you."

He shakes his head and sighs. "It's good to see you, too." He looks me up and down. "You look good. A lot better than the last time I saw you."

"When do you get off?"

"I'm off now. The calls just came in, so I told them I'd check on it on my way home. Something about screaming, cussing, and loud music," he says, narrowing his eyes at the guys.

"That was his fault," Jax points at Max with a shit-eating grin.

"That was very *lawyer* of you," Max says sarcastically.

Ryan looks around and back at us. "I'm pretty sure Max wasn't the one screaming."

My attention turns to Addison walking out of the house. Ryan notices me looking behind him and spins around.

"Everyone, hide your guns," he says, joking.

Fucking Ryan. Addison's eyes go wide and her face pales. Max growls behind me as my expression hardens. The silence is painful.

Ryan's face contorts to regret as soon as he figures out he said the wrong thing. "Addison, I'm sorry. I don't know—"

I grab his shoulder and shake my head. Max rises from his seat, putting his arm around Addison. "C'mon, Addie, let's go make Tink some hot chocolate." She slowly nods her head, letting out a harsh breath.

Once they're out of our sight, I smack Ryan upside the head.

"Obviously I deserved that, but if anyone ever *talked to me* and told me shit, I'd know how I messed up." He punches me in the arm.

"Sit," I demand. I start the same story that I told Ryker, but when Addison comes out I stop. I'm not sure if I should continue or keep going. She smiles at me and then gives Ryan a soft smile. Max and Syd come out, too. Syd's wrapped in a huge blanket with a coffee mug, steam rising from of it.

"Everyone, take a seat," Addison says. My eyebrow shoots up, wondering what she's going to do. "Everyone here is important to me and Aiden, like brother or sister important," she says, smiling at me. She sits in my lap, and I wrap my arms around her. "I feel like I need to tell y'all a ghost story. *My ghost story.*"

"Sweetheart, you don't need to do this," I softly say.

"Yes, I do," she says firmly. "I don't want what just happened to keep happening. Everyone here knows parts of the puzzle, everyone has different pieces. I need to put it together for everyone."

I nod. Syd reaches over and squeezes her hand. She knows as well as I do this is tough for Addison. She's one to keep things bottled up and deal with them herself. My heart beats faster knowing that she trusts my best friends enough to tell them her story. I didn't think I could love her anymore, until this second.

The fire crackles and the ocean waves are the only sound made for a couple minutes. I can tell Addison is preparing herself. And everyone stays quiet while she does it.

"It all started the day my mom was murdered when I was ten." I flinch, and she squeezes my hand. I despise knowing that my dad is the one she saw that day. She continues telling her story, how she met Marco and ended up at Travis's house and why. I hate hearing about Marco, but I guess that's an important detail.

"So you two were pretty much on the same life path?" Ryker questions. The guys all know that I thought Travis killed my parents. We both nod. I'm not going to spoil the surprise. I'll let Addison do it. I can't.

She tells them about how she was held captive for a week and how my job was to make sure she didn't escape. Everyone's eyes bore into me.

"It wasn't like that," I say defensively. Addison's eyebrows shoot up. "Well … you were treated well. I would never let anything happen to you," I try to explain.

"Even though that was when Aiden and I fell in love, I was still being held captive and was not allowed to leave."

"You seduced a prisoner? That's low, even for you, Aiden," Jax says a little pissed off. I fist my hands.

"It wasn't like that," Addison says, placing her hand on top of mine. "We both fought it, but it was very mutual."

"And you didn't know he was undercover?" Ryker asks.

Addison laughs. "Definitely not. And you'll believe me in a second. But before I get to that, I figured out why Travis was keeping me there. Come to find out, he didn't kill my mom. He was in *love* with my mom. And…" she briefly pauses, "…he's my father."

The guys' mouths drop as they look between Addison and me. I know what they're thinking. Keep listening, boys, it gets worse.

"When I found that out, he didn't want me to leave." She looks at me and grins.

I shake my head. "You can skip the next part."

"No, she can't," both Syd and Max say at the same time. They look at each other and laugh.

"The next part is the best part." Max chuckles.

I narrow my eyes at him. "You're supposed to be my best friend. This shouldn't make you happy."

"Shut up, Aiden. Let your girl talk," Jax says in anticipation.

I dramatically gesture with my hand to tell her to keep going. Might as well get this out. I'll never live this down now with everyone knowing.

"I love you," she says, grinning, looking at me before turning back to everyone. I squeeze her thigh where my hand rests. "I knew that I needed to get out of there. There was no way I was going to stay, *even* for a hot bodyguard."

She tells them about our run that morning, how she faked a fall. I remember feeling like shit because we were racing. The last thing I wanted was for her to get hurt.

"When he pulled me up, I …" She winces, looking at me.

"Sweetheart, it's okay. Keep going."

"With the momentum of him pulling me up, I kneed him as hard as I could." Groans can be heard around the circle. Any man cringes when they hear that. It hurts to even think about. "And when he went down, I grabbed his gun."

I look at Max and he has the widest grin on his face, waiting for it. I flip him off, knowing he's getting a thrill out of this.

"I knew I only had a couple minutes before the other guards were out there, so I needed to get out fast. I also knew if I ran, Aiden would have caught me." She clears her throat before continuing. Everyone is hanging on her every word. "So ... I shot him and ran like hell."

Not a word is uttered. They are shocked speechless. That is until Ryker bust out laughing. "You fell in love with a girl who shot you? Did you confuse that with Cupid's arrow?"

I shrug. "It was fucking hot how she handled the gun."

Ryker shakes his head. "I shouldn't be surprised. Like I said, La Femme Nikita."

Max's laugh booms around us, and he points at Ryker. "She was hot," he states, getting up. "I have to piss." He walks around the house and does his business. I don't think we'll ever grow up enough that we stop thinking it's cool to piss outside.

Syd shakes her head and rolls her eyes. "Men," she says, sighing.

Addison nods in agreement. She continues her story about how she moved to New York and finally met Agent Aiden Roberts, talks briefly about our dates, skims over the Jessie incident but explains why Ryan made the comment earlier. Then she gets to the part about admitting to me that Travis was her dad. She stops and looks at me when she starts to share that my dad was the one who killed her mom.

I nod for her to keep going. "Travis requested to meet me, and I didn't know why. So I went to visit him to tell him that I wanted him to leave me alone. He ends up telling me that he had Aiden's dad killed because he's the one who..." she swallows and takes a breath, "...killed my mom."

Gasps echo around the fire. My spine stiffens. I blow out a harsh breath. We've never discussed this. I have no idea how she feels about it. It feels like a forgotten memory that was never addressed, but now it's front and center. She turns in my lap, facing me.

"I let that go a long time ago," she says, feeling me tense. "Like you said that afternoon, we can't control what either of our fathers did. We aren't like them. You're a good man, and I love you," she whispers, leaning over and kissing me.

When she rights herself again, she continues. This is the part she takes a lot of pauses. Her voice shakes as she tells them about being kidnapped, beaten, and then raped. Her gaze never leaves the fire. The flames dance in her eyes as I watch her. I'm not sure if I'm seeing the fire or her actual anger. Thank God she doesn't go into the details of her rape.

Poking my eyes out right now would feel better than having to hear this. I read the report. I know what happened, but hearing it come out of Addison's mouth is like adding fuel to my already burning fire. I'm about to explode. I look up to the dark blue sky as my leg starts shaking.

Cool it, Roberts. She needs you to be strong.

I know she needs to get this out in the open, but I hope like hell it'll be the last time I hear it. I feel Max's hand on my shoulder, squeezing it. I don't look over. I just nod. Addison unwraps my fist and intertwines our fingers as she continues talking. Her touch helps ground me. I pull our joined hands to my lips, kissing them softly.

She tells them pretty much everything. This is torture. She talks about the rescue, the healing process, all the way up to finding Lexi. I finally release a huge breath. My heart feels like it's on speed and about to jump out of my skin. I want to stop her and take her away so I can make her feel safe. Take all the pain away. Every now and then she wipes away a tear.

But my strong girl continues. She pushes through it. The guys never stop her or interrupt her. They can see she needs this. But they're an extension of me, and I can see the anger on their faces. They hide it from Addison, but I know each of their tells.

We're close to the finish line, and I'm exhausted. My muscles have started hurting from being tense for so long. She's up to Wednesday night now. I can tell she's exhausted, too. She grabs my beer and takes a drink. I sweep my thumb against her lips, wiping the beer from them.

"Thanks," she whispers, bringing her lips to mine. I kiss her hard. Her lips part for me, and I don't even care that we have an audience. I kiss her deep. I want to make sure she knows that none of her past matters. She matters. I hear the guys snicker about needing a beer break anyway.

I weave my fingers through her hair. She moans into my mouth, and my dick twitches. The little she-devil must feel it because she grinds her ass against it. I grab her hair and pull her back.

"Sweetheart, I already want to take you away, you better stop or I'm not going to be held responsible for your disappearance tonight," I growl.

She laughs. "I love you so much, Aiden. Thank you for being here. I know how hard this was for you to hear." She looks down.

I lift her chin to meet my eyes. "Addison, I will always be here for you. *Forever.*" I pull her to me again and kiss her.

"Forever," she repeats against my lips. When I hear the sounds of chairs being filled I pull away. I know she wants to finish and the faster she finishes, the faster I can take her away.

It doesn't take her long to get to the end. But as soon as she talks about shooting and killing Marco, Ryan smacks his forehead, cursing under his breath.

"It's okay, Ryan. You didn't know," she says sweetly.

"I'm still sorry," he says. She nods in acceptance.

"So that brings me to tonight," she shrugs.

Nobody knows what to say. It was a lot to take in. Jax is first to say something.

"You definitely drew the short end of the stick in the game of life." *Ain't that the truth.*

Addison grins. "I used to think that fate hated me and sometimes I still feel like she hasn't been fair about how much I've had to go through in my life compared to others, but I have a lot of good in my life, too. I think she led me to very specific people, knowing they would be able to get me through *anything.*" She leans over to grab Syd's hand. Syd's eyes well with tears. She jumps up and lands in my lap, too, hugging Addison.

"I love you, I love you, I love you," she repeats. "You are my hero." She hiccups through her tears.

I blink back the wetness pooling in my eyes. "I love you, too," Addison whispers.

Syd gets up and bundles herself in her blanket, sitting down. "And now I have y'all," she says, smiling at everyone. They smile back and nod somberly.

Max pushes off his chair and pulls Addison into his arms. He holds her tight without saying any words for a few moments. "I love you, Annie Oakley," he finally says, kissing her on her head. Her laugh is soft.

"I love you, too, Max," she says quietly.

When he releases her, Jax is next to pull her in a hug. Max leans down over my shoulder. "I'm going for a run."

I nod in silent understanding, knowing exactly how he feels. Syd watches him go inside the house. I wonder if she'll follow, but she stays put. She chews her cheek and then turns her gaze to our direction. Blush creeps up her face. I smile wide. She rolls her eyes and looks away.

"I'm in the city, so if you ever need anything, don't hesitate to call," Jax says.

"What?" Addison's head tilts. "You live in New York City?"

Jax chuckles. "Yes. I'm usually so busy with work, I don't get out much." He shrugs, looking at me. I've always told him he works too much. He needs to enjoy life a little more. I guess that's what happens when you're a lawyer for the rich.

Ryan gives her a hug, too, and tells me that he'll be back tomorrow so we can fix all the holes. Not quite what I was planning on doing this weekend, but I guess I should get it over with. I walk him out the door as Addison talks to Jax and Ryker.

"Bring Macie tomorrow. We'll grill out in between fixing this shit," I say, looking at all the holes.

"Sounds good," he says. "You doing okay? That's a lot to take in." He looks out to the back patio.

I think about it for a minute. I sigh, twisting my lips. "A small part of me feels guilty that everything that has happened to her is a chain reaction brought on by my fucking dad."

"Aiden, don't do that," he says, crossing his arms.

"How can I fucking not?" I say, running my hands through my hair.

"Because it has nothing to do with you," Addison says from behind me. I exhale sharply.

I slowly turn around. Our eyes lock. Beautiful blue eyes plead with me. "You weren't supposed to hear that."

"Kind of glad I did," she says, her eyes softening.

"That's my cue to leave. I'll see you both tomorrow." Ryan slaps me on the back and then leaves.

"I'm sorry," she says.

None of this is her fault.

"Sweetheart, I don't know what in the world you could be sorry about."

"I should have ... *we* should have talked before I told everyone."

She sighs. "I didn't even think how you might be feeling about everything."

God, I love this woman. After all she's been though, she's worried about how *I* feel? I shake my head in astonishment. Walking up to her, I grab hold of her hips, lifting her up. She naturally wraps her legs around me, but her eyes go big in surprise. I walk toward our room. Jax and Ryker stop us before we disappear into the room.

"We're out of here," Ryker says down the hallway.

I glance their direction. "You guys staying in town?" They both nod. "Come back tomorrow for lunch. We're going to barbeque." Out of the corner of my eye, I see Addison looking at me.

"We'll be here," Jax says as he salutes goodbye.

I take Addison into the room, shutting the door with my foot. I sit down on the bed, still holding her so now she's straddling me. She struggles to get loose, but I hold her hips tighter.

"No."

She looks at me, her brows knitted together. "We're going to talk. And I don't want any space between us."

Her lips curl up, and I sneak a quick kiss. I can't look at her lips and not want to devour them, so hopefully this will hold me over for now.

"I feel like an ass," I admit. "The last thing I want is for you to worry about how I feel."

She rolls her eyes. "How can I fucking not?" she says, repeating my words earlier with a pointed brow. She runs her hands up my arms. "How we're linked together is *why* we found each other, but I feel we can't move forward until we both let go of the choices our parents made. I have. I need you to. For me. *For us.*"

"I thought I had until I heard you talk tonight. Then the feelings of guilt slammed into me like hitting a brick wall."

"I don't and have never blamed you. It wasn't because of you that I went to Chicago. I can easily say if I hadn't made that *one choice* to not find out who Travis was, I would've never been kidnapped or raped."

I loathe that my first thought is that she wouldn't have met me either. How selfish can I be? Doubt creeps up as I wonder if she regrets going to Chicago. I tense.

Her hands palm my jaw. "Stop," she pleads, pulling me from my thoughts. She rests her forehead against mine. "I can see it in your eyes that you're questioning things. Why? Why now? You've been chasing me for almost a year. Telling me to stop running. I finally say forever and *now* you're questioning things?" Tears fill her eyes.

I go to pick her up and push her aside, needing to walk around, but she squeezes her hips tight. When I find her eyes she says, "No. *No space.*"

I chuckle softly and nod in resignation. "You have to wish that you'd never gone to Chicago." It's painful to say.

She bites her lip, letting it slip out. "We would have met eventually. I was still moving to New York City ... We would have still worked together. So, if I knew that we could have been together without Chicago, then yes, I'd wish that I had never gone." Her eyes reflect a flood of emotions as she continues. "But I also believe that I was put on that course for a reason. We can't rewrite history, Aiden. There are too many unknowns. If I had never met you in Chicago, my heart wouldn't have belonged to *someone else* when I first moved to New York. I might have ended up with Dave before I ever met you."

She smiles. I cringe at the thought. Bastard still reminds me he almost had her first. "Very funny. When you put it that way ..."

"I don't regret you," she says, wrapping her arms around my neck. She spreads soft kisses over my face. When her mouth lands on my lips, I pull her bottom lip and suck on it. I deepen the kiss, coaxing a moan out of her. Her taste, her sounds, her feel is something that I'll never get enough of. She's intoxicating and addicting. I move my hands up, rounding over her round ass, and tug her closer to me.

I want her wrapped around my dick. I want to be so deep inside her that we're connected. We're one. But I'll wait until she's ready. And it definitely won't be here with people in the house. I need her to be able to lose all abandon. Let go.

But when she grinds her pussy against my painfully hard dick, it's becoming *painfully* difficult to think with the right head.

"I can't believe you did that!" Syd's voice comes from the next room. Max's room. We both freeze and stare at the wall like we're going to be able to see something. Addison looks back to me.

"I figured it'd come out eventually. She was being too quiet." She chuckles.

"I'm still freezing because of–"

The sound of someone being pushed against the door echoes in our room and cuts off Syd's yelling. Addison gasps, covering her mouth.

"Do you think …" she whispers, her eyes wide. We both lean a little toward the wall as we listen intently. At first there aren't any sounds. When I hear Max growl, it's obvious.

Addison shakes her head. "No. No, no, no," she says, trying to get off me.

"She's fine, Addison."

"She's drunk."

"She is not. She hasn't had anything to drink for the last couple hours."

"But—"

I put my finger on her lips. "Shh. She's fine," I say, lifting her out of bed. "But we don't need to listen to what's about to happen."

I grab some pillows and give them to Addison to hold. Grabbing a blanket, I head out to the patio.

Addison rolls her eyes. "I lived with the girl for years, there isn't anything I haven't heard already."

I laugh, placing Addison down on the lounger. I put some wood in the fire pit and start it again.

"What are you laughing at?" She narrows her eyes at me.

"They'll definitely be some different noises tonight."

She jerks her head back a little. "What do you mean?"

"Let's just say, Max is probably a little more *creative* than Syd's usual guys."

"What the hell does that mean?" she questions. "*Oh, my God.* Max, too?" her voice rises.

"Max, too, what?" I ask in confusion.

"You and Max," she whispers.

"Hell no," I bark out and laugh.

"Then how do you know?" she asks, lifting a brow.

"Woman, I've known Max almost my whole life. *I know.*"

I lie down beside her, covering us up. She rolls into me and snuggles into my side, putting her head on my shoulder. I feel her take a big breath in through her nose and then relax. Her hand goes up my shirt, and she rests it on my bare chest.

"I need to hear stories about Aiden and Max in the early years. You guys never talk about growing up. You say Syd and I were probably troublemakers, but I'm pretty sure we'd be angels compared to you two," she says, snickering.

I think back to our high school years and laugh out loud. "Baby, we probably made the Devil look innocent."

"Y'all were that bad, huh?"

"You don't even want to know."

She narrows her eyes at me. "I do want to know. But I'll let it go for now."

Addison snuggles against me, and we stare up to the stars. Tonight's the perfect night to sleep under the stars. Bright moon, millions of stars, and the sound of the ocean waves are the perfect trifecta to fall asleep.

"It's lovely out here," she says. Her voice is filled with exhaustion. She's had an emotional day. I start singing softly.

She looks up at me. "Are you singing Adam Levine?" I can feel her stomach muscles tighten with laughter. I nod. "Your register is a lot sexier. Deep and masculine. It's beautiful," she says, laying her head back down.

I continue my version of *"Lost Stars"* by Adam Levine until I feel her breathing even out and her body relax as sleep takes her over. It pulls me under not too long after.

30

ADDISON

"Where's the touch-up paint?" I ask Aiden. The guys are fixing the holes. I feel a little bad about us girls enjoying the sun while the men work. In my defense, I keep asking to help and he won't let me.

He looks up from plastering a hole and gives me a pointed stare. "I told you already that you don't need to help. Go enjoy the sun."

"Fine," I huff, opening the fridge and getting some more Coronas. Ryan's wife came with him today so she's outside with Syd and me. I haven't asked Syd what happened last night because we haven't had any alone time, but both she and Max are acting like nothing happened.

"We're not going to be much longer. Then we'll start the grill and join you ladies," he wiggles his eyebrows.

"Okay, Casanova, get back to work so we can finish today," grunts Ryker as he sands the spots. I laugh as they all start taunting each other.

"They kick you out again?" Syd asks, grabbing a Corona from me.

"Yes. They better not think because I'm a girl that I can't help." I pout, dropping on to my chaise lounge.

"They have this *thing*," Macie says. Syd and I look over to her. "It's like a club. Unless you're in it, you're not allowed to help." She laughs.

I keep forgetting she was around the entire time they fixed up this place. What I haven't forgotten is that Jessie is her best friend. I'm glad she hasn't come up yet in conversation, but I'm sure it's only a matter of time.

"I can just imagine how tight that boys' club was," I laugh.

"Oh, it was. They even had this ridiculous hand shake thing. Je —" She stops herself. "We used to make fun of them all the time. They all thought they were hot shit," she says, laughing.

"Woman, we were. Shit, we still are!" exclaims Ryan. We turn toward the door and the guys pile out of the house, grabbing a seat by us.

Aiden sits next to me on our chaise lounge. "A secret hand-shake, huh?" I tease, trying to hide my irritation with hearing about Jessie. He stares at me for a moment before nodding and smiling.

"We have a secret shake, too," he teases, climbing on top of me and tickling me.

"Aiden! Get off," I laugh, trying to push him aside.

"I am, baby," he says slyly, winking and pushing his pelvis bone into me.

I stop fighting and shake my head. "You're such a nerd."

"A horny nerd," he replies, attacking my neck with his lips.

My phone vibrates in my front pocket. Aiden's eyes go wide and a slow, mischievous grin spreads across his face. "Maybe we need to take this inside," he says.

"Would you get off me," I say, pushing him and trying to get to my phone. He laughs and finally moves aside. When I look to see who is calling, I don't know who it is, but it's a Dallas number. I answer quickly, afraid something is wrong with Lexi. I walk into the house listening to the person on the other end. Aiden follows me in.

"I understand. Whatever you feel is best for Lexi," I say. I twist my lips. Aiden grabs my hand, waiting for me to end my call. "Okay. Thank you for calling me."

When I hang up, Aiden stays quiet, watching me. "So, they want Lexi to stay there in Texas for a month for counseling and therapy. Her doctors feel that it'll benefit her to stay at the ranch for another month."

"Are you okay with that?" he asks slowly, winding his fingers through mine.

I shrug. "I'm sad, but I definitely understand."

"We'll go see her in a couple weeks." We both turn and see Max standing in the doorway.

"Asshole. Let *me* be my girlfriend's hero," Aiden growls, pointing at Max. I can't contain my smile hearing him call me his girlfriend.

Max flips Aiden off. "I have the plane."

Aiden narrows his eyes at Max. "We don't need your plane to get somewhere."

"Fuck you. I'm going to go see Lulu." Max crosses his huge arms and stands tall. My heart melts seeing this ginormous guy going to bat to see a little girl.

"Guys," I say sternly. "We can all go see Lexi." I pick up our joined hands and kiss Aiden's hand, looking up at him, my eyes telling him to *play nice*.

He pulls me into him. "Fine. He can go. But only because I'm saying he can."

"Whatever, ass. I'll let you *think* that," Max murmurs as he walks back out the door.

"Thank you," I whisper.

"For what? Max is the one who offered," he says, his voice bitter.

"I know you would have done the same exact thing."

"I was getting ready to suggest it," he says, playing with my ponytail.

"I believe you," I say, kissing him. "Now let's go get the food on the grill. I'm starving."

"I'm going to burn Max's," he mumbles as we walk out the door. I laugh. *These boys.*

The afternoon goes by fast. Everyone's sitting around, enjoying the sun and relaxing. I love it here. Something about being away from the city and the smell of the ocean makes me feel rejuvenated. Relaxed. The only thing that I worry about when I'm here is Jessie. And not knowing what she's doing is bugging me. This is a small town, so she has to know we are here. Which makes me feel like a sitting duck.

I'm leaning back against Aiden's chest in the lounger. A few Coronas in my system, and I blurt out, "So what's Jessie been up to these days?"

Everyone stops talking and stares at me. I feel Aiden tense behind me. I pinch my lips, looking around. "What?" I ask. Don't they know ... keep your enemies close ...

A normal person might accept the answer that she left town a few months ago and leave it at that, *but I'm not normal.* Especially when I read Ryan and Macie's body language. Ryan squeezes Macie's hand. His foot starts to shake. Oh, and Aiden's already-tense body hardens.

"She just left town? Where did she go?" I press because they obviously think their vague answer is acceptable.

"She left around five months ago," Ryan says, sighing. "We're not sure where she went. We haven't heard from her since she left."

"Ryan, what aren't you telling us?" Aiden asks as he sits up straighter.

Ryan's eyes flash to me and then back to Aiden. "Nothing. That's it." I was kidnapped five months ago so the timing has me on edge. I remember right before I was taken, Aiden came to the beach house.

I turn and look at him. "Did you see her when you were here last?"

His answer is immediate. "No," he says. His eyes never leave mine. "The last time I saw her was the last time you saw her." He pulls me closer. "Sweetheart, don't worry about her. Nothing she can do can hurt us, so why waste your time thinking about her?"

I blow out a breath. He's right. She's the last thing I need to worry about right now. Maybe she found another man to stalk. "Okay, but I'm telling you right now, something is off with her."

"I think we already knew that about her," he whispers in my ear. A bitter laugh escapes my lips as I sit back against him.

Ryker changes the conversation to football. *Jessie who?* I'm not sure if he knows this is the one subject that could easily take my mind off of Jessie or if it was just a lucky guess. Whichever, I'm grateful. We all talk about the upcoming season. It still feels surreal to be talking to the quarterback of the New York Giants. I've pretty much dropped the fan-crush mentality, but it's still awesome.

"Hate to break up the reunion, but we need to get on the road," Aiden says as he scoots me to the end of the lounger.

An hour later, the house is cleaned, packed up, and locked. We all say our goodbyes and head out. We're not on the road for ten minutes before Syd and I conk out in the backseat.

After dropping Sydney off at her apartment, we sit in Aiden's car not going anywhere. I look at Aiden. His hand is on the steering wheel, the other on the gear shift. God, his arms are a work of art.

His muscular forearm flexes as he grips the wheel. The huge Tissot watch screams rugged, sexy, confident man. I don't know why, but his watch is a freaking turn-on. Maybe because it's attached to him.

A growl grabs my attention away from his thick fingers. *What those fingers do to me.* I shift in my seat, crossing my legs to slow the building ache. When I look up to his eyes, his head tilts and a brow is arched. "You're making this really hard," he murmurs.

"Making what hard, *exactly*," I tease. He inhales sharply and moans.

"Addison," he says in a raspy voice, reaching over and grabbing the back of my head. He guides me over to him then opens his mouth to say something but instead slams his lips onto mine in a possessive kiss. When he pulls back, my senses are spinning together, out of control. I gasp for air, trying to regain composure. This is what he does to me.

He's leaning back in his seat, looking up. I can tell he's trying to regain his control, too. I smile, thinking I'm glad it's not just me.

Aiden looks over and shakes his head. "Do you have any idea what you do to me?"

I *definitely* have an idea.

"I really want you to come back to my place …"

"Aiden, I really ne—"

"Shh," he says placing his finger on my mouth. Then he runs his finger across my bottom lip. I shiver at his touch. "I know," he says quietly as he watches his finger, his expression somber.

The thought of going back to my apartment unsettles me. It'd be easy to go to Aiden's house. *Too easy.* Instead of taking baby steps, I feel I'm taking Jolly Green Giant steps. Aiden walked back into my life less than a week ago and while I have zero regrets where we are, I just need to take a breather. Not a step back, just a step away.

"I had your apartment cleaned," he says, dropping his hand. "And a security system installed." My eyes go wide.

"Really? You've been a busy man while we've been away," I say as I shift in my seat, turning my body toward him.

"Addison, I'm not gonna lie. I want to wake up wrapped around you every morning for the rest of my life," he says and then sighs, "but I know if I rush things, you'll start to run. So I need to know you're safe in your apartment."

My lips turn up. Deep down, I want that, too. But he's right, I'm not ready yet. And I love that about him, that he knows me.

31

ADDISON

"I'm assuming by those flowers, tonight's the big night," Harper says, looking at the flowers on my desk.

I glance at the beautiful pink and red roses with huge pink lilies opened up to their full bloom and nod. Aiden asked me to go out on an *official* date with him sometime this week. I remember laughing and telling him that I thought we had passed that part of our relationship. He huffed like I was insane.

Of course, I told him yes, but I made him wait until the weekend. Being gone last week, I had a lot to catch up on when I got back. It wasn't until the flowers arrived that I found out our date is tonight. And holy shit, the message on the flowers sends heat up and down my body.

Tonight is about discovery.
Holding on, never letting go.
xoxo, Aiden

ANTICIPATION of what exactly we're going to be discovering has made me worthless today. It's a good thing we didn't get a last minute crime scene.

"Do you know what you're doing?" Harper asks, pulling me from my sexual thoughts.

"Nope. He's sending a car to come pick me up at seven," I say, rolling my eyes. I don't know why he went through all that trouble. It's like a glorified taxi.

"*Aww*, that's sweet. Unnecessary, but sweet." She laughs.

"I tried to tell him that, but he wasn't having it," I say, sighing.

"Well, have an amazing night. You deserve it. Call me when you can get away from Mr. Romantic and give me details."

I laugh now. "You and your details."

"Hey! I need to at least live vicariously though you since my dating life sucks right now," she whines. I almost bring up Tony, but she might be embarrassed.

"*Oh.* I should introduce you to Jaxon. He's an attorney here. He's one of Aiden's best friends and he's hot."

"And why haven't I heard of this *Jaxon*?" she asks.

"I just met him last week," I say, standing, then pick up my flowers and purse. It's time to go get ready for my date. My stomach flutters with excitement. I've missed seeing Aiden this week. Harper opens my door for me and helps me lock it after it shuts. "But I'll find out more about him. I'll see about setting up a double date."

"Sounds like a good plan to me," she says, smiling and giving me a quick hug. "I'll see you on Monday." She walks in the direction of the subway while I head the couple blocks to my apartment.

At seven o'clock on the dot, the security guard phones to tell me that my ride is here.

Since Aiden didn't tell me what we're doing—*which I hate*—I had to figure out what to wear based on nothing. I glance at myself one last time before leaving. New York's warm weather has arrived so I chose a short, black, silk shirt-dress with a drawstring waist. I close a button showing less cleavage but then change my mind and unbutton it. I want to look sexy for Aiden. I have my strappy heels on, lengthening my tanned legs.

I take a long look at myself and I smile at my reflection. This is the first time I've dressed up since I was kidnapped. My long curls drape my shoulders. My makeup brings out the blue in my eyes.

You look amazing, Addison.

I feel amazing, too. I'm seeing things clearer and for the first time since *that day*, I'm not looking in the mirror telling myself that I'm not a victim. I see a beautiful woman who has wants and needs and nothing is going to stand in her way.

I am that woman.

THE TOWN CAR stops in front of Aiden's apartment, and the driver hops out. Aiden steps out of his building. I feel the beating of my heart increase. He comes down the stairs, his steps light, almost skipping down them but with authority. His dark jeans contrast his white button-up shirt. When he smiles, my insides sizzle. I sit back in the seat, taking a few breaths to calm my erratic heart, then scoot over to make room for him.

When the door opens, I expect him to get in. Instead, he leans in and holds his hand out for me to grab.

"Hey, gorgeous," he says as his eyes rake down my body. That is not helping calm me. Goosebumps erupt all over.

I smile, grab his hand, and he helps me get out of the car. He shuts the door behind me and pulls me into his chest. He links our fingers, moving them behind my back. The bustling city around us fades to silence as we lose ourselves in each other's gaze.

"I missed you this week," he says quietly.

"I missed us," I reply.

"You can't blame me for not trying," he says, flashing his sexy half smile. I laugh, thinking about the string of texts I receive nightly.

"If I'm basing how much you missed me by those texts, then I know *exactly* what you're missing," I say.

He shrugs. "What can I say? I'm a man. We're physical beasts," he explains, standing taller. I bite my lip trying not to laugh out loud. "But don't mistake it for *only* wanting that. I want the whole package."

He leans down, nipping my bottom lip before pressing his lips to mine. A soft moan escapes my parted lips. Our tongues meet in the middle.

The only package on my mind right now is the very large one pressed against my stomach. He growls into my mouth.

"Sweetheart." It's a heady warning.

"Yes?" I ask innocently.

His jaw tightens as he shakes his head slightly, an amused look on his face. "Let's go, my little minx."

"What?" I tease. "You said package and yours is begging to be unwrapped."

"My package is always begging when you're around," he says, smirking. "But for now, he's staying wrapped. Let's go. Our food is waiting."

He pulls me toward his apartment, but I stop him. "I thought we were going in the…" I turn and point to a now empty parking space, "…town car." When the hell did it leave? I look at Aiden confused.

"We're staying in tonight." A boyish grin spreads across his face. "I want you all to myself."

"I'm all yours."

"Damn right," he says and sweeps me off my feet, carrying me into his building. I let out a laugh as I press my dress against my legs, making sure not to flash anyone. He doesn't put me down until we are standing in his apartment.

"I think I'm a little overdressed," I say, straightening my dress as I stand in the middle of his living room.

Aiden stands in front of me, admiring my outfit. "You look perfect." He pulls on one of my curls, and we both watch it bounce back up. "You are the most gorgeous woman," he says, kissing my forehead. My eyes close momentarily while I soak up his affection that he freely gives to me.

"You're too good at this boyfriend thing. I don't believe you've never done it before," I say. Judging by his friends' reactions to me, I'm pretty sure he wasn't lying.

"I guess I was just waiting for the right one to come along to show off all my awesome boyfriend skills." I feel his lips curl up against my forehead. "I told you when we first met that I had skills."

I laugh out loud and look up at him. "When you told me that, I'm pretty sure you weren't talking about *boyfriend* skills."

He flashes a confident smile. "Okay, maybe not when we first met," he admits. I bite my lip and smile. I'm not complaining. He definitely has skills. *In all departments.*

Aiden has dinner all set out, waiting for us. We eat and drink wine, each telling each other about our week. I tell him about my conversations with Lexi. His bouts of laughter when I tell him about her crazy stories, like chicken butts and eggs or when she tried to catch a pig but ended up rolling around and playing in the mud instead. My thoughts jump to this past week. My leg starts shaking under the table.

When I talked with her CPS advisor this week, I asked what was going to happen to Lexi when she returns. It broke my heart to hear that she would be placed in foster care. I hate that for her.

Every night after talking with her, I wonder what it'd be like if she lived with me. *If I could foster her.* Having another human rely on you definitely isn't an easy decision. I've spent this week away from Aiden, analyzing, reasoning, and questioning the likelihood of my abilities to be a foster parent. And I always come back to my situation; Amy took me in when I needed someone, no questions asked. I feel like this is what I'm meant to do. Fate put Lexi in my path to help me, but I also think I'm meant to help her, too.

As soon as I decide that yes, I can be that person to Lexi, I pull back, asking myself where Aiden fits in this scenario. What if he doesn't want any part in this? He didn't sign up to date a woman with a child. Will that change my decision? *She's a child.* She needs someone there for her, fighting for her.

"Addison." I look up from my food at the sound of Aiden's voice. "Where'd you go?"

"Just thinking."

His hand reaches across the table, covering mine. "It's about Lexi, isn't it?"

I sigh, biting my inner cheek. This conversation needs to happen, but I'm scared. I don't want him to think that I don't care about us, I do. I love him more than any man I've ever known. It'll devastate me if I have to choose.

"Addison, please talk to me," he says, squeezing my hand.

I shake the thoughts from my head. "Yes, it's about Lexi." He nods, but stays quiet. I clear my throat. "I talked to her social worker this week and asked what is going to happen to her when she gets back," I say, playing with the napkin in my lap, avoiding his eyes.

"Addison, look at me," he softly commands. When I look up, he smiles. "I know how much Lexi means to you. I saw that connection the first time I saw her with you. I know what you're thinking," he says. *Oh, I'm not sure about that.* "Sweetheart, I don't want to be a reason that you don't do something. I'll stand by your side, through whatever."

Relief, excitement, questions bubble up inside me all at once. Does he really know what I want to do?

"Even if it means Lexi living with me?" I ask slowly, still afraid he misunderstood what I was trying to say. He pulls me from my chair and sits me on his lap.

"Baby, I'm holding on, *never letting go*. I don't care if you foster ten kids. You'd have to do a lot more than that to get rid of me."

"God, I love you." I crush my lips to his.

He moans into my mouth. When he pulls back he lifts me up and stands with me. "Let's dance," he says, leading me to the living room.

"Alexa, play 'Marvin Gaye' by Charlie Puth."

What the hell? *Who is Alexa?* I look around the room, confused when the sound of a woman's voice fills the air. Then the song starts to play.

Aiden pulls me into his body and starts to sway. I look up at him and smile wide. "I'm impressed."

He bellows out a laugh. Grabbing my hand, he leads as we dance around. He sings every word, his deep timbre sending sparks throughout my body. Well, it's probably the words coming out of his mouth, too. When he pushes me out and pulls me back in, I twirl into his muscular arms. My back to his front, he sings into my ear.

I giggle at the words. "Karma sutra, huh?"

It's getting hot in here. I fan myself. He thinks I'm playing, but holy hell, my body is on fire.

When he pushes me out again, this time he pulls me back into his chest. I surprise him when I start singing Meghan Trainor's part. I know I don't sound as good as him, but I hold my own. He takes advantage of this time to run his lips down my neck. My voice quivers. It doesn't last long before he's singing again.

Damn it, my part needs to be longer.

I think I have a new favorite song. When it ends, he leans me back, kissing my neck, his lips traveling down my bare chest. I'm glad I decided to leave that button open. My body trembles as chills run up my spine as his soft lips leave kisses on my breasts.

His teeth unbutton a few more, opening up my dress to my black lace bra. His hand behind me, grabs my ass, pulling me into his erection. When the heat of his breath covers my lace-covered nipple, it hardens. He flicks his tongue over it before he pulls it into his mouth and sucks. I inhale sharply and moan. I feel skin to skin on my leg as he drags his finger up, lifting my dress slowly. I focus on the path his finger takes. He moves in between my legs, running along my lace. He teases me, grazing the outside of my soaked panties, pushing up into my sex.

"Take me to bed, Aiden," I breathe out.

Without saying a word, he picks me up and takes me to his room, lying me down on the bed. His eyes are dark, laced with desire and lust. He pulls off my dress in one sweep. His eyes rake down my body. When he gets to my shoes, a growl erupts from his lips.

"You are the most magnificent sight," he murmurs. "If I was to go blind today, I'd be a satisfied man knowing that I would never see anything more beautiful than you."

My breath catches at his words. He leans down and takes off each shoe. Then he proceeds to take off the rest of my clothing. His touch is soft and tender. When he stands, he takes off his clothes, his eyes never leaving mine.

It's not until he's lowering himself, wrapping my legs around his face, that he closes his eyes. He buries his face in between my thighs as he works his tongue up and down.

As soon as two fingers tease in and out of me, I scream as my climax surprises me. I clench around his fingers as I buck against his tongue.

He slowly kisses his way up my body. His hands move up my arms, intertwining our fingers together above my head. He squeezes them when our eyes meet. His soft smile melts me. He's waiting for me. Waiting for permission. I nod, granting it to him.

"I want you to fill the only empty space in my body, claim it as yours," I whisper. "I need to feel you inside of me, Aiden."

I can feel his hardness at my entrance. "Do I need a condom?"

Confusion turns to panic. Does he want to wait until next month for my six-month checkup? I was tested for everything under the sun after the rape, but they redo the tests at six months. Of course he wants to shield himself against possible sexual diseases.

"Addison, stop." I look at him. "All I wanted to know was if you were still on the pill," he says softly.

"Oh." I close my eyes and blush in embarrassment. "Yes. But if you want to—"

His lips on mine stop me. He slowly pushes into me, stretching me as I feel his length filling me. I groan into his mouth, spreading my legs, opening for him. Once he's seated all the way in me, he stops kissing me.

"Breathe, sweetheart," he says as his eyes soften. I exhale the breath I didn't even know I was holding. "Keep your eyes open, baby. I need you to see that it's me filling you, loving you, becoming one with you."

I nod as he slowly pulls out. A moan slips from my parted lips. My back arches as I feel every stroke caress my inner walls. His unhurried pace lets me adjust to the feeling of being filled. Our bodies move in sync to the slow, sensual ride.

Our gaze never breaks. His whispers of loving words penetrate deep inside me. *He consumes me.*

My heart.

My body.

My mind.

A sense of nirvana flows through me. He's never owned every part of me at the same time. There's always been a piece of me that has held back. I'm giving myself to him.

Completely.

I squeeze his hand in mine and wrap my legs around his waist, pulling him in deeper.

"I love you," I whisper, looking into his eyes. His lips curl into a smile. "Now kiss me."

His mouth slams down on mine without hesitation. The quick movements of his hips intensify his thrusts. I hold my legs tight around his waist, causing his strokes to be small and fast.

Pleasure explodes through my body as my heat spreads around Aiden. My toes curl as I pulse around him, squeezing him tight. His head falls to the curve of my neck as he growls though his release. He thrusts a couple more times before collapsing on me.

"Alexa, play 'Die a Happy Man' by Thomas Rhett," he commands, lifting his head from my shoulder. Music fills the air.

"Who is Alexa?" I ask.

All of a sudden the music stops playing. Oops. What did I do? I look around the room.

"Shh," he says, chuckling. The music begins to play again. "If you say her name, she stops what she's doing and waits for a command."

"You like that, don't you," I say, smiling. "Obedient woman, waiting for your command."

"If I liked that, I'm with the wrong woman." His voice is laced with humor. He lays his head down on my shoulder and softly sings the song to me. He pours his feelings into the song, word by word. It takes me back to when he first sang the song to me in Central Park. Then, it was just the song that happened to be playing at the concert so I didn't know if he meant those words.

Right now the words send sparks to my heart, making it beat to a tune only Aiden can carry.

When the song ends, I exhale slowly. "Aiden, I've already told you that the love I feel for you scares the shit out of me," I say softly. He pushes up on his elbow, lying on his side. "I need you to know why." He nods, keeping quiet. "I've never felt a love so deep that I felt I couldn't…" I pause to catch a breath, "…live without it." I look around the room, trying to gather my thoughts. "When Joe told me that he had killed you, I lost all desire to live. I wanted to die so I could be with you. Forever."

I find Aiden's eyes and tears fill them. I need to keep going to get this out in the open. "Then when I found out you lived … I felt like I wasn't good enough for you." I look away from the pain in his eyes.

He clears his throat. "Addison, you weren't in the right state of mind to have made a clear decision in both those instances," he says with a shaky voice.

"Even so, I wanted to die *for you*. This kind of love scares me." My breath hitches. "But, I also see now that's what love is. Someone you would do anything for. I'm fully aware that my decisions were … *extreme* because of the situations I was in, but it still scares me."

He wraps me in his arms and squeezes me. "Sweetheart, it scares me, too. I would do anything for you," he whispers into my hair.

We hold each other in silence. The love between us wraps all around us, binding us together in invisible ropes. Love is an actual thing. It makes us do irrational things, blinds us even, but in the end it's the most beautiful thing that can happen between two people. And I wouldn't want it with anyone else.

My eyes get heavy as the warmth of Aiden's embrace relaxes me. I'm startled when Aiden jumps up on his knees and bends over me, reaching for his nightstand.

"What are you doing?" I ask Aiden, watching him search the top drawer of the nightstand. I giggle when I wonder if he'll pull out a vibrator. I mean, isn't that what all nightstands are for? *It's where mine are.* Hmm … I guess I might want to hide those if Lexi lives with me.

He finds what he's looking for and waves it around in the air. A deck of cards?

"Well, I hope you're not wanting to play strip poker, because you're a little too late," I tease, looking down at my naked body.

He pushes back to a seated position and pulls me up so I'm straddling him. I wrap my legs around him and sit back enough to steady myself.

He stares at me, like he's contemplating what to say. "I know your body, probably better than my own," he says seriously. My eyebrow lifts. "Every erogenous zone you have. I know exactly where it is and exactly how to touch it to make your body ignite."

"Is that right?" I say, looking at him with a dare. He throws the deck of cards down, obviously taking my dare.

"Mmm-hmm," he hums as he runs his fingers up my leg. When he gets to my knee, his fingers brush behind my knee. The slight touch sends a current straight up to my sex, and I shudder.

"Okay, you got lucky," I say as my voice hitches.

"Sweetheart, it's not luck," he rasps, looking up from where his hand now travels up my thigh. It stops right on the inside of my thigh. With soft strokes of his thumb, he starts to move higher, my mind and body buzzing with the imminent destination of his thumb. I watch each stroke, my pulse quickening. *Until it stops.* When his hand retreats, still circling his thumb but now moving away from my building ache, I glare up at him.

He flashes a devilish grin. He continues his tantalizing, torturous exploration of my body. Proving time and time again that he does know my body. He owns my body.

It's his to take.

It's not until he finds the spot above my pelvic bone that I concede. He lays me down. The burning ache deep in my belly is so intense that I wonder if I'll ever be sated. I look at my body, his fingers tormenting that erogenous zone, but it's his hardened cock that gets my attention.

"Aiden," I breathe out in desperation. My hips move, trying to rub his head against my throbbing clit. He looks at me with dark and pleading eyes. I moan out and slam my eyes shut when he grabs his cock and presses it against me. My back arches off the bed as I grab hold of the sheets around me.

"Nobody knows your body like I do, Addison," he growls.

"Only you, Aiden."

His restraint breaks as he slams into me. He exhales sharply and groans. I scream out as he fills me, stretches me. His hands grab my hips, pulling me into him, as he thrusts wildly.

Getting on his knees, he spreads me open wider, holding my feet out. Noises of grunts and our bodies slapping together fill the room as our orgasms rip though both of us. Our bodies dance to the erotic ride. A ride I don't want to ever get off.

A half hour later, Aiden has the cards back in his hand. This time, he's got a pair of shorts on. And I have a T-shirt on, one I didn't put on myself. I bite my lip and lift my brow, watching him when he sits across from me on the bed.

"I can't do what I want to do when you're distracting me with your naked body."

I exhale, looking at his sculpted chest and abs. He is so gorgeous. And he thinks *I'm distracting*.

"Do I need to put a shirt on?" he jokes.

"Yes." There is no humor in my voice. My body is tingling already.

He flops back onto the bed, with a shirt on, and takes out the deck of cards and shuffles them. "As I was saying, I already know your body …" He pauses and tilts his head. My body is screaming for me to contradict it, hoping he'll prove it again. He laughs, shaking his head, knowing what I'm thinking. "Woman, I will show you *repeatedly* what I can do, but later," he rasps. I will definitely make sure he follows through with that promise.

He pulls me in his lap so I'm straddling him *again*. Doesn't he know how this ended last time?

"I know your heart," he says, leaning his head down, pressing his ear against my chest.

"You know it because it's yours," I whisper, running my hands through his hair.

"But," he says, gazing into my eyes, "I feel there is so much more to know about you in here." His forehead touches mine as he cups his hand around my head and his thumb rubs my temple.

I understand what he's saying. There have been many times that I hear something about Aiden that I think, *I didn't know that. I should know that.*

I nod in agreement. "So I thought we'd play poker. Winner gets to ask a question." I smile wide. *We've played this game before.* "This time," he says, interrupting my memory, "we only tell truths."

"Truths," I say, agreeing.

It's the simplest of questions, but it's what make us, *us*. It's the building blocks of our foundation. The reason we tick the way we do. The questions are limitless. Childhood dreams to future fantasies. The latter ends with us and lots of kids. Well, the *lots of kids*, was his truth. My truth was two of them. We'll have to work on that.

"I've never even thought of having kids. But just thinking about you growing part of me in that body of yours …" He stops, pushes me back, lifts up my, shirt and presses soft kisses across my stomach sending tingles down my spine. "Before you, nothing mattered. Revenge poisoned my mind to the point I didn't even care for my own life. I was reckless." A bitter laugh escapes his lips as he lays his head down on my stomach. "When I tell you that Max and I were crazy, that's an understatement. I can't even admit half the stuff we did."

I smile, just imagining the crazy stunts they pulled. "I think you're selling yourself short," I say, pushing up on my elbows. "You made it into the FBI. That's not a small feat. Even if it was fueled by revenge, something good came from it."

He doesn't say anything. With his hand on my side, he brushes his thumb back and forth against my hipbone. "What prevented you from taking revenge?" I ask.

He looks up at me. "You."

I swallow at his heartfelt answer. But it wasn't the one I was looking for.

"No," I respond. His brows furrow. "You were living with Travis for a year before you met me. If you truly wanted reckless revenge, you would have done something long before I came around."

He smiles into my stomach and then lays his head back down. I can feel his heated breaths through my shirt. "I liked the *bastard* too much," he admits with a chuckle.

Mixed feelings stir inside of me and not because of his revelation. That isn't surprising. Travis seems to be a likable guy. It just feels weird talking about him.

"When I first got there and couldn't find a damn thing linking him with my parents' death, the more time I spent with him, the more I questioned if he actually did it. Deep down, I knew he did, so I decided at that point to do the job I was actually sent there to do." He pauses, getting lost in thoughts. "Travis is a very intelligent guy. He seems to only make mistakes when it comes to the women in his life," he says, pushing his body back up against mine.

Our eyes meet and I nod. It's true. It's a hard fact to accept when you're on the receiving end of those mistakes. There have been a couple times that I wish I knew him better. That maybe we can get to know each other.

Then the thoughts pass and I realize I must be getting ready to start my period because there is no way in hell that we can ever be close. *Damn hormones.*

"But it was *you* who made me see that I wanted more out of life than revenge," he says.

"You were always a good man, Aiden, just misguided. Your compass was broken. It just needed a good shake."

"And it was a damn good shake." He leans over and kisses me. He pulls back fast and sits up. "Back to cards, woman. We're not done," he says, shuffling the cards.

With his next winning hand he says, "I want to hear about your mom."

"That's not a question."

He shrugs. "I still won, so talk," he demands, poking me in the stomach.

The next hour we exchange stories about our moms. Never with hesitation. Never with regret. We talk about our moms with the love in our hearts set aside just for them.

"My mom would have loved you," I say.

"Why is that?"

"Well, you're gorgeous for one." He shakes his head, dropping it. "*And* you're intelligent, you're passionate, you challenge me, you entertain my stubbornness, and you love me. Scars and all."

"Do you know what I think?" he asks. I shake my head. "I think fate led us to each other. But falling in love ... that was our mothers' doing. They're probably together, looking down on us, celebrating."

Tears well in my eyes as my smile widens. A laugh escapes my lips, imagining them dancing around and high-fiving each other.

"Thank you for that," I hiccup. My voice hitches with

emotions. He climbs on top of me, kissing me passionately. I bite his lip, ending the kiss. "So, I wonder what your mom was thinking when I shot you?"

He barks out a deep and sexy laugh. "She was probably you're biggest cheerleader, saying I deserved it."

32

ADDISON

It's been two weeks since I've seen Lexi, and it feels like it's been forever. Aiden and I have connected more and more each day, but hearing Lexi's voice completes my day. We have video chatted almost daily and for those five minutes, just seeing her light up when she talks to me, makes everything right in my world.

I started my application to be Lexi's foster parent the other day. Aiden and I went together to the agency. When I think about the support Aiden has given me through all of this, I can't think of a better man to spend the rest of my life with.

I lean over and kiss his cheek. We're on Max's plane going to Texas to see Lexi.

He squeezes my hand that is intertwined with his. "What was that for?" He flashes a half-sexy smile.

I kiss his dimple, and he turns his face to mine. Our lips brush. "I love you," I whisper.

"Sweetheart," he breathes out on my lips. He pauses like he's going to say something. Instead, he slams his lips onto mine in a passionate kiss. A kiss that tells me everything he wanted to say.

"I'd tell you to get a room, but then you'll go back to the bedroom, and I don't need to hear you fucking. On my plane," Max grates out.

I laugh against Aiden's mouth. When I pull back, I stick my tongue out at Max. Aiden chuckles and mumbles "cock blocker" under his breath. Max shakes his head at our less-than-adult responses. We start our descent and my leg starts shaking in excitement. We're almost there.

After throwing our bags in the back of the SUV, I hold out my hand to Aiden. He tilts his head in question.

"Keys," I say, wiggling my fingers.

His head jerks as he straightens. "Woman, you are not driving."

"Yes, I am." He shakes his head like I'm crazy.

Max barks out a laugh, hopping into the backseat.

"I miss driving and I want to drive," I say forcefully and stomp my foot, not backing down.

"I'm a little scared right now," he admits but hands the keys over slowly. I jump up and down, skipping to the driver's door.

Aiden is staring at me in wonderment as I adjust my seat. When I start the engine, it snaps him out of it, and he dramatically puts on his seat belt.

I glance at him out of the corner of my eye. "*Jerk,* I have been driving since I was sixteen. Actually as long as I've shot a gun and look how good I can do that." I turn and stare at him, raising both my brows.

He looks at me stunned. *Well, shit.*

"Too soon?" I wince. Aiden is still worried about how I'm dealing with the Marco incident. I'm still meeting with my therapist three times a week. I'm dealing with it. But just now, I wasn't even thinking about Marco. I was thinking about *him*. God, that makes me sound like a gun-toting lunatic. *Oh, which shooting were you talking about, Addison? You've been involved with so many.*

"Addison …" He pulls me from my self-deprecating rant.

Reaching his arm over the console, he rubs my head. "Sorry. I didn't mean to take you there."

"I'm fine," I say, putting the SUV in drive. "I'm thinking maybe I need to stay away from guns."

"It was self-defense," he says firmly. "Both times."

I laugh out bitterly. "I was not in danger with you."

"You were very well in a dangerous situation, Addison," Max says, scooting up between our seats. "You shot Aiden for a reason. You escaped from being held prisoner without causing a lot of harm to Aiden."

"So, why didn't I just immobilize Marco and wait for the police to get there?"

"I think we all know that answer without needing to say it," Max says, sitting back.

I nod because I know. The bullet placement shows my intent, but there is no way they can prove that.

I hate that he tried to rape me: shot to the groin.

I hate that he killed because of me: shot to the heart.

I hate him for making me kill him: shot to the head.

And he was never going to touch Lexi again. She can grow up without having to look over her shoulder like I did my whole life. No more worrying that someone will be coming back for her one day. I was going to make sure of that.

Silence fills the air the remainder of the car ride. My thoughts make enough noise that I don't even notice. When we pull into the driveway, Max hops outs first.

Before I'm able to open my door, Aiden stops me and grabs my hand. "Don't second-guess yourself. Nobody has ever questioned why you did what you did. He killed *twelve* people, Addison. He would've killed you, too," he says in a serious tone.

I blow out a harsh breath. "I know."

He leans over and kisses me. "Now, let's go see our girl."

Those words, coming from his mouth, erase all my doubts. I flash a smile as my heart beats faster. *Our girl.*

Max is waiting for us on the porch. I knock on the door and walk in.

"Hello?" I say loudly.

Giggles and screams come from the kitchen. Then a streak of caramel comes running straight for me. "Addie," Lexi yells, jumping into my arms. I pull her up, taking in a deep breath through my nose.

God, I've missed her smell.

I hold her tight as she wraps her legs around me. "I missed you, Addie."

"I missed you, too, sweet girl." Aunt Amy comes in from the kitchen. She smiles brightly as affection glows in her eyes. She leans against the doorjamb, placing a hand over her heart. I tear up, watching her.

Lexi pulls back and then a million words spill from her mouth. I laugh because I caught maybe a third of them. She wiggles to get down and then runs to Max. He throws her up in the air. I immediately feel a little bad for Aiden. When I look at him he winks at me. He's trying to reassure me that he's okay.

"Max, did you fly on your plane?" Lexi asks excitedly.

"We did, Lulu."

"You haven't gone to Disneyland without me, have you?" She puckers her lips and stares him down. Her expressions are priceless.

"No. I would never go without you," he says, touching her on her nose. She scrunches up her nose then gives him a hug and wiggles to get down.

Aiden's her next stop. I take a silent breath of relief. He's being so supportive of me taking in Lexi, I would hate it if Lexi didn't like him. I shake my head. That's ridiculous. Lexi loves Aiden, too.

"Aiden, guess what?" Her eyes go round and her little face beams.

"What?" he asks, squatting down to her level.

"I got my own horse. And he's red. Guess what I named him?" she asks so excited. *She got her own horse?*

"Um ... Mr. Ed?" he says, smiling.

She pulls her head back, looking at him like he's got two of them. "No, silly." She huffs adorably and rolls her eyes.

He laughs because she has no clue who Mr. Ed is. "What did you name him?"

"Ketchup."

He twists his lips trying to figure out the meaning. "Why did you name your horse Ketchup?"

"Because, ketchup *always* goes with tater tots," she says, throwing her arms out wide.

The smile on Aiden's face is probably the biggest I've ever seen. My heart beats faster looking at them together. Together they make my heart whole.

"I want to show you him," she says, pointing out the door.

"Amy?" Aiden looks toward my aunt. She nods her head. Lexi pulls him to the door, jumping up and down the whole way.

"Come on, Aiden. You're too slow," she whines. Once they're out the door, I see him throw her on his shoulders and start running. Her giggles fill the air.

Max stays inside with me. Amy comes up and gives me a huge hug and then Max.

"It's so good to see you," she says, grabbing my hand. "Can I say that you've aged me far too fast?" she laughs, bringing our joined hands to her heart. "You're going to give me a heart attack soon."

"I'm sorry," I say, looking away from her tears. "I really don't mean to."

"I know. And really, I should be used to it by now." She jokes to lighten the mood. I laugh and give her another hug.

"So what's this about Lexi having her *own* horse? She's five."

Amy flashes a knowing smile. "She doesn't have her own horse, Addison. She just renamed *another* one."

"Rusty?" I whisper. Amy nods her head, smiling softy. I'm not surprised at all. I think Rusty is an angel of healing. Memories of all the time I spent with him after I was rescued surface. Riding him allowed me to stop thinking about the past and made me feel free. Made me want to move forward.

And now he's helping heal Lexi.

My hand goes to my heart. I feel Max's arm wrap around my shoulders as he pulls me into his side. I lay my head against his shoulder. Max knows how important Rusty is to me.

"He's so gentle with her," Amy says, pulling me from my thoughts. "The therapist wants to use him for more of her patients."

"I love it. He's meant for that, he's perfect."

Aiden and Lexi walk into the house hand in hand. She bounces on her toes, running to the bathroom. Aiden walks over and removes Max's arm from me.

"I leave for five minutes and you move in on my woman," he jokes, pulling me back into his chest. He wraps his arms around my waist, and I weave our fingers together, leaning back into him. Max laughs, shaking his head.

"Did you see Rus— Ketchup?" I ask.

Before Aiden can answer, Lexi's back and runs up to us. "Can you watch me ride him later?" I release one of Aiden's hands and brush through Lexi's long, caramel locks.

"I wouldn't miss that for anything, sweet girl."

Her smile brightens, and she wraps her arms around my legs. "I missed you, Addie."

I lean down and pick her up. "Oh, my gosh. I missed you so much." I squeeze her.

"Dr. Frank says that I'm going to go to a new family," she says, sticking out her bottom lip. "I don't want a new family. I want to stay in this family." Her big eyes water as her lip quivers.

My chest tightens. Aiden's hand squeezes my hip. I want to tell her that she's going to live with me, but I just filled out the application so it's not a sure thing. The last thing I want is to give her false hope. Ugh! Why did the doctor have to tell her that?

"Lexi, don't cry," I say, wiping away a tear. "We're working with the agency in New York to find the best home for you. I promise you that I will always be a part of your life. We'll still see each other. Okay?" She sniffs and nods her head fast, sucking on her bottom lip. "But you still have two weeks here on the ranch. With Amy and Ted."

"And Ketchup!" Her eyes light up.

"And Ketchup," I repeat, brushing my nose against hers.

"Lexi, I need to go out and get the eggs for today. Do you want to help me?" Amy asks, holding a basket. Lexi's eyes get large. She claps and wiggles to be put down.

"Yes!" she squeals, running to Amy. "I promise I won't hide any in my pocket this time," she says, looking down. You'd think she was sorry for doing it, but the huge smile she has says otherwise.

Amy laughs, looking at me. "So, Lexi tried to hatch an egg herself. But as soon as she sat on it ..."

We all bust out laughing. Lexi blushes but then shrugs. "It didn't work," she says in a serious tone. Aiden laughs harder. She puts her hand on her hip, showing her sassy side. "You try and sit on an egg without breaking it. It's *not* easy," she says to Aiden. I slap my hand over my mouth trying to contain my laughter. Aiden's head leans on my shoulder as he silently laughs.

"Come on, Lulu, show me how you collect eggs," Max says. She jumps up and down in excitement. I'm quickly learning that little girl's emotions are bipolar.

As soon as she leaves, Aiden straightens. "Are you sure you're ready for that?" His voice is laced with humor.

I elbow him in the stomach, "Are you?"

He spins me around and pulls me in tight. "I want ten of those." He flashes a megawatt smile and winks. I shake my head.

"Ten? We've talked about this." My voice cracks. I can't even imagine.

"Let's just say we'll never stop trying."

"I'll agree to that," I say, standing on my toes and kissing him. "*Ten*, not so much." I pull away and tickle him in the stomach. There is one spot where Aiden is ticklish.

He laughs, grabbing both my hands and throwing me over his shoulder. I squeal in surprise. His hand smacks me on the ass. Hard.

"Aiden," I warn. He barks out a laugh, slapping me again. *Okay, asshat. You're going down.* He walks out the door, heading toward the barn.

When we get to the field of grass in front of the barn, I push up so I'm straight and throw Aiden off balance. He lets go of my legs just in time for me to push against him. He tumbles back into the grass, and I land in a squatted position. He stands quickly in a defensive position. I mimic his stance.

"I told you what would happen." He flashes a wicked smile, hunger in his eyes. My body starts to hum. His strength, confidence, and sexiness ignite sparks of desire. He's playing dirty as he takes off his shirt, throwing it to the side. His perfectly sculpted chest and abs flex, and I can't help myself from gazing.

I bite my lip. "You don't play fair, Agent Roberts," I say, dragging my eyes up to his. He lifts his brow in challenge. I quickly look around to see if anyone is nearby. The chicken coop is on the other side of the house and it seems to be just us out here. The barn is on higher ground and with the tall grass growing around, it'd be hard to see us unless you were headed this way.

I hear Rusty neigh. *Don't worry, buddy, I'll come see you next.* I have to take down this ass-slapping, gorgeous man first.

"Am I too *distracting?*" he teases, circling me. I spin in place, keeping my eyes on him. He knows how I react to his body. So yes, distracting is an understatement. My body is ready to lie down and say "*take me now.*" My head, though, wants to take Aiden down to prove a point.

Two can play this game. I grab the bottom of my shirt, lifting it slowly. Aiden stops abruptly. I innocently smile. When I meet his eyes after slipping my shirt off, they blaze with heat. I hold his stare, talking a step toward him. The desire radiating off of him slowly unravels me. Knowing how *I* affect *him* is a potent feeling. I'm drenched and throbbing already.

Another step forward. He stays rooted, not moving an inch. I reach behind me and unfasten my bra. I can see the dilation of his pupils, his chest moving up and down a little bit quicker. I drop the bra on the ground and his eyes drag their way down to my breasts. They're already hard and yearning for his touch. When I step up to him, I take his hands and put them on my breasts.

A deep, low growl erupts from the back of his throat as he grips them. His thumb grazes a nipple, causing me to moan.

Addison, you better hurry the hell up, my inner voice yells at me. Obviously that voice is on my head's side. As I gain a little semblance of control, I reach out and grab his balls—hard. He jumps at my invasion.

He laughs nervously. "Sweetheart?"

"I told you not to slap my ass," I say, putting a little more pressure on my grip. His hand is on top of mine as fear flashes in his eyes now.

He hunches over a little and winces. "Okay."

I look at him with a raised brow. "Okay, what?"

"I'll stop slapping you on the ass," he says, smirking, "unless you ask for it."

I narrow my eyes. His tongue darts out to lick his bottom lip.

My resolve weakens. He flashes a knowing smile. Well, *I think* I got my point across.

His hand starts massaging my breast again. It's not until he leans down and takes my hardened nipple in his mouth, sucking, do I release his balls. I look up to the sun, closing my eyes, letting my body succumb to his touch. Warmth spreads through me. His hand that is currently on top of mine moves up to his hard shaft. He guides my hand up and down his hardened member. When we get back to the top, I take control of my hand and slide my fingers between his underwear and warm skin. I graze the head with my fingertips. The slight twitch at my touch sends a surge of need through me.

My fingers work at lightning speed, freeing his glorious cock. He groans when my hand wraps around him.

"You better hope no one comes out here," he says, lifting me up and carrying me into the barn.

"It's just you, me, and Rusty … and some of his friends," I giggle. He looks at me confused, looking around the barn. "Horses," I say, biting my lip.

He takes me to an empty stall and lays me down on a bed of hay. His hands are in my pants within seconds, sliding through my wetness. His fingers plunge inside me, and I arch my back, moaning out in pleasure. He slams his lips to mine. I gasp when he pulls his finger out and starts assaulting my clit. He makes it a game to get me on the verge of nirvana before pulling out and starting over.

Frustration builds after the third time. I think he's trying to get revenge. "If you don't finish, I will," I whisper the threat into his ear and then bite his earlobe.

He chuckles, which makes me bite down a little harder. He sits up on his knees and watches as his fingers slide back into me. I look down at my body, watching his glistening fingers work me. His hard cock strains against his boxer briefs.

"Aiden, I need more. I need to feel you inside of me," I breathe out.

He wiggles his fingers against my insides making my whole body shiver. "Baby, I am inside you." His pace increases, his fingers moving in and out faster. His thumb rubs my sensitive nub. I can't speak to tell him that isn't what I meant, but I think he already knows.

My whole body convulses as my orgasm rips through me. I scream out his name and other mumbled words and sounds that I can't even comprehend.

As soon as his fingers retreat, he slams into me with one hard thrust. Wrapping my legs around his waist, he grips my hips as he grinds into me. I suck in a breath, closing my eyes. I writhe beneath him as he hits the perfect spot. I grab onto some hay, needing something to ground me. It doesn't help.

"Is this what you *wanted*, sweetheart?"

"Yes. Oh, God!" I gasp as he pulls back and slams into me again. Over and over until both our toes are curled from our explosive orgasms.

We laugh as we collect our clothes, which are thrown all over the place.

Music comes from the house as we approach. I hear Lexi singing. I still can't get over how *that* voice comes out of a five-year-old. I could barely talk without a lisp at that age.

When a male voice starts singing, Aiden stops unexpectedly, yanking me back.

"What the h—"

"*Shh*," he says, bringing a finger to my mouth. He turns his ear toward the house and listens a couple seconds more before breaking out into a run, dragging me behind him. What in the world? He takes the three patio stairs all at once, almost sending me through them. I trip but catch myself and make it up to the top in one piece. He looks down at me, scrunching his nose up.

"Sorry, baby," he says, kissing the hand that I caught myself with, "but I can't miss this." *Can't miss what?*

He starts to pull me again guiding us into the house. He stops short at the sight of Max and Lexi singing into a karaoke machine in the living room. Max hasn't seen us yet. I tilt my head as I watch him dance around with Lexi. He's pretty good. Aiden pulls out his phone and starts recording.

I elbow him. He smiles a huge grin down at me, shaking his head. "Fucking priceless," he whispers. He must not have been quiet enough for Max. He whips around and stares at Aiden. *While he records him.* The look Max gives Aiden has me stepping a few feet away. I'm not going to lie, I'm a little scared. Aiden laughs.

Lexi is clueless as to what's going on. She grabs Max's hand. "Max, this is your part," she says, tugging on him. Max's jaw clenches tightly. He looks down at Lexi's large eyes and exhales loudly. There *might* have been a little growl, too.

"What's wrong? Do you not want to sing with me anymore?" Her bottom lip sticks out. He closes his eyes for a moment, taking in a breath then releasing it. I can see the second he plans on giving in to Lexi. He rolls his shoulders and when he opens his eyes, he smiles wide and grabs the microphone.

He looks up to Aiden before singing and mouths, "Payback's a bitch." He jumps right back in singing and dancing, not missing a beat. He's definitely not embarrassed, so I wonder why he freaked out.

When the song ends, Max hands Lexi the microphone. My eyes go wide and I yelp when he runs, jumping over the couch toward Aiden. Aiden slams the front screen door open, running out with Max trailing right behind him. Lexi giggles at the guys.

I run to the window and watch. Unfortunately they run in a direction out of my view. I laugh, thinking how two men who are almost thirty can still act like teenagers.

"What in the world was that sound?" Uncle Ted asks, coming from the hallway.

I turn. "That would be Aiden running from his death wish," I say, laughing.

"Seems he's not the only one who has a death wish," he deadpans, walking toward me. He's stone faced but his eyes tell a different story. The emotions swirling in them is like a punch to the gut.

I hate seeing it. The worry. The pain. The sorrow. I want to scream and stomp. We were just getting past the kidnapping, but now we're here again. I want to yell I'M FINE so everyone will stop looking at me like this.

Ted pulls me into a tight hug. I wrap my arms around him and sigh. The tension melts away from my body as soon as he hugs me tighter. I know the emotions are coming from love. I can't fault anyone for that.

"Hey, at least you can't blame my job," I joke, trying to lighten the mood. He didn't want me to work in law enforcement, thinking I'd be in constant danger. He's a retired cop, so he knows how it is. Seems the joke's on him, though. Things that have happened to me have nothing to do with my job. *Which I'm sure doesn't help ease his mind.*

He looks down and chuckles. After placing a kiss on my forehead, he stands tall. His hand tugs at my hair, and I tilt my head wondering what he's doing.

"Seems you have some hay in your hair," he says, humor filling his voice as he pulls out a piece of hay. "Wonder where that came from?"

My face heats, and I'm pretty sure it's as red as a tomato right now. Please tell me he didn't see us. I cover my face with my hand, shaking my head.

I hear the screen door open and Aiden grumbling. "Asshole broke my phone."

I lift my hand, meeting Aiden's eyes. My mouth hangs open at the sight of Aiden's face. His lip is bleeding and his face is covered with dirt. There's grass in his hair.

"*Really?* Sometimes I wonder if y'all are really almost thirty."

"Don't worry, sweetheart. He looks just as bad," he says proudly, jerking his head in the direction of outside. He lets out a laugh. "Why were you so red when I walked in?" he asks, shaking out his hair.

My gaze flicks to Ted. He barks out a laugh. I don't even want to know what he might have seen or heard, so I take off for the kitchen.

I hear Ted say, "Son, it's good to see you." I turn and see them hugging. Aiden winks at me. I smile at two of the most important men in my life.

I walk into the kitchen and Lexi is helping Amy make cookies. I chuckle when I see that she's wearing more flour than what's on the counter. "Look, I'm making balls," she says, showing me by sticking out her hand.

I hear the screen door open again.

"Asshole, you're buying me a new phone," I hear Aiden say.

"Maybe next time you'll know better than to film me." Max grunts.

"It's too bad that the video already uploaded to the cloud," he says, taunting him. I shake my head, wondering why the hell he's egging on Max.

Max grunts again, and then I'm assuming he's on the phone. "Break into Aiden's cloud account and delete a video."

"Stone." Aiden warns loudly.

"Don't listen to him. I sign your check."

Lexi's movement catches my eye. She wipes her hand down her shirt, picks up a jar, and walks into the living room. My eyes shoot to Amy's and she nods. We both hurry behind her, not wanting to miss this.

Max is hanging up and smiles down at Lexi. She stands in between the two huge guys and holds up her jar.

"I've missed you guys."

Oh. My. God. My head falls and I can't contain my laughter. Max and Aiden both look in the jar and start laughing while they pull out their wallets.

"I'm not making any money here," she huffs, looking in the jar, too. There's a lonely dollar bill at the bottom.

I look to Ted with a smirk. "Don't look at me, it was that one," he says chuckling, pointing to Amy.

"Hey, I stubbed my toe. It hurt," she says defensively.

"It's okay, Amy," I say, wrinkling my nose. "We've all fallen victim to the bad word police."

"Yes, but obviously y'all are going to fund her college," she says, pinning the guys with her stare.

They both immediately apologize. *Hmm, I need to work on my stare.*

Later that evening, I tuck Lexi into bed and read her a bedtime story. She can barely hold her eyes open, but I can tell she is trying her hardest to stay awake.

"I don't want you to leave, Addie," she whispers.

I want to tell her that hopefully she'll be coming home with me the next time I see her, but I hold my tongue.

"Sweet girl, I'll be back in two weeks."

"Two weeks is forever away. How many bedtimes is that?"

I smile. It does seem forever away. "It's thirteen bedtimes," I say, running my hands through her hair.

Her eyes flutter closed. I lean over and kiss her on the forehead.

"I love you, Addie."

Any doubt I had about fostering Lexi dissolves in that instant. I love this little girl with all my heart. I don't even want to think about what I'll feel if I'm rejected.

"I love you, too, Lexi," I whisper.

I have to pull myself away from her. I want to snuggle up to her and sleep right beside her. I push myself off the bed and notice Aiden standing in the doorway. He's leaning against the door-frame with his arms crossed.

He smiles as I walk up to him. He turns me around where we both can see Lexi and wraps his arms around my waist.

"She's lucky to have you," he leans over and whispers in my ear.

"I'll be lucky to have her," I say, leaning my head on his chest. I know one thing is for certain, I want more time with her.

33

ADDISON

Lexi isn't ready to say goodbye, and truthfully, neither am I. Promises of seeing her in a couple weeks and that we'd talk every day is the only thing keeping Lexi from breaking down. I think I said it to keep myself from breaking down, too.

On the plane back to New York, I start making a list of everything that I need to get ready for Lexi to come live with me.

Reality hits me and I drop my pen. Aiden looks over from his laptop. "I can't cook worth shit. How am I going to feed her?"

His lips curl up. "Well ... I guess our girl will have to live off Cheerios and applesauce," he says, mocking me.

I elbow him and twist my lips. "She'd love that," I say, rolling my eyes. Those are her favorite foods right now.

"Exactly," he points out. "She's five. She's not expecting five-course meals. Stop worrying," he says, closing his laptop and pulling me onto his lap.

I run my hand through his hair, kissing him gently on the lips. "I just don't want to mess up with her. She's been through so much already."

"In her eyes, you can do no wrong. Even if it's burnt toast and over-cooked macaroni." He chuckles.

"*Hmph.* Maybe I can hire a cook," I say, smiling.

Aiden's finger slowly starts circling my bare inner thigh. I glance down as the circle starts to get bigger. Heat shoots up my leg, straight to my sex. I will his finger to move higher, but it stays in that exact spot. The desire builds. I fight fidgeting because I don't want him to remove his hand. I'm almost to the point of moving his hand myself.

I lift my head and look in Max's direction. He's busy on the phone. I snicker to myself when I notice his darkened eye from Aiden's elbow when they were wrestling yesterday.

I look back to Aiden. He's leaning back against the seat, eyes closed. One might think he's taking a nap. That *one* is not me. I feel his hard cock pulse against me. I watch his Adam's apple move as he swallows. His gorgeous soft lips curl up.

"See something you like?" he whispers.

I lean over, running my mouth along his jaw to his ear. "Just wondering what you're doing?"

He shrugs, shaking his head. "Nothing."

"Then you need to do *nothing* a few more inches higher." His finger stops moving. *No! I didn't mean stop!*

Relief runs through me when he squeezes my inner thigh, and his hand begins to move north. His fingers move under my shorts. I part my legs a little more, giving him easier access. I close my eyes as they run along the lace of my panties.

I can't get enough of him. My hunger for him has become insatiable. I hope this feeling dies down because wanting sex all day can't be healthy. This morning we had slow, seductive sex in the shower. Our bodies melded together as one, and we cried out in each other's mouths, not wanting to wake anyone. The water hitting our bodies was the only sound. If passion could be heard, it would've broken the sound barrier. *It was that amazing.*

But here I am, wanting more. Wanting his finger to move my panties to the side and push inside me. Just thinking about his finger skills has me reaching for his arm and giving it a little push.

Aiden's chuckle has me opening my eyes. "My greedy little minx. What am I going to do with you?" he says into my neck, kissing and nipping.

"I think I've been pretty clear about what you can do," I say, biting my lip.

He glances at Max, who thankfully isn't facing us now. He's still on the phone. Aiden moves his hand out of my shorts, and I pout. A half-sexy smile crosses his face, displaying one of his dimples. He brings his finger to my lips, mouthing for me to be quiet. I nod quickly in anticipation.

Holy shit. *I've become a hussy.* I want it so badly I'm okay that Aiden is about to do *whatever* and Max is five feet away from us.

Aiden shakes his head. My brows furrow. Why is he shaking his head? Before I can ask, he lifts me up in his arms and walks with me to the back of the plane. I'm all about trying to fit in the bathroom if it gets me what I need. It'll be a tight squeeze, because well ... Aiden's huge. I giggle to myself. I'm really talking about the bathroom, but it applies to Aiden's cock inside my pussy, too.

I cross my legs in Aiden's arm and squirm a little. His arms squeeze me tighter. My eyes flash up to his. His eyes are dark and pleading. We only break our connection when we come to a door. When Aiden opens it, I'm surprised to see a double-sized bed. It's situated on one side with a chair along the other side.

He lays me on the bed and closes the door softly, locking it. I don't even wait for him to return to me before I'm taking off my clothes. Instead of sitting on the bed with me, he sits on the chair facing me.

I tilt my head, watching him. He's flashing a salacious smile. "Sweetheart, you're going to be the death of me," he says, slowly unzipping his jeans. His black boxer briefs are pulled tight as his hard cock tries to get out. His eyes never leave mine. I face him, lying back on my elbows. He clenches his jaw when he looks down my body. I spread my legs wide. He takes his cock out and runs his hands up and down it. "Your pussy is fucking perfect," he growls. I clench my sex as a bolt of heat runs through me. His eyes are hooded and his look alone could probably set me off. I watch his hand stroke himself.

I need those hands on me. Now. "Aiden," I moan desperately.

"Touch yourself," he rasps. "Show me with your fingers where you want me."

I lie back. My chest moves rapidly as I run my hand over my pebbled nipple and down my body. I shiver at my own touch. His groans fuel me. My finger hits my sensitive nub and my hips move of their own accord. I bite my lip to keep from moaning.

"That's it, baby. You're dripping wet."

My eyes roll back in my head when I stick my finger inside. A moan escapes my lips. I add another finger. It's still not enough. I hear Aiden taking his clothes off and continue, knowing he's watching. Knowing it's affecting him as much as it is me.

When I feel his hand removing my fingers, I open my eyes. He's on his knees at the end of the bed. He sticks my fingers in his mouth. His tongue circles my fingers, licking them clean. When his mouth slams down on my clit and he sucks, I scream out.

Music fills the cabin. Aiden laughs, but his tongue never slows down. I buck as his tongue goes from my clit to being inside me. He tongue-fucks me, making every nerve ending down there spike with pleasure. His tongue moves down farther, softly licking around *that spot*. I about jump off the bed in surprise, but he holds me down with his arm. I'm so flustered that the words I want to say don't come out. Then again, maybe they don't come out because it feels good. *Dirty, but good.*

I'm a little relieved when he moves back up though. When his tongue hits my clit again, I grab his hair. I grind my hips needing more friction. As soon as two fingers move inside me, I'm lost to the orgasm ripping through me. I lose all control as my mind goes blank and my body takes over, surrendering to the feel of Aiden.

When the music gets louder, a blush spreads over my cheeks. I move my hand to cover my face, but Aiden grabs it, putting it above my head. One of his hands holds them both above my head as he slides the other one down my body. He gazes into my eyes, searching for something.

Deep down I know what he's asking. *Is this okay?* I can promise him that there is not one cell in my brain that isn't focused on his cock that is slowly gliding into me. I wrap my legs around his waist, pulling him into me deeper.

I'm pretty sure he got his answer. I gasp at feeling filled to capacity. My mouth gapes open as he plunges wildly into me. His free hand is all over my body. Grabbing, pinching, rubbing. I want to touch him, but he holds my hands in place tighter when I try to move. It only makes me writhe under him more.

He digs his face into my shoulder. His face is damp with sweat and his breathing is erratic.

"I love you, Addison," he rasps into my ear. His hand moves down to my clit. He pulls out of me and his finger dips into my wetness. It doesn't stay there long, before he's sliding back into me. He nips my jaw and neck. His hand reaches around, grabbing my ass, pushing it up into him to get deeper. I can feel my orgasm ready to spill over. He picks up his pace. His hand moves over between my ass cheeks, his finger putting pressure *there*. My hands jerk.

"Sweetheart, it's just me. I'm not doing anything more than just this," he whispers. He circles the area, adding pressure but not going any farther. When my body takes over and pushes against his finger, I moan out in pleasure.

When my hands relax, his lips find mine. He devours my mouth. I am at his mercy as almost every orifice is being explored and my nerve endings explode throughout my body. My body starts to shake involuntarily as pure ecstasy burns through me. I can feel the heat from the wetness coat Aiden.

His head falls on my shoulder. He lets go of my hands and wraps his arms around my body, pulling me tight against his chest. His body convulses as he slams into me one last time, riding out his orgasm.

"Addison," he rumbles in my ear, falling on top me. His chest heaves against mine. I run my fingernails up his back, and he shivers. When his breathing settles, he says, "I hope I die fucking you, because it's the most amazing feeling being inside you." I giggle. "And I would die one happy man."

"That's a little morbid," I say. He pulses his still-hard cock inside of me. I gasp and my muscles squeeze.

"Fuck, baby, you keep doing that and I'm never pulling out." He grinds his hips into me. I let out a whimper at the delicious pain. He gets on his elbows. His gorgeous, emerald green eyes find my eyes. He kisses my nose before putting his forehead against mine. "You okay?" he asks softly.

"Yes," I reply with certainty. I breathe a sigh of relief knowing he didn't hold back. And I didn't *go there*. I lift my head up, meeting his lips. I suck on his bottom lip, pulling him back down toward me.

The music stops. "This is your captain speaking. Actually the owner of the plane," we both chuckle at the sound of Max's voice. "We will be landing within the next hour. So please finish your business and find your seat so we can land. Thank you."

"Holy shit! Max *had* to have heard us," I say, blushing from embarrassment. I cover my eyes with my arm. "It's all your fault. You make me act like a hussy."

"My fault?" Aiden asks, picking up my arm. "You're the one who makes *me* go crazy. I can sense the second you get wet. And as soon as I do, my dick is cocked and ready. Literally." He smiles wide.

He pulls out of me, and I mewl. "See," he says, pointing at me. "That *right there* just made me hard." I look down. Yep, he's hard again. "Sweetheart, knowing how I make you feel, especially when I pull out, is the biggest turn-on ever. Nothing is sexier than knowing you want me inside you."

I bite my lip, trying to steady my out-of-control libido. What the hell is wrong with me? My whole body tingles knowing that he's hard.

"*Goddammit,* Addison," he growls, resting his head on my chest. "You better hold on fucking tight because this is going to be hard and fast." He bites my nipple, and I gasp loudly.

The music comes on again. I don't even have time to laugh as I'm being impaled just like he said. *Fast and hard.* And I love every second of it.

34

ADDISON

Does everyone have that moment in their life when they feel they are doing something bigger than themselves? Like they were put on this Earth specifically meant to do that one thing? That's how I feel right now. I just hung up with the social worker, and I'm screaming.

Literally screaming, jumping up and down.

Lexi is coming to live with me.

Then I freeze. *Oh, shit.*

Lexi is coming to live with me!

In one week.

I run to the guest bedroom and look around. This is not going to work for a five-year-old. I need to go shopping. *Like right now.* I call Aiden and tell him the awesome news. He wants to come over and celebrate, but then I mention that I need to go shopping today for everything and he suddenly has things he needs to do. Ha, typical man.

But I know who will go with me.

"Sydney, we're going shopping today!" I scream into the phone, skipping the hellos.

An hour later, I've written my list of stuff I want to get for the room and have gone on Google to find the places that we need to go.

"I'm all for what you're doing, Addie. But isn't this kind of … excessive?" Syd questions, looking at my total bill.

We're leaving Pottery Barn Kids, and I admit I probably went a little overboard. When I look at the total and it doesn't even faze me. I can't wait until Lexi sees it all. She's been through so much, I want her to have everything.

"She deserves it," I say.

"What happens if she gets adopted?"

A pain in my chest starts to ache. That day will definitely suck for me, but it'll be great for Lexi to find her forever home. I blow out a breath. It's what is best for Lexi. I can't be her foster parent forever.

I shrug. "She can take it with her. It's hers."

"Mmm-hmm," she says, narrowing her eyes like she doesn't believe me.

"What?"

"Nothing," she answers vaguely, but smiles wide.

I ignore her weird behavior. I'm too excited to move on to the next store.

"So, what's next?" Syd asks as she follows me on my mission.

"The paint store."

"HOLY SHIT." Aiden's eyes widen in surprise.

"It's amazing, isn't it?" I ask, bouncing on my toes. The painters did an awesome job. All the walls except one are a butter cream and the accent wall is a dark gray. The furniture was delivered this morning. I took the day off to get everything set up. It looks like a scene out of a fairy tale—or at least the Pottery Barn catalog.

We go get Lexi in two days, so I want to make sure it's all done before she gets here.

"It is. But that isn't what I was thinking," he says, looking around slowly.

My smile turns down. "What's wrong with it?" I ask, taken back.

"Does a five-year-old need all this?" he asks, opening the play oven and refrigerator. His eyes scan everything in the room.

I stiffen. "Well, I really don't know because I haven't been around many five-year-olds," I huff. "But I think she'll love it."

"Oh, sweetheart, there's nothing wrong with it," he says, trying to backpedal. He walks up to me, pulling me into his chest. "She'll love it."

"She will." My eyes start to water. "I just want her to feel wanted and like she has a place of her own right now. She's been shuffled around so much, I want her to have a place that she feels safe and loved." I dig my head into Aiden's chest. "Did I go overboard?" I mumble. My shoulders fall.

"No, Addison," he says, lifting my chin up so I can look at him. His lips curl as his eyes soften. "I'm sorry, I was just surprised. And I'm a guy who doesn't know anything about little girls and what they need."

"*That is true*," I say, sighing. "But when Syd, who's the queen of shopping, thinks I went overboard, I probably did."

"Do you know what I love?"

"Me?" I know that isn't what he's asking, because I know without a doubt that he loves me.

"More than you know," he says. "But I especially love what you have in here, set aside just for Lexi." He places his hand over my heart. "The part that will do anything to make her happy. You are an incredible woman. And anyone who knows you is incredibly lucky."

I fight the words that want to come out of my mouth. I'm

not sure if lucky is the right word. I come with a lot of baggage and most of the people who I'm close to are a result of said baggage.

"Addison," he says as a warning. Of course he can tell what I'm thinking.

So, instead I say, "Thank you."

"That's better." He leans in and kisses me, biting my lip before he pulls away. "Now let's go get some food so I can show you all night how lucky I am."

Max WANTS to follow through with his promise to take Lexi to Disney. I would have rather waited until we settled into a routine, but when it comes to Max, he doesn't change his mind once he gets an idea in his head. Aiden and I had already taken the week off, so I gave in.

As we're walking through the hangar to board the plane, we hear, "Wait for us."

I turn around and see Damon and Sydney running toward us. Aiden mumbles something under his breath. I didn't catch it, but it doesn't sound very happy.

"What are you guys doing?" I ask when they catch up.

"You can't go to Disney without me," Syd says, trying to catch her breath. I look at Damon, wondering what his reason will be.

He shrugs. "I needed a vacation. Florida sounds fun," he says with a huge smile. Max decided to go to Disney World instead of Disneyland because he has some business in Florida he needs to take care of. Lexi won't even know the difference. Katie is going to meet up with us, and I get to meet their grandparents.

"Oh, look, Tink and Peter Pan are wanting to go see their friends at Disney," Max says, chuckling.

Damon flips Max off, and Syd rolls her eyes. Well, this trip is going to be interesting. Max doesn't seem to mind that Syd and Damon are going.

"Don't you have to work?" I ask Sydney.

"Nope. Summer break started yesterday," she says, hopping up and down, grabbing me in a hug. "When Damon told me where y'all were going, because *hmph* … someone else didn't … I called Max and begged."

Max chokes on his laugh and looks down at his watch. "Okay, boys and girls, we need to get this shit on the plane," he says, clearing his throat and picking up luggage.

As we start walking to the plane, I lean over to Syd and say, "I'm glad you're here." I did feel a little tinge of guilt when Max told me we were going.

I have both metal pieces of my seat belt in my hand, ready to snap them together, when Aiden yells out, "No fucking way. You are not going."

My head jerks up to see who he's talking to. I yelp out in pain as the seat belt buckle pinches the skin between my index finger and thumb. I don't even get a chance to find the person Aiden is barking at because I'm trying to suck the pain out of my hand.

"Sweetheart, are you okay?" Aiden says, dropping back into his seat, trying to grab my hand out of my mouth to see how bad it is. I nod my head yes but firmly keep my mouth on my hand. "Let me see." I shake my head.

Then I see who came on the plane. "Jaxon?" I say, releasing my hand to unbuckle my seat belt so I can stand back up. I shake my hand in the air as the pain starts to throb again. "What are you doing here?" Aiden stands right behind me, which reminds me about his outburst. I turn and look at Aiden, confused.

Jaxon leans in and gives me a hug. "Who doesn't want to go to Disney?" he chuckles.

"You guys all suck as fucking friends," Aiden bellows, grabbing my injured hand and dragging me to the bedroom, slamming the door shut. I hear loud laughter coming from the other side of the door.

He sits on the bed and inspects my hand. A blood blister is already forming. "I'm sorry, baby."

The pain is already subsiding. "It's okay. But what in the world was all of that?" I say, looking at the door. He kisses my hand softly. I see his shoulders drop and he takes a deep inhale and exhale.

"This trip is supposed to be about Lexi," he says, looking down. I look around the bedroom. When did it *not* become about Lexi?

"Fuck," he rasps. He stands and paces back and forth, running his hand through his hair. I stand there speechless. I have no idea what is going on in that head of his. "Jaxon is in love with my sister," he finally says. That must be who she was there to see a couple months ago.

Oh. Well, I guess that means I can't set him up with Harper. *Hmm*, who else can I set her up with. Ryker? No, he's too much of a player. I'll have to think about this one. Aiden is still pacing, obviously bothered by this.

"Aiden, I don't see what the big deal is."

He growls. A deep, hard growl. I stand straighter and wonder what the hell is wrong with him. "The big deal is I don't want my sister anywhere near him," he seethes. *Whoa.* "I already have to deal with the fucking love triangle between those three out there." He spears the air with his finger in the direction of the door. I don't know why, but a laugh escapes my lips. This is why he's so bent out of shape?

"It's not funny, Addison. The only reason Jaxon is going is to see Katie."

"It kind of is," I say, pursing my lips to stop from laughing. "First of all, Katie is a grown woman and Jaxon seems like a great guy. Hell, I was going to try and set him up with Harper, but I guess that's not going to happen." Aiden grunts this time, and I laugh again.

"Stop trying to hook up your friends with mine. We'll always be in the middle of that shit if it goes badly," he says, plopping down on the bed, lying back.

"I see where you're going with this, but it's bound to happen if my friends are always around your friends. Especially since all of you look like that …" I gesture up and down his body with my hand.

"We don't all look like this," he jests, wagging his eyebrows. Seeing him lie on the bed, his hands resting under his head, brings back memories of a couple weeks ago.

I straddle him, leaning over to get close to his face. "No, you definitely don't all look like this. This …" I say, grinding my pelvis into his semi-hard dick, "… is one of a kind and all mine."

His hands are on my hips, helping me grind harder against him. My pulse quickens as I feel his arousal, now completely hard. He moans out when I slip my hand down his shorts and stroke him.

Max's voice comes through the speakers and stops my movement.

"We leave in ten minutes," he states.

I giggle against Aiden's chest. But instead of stopping, I increase the pressure of my stroke. I don't want to stop. I need Aiden to loosen up.

So, I don't. But instead of my hand, I push down and finish with my mouth. After we're done, I still have five minutes to clean myself up. *Go, Addison*, I internally high-five myself.

We slip into our chairs in the back of the plane. Aiden buckles my belt for me this time.

"Feel better?" I whisper in his ear when he's leaning over me.

He chuckles. "I need to get mad more often."

FLYING INTO ORLANDO, I immediately felt the humidity hit me when we step off the plane. I breathe in the thick, fresh air. It makes me miss Texas, especially when I have to breathe in car exhaust, garbage smells, random food street vendors—well, those aren't all bad—and other unknown smells daily. Watching the palm tree-lined streets whisk by on our way to our rented house, it reminds me of Galveston where Syd and I spent many spring breaks.

Lexi has exhausted herself from being so excited. She's passed out in the backseat. I love watching her sleep. Aiden turns his head and sees me. "She's so awesome," he says quietly as he grabs my hand.

"She is. Her excitement is contagious. I can't wait to ride Dumbo or It's a Small World with her and see everything through her eyes."

Aiden chuckles. "Syd warned me about you and It's a Small World."

"So, it's not my favorite ride," I say, throwing my hand up. He narrows his eyes at me. "Okay. I *hate* that ride, but I'd do it for Lexi. I'm sure she'll love it."

Although we rented a huge house for everyone, we rented three cars to shuttle us around. When we get to the house, we all pile in and find our rooms. One of the rooms is all Disney themed, which Lexi called *dibs* on as soon as she sees it. It's her new favorite word thanks to Max.

Amy made homemade biscuits and gravy for everyone this morning for breakfast, and Max called dibs on the last one. Ever since Max told her what it means (because she wanted to know if she should be getting money for a bad word), she's been calling *dibs* on everything.

"What if me and Sydney wanted to sleep on the bunk beds?"

Damon jokes, standing behind us. Lexi is sitting on the top bunk, scowling at Damon.

"I don't think so! I called dibs!" she snaps through gritted teeth, hands on her hips.

"You tell 'em, Lulu," Max calls, walking past us as we all burst into laughter.

The house has eight rooms. There is plenty of room so we don't have to double up. I tell Aiden I think it's a good idea that we sleep in separate rooms because of Lexi. He moans and groans until I tell him that we don't *actually* have to stay out of each other's room. I shake my head at him. He's going to need to get better at this when Lexi lives with me.

Katie decides to stay in one of the rooms, too. I do remind the others that we have a child with us, so I better not hear one damn moan coming out of *any* bedroom.

"How's that going to work? You're usually a screamer, baby," Aiden whispers in my ear.

Katie covers her ears. "You did not whisper that quiet enough. My ears are bleeding," she says sarcastically.

I elbow Aiden in the ribs. "Well, I guess that means you'll just have to *wait* till we get home."

"Yes, that's a great idea." Katie laughs.

"Shit. We'll find a way to make you quiet," he says, biting my ear and ignoring Katie all together. Goosebumps spread over me. I take a few steps away from him. I look over my shoulder, and he wiggles his eyebrows and flashes a wicked smile.

I mouth, *"Stop,"* when Lexi comes bouncing into the room. He laughs loudly. "Tater Tot, you ready to go ride some roller coasters?"

Her eyes go wide. "Only if you hold my hand. Really tight," she says in a small voice.

He flips her over, putting her on top of his shoulders. "I think you're going to need to hold *my* hand really tight. You're braver than me," he says, jumping around. She squeals, holding onto his hair.

An hour later we're standing in line to enter Disney World. Max bought everyone three-day, park-hopper passes, so Lexi is looking at the map, rambling on about what she wants to do. We all split up into three lines, hoping to quicken the park entrance experience, because this sucks.

We all end up going through together. And I'm not entirely sure this wasn't planned, but Max, Damon, and Aiden all go through their designated metal detectors. Buzzing and lights flashing like a carnival ride causes everyone to look our direction. I drop my head, slapping my forehead.

Security is there almost instantly. Of course people are nosy, so the noise level has dropped to almost a whisper. Lots of them are wondering what's going on. Aiden and Damon take out their badges, and Max takes out a piece of paper. They're escorted to the side so the employees can continue pushing us through like herds of cattle.

"That's a bunch of bullshit," Damon snaps as we walk into the park. Lexi clears her throat, holding out her hand. He doesn't even question it, he just pulls out his wallet and hands her a ten-dollar bill. "Just call that my deposit for the day, Lulu."

"Thanks, Peter Pan," she says, shoving the money in her pocket.

The guys had to put their firearms in a lockbox, so we have three grumpy guys.

"Do you know the last time I went without my gun?" Aiden whines, threading his fingers through mine. I shake my head wondering if I've ever seen him without it. "I can't either! I feel naked."

Lexi goes to his other side, grabbing his hand. "Don't be sad, Aiden. You got the bad guy," she says, looking up at him with big eyes.

He nods his head as he looks down at her. He pockets his feelings and flashes a big smile. "You're right, Tater Tot. We don't have anything to worry about here."

All three guys paint on smiles for Lexi and take off running around. She's passed from guy to guy, and they spoil her rotten all day. Lexi just mentions she wants something and it magically appears. She really thinks Disney is magical.

"He's so good with Lexi," Katie says as we walk around. "He's going to be a great dad someday."

I smile wide, watching them ahead of us as they stand in line to meet Tigger. Lexi's bouncing up and down, calling Tigger's name over and over to get his attention. I laugh, seeing four huge men stand in line with a little girl.

When she can't get Tigger's attention, Aiden yells loudly, "Hey, Tigger." He looks over quickly at the deep voice, and Max points to a jumping Lexi, waving her hand. He must decide it's probably best to wave to Lexi when he sees the guys taking up half the line. She squeals excitedly.

"He's going to be amazing. He *is* amazing," I say, wrapping my arm through hers. "I'm so happy you're here. I'm sorry I didn't call. I've been so busy."

"Addison, don't apologize. I understand," she says softly. "I'm just glad you and my brother found your way back to each other."

Me, too.

"So what's this I hear about you and Jaxon?"

She sighs heavily. "It'll never happen. Jaxon is too loyal to Aiden, and Aiden *won't* allow it."

"I think I can make him change his mind," I say. At least I have *goods* to barter.

Sydney comes skipping over from the bathroom. Our feet are killing us already, so we sit down on a bench. I can't believe this is just day one. How did we do it when we were little?

The next two days are rinse and repeat, just at different parks.

I am exhausted. So exhausted, that last night I fell asleep on the bottom bunk in Lexi's room. You'd think I was out of shape, because today I feel like my body is protesting from doing anything. I think it perks up a bit when I tell myself we're going home today. The best thing about this vacation? Lexi hated It's a Small World.

As I pile everything into our rental car and all the other rental cars, too, I laugh at how much *stuff* the guys got Lexi. And Aiden thought *I* went overboard with her room. Holy shit, how are we going to get this all on the plane?

35

ADDISON

"Addie, are you coming home soon?" Lexi asks me on the phone. I'm at work, but I'm taking the afternoon off to register her for school. Aiden took it off, too. He wants to check out the school. *Make sure its security is up to par.*

We've been home a week and the transition has gone smoothly. Lexi loves her room. So much so, that she doesn't have any problems sleeping in her own bed now. Except, it doesn't resemble the Pottery Barn, picture-perfect bedroom anymore. It's more like Disney threw up all over that picture. But she's ecstatic about it, so that is all that matters to me.

Syd is helping me learn how to cook simple things like spaghetti, and chicken without it being dry. We're learning as we go. And like Aiden said, she doesn't care what I cook. Thankfully, Aiden is a better cook than I am, so when he has come over this week we have had fantastic dinners.

I put up pictures of Lexi and her family on one wall in her room. I want her to remember them, to know where she came from. It's important to me, knowing how fast the memories will fade. She cried when she saw them, and I started to doubt if it was the right thing to do. Now, it's her favorite place to sit and read. She talks to them frequently. Every night I have Lexi tell me something about her parents or her brother.

"Sweet girl, I'm leaving here in just a few minutes. Are you all dressed and ready to go?"

"Yes, I'm ready," she says excitedly. "Just don't forget to wash off the DNA from work, I don't want to touch it."

I laugh into the phone. "Okay, I'll wash my hands." It's funny the things kids remember.

When we got back from Disney, Syd talked about getting a summer job since living in New York was so expensive. I asked her if she'd watch Lexi for me and I'd pay her. She didn't want to at first, but I talked her into it. Actually, it didn't take much convincing; she loves hanging out with Lexi. It's a win-win for everyone.

"Hey, gorgeous," I hear and look up from my computer to find Aiden leaning against my doorframe with his arms crossed. God, I *love* having a boyfriend. A very sexy boyfriend, with muscular arms. He flexes causing me to blush. He obviously caught me gawking at his arms.

I push my chair back and stand, grabbing my purse from my desk drawer. "Is there a reason you're wearing your FBI shirt?" I chuckle as I push him out of my doorway so I can close it.

"I came from work," he says, shrugging.

"Mmm-hmm."

He shrugs. "You should wear your CSI vest," he suggests as he grabs my hand.

I snicker, shaking my head. "And why would I do that? They are already going to know that I work for NYPD."

"It's about appearances. I want to make sure they know not to mess with our Lexi," he explains. Even though I think he's being ridiculous, my heart skips a beat when I hear *our Lexi*.

"She's in kindergarten, Aiden. You think because you look like a big badass in your *FBI shirt*, a boy isn't going to throw dirt at her," I say, rolling my eyes.

"That's what I'm hoping for," he says confidently.

"This is where her parents wanted her to go, and Syd tells me getting into these schools is as easy as climbing Mt. Everest. So keep that macho attitude of yours in check. We need to make a good first impression," I say, squeezing his hand. I'm scared as hell.

I've never felt so insecure as a person as I feel right now. What if they don't like me? What if they use my past as a reason to not let her go there? What if being a single, foster parent reflects badly? So many *what ifs* flow through my mind in the cab.

"Addison."

"What?" I look up at his soft eyes.

"Stop worrying. She's already been accepted. We're just going to meet the principal."

I nod. He's right. They won't *un*-accept her because of me. Right? I stand up straighter. Well, they better not.

"I CAN'T BELIEVE YOU," I say to Aiden after we lie Lexi down for a nap.

"What?" he says innocently. I stare at him.

"Really?" He shrugs as he sits on a barstool. "You basically threatened the principal."

"I did no such thing," he says with a slight twitch at the corner of his mouth.

"There," I say, pointing to his mouth. "You *know* you did."

"Well, that guy was a total douchebag. I mean for him to even mention that Lexi still might be in danger and he's worried for the staff all because he's an idiot who doesn't already know we took care of that situation."

My eyebrow shoots up. "*We?*"

"Don't remind me," he says, pulling me at the waist and settling me in between his legs.

"Still, you didn't need to tell him that you knew about his cross-dressing habits."

"*What?* I found that interesting tidbit when I was looking into him." He flashes a mischievous smile. "I'm pretty sure Lexi will never be in trouble." He winks at me before slamming his mouth to mine.

36

AIDEN

"You know she's going to kill you when she finds out, right?" Syd says on the other end of the line.

I laugh. Because I'm almost certain she will.

"Does that mean you're out?" I prod her, knowing she won't be able to resist.

"Absolutely not," she huffs. Even though we're on the phone, I can see her hand on her hip as she puffs out her chest.

Damon walks into my office and sits down. I hold up my index finger. He nods, waiting for me to finish.

"You better not tell her, Syd." Damon's eyebrows go up when he hears her name.

I shake my head, covering the mouthpiece. I whisper to him, "That ship has sailed." He flips me off. I still don't know why he acted like he was dating someone when he wasn't. It's not like him to try and make a woman jealous.

"I promise, I won't. You don't know how many times I've tried to surprise her, so I'm invested as much as you are," she says. "But you know Addie, she's like a freaking bloodhound. She knows when things are amiss."

"I'd say more like a German shepherd," I chuckle, thinking about my gorgeous girlfriend. "She can kick some ass."

We end our call after we go over a few more details. The place and date are set. Now all we need to do is keep it under wraps. Damon is sitting back with his foot over his other leg, his fingers tented against his lips.

"What's up?" I ask him.

He takes a few moments before he answers. I narrow my eyes, surprised by his serious expression. He's probably wondering the same thing as Syd. Can I actually get away with this? *Fuck yes*, I can. My job is lying, and I'm damn good at it. This is officially my next assignment.

But when he starts talking, I'm taken by surprise. "Do you really think that ship has sailed?"

I don't even know how to answer that. He knows about Max so the fact that he's asking this floors me.

"*What?*" I say, looking at him with utter shock.

"I was stupid for saying I was dating someone." He sighs. "I thought she'd be jealous or something like that. I never would've thought she would have hooked up with Max."

"But she did."

"I don't need the reminder, asshole."

I sit back in my chair, crossing my arms. I look around the room because *fuck*, I'm at a loss for words. I don't want to be part of this situation. They're big boys. They can deal with it between themselves. I just hate that a girl is getting in between a friendship. In all the years we've been friends, we have never gone down this road.

"They both say it was a drunken night. It meant nothing," he says, trying to justify the need to further pursue her.

It might have meant nothing to Syd, which I find hard to believe in the first place, but I know it meant more to Max. Unfortunately, he won't act on it, especially knowing that

Damon still likes her. *And* Syd made it pretty clear that it was just sex.

I run my hand through my hair. If Syd wasn't Addison's best friend...

"I know what you're thinking," Damon grunts, pulling me from my murderous thoughts.

No, buddy, I don't think you do.

Don't get me wrong, I love Syd like an annoying little sister. She definitely gives Katie a run for her money in that department. But she's coming between two of my brothers. Which is why I have always had the rule: *never date my fucking sister.*

"I just can't get her out of my mind. Every time I see her, there's this connection."

I get it. I know what that slap in the face—like your life is saying wake the fuck up and look at what's in front you—feels like. I just don't understand how he thinks Syd feels that connection, too, when she slept with one of his best friends.

I sigh. "Damon, I want to say she's not worth it, but Addison would probably rip my nuts off if she heard me say that." He chuckles and nods, automatically covering his groin with his hand. Yeah, I know firsthand how it feels to have your balls in a vise grip, literally. *No, thanks.* "I can't tell you what to do. I don't even know what you *should* do. I've had one relationship my entire life. And we've seen how smoothly that's gone."

He laughs out loud. "Smooth as a fucking roller coaster."

"Exactly." I smile, thinking about Addison. "But it's about to be smooth sailing."

"Aiden, for all that you've both been through, I wish nothing more than that to be true," he says. My smile widens just thinking about our future. Together. It's my job to make that happen.

"So what do you need me to do for the party?" he questions.

"Just make sure everyone gets there by seven o'clock. I'll need you to do airport shuttles for everyone coming in," I say, mentally checking off lists.

"Done."

"Thanks," I say, standing up. "Now get the hell out of here so I can go have lunch with my girlfriend."

"HEY, HARPER," I say, walking off the elevator on Addison's floor. Harper stops from getting on the elevator when she sees me. She looks around quickly and pulls me back on, hitting the lobby floor level button.

Guess I'm taking another elevator ride.

As soon as the doors shut she starts talking in a hushed voice. "Okay, so I have everything taken care of with the office people."

I lean my head against the elevator wall. Thank God the party is just a week away. I don't know how everyone is going to be able to keep this from Addison.

"Don't worry, no one will say anything. I've threatened them." I glance at her with a pointed look. Harper is attractive, smart, and fun. Lethal? Scary? Not by a long shot.

She giggles. "Obviously I didn't threaten them that *I* would do something." With a slight tilt to my head, I have a feeling this has something to do with me. "I told them that you'd sick Max Shaw on them," she says proudly. "They won't say a word. They're scared of *that* man."

I chuckle. "Don't tell him that. His head is big enough."

She bites her lip as her face flushes red. "Oh, fucking *come on*. I don't want to know," I say, pushing her out of the elevator as soon as the doors open. If another woman in Addison's circle of friends starts fucking one of my best friends, I'm going to lose it.

I slam my finger down on the third level button, letting out a grunt. The man who got on as I was pushing Harper out looks at me through the corner of his eyes. He glances down to my gun and back up. His back straightens. I want to laugh at the suit-wearing stiff. I look to see what floor he pressed, seventh. *Accounting.* No surprise there. But he shouldn't be surprised by my gun. That's the norm around here.

Smiling, I bite my lip, looking straight ahead. I could easily mess with this guy. I glance down at my watch and notice I'm already five minutes late. I guess not today. The elevator dings and doors open to the most magnificent sight ever. My smile is huge as Addison steps onto the elevator.

"Agent Roberts," she addresses me formally, standing at my side but looking forward. She reaches out and presses the lobby button. I inhale her scent as she reaches in front of me. It's always cherry with a touch of vanilla. It has to be her pheromones because I have smelled every lotion, hair product, and perfume in her entire bathroom so I could steal some to have at my place. Unfortunately, nothing smells as good as her.

"*Oh.* I thought this was going down." She glances at the guy standing in the opposite corner as me. He smiles at her and then quickly looks forward when our eyes meet.

"Hey, beautiful," I say into her hair, kissing the top of her head. I notice suit-boy stiffen again. His lips purse together.

What the hell? Not into public affection? Well, keep watching then, asshole. I slide my hand down her arm. She shivers as I slip my hand in hers. I see her back rise, her breath catch from just my touch. *My fucking touch.*

I lean down and dig my face into her neck. "I've missed you," I whisper. Her other hand grabs my thigh and squeezes. I flex my thigh and her head shakes. I chuckle into her neck. She's trying to act unaffected, but she's failing. I stand taller and suit-boy is staring at us. With disgust on his face.

I jerk back a little, confused by his expression. He seems to *really* not like me. I search my memories trying to place him. Nope, not a clue.

When the elevator doors open to his floor, he pushes off the wall. He leans in Addison's direction when he passes her and says in a tight voice, "He's not worth it." *Excuse me?*

Addison puts her arm out in front of me, stopping me from moving forward. She turns to me when the doors close. "What in the world?"

"Who the fuck was that guy?" I ask, fuming, seeing myself in the reflection of the closed doors. *I'm not worth it?* Who says that to someone they don't even know?

"I don't know him personally, but he works with Bryn, the accountant assigned to our department," she says, looking up at me. "I'm guessing you don't know him?"

I finally look away from the closed doors down to her face. "No, I don't know him."

"He must be jealous," she says, running her hand up my chest and into my hair, obviously trying to distract me. I moan a little as her fingers comb through my hair. "Because you are *definitely* worth it."

She lifts up on her toes and her lips brush mine before she presses into me. I lean against the wall, pulling her with me. I savor her taste with my tongue, taking it slow as I explore her mouth. The ding of the elevator makes Addison jump.

She whips around, quickly running her hands down her body, making sure her clothes are straight. A man joins us on the second floor. He glances between us and smirks as he turns around. I look down to Addison and see her face flushed red. She doesn't say anything though, just looks straight ahead. A chuckle escapes my lips.

I grunt as an elbow makes contact with my ribs. So I grab her ass. Hard.

"Aiden," she warns, looking back to me. I put my hands up in the air and wink. In no time the door opens and we step off. I grab her hand, linking our fingers as we walk outside.

"You look hot," she says, dragging her eyes down my body. "Court?"

"No. I just thought you'd like to see me in a tie," I say, wagging my eyebrows. I did have court this morning. It's my least favorite thing to do. Lots of sitting and waiting. It sucks. Of course dressing up in August is a beating, so I left the jacket at the office and rolled up my sleeves. Right now, I'm glad as fuck I left my tie on. I think I'll be wearing a tie more often just to see that gleam in her eyes right now.

"I have a few ideas that you can do with that tie," she says and bites her lip.

"Care to share?" I ask, stopping her in the middle of the sidewalk. I hear people cursing under their breath as they walk around us. Fuck if I care. I want to hear these ideas.

She laughs out loud. Is she serious? There is nothing funny about this. My dick is listening intently, too. Inquiring minds want to know.

"It's more of show rather than tell," she says softly.

I look up to the cloudless sky. "Why, God? Why is she trying to kill me when she knows..." I pause to look her directly in the eyes, "...when she knows I'll think of nothing other than her naked body and this tie. All. Day. Long."

She swallows hard. I swear I can feel the swells of her breast, her hardened nipples under her purple shirt against my chest.

"Feel like taking the rest of the day off?" I ask, struggling not to sound desperate.

She puts her hand on my chest. "I wish I could," she says, regretful. "But we're working on an important case right now. I have to go back." She sticks out her bottom lip.

I let out a heavy sigh. "I have stuff I need to do, too, but I'll have shit for brains now thanks to you," I chuckle.

"I'll make it up to you later." She stands on her toes and presses those plump lips to mine.

"My tie and I will be looking forward to it," I say. "Or should I bring a gray one?" Her brows furrow as she tilts her head slightly. "So we can Fifty Shades of Grey it."

She giggles, shaking her head. "Do you have a red room of pain that I'm not aware of?"

"I can," I say quickly. My dick is hard and my balls are bordering on painful just thinking about stuff we could do. I'm not into BDSM, but I'm all for a good slap on the ass. *Or toys.*

She grabs my hand and starts walking. "Come on, Mr. Grey. We can explore that room later. I'm hungry."

"Thanks to you and your tie fetish, I'm a different kind of hungry. Starving," I groan, loosening my tie. I can feel sweat beading along my forehead, and it's not from the weather.

When we turn down the street headed to her apartment, I look at her, wondering where we are going.

When she smiles up at me, her eyes shine with mischief. She licks her lips and says, "I'm pretty sure I have stuff to eat at my apartment."

Words escape me at the moment since I can't seem to think past the feeling in my pants, so I just nod. Instead, I pick up our pace. She laughs out loud as I practically drag her. My mouth waters thinking about what I'm about to *eat*. She's like a saint, ready to feed a starving man.

37

ADDISON

I hate feeling like this. Like something big is about to happen. As much as I tried to push down those thoughts, there's something banging on the inside of my brain telling me to watch out.

People are acting strange. And I don't know if that is me reading into everything because of that damn banging noise or if it's a warning.

It's Thursday and we're really slow today. Bryn from accounting asked me to go to lunch with her. I recall our phone conversation and it sounded urgent. I'm a ball of nerves now. I'm feeling off, people are acting off, and now this.

I hate this feeling.

We meet in the front of the building. The sun is trying to peek around the clouded sky. I feel like the sun as I try and burn off the clouds in my head.

"Hey, girl," Bryn says, giving me a hug.

"Hey. You're looking pretty sexy," I tell her, looking at her gray pencil skirt and white, ruffled, silk top. Her hair in a twist, looking very professional. I envy that she gets to look like a woman at work. Unfortunately, I work in a lab or out in the field. Wearing a skirt or dressing up is definitely not practical.

"Thanks! But I secretly wish I could put your CSI jacket on and walk around so I look like a badass."

I laugh out loud. "It's not as sexy as you would think."

"Oh, be quiet! You look *hot* in your CSI jacket. You're a rock star and you know it," she says, smiling.

I shake my head. I'm definitely not a rock star. Sexy nerd is more like it. Our chat to the deli is easy. We both like to people watch, and New York City is definitely the place to do it. We laugh as we pass someone dressed up as Mickey Mouse. *A really deranged Mickey.* They probably scare more kids than they get to take pictures with them. And then one block over we have the women who are naked on top with painted breasts, and right across the street we see The Naked Cowboy. Oh yes, we are in the land of equality. Something for everyone.

The smell of fresh bread hits my senses as we walk into the deli. I can taste the sour dough bread already. By the time we sit down, I start to second-guess the urgency of our lunch. Bryn hasn't said anything to make me think something is wrong. Am I getting ready to start my period? I start counting days in my head. Maybe that's why I'm being so sensitive. As I calculate, I shake my head ... nope, not time.

We squeeze into a table that'll fit just two. This is always a busy place for lunch. And loud. Chatter fills the air from every direction.

I bite into my roast beef sandwich and moan. I could eat this sandwich every day, it's that good. Bryn laughs at me, and I shrug. I can't help it.

I swipe my mouth with my napkin before I ask, "So, why did you sound so urgent on the phone?"

She just stuck a fork full of salad in her mouth, so she holds up a finger. I laugh. "Sorry. Why does that always seem to happen?"

She takes a quick drink of her tea and then laughs. "I know, right? So, do you know Ned?"

I twist my lips and think. Ned? Hmm … I shake my head when I can't place the name.

"He works with me. Stiff asshole and not very good looking."

"Oh, him," I say, laughing. "I guess I never knew his name. But hey, he's the one who was on the elevator with me and Aiden on Monday and get this … he leaned over and told me that Aiden wasn't worth it on his way out." I had forgotten all about him after our *lunch* that day.

She rolls her eyes. "Yeah, that's him."

"So, is he always an asshole? Aiden was about to kill him."

"Well …" she says, grimacing, "I'm pretty sure once he hears what he said, he'll still want to kill him."

My eyes go wide. "What did he say?"

She crinkles her nose. "He, um … he told people that Aiden and Harper, are um … having an affair."

I jerk back. "What?" I say loudly. People around us stop talking and look our way. "Why the hell would he say that?"

"You know it's not true."

I do. I know that Aiden would never cheat on me. Well, I hope he'd never cheat on me. I'm not stupid. I know it's always a possibility, but after all we've been through, it's not happening right now.

"Addison, that man loves you. I mean *really* loves you. The love you hear about in Cinderella stories."

I chuckle at her comparison. "I know he loves me, but people have been acting weird the last couple days. Do you think they've heard this rumor and are afraid to tell me?" This has to be it. Poor Harper. Oh, my! If she's heard the rumor, she'll be so upset.

"How did you find out?" I ask her.

"Unfortunately, I heard from someone down in records." I wince. If it has gotten to the second floor, it has gotten around.

"So, I went straight to the rotten bastard and confronted him about it. He said he saw it himself. He said it happened on the elevator on Monday," her voice lowers.

I think back to Monday and laugh. "I'm not exactly sure what he saw, but Monday Aiden and I were having sex in my apartment at lunch and then we both went back to work. Then after work, he came over for dinner with me and Lexi and stayed until bedtime. I'm not sure when he *saw* them, but it didn't happen," I say, using air quotes.

Her smile spreads across her face. "Why are you smiling?"

She sighs dreamily, sitting back in her chair. "I want a boyfriend to come sweep me off my feet and have sex with me for lunch." I run my finger around my water glass thinking back to Monday and *his tie*. Blush spreads across my face when I meet Bryn's eyes. "See? I want *that*, whatever just made your whole body light up."

"Why don't you have a boyfriend? You're a great catch." I take a drink from my water, hoping we can move to a different conversation.

She waves her hand around. "Men suck," she declares. "I don't sleep around, so that eliminates half the male population right there. I'm intelligent and independent so that takes care of a huge chunk of men who want needy women, and I won't chase a man so there's the rest." She shrugs. "I'm going to end up being the cat lady."

"Do you have cats?"

"No! I hate cats," she huffs. "Well, not really hate, just really allergic to them."

"Well, then you really can't be the cat lady," I tease.

She throws a chip at me. "You know what I mean."

"I think you just haven't met the right one," I say, tossing the chip back at her.

"Aiden have any friends?"

"Oh, he has friends. *Hot friends*. But according to Aiden, they're all off limits to my friends." I laugh.

"Well, that sucks."

"We'll find you someone," I say and then look around the deli, noticing a couple cute guys a few tables over.

"Not here," she whisper yells. I laugh at her freaked-out expression. "So do you have any amazing plans this weekend. Like jumping out of a plane or going to a beach house?"

I tilt my head. "How do you know that?" Being a closed-off person, there are very few friends who I talk openly with. Bryn isn't one of them. I like her, but we just became friends a couple months ago.

"Oh. Was it a secret?" she says hesitantly. "Harper told me one day at lunch. I hope that's okay." Her shoulders droop.

I'm happy to hear it was from Harper. I definitely don't want to become gossip at work. I balk at that. Who am I kidding? I've been the talk of the whole building for months.

"No, it's okay, it wasn't a secret." She blows an errant hair out of her eyes and seems to relax. "So, about this weekend. Nothing spectacular. Aiden is taking me on a date tomorrow night. Sydney is taking Lexi. We try and go out at least once a week by ourselves since Lexi started living with me. Well, other than our trysts at lunch times." I bite my lip and smile.

Tomorrow is my birthday, but when Aiden mentioned taking me to dinner, he didn't say anything about my birthday. And I'm okay with that. I'll tell him at dinner and he'll probably be mad at me for not reminding him. I just hate for people to feel obligated to do anything for me. Syd always made a big deal about it, so I'm surprised she hasn't said anything. But she's been busy getting ready for school to start.

When I get back to the office, I look around for Harper. I need her to know that I would never believe that she and Aiden are having an affair. But I can't find her. Her door is closed and looks like she's gone for the day. Weird. She usually tells me if she's leaving.

I pass CJ's office, sticking my head inside. "Hey, is Harper gone for the day?"

"Yep, she took some vacation time off. Since we're slow, she took tomorrow off, too," she answers, not even looking away from her computer.

"Oh." Well, shit. I hope this has nothing to do with the rumor. "Okay, thanks," I say and walk back to my desk. I try and call her but it goes straight to voicemail. Well, this isn't good. I decide to call Aiden. I'm not going to be the one to tell him about the rumor, but at least I can gauge his behavior to see if he's upset about something.

"Hey, gorgeous," he answers. His deep voice is so sexy. I don't think I'll ever get tired hearing it.

"Hi."

"I wish we could've done lunch today," he says suggestively.

"Oh, I bet you do," I laugh.

"Seems you had other plans."

"Following me, Agent Roberts?"

"Nope. But I have eyes and ears, everywhere," he says jokingly. I search my memory of the people in the restaurant. The two guys sitting a couple tables over. The ones I thought were cute. They did look familiar. Shit. I can't place them. I tap my finger on my desk.

"You're trying to figure out who was there, aren't you," he asks.

"Um, *yeah*. There were two guys there. I noticed they looked our way a couple times. I didn't think about it then, but now that I am, they did look familiar."

He scoffs. "Are you checking other guys out, Addison?"

"Who are they?"

"You didn't answer my question."

"I don't think it warrants an answer," I say defensively. Yes, I noticed them, but for *Bryn*. It kind of pisses me off he's accusing me of checking out other men yet there's a rumor of him and Harper going around.

The line is silent. I continue tapping my finger, waiting him out. We can play this game all goddamn day. I didn't do anything wrong.

I hear him sigh heavily into the phone. I know he's a jealous man, but I hope he doesn't think I would ever do something.

"You know you're all I see, right?" I say softly, breaking the silence. "You're the only man I want."

"I'm sorry," he murmurs.

"I had noticed them because I was scoping out a guy for Bryn."

"Who?"

"Bryn from accounting. She's who I had lunch with." I wait to see if there is a reaction when I mention where she works.

"The guys are the newbies who just started last month. They know who you are so they told me they saw you at lunch."

"Answer me. You *know*, right?" I ask again. I need reassurance from him that he understands he's the only man I need. Maybe I'm looking for it in return, too. Especially with a stupid rumor running around our halls.

"I know," he replies. *That's it?* He's acting different. He's definitely a jealous man, but for him to get jealous from me looking at someone seems a little extreme coming from him.

"Well, I have to get back to work," he says. I can hear voices in the background and then him telling someone that he'll be right in. "I'm going to have to work late tonight, too, so I won't be able to come over."

"Oh. Okay," I say a little surprised. A small voice way back in a dark corner of my mind is making me question things. Harper took off early. Aiden won't be available tonight. And add to it the rumor, it's a mixture for disaster in my head.

"I'll call you later though. I love you, Addison," he says and hangs up before I can respond. *See, he loves me*, I tell the small voice creating havoc in my head right now, making me question things.

The rest of the afternoon I notice people whispering, watching me. I don't know what the hell is going on, but I'm driving myself insane. I call Syd to try and calm myself.

"Hey, girlfriend," she says.

"Hey."

"What's wrong, Addie?"

"People are acting weird. Do you think Aiden would cheat on me?" Sydney starts choking and coughing. "Are you okay?" I ask.

"Sorry, I was taking a drink of water. Went down the wrong pipe," she replies, clearing her throat. "What in the world are you talking about? Why would you ever think that?"

"Never mind. I'm being stupid."

She's right. I'm being ridiculous. People are just whispering because I'm sure they've heard the rumor. But it's not true. *It's not.*

Aiden ends up not calling me tonight. Instead I receive a text.

Aiden: Can't wait for our date tomorrow night. Miss you.

I don't text him back. I'm a little upset he didn't call me. I'm irritated with myself because he hasn't done anything. But I can't stop myself from feeling mad. Sydney comes over with pizza, and we have a girls' night in with Lexi.

After we put Lexi to bed, Sydney pours a couple glasses of wine. I'm going over everything about today in my head when she hands me a glass and sits down on the couch beside me. I take a big drink and sigh.

"What's going on?" she asks.

I look at the wine as I swirl it around in my glass. "There's a rumor going around the department that Aiden and Harper are having an affair."

Syd spews her wine all over, choking. I jump when I feel wetness on my legs. "What the hell? Are you having issues swallowing drinks?" I ask her, jogging to the kitchen to get paper towels. Thankfully it's white wine.

She pats her chest. "Sorry," she coughs. "Where the heck did that rumor start? And is that why you asked me that earlier?"

"Yes. And I don't think it's true. Well, I'm ninety-nine percent sure it's not true."

I tell her what Bryn told me and how everyone is acting in the office. And how Aiden seemed to get jealous over something so stupid.

"You need to stop over-analyzing everything. You know Aiden would never do anything to hurt you. Ever," she says as she grabs my hand.

I push off the couch and throw my hands in the air. "I know that. I do. But something feels off. And I *hate* when things feel off."

Syd tries to hide her smile. I narrow my eyes at her. "Why are you smiling?"

"You're just being silly. Are you getting ready to start your period?"

"If you were a man, I'd hit you over the head," I say, plopping back down on the couch. She laughs out loud. I can't really be mad at her for asking. I had that same thought.

She reassures me that I have nothing to worry about before she heads home. As I lie in bed, I think about Aiden. I feel bad for not responding to him, so I fumble around for my phone on my nightstand. Finding it, I open up the texting app.

Me: I wish you were here right now. xoxo
Aiden: Me too, sweetheart. Is it tomorrow yet?

I smile wide. *I wish it was.* I don't know why I'm feeling so needy. I place my phone back on my nightstand. Tomorrow can't get here soon enough.

38

ADDISON

It's tomorrow and it's not any better than yesterday. People are going out of their way to avoid me. I feel like I should stand up and scream, "*Aiden is not cheating on me.*" I push back in my chair, staring up to the ceiling.

Happy birthday to me.

I rub my temples as a headache threatens to surface. At least I had a great morning. Syd came over with my favorite breakfast food—donuts—and sang Happy Birthday to me.

A smile spreads across my face remembering how excited Lexi was. She woke me up, jumping up and down on my bed. Her homemade card brought tears to my eyes. It was a picture of her standing with Aiden and me. We were all holding hands.

Syd took Lexi for the day to do girly stuff. I really wanted to play hooky with them, but with Harper taking vacation, I really need to be here. So now I'm stuck in rumor hell. I tap my spacebar to wake my computer. Two thirty-five. I blow out a breath, not much longer.

At four, I decide I'm done. I've finished everything so I tell CJ that I'm going to leave a little early. She's more than happy to let me leave. She's probably sick of the rumor mill, too. If I'm not here, at least the whispering might stop.

The only thing I've heard from Aiden today was in a text. It said to be ready at six-thirty and where we're going is dressy, but not too dressy. *Details, Aiden. I need more details.* When he doesn't answer my text, I guess I'm on my own.

I feel a little retail therapy will help my mood. I take a taxi to a small boutique that I love in SoHo. An hour later I have a dress in hand and some new Jimmy Choo, strappy, nude heels. My day is already getting better.

Syd texts me that she and Damon are taking Lexi to a movie and dinner so they'll see us tomorrow. Huh. *She and Damon?* I chuckle to myself. That girl is going to give Aiden a heart attack. I get home and crank up the music, pour myself a huge glass of wine, and get ready for my date.

The knock on my door right at six-thirty makes my heart flutter. I've yearned to see Aiden and ache for his touch. It's been too long. Yet it's only been two days. Aiden is my addiction. And it's time for a fix.

I open the door and my breath hitches seeing the gorgeous man standing in front of me. My heart beats faster. He has his hands in his black slacks. He's wearing a white shirt and a gray freaking tie. I bite my lip as I appraise his body. When my eyes flash up to his, his nostrils flare. His gaze is burning with lust and desire. A shiver runs up my spine as he takes a step forward. A low, rumbling, deep throat growl erupts from his lips.

"*Fuck me*, Addison." Yes, please. "You look stunning," he says as he takes his hands out of his pockets. He grabs one hand, putting it over my head, and spins me around slowly. His other hand brushes my midsection as he turns me. I hear him exhale sharply when he gets to my backside.

My go-to dress is usually black. They're simple, always in style, and you can never go wrong. But the sales girls swore this dress would look good on me. The halter dress contours my body, hitting me at the knees. It's navy rosebud lace over a nude lining that isn't as long as the lace. The back is exposed and gorgeous. I'm so happy she pulled me out of my comfort zone because the look on Aiden's face right now is intoxicating.

"You like?" I flash a knowing smile.

"No," he says, pulling me into him. "I *fucking* love."

He presses his lips softly on mine. I can feel his hard body holding back. His restraint is evident as he growls again, taking a step back. His jaw clenches as he exhales sharply again. "We need to go. Now," he demands.

"I love your tie," I say seductively, running my hand down it. Memories of how the silk felt around my wrists excites me. It's been eight months now and every gut-wrenching memory has now been replaced with Aiden's loving touch. Unfortunately, those memories will never die, but they are buried. It's one period in a book full of beautiful words.

"*Sweetheart*, you and that new tie fetish of yours is going to have to wait," he rasps.

THE RESTAURANT IS AMAZING. The Japanese brasserie's dark red ambience and lit lanterns all around create the perfect romantic setting. We're in a private semicircle booth, which allows us to sit *really* close. Aiden hasn't stopped touching me since we sat down.

"That dress is my new favorite," he says, leaning into me. "But right now, I hate it." He squeezes my lace-covered thigh. Having a body-hugging dress down to one's knees doesn't make for easy access.

"Don't you know good things come to those who wait?" I whisper in his ear as I slide my hand up his tie.

He nods his head. "Oh, I know, baby. I know."

He glides his hand over my jaw then tugs me over to him. His lips are soft as he kisses me sweetly. When he pulls back, I let out a small whine.

"Seems like I'm not the only one who has to work on their waiting skills." He chuckles.

I'm grateful for the interruption from the waiter. "Welcome. Are we celebrating anything?" he asks, looking down at us.

"Nope," Aiden replies.

I purse my lips. I guess I should tell him today is my birthday. Ugh. *Addison why did you wait?* I know why. I didn't want him to feel obligated to get me anything or make a big deal of it. I'm not a big birthday person. I shake my head and blow out a breath.

Aiden orders our drinks and an appetizer. After the waiter leaves, he looks at me. "What's going on in that head of yours? I can always tell when you're having a conversation with yourself."

"So, don't be mad," I say quickly. He stays quiet. "Today is my birthday." His eyes go wide in surprise and then he drops his head. "I'm sorry I didn't say anything."

When he looks up he says, "Well, now I feel like the worst boyfriend ever." He picks up his water and takes a drink. I watch his Adam's apple move as the liquid goes down.

"No, you're not. You're perfect," I say, scooting closer to him. "If anyone is failing in that department, it's me." I sigh.

"*I* should have known. You told me a few months ago. I should have remembered. I'm sorry."

"It's okay. I swear. I won't hold it against you. I've just never been the person who has loved celebrating her birthday," I say, shrugging. "Well, I used to when my mom was still here, but that was a long time ago. Syd has tried repeatedly to surprise me. She's just too easy to read." We both laugh.

"I promise to make it up to you tonight," he says, placing a soft kiss on my lips again.

The food is divine here. I savor every bite, each better than the last. I've always wanted to eat here, but the wait list for a reservation is six months out. I wonder how many favors Aiden had to call in to get one. Little does he know this is the best birthday present he could have given me.

While he pays, I go to the restroom. As I walk up to the table, he's texting someone. I scoot in around the bench and he puts his phone away.

"I was texting Damon to ask how Lexi is doing," he says quickly. While it warms my heart that he's thinking about Lexi, he almost sounds guilty of something.

"Okay," I say slowly.

"I just don't want you to think I'm working on our date," he says. "It's just you and me tonight." He wraps his arm around me and pulls me into him. The kiss this time isn't soft or sweet. It hard, deep, and possessive. I hope it's a precursor to the rest of the night.

"Are you ready to go?" he asks, leaning his forehead against mine. My voice is hidden under my heavy breaths, so I just nod. I'm not wearing a bra so the brush of the fabric against my pebbled nipples has me clenching my thighs. *I am definitely ready.*

We took a cab down here, so I'm surprised when we start walking. "What are we doing?"

"Just taking a walk," he says, smiling down at me. "I want to see you in that dress for a little longer before I rip it off."

"You know I can wear it for you whenever you want, right? I am not opposed to going straight home."

He belts out a sexy, deep, throaty laugh. I know I sound desperate. *I am.* I need to feel him, all of him. I'm about to pull the birthday card. We should be doing what *I* want.

"Patience, sweetheart."

I roll my eyes. "Fine," I huff. Even though it does feel nice walking hand in hand with Aiden, I won't admit it right now. I see the karaoke club coming up, and I laugh out. Aiden follows my line of vision and smiles. "That night seems like forever ago. You were so hot up there singing to me."

"You were so drunk," he chuckles.

I wave my hand around. "I don't remember that part."

"You want to go in and have a drink? Maybe I'll sing something to you again," he says wiggling his eyebrows.

"If you promise to sing something, I'll go."

"I promise."

I'm trying to think about what I want him to sing me. He opens the door for me to walk in and I turn back toward him. "How about you si—"

"SURPRISE!"

I jump at the sound, tripping myself when I turn around. Aiden grabs me and sets me upright. I feel my cheeks burn as I look around and everyone is staring at me. It takes me a couple seconds to fully grasp what is happening.

I cover my mouth as I notice who is here. I look around and see the large banner that reads HAPPY BIRTHDAY, ADDISON!

Oh, my God!

I spin around to Aiden, and he's flashing his megawatt smile. "You!" I yell, pointing at him.

He picks me up, laughing. "Happy birthday, sweetheart." He kisses me and the crowd goes wild. I shake my head as he puts me down. I can't believe this. I can't believe they pulled this off without me knowing.

Sydney runs and jumps in my arms. "We did it! We surprised you!" she screams, jumping up and down.

"Either you're getting better at hiding stuff or I'm losing my touch," I say.

"You about killed me last night when you were saying you felt things were off," she says, pushing my shoulder.

That's it! This must be why I felt something was going on.

"So, there was never a rumor?" I ask, thinking maybe it was a diversion.

"No, the asshole did start that rumor," Syd says flatly, rolling her eyes.

Aiden leans his chin on my shoulder. "What rumor?" I look at Syd. Oh, shit. I guess it hadn't made its way to Aiden.

"Um … nothing," I say.

Aiden whips me around. "What rumor, Addison?"

"It went around the office that you and Harper were …" I don't even finish. I can't say it out loud.

His eyes widen and he tilts his head a little. "What! Who spread around that rumor?"

I scrunch my nose. "I never believed it," I say.

"Who do I need to kill?"

"When you put it that way, I'm not going to tell you. He's not worth your time," I say crossing my arms.

"You're not going to go enjoy your party until you tell me." His hands on my hips increase their grip.

I tell him the story that Bryn told me. When he thinks back to that day of the elevator incident, he remembers why Ned might think something was going on. He tells me he pushed Harper out of the elevator, and she was giggling and blushing because she had been talking about Max. He understands why there was a misunderstanding, but he's still pissed.

"Baby, I would never."

"I know. Well, I was *almost* certain." His eyebrows shoot up. I shrug. "People were acting weird. And then you and Harper disappeared suddenly. I'm sorry I had any doubts. I knew you weren't, but there was a tiny doubt," I say, sighing. "I was going to talk to you about it this weekend."

He pulls me outside and waits for the door to close to drown out the noise from the party. "Addison, I hate thinking that something I did caused you to doubt us." He stares at me while holding both my hands.

"Aiden, this is silly. I *really* didn't believe it. I love you and you've proven to me over and over how much you love me. *We're forever.*" I stand on my toes and kiss him. Our bodies start to sway to the music in the club.

"I love you," he mumbles on my lips.

"Enough hogging the birthday girl," Uncle Ted says. I do a double take when I hear his voice.

"Ted!" I scream and jump into his arms.

"Happy birthday, Addison," he says warmly, wrapping me in a hug. He looks at Aiden. "You did good, son." Then he shakes his hand.

I look back at Aiden and say, "He did, didn't he?"

Back inside, I'm stunned how many people came for my birthday. Lexi runs to me as soon as she sees me.

"You look so pretty, Addie," she tells me, giving me a big hug.

I look at her new dress and twirl her around. "You do, too, sweet girl. Looks like you and Syd went shopping." She smiles super wide and nods her head.

She pulls me around to different people she knows, and I introduce her to the people she doesn't.

I look around at how many people are here and there has to be at least a hundred. Tony waves at me from the stage while he and Harper sing. I can't help but laugh as they dance around on stage and sing with their pitchy voices.

Syd takes Lexi, so Aiden and I walk around talking to everyone. Ted comes up behind me and whispers in my ear, "Why is the quarterback from the Giants here?"

I find Ryker with a group of people around him. Mainly women. I wrap my arm through Ted's. He's a huge fan of Ryker's, not so much the Giants. *I know the feeling.*

"Come on. He's one of Aiden's best friends," I say, leading him over.

"There's the gorgeous birthday girl," Ryker says and pulls me into a tight embrace. "Let's see how long it takes for—"

I'm being pulled back and arms are wrapping around my waist as a growl comes out of Aiden's mouth. Ryker barks out a laugh. "I guess not long," he says, grabbing Aiden's shoulder and patting him on the back.

"Ryker, I want you to meet my uncle Ted. But he's more like my dad," I say, looking warmly at Ted. They shake hands.

I don't even notice the man to Ryker's side until he says, "Aiden, it's great to see you. I'm assuming by the possessive embrace, this is Addison."

It's Aiden's turn to laugh. He doesn't release his hold but does take one hand off my waist to shake the guy's hand. I tilt my head looking at him closer. He looks familiar. It's Ted who gives it away. "No shit! You're Shane Jacobs, the owner of the Giants." I look at Aiden, and he shrugs. I wonder what other famous people he knows.

We all start talking about the upcoming season. And I'm actually surprised that Ryker is even here because it's preseason. "I wasn't going to miss this. Plus, I'm the quarterback, they're not even playing me," he says, throwing his hands in the air.

I'm surprised by his comment. It's just my birthday. It's not that big of a deal. He acts like it's the party of the century. I'm about to say something when a certain voice singing stops me. I look to the stage and Sydney and Lexi are on stage. Lexi is singing *Party in the U.S.A.* by Miley Cyrus. She's swinging her hips with so much sass that I think she's going to fall off the stage. Hoots and hollers only spur her excitement. All eyes are on them right now. My hand is on my heart as I watch her. This is her thing. She's come so far from three months ago. I'm sure her mom is looking down on her right now, so proud of her.

She sees me and waves. Aiden and I both wave back. "She's a

natural on stage," Aiden says, leaning on my shoulder.

"She is," Shane says. "It'd be awesome if she came and sang the National Anthem one game."

I jerk my head in his direction. I open my mouth and then snap it shut. "I'm not sure if she needs to be in the spotlight right now. She's been through so much this year."

"Well, if you change your mind, you know how to get a hold of me," he says, smiling and looking at Aiden.

"Any other famous people going to be coming to my birthday party?" I joke, leaning my head against Aiden's resting on my shoulder. He chuckles.

Everyone important to me is here. I can't even imagine how much work went into making this happen. People from all over are here. Aiden's sister, Katie, is talking with Jaxon across the room, trying to be discreet. Aiden's grandparents are talking to Amy and Ted. Friends from both our worlds are enjoying themselves. This is our world, combined.

I squeeze Aiden's arm that is wrapped around my waist. "Thank you," I say, turning my head toward him and kissing him on the cheek. "This is the best birthday present ever."

"You're definitely worth it," he says.

My cheeks are hurting as the night goes on. I'm trying to pace my drinks so I don't miss a second of tonight.

"I am borrowing that dress," Harper says while we dance around. "Although I'm pretty sure I won't look half as stunning as you in it."

"Shut up. You are drop dead gorgeous. You'd rock this dress."

Aiden comes up behind me. "That dress never leaves your closet, unless you're wearing it or it's on the floor," he whispers. "Got it."

I giggle and push him away. "Go away, Tarzan, I'm dancing with my girls." He beats his chest and yells as he walks away. We all bust out laughing.

Not long, Syd and I are walking to a couple chairs to sit down. My feet are starting to hurt. A table right in the middle is reserved for me. They didn't miss anything.

I look around for Lexi and she's on Max's shoulders, entertaining a group of people. She's definitely a shining light. *My shining light.*

The sound of a guitar has me turning my attention to the stage. Butterflies inside me flutter at the sight of Aiden in the center of the stage, sitting on a barstool. His sleeves are rolled up and his tie is loosened so the shirt's first button is undone. He looks right at me and smiles. I cross my legs and fan myself.

He's gorgeous. *And mine.*

He shakes his head, chuckling to himself. "This is for you, sweetheart. I love you."

I mouth back, "I love you."

His fingers move effortlessly across the strings. I'm not surprised in the least. They *are* experts at strumming me. Heat spreads through me, thinking about later and those fingers.

I look quickly at Sydney. "You are still keeping Lexi, right?" She nods and giggles.

When the words start, Aiden's voice is husky and sexy. It reverberates deep down inside me. Tears pool in my eyes as he sings "H.O.L.Y" from Florida Georgia Line.

He closes his eyes momentarily. When he opens them they glisten. The words strip me naked and then cover me line by line as he pours his heart into them.

By the time he's done, tears fall freely. Syd hands me a Kleenex. It's then I notice that everyone has gone silent. I don't even care. All I care about right now is the man stalking toward me.

When he stands in front of me, words have a hard time coming out. How do I tell him everything I just felt?

"Hallelujah," I say in a singsong voice. Not quite what I was going for, but it was definitely a good part of the song.

His booming laugh echoes in the silent room. "God, I love you and your dirty mind."

"Aiden, there's so much more I want to say," I say, sliding off the chair.

"Wait. Let me say what I need to first." He grabs my hands and kisses each knuckle.

"Addison, I don't even know where to start. Two years ago you jump-started my heart. You opened my eyes to a life I never knew existed. You told me once that my compass was stuck. *Sweetheart*, it wasn't stuck. It was showing me exactly where I needed to go. Straight to you." I can't control the tears as he continues. "I can't imagine doing life without you. I want to be there for you, *especially* when danger knocks on your door, which seems to be frequently," he says, smirking, and the crowd laughs.

I narrow my eyes at him and stick my tongue out. "I know you don't need a hero or a protector, even though I'd do that in a heartbeat, and I *really* wish you'd let me at least once." I laugh this time, shaking my head. He's my hero every day. He wipes away some of my tears as his thumb caresses my cheek. "Addison, I want to be your partner, your lover, your everything as long as I'm yours. The first chapter of our love story was dictated by fate. Let's write the rest of it ourselves." My breath hitches as he pulls out a black velvet box and kneels down. I have to cover my mouth to hide the sobbing sounds. "Addison Grace Mason, will you marry me?"

He opens the box and *holy shit*! It's a huge solitaire outlined in tiny diamonds on a thin platinum band. I don't know much about engagement rings; hell, I don't know a damn thing about them because I've never even thought about them, but this ring is *perfect*.

I pull Aiden off the ground, my hands shake as I bring my hands to his jaw. "I love you." I'm having problems forming words. I'm frozen, wanting to preserve this moment forever. He looks at me, waiting. "Oh …" I nervously giggle. "Yes, yes, yes," I say, wrapping my arms around his neck. Cheers explode around us.

He lets out a ragged breath and then pulls back, kissing away all my tears. He lays his forehead on mine. Our eyes lock. "I can't believe I'm getting married," I whisper. I pull back quickly. "Wait."

"What?" he asks, an eyebrow pops up.

"You know I come as a package now, right?" His eyes soften.

The crowd goes quiet as Aiden looks around. Spotting Lexi on Max's shoulders he yells out, "Hey, Tater Tot, what do you think? Are you okay with Addison being my wife and you both living with me?"

She claps and bounces. Max grabs her legs so she doesn't fall backwards. "Yes. Yes. Yes," she says, mirroring my own words. "But I call dibs on flower girl."

I thought the cheers were deafening before, well the decibels just shot through the roof with laughter.

"You heard it," Aiden says, taking out the ring. I open my hand, spreading my fingers out, and he slips on the ring. It fits perfect.

He picks me up and twirls me around. This is the best night of my life.

The happy birthdays now turn to congratulations. The drinks seem to come more frequently now. I guess Aiden was making sure I wasn't going to be drunk for his proposal. Probably a good thing.

"Addison," I turn around to Amy and Ted, who's holding a sleeping Lexi in his arms. "We're going to take Lexi back with us to the hotel. We told Syd to stay and celebrate with you both."

"I love you both so much. Everything you've done for me in my life, I can't thank you enough," I say. I give them hugs and kiss Lexi on the cheek.

The celebration is turned up a notch. Syd, Harper, Bryn, and I take the stage a few times. As well as Aiden and the guys. Bryn finds me. "So the quarterback is hot," she slurs a little.

I giggle. "I think he probably fits into the first fifty percent of men looking for only one thing, sweetie."

She rolls her eyes. "With that, I'd be willing to find out." She struts away, probably to go find Ryker.

Aiden slips behind me, holding out my ring finger in front of us. "I can't wait for you to be Mrs. Roberts." I wiggle my ass against him.

"What if I—"

"Bullshit. You will take the name Roberts," he says, tickling me.

"Okay, okay." My voice softens. I turn in his arms. "I can't wait to be Mrs. Roberts." He nibbles on my bottom lip, then sucks on it. Tingles run down my spine. I press into him and open, allowing his tongue to dance with mine.

"What the fuck are you doing here?" Max's booming voice has us separating and looking around for what's going on. Toward the front door, there's a wall of men all facing it. Max, Ryan, Ryker, Damon, and Jaxon. Aiden grabs my hand as we start to walk that way. Ryker turns and focuses on Aiden. A slight shake of his head halts Aiden.

I look at Aiden's concerned look. "Maybe we should let the guys handle it," he says quickly.

"This is my night so I'm going to go see why there's a wall being built between *whomever* is on the other side of it and *us*," I say, trying not to slur. I'm a little drunk. Aiden holds my hand and we both walk over.

"Alright, boys, move," I say and gesture with my hands for them to step aside. Max looks at me, winces, and then looks at Aiden. They slowly step aside.

I gasp. This cannot be happening.

NOT ON MY FUCKING NIGHT!

"Hi, babe," Jessie squeals, rubbing her *very* large pregnant belly. "Guess what? We're having a girl."

PROLOGUE PREVIEW BOOK #3

I can't believe of all the nights to ruin, it's this one. I can't believe Jessie would do this. I pace my apartment, practically pulling my hair out. How did this happen? Why is she doing this to me?

I don't know what Addison is thinking right now because she won't answer my fucking calls. Five sets of eyes watch me walk back and forth. The only thing that can be heard are the curse words flying out of my mouth and my heavy steps across the hardwood floor.

"Aiden," Ryan says, clearing his throat. I watch him sit forward on his knees. "Are you sure you didn't—"

"What the fuck kind of question is that? I think I know where I dipped my stick," I grind out, wondering why he's asking me this. I would never have cheated on Addison.

His eyes bore into me like he knows something. Well, clue me in, asshole, because I don't know where you're going with this.

"Aiden, you saw Jessie a little over eight months ago."

"I fucking did not," I bark, crossing my arms over my chest.

He stands up, mirroring my stance. "When I came to the beach house, when you decided to use the walls as a punching bag ... when I got there, Jessie was leaving the house and she made it pretty clear that you two ..."

Click Here to find out what happens in Fate Loves.

ALSO BY TINA SAXON

TWIST OF FATE Trilogy

Aiden and Addison

Fate Hates

Fate Heals

Fate Loves

Twisted Wings

Max and Sydney

Blinding Echo

Kase and Ellie

Wild Distortion

Ryker and Aspen

Engaging Chaos

(Coming soon!)

Brooks and Reece

Join my reader group to get to know me and get early access to what I'm working on! Saxon's Sirens on Facebook

FOLLOW ME!

Facebook

Instagram

Website

ACKNOWLEDGMENTS

Thank YOU! If you're reading this, this book is dedicated to YOU! The love and encouragement from you, my readers, has been mind-blowing. It still feels surreal to have published two books now and your praises makes this new author feel amazing.

To my family who has put up with me disappearing to write, thank you for your patience and understanding. I couldn't have finished this book without the help of my husband. Your extra help with the kids and the house, your support and encouragement to keep going no matter what, the constant love you show me (especially after eighteen years of marriage) has made me feel like one lucky woman.

My book wouldn't be what it is without my professional team behind me. Max and Elaine, thank you for making my words come alive and shine. You both rock! Sarah, thank you for putting up with my controlling tendencies and creating an awesome book cover.

I could never forget to thank my number one fans, my Alpha and Beta readers. Tiffany, Lori, Traci and Michelle, the time you take out of your life to read my book, give me feedback and help me promote means so much to me. You have made my books better and I can't thank y'all enough.

Now on to finish Aiden and Addison's story ... *Fate Loves*.

Xoxo,

TS

ABOUT THE AUTHOR

Tina Saxon lives in Dallas, Texas, with her husband and two kids. She's not afraid to try new things because it's outside the box of *typical housewife*. CEO of her home is by far the most rewarding job she has ever had. Her jobs include, but are not limited to, seamstress, carpenter, craft extraordinaire, PTA President, chauffeur, dance mom, mediator *of mentioned kids*—and author. Once upon a time she was a Financial Analyst but traded budgets and forecasts in for diapers and bottles. The former was definitely easier but the latter more fulfilling.

Tina's love for reading surged into her passion for writing. Wanting to bring the reader an intriguing story that's hard to put down with steamy love scenes that heat you up, she's always thinking of the perfect way to take you down that path.

She loves hearing from her readers! Contact Tina Saxon at:
http://www.tinasaxon.com